"Progress, Mr. McQuaid. I'm a great believer in progress."

"Bear," he reminded her.

"Bear." Her breath quickened. "And in the men who make progress happen."

"Men who make progress." A wicked grin curled one side of his mouth as it lowered toward hers. "Does that include me? Am I making progress?"

"Progress?" Her gaze sought his as she felt his breath bathing her lips. "I believe you're one of the most *progressive* men I've ever met."

Shameless hussy, some small prune-proper part of her whispered. But the pounding of her heart and the stark new sensitivity of her skin inured her to it.

He dragged his lips lightly across hers, back and forth, mesmerizing her with the "almost" of the kiss that was coming. If she raised her chin just a fraction of an inch, she would fulfill that luscious promise of contact, but she would also end this delectable suspension in time and desire. And it was so entrancing to hover just at the threshold of pleasure, experiencing new sensations of wonder and longing.

Then, with a soft rushing sound that might have been her breath escaping—or his—he ended the suspense . . .

THE SOFT TOUCH

Betina Krahn

BANTAM BOOKS

NEW YORK · TORONTO · LONDON · SYDNEY · AUCKLAND

THE SOFT TOUCH

A Bantam Book / June 1999

ISBN 0-553-57618-6

Published simultaneously in the United States and Canada

Bantam Books are published by Bantam Books, a division of Random
House, Inc. Its trademark, consisting of the words "Bantam Books" and
the portrayal of a rooster, is Registered in U.S. Patent and Trademark
Office and in other countries. Marca Registrada. Bantam Books, 1540
Broadway, New York, New York 10036.

PRINTED IN THE UNITED STATES OF AMERICA

OPM   10   9   8   7   6   5   4   3   2   1

*For Nathan O. Krahn and Zebulun A. Krahn
whose love has sustained my heart.*

THE SOFT TOUCH

ONE

Baltimore
Late April 1887

"YOU DON'T NEED a loan, Mr. McQuaid, so much as you need a miracle."

The diminutive loan officer looked down his gold-rimmed spectacles at Bear McQuaid and gave him an excessively polite smile.

It was the second time in as many days that Barton "Bear" McQuaid had seen that look on a banker's face. He wanted nothing more than to replace it with a grimace of pain from a fist connecting solidly with a nose. Instead, he rose and tucked his maps and documents under his arm, thanked the man for his time, and walked out. Moments later he stepped onto the street where his partner, Halt Finnegan, was waiting for him.

"How did ye get on?" The big Irishman pushed off from the lamppost he was leaning against, but stopped at the sight of Bear's grim expression. "We didn't get it, did we?" He ripped off his Western hat and slapped his thigh with

it, releasing a small cloud of dust from the brim. "Miserable . . . sidewindin' . . ." He trailed off into a blistering
curse that was all the more potent for being soundless.
"Makin' ye get an appoin'ment, to get delivered bad news.
We oughta—"

"No, we oughtn'ta." Bear grabbed his partner's arm and
kept him from charging back into the bank. "Look—you
bruise a knuckle or two on him . . . then the police will
bruise a few on you . . . then I'll have to stick up for your
mangy hide . . . and ten years from now we'll both be
toothless, scarred up, dead broke, and just getting out of
prison." Halt eased and Bear released him.

"What do we do now?" Halt demanded, rolling the lingering tension from his shoulders. "We ain't got much
time. Them land office boys won' wait long for proof of our
ownership of th' right-o'-way land. Them grants depend—"

"We'll find another banker." Bear settled his wide-
brimmed Western hat on his head and searched the street
for a sign of another financial institution. "Then another.
Then another, if necessary. The city's lousy with bankers,
and we only need one. The right one. A man with a soft
spot in his heart for railroads." He grabbed Halt's arm and
dragged him along. "Or a soft spot in his head. Anyway
. . . the next time I try to put the touch on a banker,
you're coming with me."

"No I ain't." Halt stopped dead on the pavement and
glared at Bear, who squared off and glared back. It was a
contest for a moment, but the outcome was never really in
doubt; the power of Bear McQuaid's stare was legendary
around Billings, Montana. Almost as legendary as his independence.

Barton McQuaid had had to make his own way in the
world from a tender age, and as a result, had made it his
policy not to ask anything or expect anything from others.
But as he worked to put together the land and resources

he needed to build his railroad line, he learned there were some things a man simply couldn't do by sheer force of will no matter how capable or determined he was. Funding something as costly and complex as a railroad line was one of them.

For the last six months he and Halt had worked their way across the country, in search of the money they needed to exercise land options they had contracted and use those options to secure government grants. Over and over they had come close to securing loans, only to have the deal fall through when their potential investors insisted on taking charge of the enterprise. Colorado silver men, Kansas City beef barons, and St. Louis bankers alike watched in frustration as Bear McQuaid headed farther east in search of loans with fewer strings attached.

The simple fact was that it strained every fiber of Bear's being to have to ask for money from strangers . . . citified strangers, at that. His Westerner's self-reliance chafed at having to submit his hard-wrought plans to the judgments of men who had never had to raise calluses in order to eat or to wonder if they would ever see another sunrise during a frigid winter night on the high plains. But if he had to bend his stubborn will, he would do so in order to build something of his own, something lasting, something that would make both his fortune and his mark on the world. And if he was willing to make that sacrifice, Halt Finnegan had better be prepared to make it, too.

"Oh, you're coming, all right." Bear's face hardened to weathered bronze.

"Come now, Bear, me lad," Halt said in a brogue suddenly as thick as potato soup. "Ye know these Eastern bank fellas don't like doin' business with Irish."

"Yeah, well . . . if you're so damned Irish, then brush up on your blarney. Because I'm not going in there again without a partner." His legendary stare intensified. "I've got a partner . . . don't I?"

THE NEXT AFTERNOON they sat together in the spacious walnut-paneled office of the president of the Mercantile Bank of Baltimore. Across a huge, highly polished desk sat a rotund and impeccably dressed man, templing his fingers and studying them with a gaze that was somehow both unnerving and disarming.

Philip Vassar, they had learned, owned one of the three largest banks in Baltimore and, despite his enormous personal wealth, continued to run the bank on a daily basis and make most of the decisions about major business loans. Bear took that information as a good sign; it meant Vassar was a man who understood the value and satisfactions of hard work. When their letter of introduction—from the territorial governor of Montana—was taken seriously and they were shown into Vassar's presidential office, Bear shot a hopeful look at Halt. The Irishman tucked his chin and shoved his hands deeper into his pockets, wearing a look that said he would rather be shoveling boiler coal than sitting down to talk money in a banker's office.

"We are launching a railroad venture that you should find quite interesting, Mr. Vassar," Bear began. He went on to describe their proposed railroad line, unrolling his maps, detailing their meticulously drawn estimates, and laying out the option contracts and promissory letters from the land office in Washington. Vassar asked pertinent questions and seemed genuinely interested in the spur line they intended to build. He stroked his chin thoughtfully, nodded, and even smiled once. More hopeful signs.

But when the presentation was over, a deep silence descended. Bear shifted uncomfortably in his chair and glanced at Halt, who squirmed more or less discreetly.

Vassar seemed to be measuring them inch by inch, turning them inside out, examining them as men as well as financial risks.

"Well, gentlemen," Vassar finally began, then paused to clear his throat. "Yours is a most interesting proposition. Railroads are opening all of the riches of the West to us and this project would certainly make lucrative connections. Who is your primary competition for these right-of-way grants?"

Bear tensed. Vassar was nothing if not astute. He obviously knew enough about men and railroads to understand that the possibility of free land alongside every mile of track laid would draw not only great interest, but also fierce competition.

"To be honest"—Bear shot a glance at Halt—"there are two major competitors. One is James J. Hill and his Chicago, Milwaukee and St. Paul. He likes to build his own spur lines. Then there is Jay Gould of the Northern Pacific, who would like nothing more than to move in on Hill's operation. A couple of lucrative spurs or short lines would give him bargaining power with Hill. But we got there first, optioned the land on the only logical route through two major valleys. Our right-of-way will cut through some of the finest wheat land in the West. Once the track is in place, that land will be golden in more ways than one. And of course, I've already mentioned the timber in the upper reaches."

Vassar thought about Bear's response for a moment, then frowned. "A tempting proposal, gentlemen, assuming all is as you said." He canted his head, regarding them from a different angle. "If only it were in the next county, or even in this state, you would have your money within the hour. But I am afraid I must decline the opportunity. I simply cannot invest the kind of capital you require on a venture so far from here . . . in such perilous country

. . . in competition with men whose reputations and resources far outstrip your own."

"Of course it's far away." Bear shot to the edge of his seat. "That's where railroads need to be built—where the money is to be made!" He clenched his hands resting on the maps covering the banker's desk. "Look, Mr. Vassar . . . as a full partner, your profit from the land sales alone would far exceed the profit from any sort of investment you could make here in Baltimore."

"I simply cannot commit my shareholders' money to such a risky venture. And my own personal holdings are not liquid enough to permit me to back you at the level of your needs. I'm afraid you'll have to find your funding elsewhere." Vassar watched the exchange of glances between Bear and his partner. "Perhaps Gephardt, over at the First Baltimore."

"We a'ready seen th' little bas—" Halt muttered.

"He's . . . not interested." Bear glowered at Halt, who clamped his jaw shut and lowered his scowl to his boots. "We would appreciate any other suggestions you might make . . . another bank . . . perhaps a private investor." He stood, ran his hands back through his hair, and began to gather up the documents.

Vassar gave a contemplative "hmm" as he watched Bear's movements and assessed his reaction. After a moment, he reached for a pen, dipped it in a silver ink pot, and wrote something down on a small vellum card. "I believe I do have a suggestion for you. You seem knowledgeable and well-spoken, a presentable enough fellow. If you won't take this ill—" He handed Bear the card, and Bear studied his expression before glancing down and reading the names aloud.

"Martene and Savoy." He looked up with guarded relief. "Are they bankers or investors?"

"Tailors." Vassar got to his feet and stuck his thumbs into his vest pockets. "The best in Baltimore."

Bear scowled, then stiffened as the sense of it struck. Tailors? He asked for financing and got clothing advice instead?

"I like you, McQuaid. You're a forward-thinking fellow. I believe you will take that suggestion in the spirit in which it was intended. Now as to your funding . . ." Vassar indulged in a quirk of a smile. "I doubt you'll find a banker in Baltimore willing to give you the kind of money you need. However, there are other avenues to acquiring such assets . . . other sorts of 'alliances' that can prove most profitable for a presentable fellow such as yourself."

Frustration rose with a bitter taste up the back of Bear's throat, preventing him from catching Vassar's meaning at first.

"I take it you are an *unmarried* man?"

The suggestion so astonished Bear that it took him a moment to be able to respond. Better clothing . . . other "alliances" . . . He looked to Halt and then back at the banker with disbelief.

"I want no part of that sort of 'funding.' " His voice sounded choked. "I am a railroad man, not a fortune hunter."

Vassar sighed. "Pity. You would find Baltimore brimming with possibilities. We seem to have a surfeit of eligible females just now. However, if you are determined against—"

"I am." Bear's voice vibrated with conviction.

Vassar shrugged. "Well, then, I suppose your best chance in Baltimore is probably Diamond Wingate. She has been known to be accommodating in such matters. Come to think of it, my wife is giving a little party next Saturday and she will most certainly attend. I could introduce you to her there, if you'd like."

"I repeat, I'll have no part of romancing a female for money."

Vassar gave a short laugh. "You mistake me, Mr. Mc-Quaid. Miss Wingate is an investor. She has considerable assets, many of which are suitably liquid. And she is known to be generous. She supports a number of philan-thropic and entrepreneurial projects, and is widely known as Baltimore's foremost . . . proponent of 'Progress.' Of all the investors in Baltimore, I truly believe her to be your best hope for funding your railroad line." The banker's di-rect and unwavering regard caused some of the heat in Bear's temper to drain.

"We appreciate your offer, Mr. Vassar, but by next Sat-urday we should have letters of credit in hand and be on a train bound for Washington."

Vassar seemed to take the rejection in stride. He rose and extended his hand to both men, wishing them luck.

By the time they reached the street, Halt could no longer contain his outrage. "Nervy bastard. We ask for a loan an' he gives us a *tailor!*"

But Bear was staring at the card in his hand, caught hard in the grip of something he hadn't experienced in a very long time: embarrassment. He had a sketchy idea of what his face looked like, and that only because he had seen it in the peeling mirrors of the bathhouse he used every morning. But what he had seen was enough now to shame him.

He looked rough, edgy. His sun-darkened skin resem-bled weathered stone and his hands were as hardened as a ditchdigger's. He looked down at his callused palms and for the first time noticed how much of his arm showed below his too-tight sleeves and how much of his boot showed below his too-short pants. The sight shocked him. He must look as if he'd been melted down and poured into somebody else's clothes.

Clearly, he'd been out West too long, where a man was judged mainly by what was inside him, his strength, skill, and character. He had forgotten the most basic tenets of Eastern society: appearance determined acceptance, and acceptance determined opportunity.

He spotted the darkened glass of a nearby shop window and made for it. His full-length reflection caused him to wince. The fellow looking back at him was tall and rangy, with hair that was too long and a suit that was too tight. His tie was knotted, his buttons were straining his coat fabric, and his worn Western boots were beyond the aid of brush and polish. Halt stood alongside him in a dusty Western hat, chambray shirt, and ancient string tie . . . looking done up like a sore thumb and acting every bit as touchy.

Who in his right mind would lend money to men who looked like them?

"How much traveling money do we have left?" he demanded.

"Three hundred or so." Halt was puzzled by the way his partner glowered at the pots and pans in the dry-goods shop window. Then he realized Bear was using the glass as a mirror, and he too began to examine their reflections . . . making a face at himself.

"It might be enough," Bear muttered.

"For what? What are we goin' to do?"

"We're going to find a barber." Bear wheeled and struck off down the street, searching the sign boards and shop fronts for evidence of the familiar red-and-white-striped pole. "Then we're going to find this 'Martene and Savoy.' And *then* we're going to find us another blessed banker!"

FOUR DAYS PASSED before Bear McQuaid was again shown into banker Philip Vassar's office. This time, his dark hair was neatly trimmed, a handsome new coat skimmed his big frame, and a pair of new shoes padded softly over the Aubusson carpets. His face, however, was drawn and his mood was nothing short of grim.

"I won't take up your time, sir." He came straight to the point. "I would like to know if your offer to introduce us to that investor is still open."

Surprised, Vassar lowered the document in his hand, removed his spectacles, and leaned back in his chair. "Why, yes, it is." He ran his gaze over Bear and nodded, clearly pleased by the improvements in his appearance. "However, the party is only four days away, and you would need evening dress."

"By Saturday, I'll have it," Bear declared fiercely.

Vassar assessed his crackling determination and gave a chuckle.

"I just bet you will."

"WELL?" HALT ASKED when he stepped out into the street.

"It's all set. Saturday night I'm going to Vassar's house to meet this rich old lady. What the hell was her name? Sparkle? Twinkle?"

"Nah . . . Ruby or . . ." Halt squinted and scratched his bristled chin as if it helped him remember. "Diamond something. Yeah, that was it." A bit more scratching and he had the rest. "Diamond . . . Wingate."

"Miss Diamond Wingate." Bear winced at the name and struck off down the street. "I never thought I'd have to sink to charming money out of women." He realized Halt wasn't beside him, and turned to locate him. Finnegan stood on the pavement with his fists propped on his waist.

"Yer not meanin' to romance th' woman?"

"If you weren't my partner, I'd lay you out flat," Bear growled, grabbing him by the arm and dragging him along. "Besides, she's probably old enough to be the 'ol' granny' you're always swearing by the grave of. Come on. We've got four days to get me some proper evening clothes and to figure out how to make old Miss Wingate forget how to say the word 'no.'"

"THAT AWFUL RABBLE collected around the gates . . . Basil Wingate would never have stood for it." Evelyn Stanhope Vassar sat glued to the carriage window the next day, as she and her family passed the Wingate estate on their way home from a day in the city. When the motley assortment of indigents and hopefuls loitering around the entrance to Gracemont were completely out of sight, she settled back into her seat and felt her daughter's stare. "Sit up, Clarice," she said defensively. "And don't slouch. Gentlemen don't like girls who slouch."

A sigh issued from behind the open newspaper beside her, and she cast an irritable look in her husband's direction.

"If she would just choose someone and get it over with. It's simply not fair to the rest of the girls for Diamond to keep the eligible men in Baltimore in suspense." Upon further reflection, however, she had to admit there was plenty of blame to go around.

"Ridiculous men. Do they think they all can marry the same girl? You know, don't you, Philip, that there hasn't been a single engagement announced in Baltimore this season. Not one." She raised her chin and looked balefully at her dimpled dumpling of a daughter. It was her one ambition in life to see her only offspring happily and advantageously married.

The paper lowered enough for a canny pair of eyes to become visible.

"It won't be much longer, my dear," Philip Vassar said.

She started and turned to him. "What makes you say such a thing?"

The paper crumpled toward his lap. "You will be ecstatic to know, dear wife, that your relentless wheedling has finally borne fruit." He gave his daughter a covert wink and she blushed. "I have taken *steps*."

"Steps?" Evelyn's eyes widened and her maternal instincts rose to a full quiver. "What sort of steps?"

"I have invited a business acquaintance to your little party on Saturday."

"A business acquaintance?" Evelyn deflated.

"A *gentleman* acquaintance," Vassar clarified, giving her a meaning-filled glance from the corner of his eye.

"A gentleman?" She brightened and glanced at Clarice. "Is he rich?"

"About as rich as a church mouse, I believe."

Evelyn grew annoyed with his inscrutability. "How, pray, does my entertaining this *pauper* of yours help our Clarice?"

"He needs a loan. He's building a railroad out West and needs funds. I've promised to introduce him to Diamond Wingate." He smiled with a hint of satisfaction.

"Don't be obscure, Philip." She grew impatient. "How can you possibly think she'll be interested in a penniless fellow who wants to take buckets of her money out West and pour it all over the ground in some wild railroad—" She halted, remembering the nature of the young woman in question.

"Oh." Her eyes widened further. "Ohhh."

Vassar enjoyed watching his wife discover his genius. He started to raise his paper again, but Evelyn stopped it halfway up.

"But if he really is penniless . . ."

Vassar fixed her with the long-suffering look of a prophet trapped in his native land, then returned to his reading.

"I believe the fellow has . . . *other* . . . assets."

Two

THE WALNUT-PANELED boardroom was filled with the light of the afternoon sun, the scents of waxed wood and India ink, and a low, continuous drone of numbers.

More money, Diamond Wingate realized.

"The electrical water-bath can-sealing process . . . one hundred thirteen thousand. The new valve-and-jet combination for using gas in cookstoves . . . fifty-seven thousand this quarter. That new man-made medicine, 'aspirin' . . . only seventeen thousand. But they plan to advertise in ladies' journals, business quarterlies, family magazines, newspapers. The Remington Company investment . . . profit distributions amount to—"

A lot more money.

"—a total of ninety-six thousand. Those 'typewriting' machines are selling hand over fist." There was a corroborating murmur from around the room and a muted crackle of dry paper as a page turned in a ledger. "Swift's refrigerator cars"—the voice droned on—"one hundred seventy-two thousand. Guardwell safety pins . . . twelve thousand . . . and branching out into other sewing no-tions. Proceeds from the new Baltimore glassworks . . . twenty-nine thousand. People seem to have taken to getting their milk from glass bottles. Ives's photoengraving process . . . thus far, only eight thousand. But every major newspaper and magazine up and down the coast is clamoring for the process."

It was a blessed avalanche of profit!

The litany of incomes halted as Diamond looked up from the ledger and into the faces of the men seated around the long table.

"In short," she said, eyeing them through the demiveil of her elegantly feathered hat, "we've made another pile of it."

"I should say so, miss." The secretary of the board, standing by her chair, lowered the ledger he held and smiled proudly at his fellow directors. "Another *whopping* pile of it, in fact." The others around the table nodded and murmured to each other in congratulatory tones.

Diamond sat back in her chair at the head of the board table, staring at the balance sheet and considering the report. It wasn't exactly unexpected news. She always made money. Not on every investment or venture, true; but she made a large-enough profit on enough of her investments that her fortune had grown from sizable to nothing short of extraordinary in the last eight years.

A smothering feeling settled over her chest at the sight of those long, complex figures on the balance sheet. More . . . there was always so much more . . . She took a deep, determined breath and dispelled that feeling.

"Excellent," she said, with conviction. "Just excellent."

Smiles of relief, arm-clasps, and handshakes were exchanged all around the table . . . only to stop dead when she continued.

"Now, let's get down to business."

The secretary frowned. "But we have been down to business."

"*Old* business," she said, closing the heavy book on the table before her. "I can take the general books with me and look them over this evening. I think it's time for some *new* business."

Every man in the room tensed at those words and glanced at the door, recalling the collection of people they had waded through as they arrived for the meeting. She was going to give away money. Again.

This had happened after each of the last several meetings of the Wingate Company Board of Directors. Perhaps it was a reaction to the numbing recitation of accounts, or a realization of the staggering sums that her wealth involved, or simply the excessively charitable taint of her upbringing . . . whatever it was, *something* caused Diamond Wingate at the end of each glowing financial report to suffer a raging bout of philanthropy. She insisted on throwing open both the doors and the treasury of the Wingate Company and inviting the enterprising elements of Baltimore to make her a proposition.

And the enterprising elements of Baltimore responded. Aspiring financiers, market speculators, would-be investors, social reformers, commodity brokers, charity mavens, down-on-their-luck businessmen, itinerant preachers, and get-rich-quick schemers . . . everyone, it seemed, had a proposition of some sort for Baltimore's "Patroness of Progress." Since daybreak that morning, a crowd of citizens in the grip of a determined entrepreneurial spirit had been collecting outside the doors of the Wingate Company offices . . . crowding into the upper hallway, clogging the sweeping staircase, filling the downstairs lobby, and spilling out into the street.

Diamond turned to a chair by the windows where a portly older fellow with enormous muttonchops had been reduced to a semiconscious state by the combination of a comfortable chair, warm sunshine, and boredom.

"Hardwell," she called. "Hardwell!"

"Whaaa . . . ?" He snapped upright, blinking against the bright light.

"The numbers," she prompted.

He rubbed his face, looked around, and scowled as he recalled where he was and why he was being called. Retrieving a glass fishbowl from under the side of his chair, he carried it to Diamond at the head of the table.

"Are you sure you want to do this, my girl?" Her erstwhile guardian frowned as he placed the bowl on top of the ledger in front of her.

"Absolutely," she said, rising to address her gentlemen directors. "You'll be relieved to learn that I've come up with a plan to avoid the . . . *problems* . . . we had after the last board meeting." The tension around the board table was palpable. "I know you're probably remembering that little misadventure with the soap suds in the outer office. . . ."

"It took weeks to restore the files and paperwork," the secretary declared.

"And what about the disaster caused by that lunatic on buffalo back who wanted to start a wild animal park?" Hardwell added with a glower.

"Well, it wasn't his fault the poor beast didn't take well to green corn feed," she said, though with a bit less certainty. "And anyway, the rug was probably due for a good—" She waved it impatiently aside. "That is all in the past. I've come up with a much tidier and more efficient way to hear business proposals. I've decided to hold"—the gentlemen board members seemed to be holding their breaths—"a *lottery*."

"A lottery?" The secretary exchanged puzzled looks with the others.

"Over the last three months, whenever I was approached regarding a business proposition, I responded by giving out a numbered business card. I informed the applicants that they should present both that card and themselves here this afternoon to participate in a lottery. The ten people holding cards with numbers corresponding to the numbers we draw from this bowl will each have a chance to present business proposals to the Wingate Companies."

She paused, searching their faces and finding only reserved judgment.

"Don't you see? This will eliminate the chaos that occurs when people feel they have to compete for the opportunity to make us a proposal."

After a moment, the secretary of the board looked at the others around the table and shrugged. "Well, I suppose it has to be better than . . . What can it hurt?" Following his lead, the others gave hesitant nods.

Visibly pleased, she stirred the pieces of paper on the bottom of the bowl, then pulled out one after another, until ten numbers lay on the tabletop.

"Number fourteen will be our first applicant." She turned to Hardwell Humphrey. "If you'll be so good as to summon our first presenter."

Diamond's first lottery winner proved to be a big German meat cutter who smelled faintly of schnapps and proposed a novel method for stuffing sauerkraut *inside* of wieners. Number thirty-three was a pair of genteel older ladies who had come to plead the plight of "barefoot" natives in tropical regions. They wanted funds to buy and ship shoes to missionaries . . . shoes, in their cosmology, being somehow fundamental to both salvation and godly behavior. Number forty-seven clanked and rattled through the door with a prototype of a mechanical chopper which could be used on an astonishing range of edible material, from cow silage to cannery beets. His demonstration with a bag of said beets left a worrisome crimson-purple puddle on the floor. In every case, she wrote out a bank draft and assigned a director to oversee the project.

Next came number sixty-four, a fellow with an idea for a mechanized bread bakery, who also left the boardroom with a bank draft in his hands. Then came an enterprising young chemist with a new formula for bug spray . . . which he demonstrated by attaching a jar of it to a hand bellows and pumping the room full of noxious kerosene-based vapors. The directors staggered to the windows with handkerchiefs over their noses and frantically fanned away the fumes while Diamond dabbed at her tearing eyes and wrote out another draft.

When the air had finally cleared, Diamond looked up to find several board members standing shoulder to shoulder, staring at her.

"Sauerkraut *inside* wieners . . . mechanical food choppers . . . bread from a machine . . . now we've nearly been suffocated by poisonous vapors." Only one spoke, but they all glowered. "You'll never see a penny from such nonsense."

Diamond assessed their forbidding expressions, smiled, and played her trump card. "I believe that was exactly what you said about the electrical water-bath can-sealing process. And if memory serves, it made us one hundred thirteen thousand this quarter alone."

That gave them pause for a moment. Then another director spoke up.

"But five thousand dollars just to peel a few beets—"

"Is a bargain . . . if it leads to an efficient new machine for peeling and processing food," she answered, sensing that their uneasiness required a broader response. "I know it is sometimes difficult for you to understand why I feel so strongly about this. But I've been blessed with means far beyond my needs, and with that blessing comes a great responsibility to use my wealth for the benefit of others. Progress can be a very expensive thing. And it has to start somewhere."

They lowered their gazes and shifted their feet and, one by one, retreated to their chairs to see what else Diamond Wingate and "progress" had in store.

"That's ten," Hardwell said with an air of finality, an hour later, ushering the tenth lucky presenter to the door. "I'll send the others home."

"You see?" Diamond, feeling somewhat vindicated in her largesse, rose, checked the pinning of her hat, and began to draw on her gloves. "No major catastrophes. And you must admit, we discovered some interesting prospects in our lottery." She looked to her treasurer. "How much did we spend?"

"I'll have the number for you in just a moment." The treasurer adjusted his spectacles and began a quick bit of arithmetic, which had to be redone when something disrupted his concentration. By the time he looked up with the answer, Diamond and everyone else in the room was staring at the door in alarm.

Noise was rising beyond the heavy walnut panels: a cacophony of voices and scuffling sounds, overlayered by Hardwell Humphrey's beleaguered voice.

"Please—go home! I'm tellin' you, Miss Wingate and the board are not seein' anybody else today!" The door flew open, admitting both the sound of the chaos from the outer office and Hardwell . . . who careened around the edge of the door and then planted his back against it, slamming it shut.

"They've gone mad—the lot of 'em!" Hardwell panted as the other directors rushed to help him hold the door against the mob outside. "Stark ravin' looney—wavin' cards an' demandin' to see you!"

Thuds from the other side threatened to force open the door as more directors rushed to pile hands and shoulders against it. Diamond was distraught at the demands of the unruly crowd on the other side.

"It was a lottery," she said in disbelief. "I told them they would have a chance . . . I never promised them that we would hear and fund them all."

The door thudded back a few inches and the people outside spotted Diamond through the opening.

"There she is!"

"Miss Wingate, we need yer help!"

"Miss Wingate—you've got to look at my fertilizer spreader!"

Arms and legs snaked through the opening, forcing the door back despite the gentlemen directors' best efforts.

"This way!" Hardwell grabbed her elbow and dragged her toward a door half hidden by a drape at the far end of the room. It was an exit onto a rickety set of fire stairs that led to the alley behind the Wingate building.

"I have to talk to them, Hardwell." Diamond's resistance stopped him at the door. "I have to make them understand."

"They're not of a mood to listen," he declared with a glance past her. "She who gives and runs away, lives to give another day! Come on!"

The board members, unused to such primal exertion, suddenly gave ground. The door swung open and people surged into the room. "There she is!" They spotted her near the exit and headed for her. The Wingate directors scrambled to re-form ranks, but their struggles bought only a short delay. It was just time enough for Hardwell to throw the bolts and plunge out onto the narrow iron scaffolding.

Clinging tightly to the railings, they descended the precarious stairway to the floor of the alley. As they hurried toward their carriage at the far end of the narrow lane, they saw Ned, Diamond's veteran driver, rushing around the corner beside the coach with a frantic look on his face. Behind him came a small crowd of people . . . carrying rolled-up blueprints, legal folios, and contraptions, and waving Diamond's business cards. Spotting Diamond and Hardwell, Ned jerked open the door, vaulted up onto the footman step, and beckoned them on.

The crowd reached Diamond and Hardwell just as they reached the carriage. There was a moment's confusion in which Diamond was buffeted and momentarily deafened by the shouting. Ned and Hardwell were able to keep their feet, and with their help she hoisted her skirts and climbed into the carriage. Hardwell hurtled in after her, the door slammed, and a moment later the heavy black landau lurched into motion. A howl of disappointment rose from the crowd and followed them down the street as they sped away.

Inside the coach, Diamond and Hardwell Humphrey sat in stunned silence for a moment then slowly began to right hats, tug jackets back down into place, and brush skirts and trousers. Diamond looked up at the broken egret feather hanging over the brim of her tailored hat and gave a long-suffering sigh. Some days it just didn't pay to be the richest young woman in Baltimore.

A stifled sound of surprise caused her to look up. Hardwell was staring out the carriage window wearing an incredulous look.

"Gawd A'mighty. Don't they ever give up?"

Diamond leaned to the window to see what had caused his reaction. Someone was pursuing the coach on foot down the dusty street.

"Miss Wingate—I implore you!" The fellow's lanky arms and legs churned as he came abreast of the coach. "If only you will have a look at my . . . motorized steps . . . see how practical . . ." He managed to launch a bundle of papers through the front window, and it rolled onto the floor between their feet.

Hardwell's response was to stick his head out the window and shout: "Go away—d'you hear?"

"If she will only"—the fellow panted, clapping one hand over his jiggling bowler and rescuing his spectacles with the other—"*listen* to my proposal . . ."

"Miss Wingate is not acceptin' any more blessed proposals!" Hardwell struggled briefly to raise the stubborn window glass, then abandoned it to thump the roof of the coach with his fist, signaling their driver to go faster. The petitioner matched the coach's quickening pace for only a few more strides.

"Miss Wingate!" His strained voice began to fade. "You're my last hope!"

Diamond turned to look through the oval rear window at the fellow's spent and doubled figure disappearing into the dust. When he was no longer visible, she sank back into her seat and smoothed her skirts again, finding her roused feelings harder to settle.

The plaintive edge in the man's voice—in all those disappointed voices—permeated her thoughts until it seemed to echo through every chamber of her heart. ". . . *my last hope* . . ." The sight of his heroic effort refused to fade from her mind. He was one of many, so many, who were desperate for help. And she always seemed to be their last hope.

Why was it that she was never anybody's *first* hope or *best* hope?

She knew the answer, had known it for a long time. It seemed to be her destiny in life to be a safety net for others, especially those on society's leading and trailing edges. Why else would she have been saddled with such a huge fortune, unearned and undesired?

She looked up to find her former guardian watching her troubled expression through narrowed eyes.

"I could have at least listened to him," she said.

"Motorized steps." Humphrey snorted. "Of all the silly—you just got finished givin' away thousands of dollars to fools like him."

"Invested," she corrected. "And I could have invested thousands more."

Hardwell stared intently at her, then threw up his hands and gave a huff of exasperation. "You can't fix the whole world, you know."

"I'm not trying to fix the whole world." She lifted her chin. "I'm only trying to make the world a little better . . . doing what I know to be right . . . what I was *raised* to do."

Hardwell reddened and grumbled wordlessly before sinking back against the seat and crossing his arms. She had him there and they both knew it.

Hardwell Humphrey and his wife, Hannah, had to take much of the blame for Diamond's excesses of generosity. They had been appointed her guardians upon her father's untimely death, eleven years ago, and—having had no children of their own—did their best to raise Diamond in accordance with what they believed to be a proper Christian upbringing. To see that she wasn't spoiled and made selfish by the luxury around her, they exposed her to the needy of the world and instructed her in the grave responsibility that accompanied her wealth.

Their efforts were richly rewarded. From her earliest days with them, she showed a remarkable aptitude for compassion and philanthropy. She eagerly gave money, food, and clothing to whoever asked and understood, at an exceptionally young age, the idea that helping people to make their own way in the world was infinitely more desirable than just giving them handouts. By her sixteenth birthday she had already helped to start several new businesses and charities through personal donations and unsecured loans.

But as she neared the fateful age of eighteen, her generosity had developed a worrisome notoriety and Hardwell and Hannah began to suspect that they might have overdone the "take-off-thy-cloak-and-give-it-to-them" aspects of her training. Hoping to remedy their miscalculation and prepare her for the life she would lead in Baltimore's highest society, they approached the wife of one of Baltimore's leading financiers for help. Evelyn Stanhope Vassar, having a daughter near Diamond's age and thinking it might be good for her daughter Clarice to have a companion in her first season, agreed to oversee Diamond's entrance into society.

Diamond's debut, near the end of her eighteenth year, was a success by every possible standard. She was the phenomenon of Baltimore's social season; well liked by her peers, adored by matrons, fawned over by gentlemen, and sought out by the scions of Baltimore's elite. But there her progress along an orderly and predictable course of feminine expectations stopped.

She had become not only the wealthiest young woman in the state, but also the most stubbornly and legally independent. Whether by intention or oversight, the wealthy and powerful Basil Wingate had left his entire estate to her unentailed and unencumbered. Since the day she reached the age of eighteen, there had been no one to tell her no . . . or to require her to say it.

"You know, don't you . . . it's not that we're opposed to your improvin' things for people?" Hardwell said, his amicable face growing somber with concern. "It's just got all out of hand. You can scarce set foot outside the house without bein' set upon. Down-and-outers forever collectin' around the blessed gates. And then every time you go to town it's somebody like that sob-sister orphanage female with her gaggle of glum-faced kids layin' in wait for us at Hurst Purnell last week. And that lunatic who stormed the carriage house—"

"He only wanted to show me how his machine could shine my boots."

He wagged his head and engulfed her slender hand in his. "Yer too softhearted, Diamond girl. Look at what happened with those people whose houses burned in the Hampden Street fire. It took a full week to clear out the mess they left in the outbuildin's." He shook a parental finger. "You can't go on forever handin' out money as if you're the world's sweet auntie and your money is penny peppermints."

She frowned at him. *If only her money were just penny peppermints. One huge pile of sugar candy that could be left out in the rain . . . to melt away . . .*

"You have to learn to say no, girl." He studied her face and the look in his eyes betrayed his conclusion about the likelihood of that happening anytime soon. "Or find somebody who can say it for you. A husband, for instance." His gaze and tone both sharpened. "Seems to me the only thing you haven't said yes to in the last five years is a *proposal of marriage.*"

Diamond squirmed under his stare.

"Ohhh! We almost forgot!" She lurched to the window. Holding on to her hat by its narrow brim, she stuck her head out and called up to Ned: "Be sure to stop at the tailor's for Robbie!"

Hardwell groaned quietly. "As if we haven't had enough trouble today."

Having effectively diverted Hardwell, Diamond settled back in her seat and proceeded to finish the conversation in her own head . . . at least her half of it.

A husband. Her eyes narrowed. She needed one like a

duck needed overshoes. Imagine her having to bend her knee and bow her will to a tightfisted man with a passion for naysaying. Imagine having to put up with someone telling her how, when, and where she *couldn't* spend her own fortune. Spending money was the only thing that made her life bearable.

True, there had been a time—not so long ago—when she had considered marrying. A husband, she had believed, was her only hope of having children and creating a family. And "family" was the one thing that for all her wealth and privilege, she had never had. The possibility of creating a family of her own held such powerful allure for her that she had sat atop the matrimonial fence for four long years, unable to surrender to the expectation that she must marry and turn control of her life over to a man, but equally unable to renounce her desire to have children and make a family of her own.

Then, three months ago, her cousin Robbie appeared.

A woman of questionable appearance and background arrived on her doorstep with the orphaned boy in tow, claiming the coarse little urchin with the atrocious grammar was Diamond's first cousin and insisting on a reward for returning him to the bosom of his family. On the basis of the ancient letter the woman produced and a striking physical resemblance between herself and the boy, Diamond had taken him straight into the placid and predictable household she shared with her aging guardians. And things hadn't been the same since.

She thought of Robbie's energy, his enthusiasm, and his irreverence for the rigid conventions of the society into which he had been thrust. He was a light-fingered, quick-witted, ill-mannered disgrace. She smiled.

She now had the makings of a real family: Hardwell and Hannah as companions and surrogate parents and Robbie on whom to vent her maternal urges. Her life was virtually complete. What on earth would she do with a *man*?

Her pleasure faded to a pensive frown as she slid her fingers over the outline of folded envelopes through the embroidered velvet of her purse.

What on earth was she going to do with *three*?

THREE

MARTENE AND SAVOY were the finest tailors in Baltimore. Their shop was a masterpiece of understated ele-
gance, lined with pristine mahogany shelves containing
bolts of the finest fabrics and set with marble counters
bearing a sumptuous array of gentlemen's haberdasheries.
It was as close to a gentlemen's club as any establishment
of that kind in Baltimore. Only the very well-to-do could
afford the expensive imported fabrics and fastidious tailor-
ing offered there.

Diamond paused on the step, before the etched-glass
doors, to smooth the peplum of her jacket and check the
tilt of her high-crowned hat. When she stepped inside, the
smells of the place—the tang of dyed woolens, the smell
of hot irons on starched linen, and the pungent taint of the
spent pipe tobacco in the smoking stands—filled her head,
rousing memories of when she had come here years ago
with her father. She scanned the shop for Robbie. Surely
they had completed his fittings by now; it had been more
than three hours since they dropped him off on their way
to the board meeting.

She called out to the proprietor, Monsieur Martene, who made it a habit to greet each of his wealthy and influential customers personally. When there was no response, she strolled among the counters and tables, peering this way and that, investigating. The place was eerily silent, without even a clerk or apprentice in sight.

Then from the rear door that led to the fitting rooms and workshop she heard muffled thuds, the sound of rising voices, and Robbie's fear-tightened tones denying that he had anything to do with . . . something.

"Robbie?" She rushed for the door to the fitting rooms, using the sounds of growing conflict as a compass. "Robbie, where are you?"

In the doorway she bumped into a harried Monsieur Martene, who recoiled, recognized her—"Mademoiselle!"—and was so overwrought that he seized her by the wrists and pulled her through the curtains.

She was dragged down a short passage toward the fitting rooms, which were actually a series of cubicles set apart by standing mirrors, dressing screens, and the occasional set of sagging curtains. Dust filled the air in a visible haze and Monsieur Martene put out an arm to halt and keep her from stumbling over something on the floor. When she looked down, she found an aged dressing screen lying in ruins at her feet.

The center of the row of fitting rooms had collapsed. Screens and mirrors had collided and toppled like dominoes, taking down with them all but a few faded drapes, which could be seen clinging by one end to their dangling supports. From the shocked, unnatural silence and the amount of dust still in the air, the calamity seemed to have just happened.

"Lemme go, mister!—I—I swear—I didn't do nothin'—honest!"

Small, wiry Robbie Wingate, hanging by the neck of his

velvet-bound riding jacket—arms and legs wriggling—was held aloft by a tall, disheveled man wearing a layer of dust and a glare of outrage.

"You didn't do nothin'? Where do you think this mess came from?" The man raised him even higher off the ground, which set him flailing. "You were climbing around on the damned things and caused them to fall over!"

"Robbie! Let him go this instant!" Diamond demanded, straining against Monsieur Martene's grip. At the sound of her voice Robbie began to wail.

"Help—help me—he's gonna kill me!"

"Don't give me ideas," the man ordered, narrowing his eyes.

"*Non, non,* please, monsieur—there is no harm done!" the tailor cried, struggling to restrain both Diamond and the anger of his beleaguered patron.

As Diamond wrenched free, the man thrust Robbie out to arm's length, glowered at her, and drawled, "Is this *yours*?"

The fear in Robbie's face and the fact that his accuser was standing knee-deep in chaos struck her at the same time and she hesitated . . . just long enough for the man to drop Robbie on his rear.

"Owww!" The ten-year-old scrambled to his feet, rubbing his bottom, skittered across a collapsed screen, and threw himself into Diamond's arms.

"Are you hurt?" She raked her fingers through his dusty hair and did a cursory visual inspection of him before wrapping him in a protective hug. Looking up, she she met the stranger's fiery gaze head-on. "How dare you handle him like that?" she demanded. "He's only a child."

"Who has climbed the walls, swung from the curtains"—the man's voice lowered until it vibrated like rolling thunder—"and made a first-class menace of himself for two solid hours."

"He is ten years old," she declared hotly.

"Condolences, ma'am." He gave her a sardonic nod. "Imagine what he'll be like when he's twenty."

Her mouth opened but his unthinkable rudeness had momentarily deprived her of words. She looked down at Robbie's face, cradled in her hand, and found his blue eyes rimmed with unaccustomed moisture. "It's all right, Robbie." She directed him to the door and gave his back a pat. "Go . . . join Hardwell in the coach. I'll be there shortly." Robbie swiped his eyes and, with a chastened rounding to his shoulders, hurried out.

When he was gone, she turned back to the big stranger and found him pushing wrecked furnishings aside and stepping across them, headed straight for her.

"That's it? Just a hug and a pat and a 'Mommie'll make it better'?" He gave a snort of disgust. His drawl suggested Southern origins, but was nothing like the mid- or deep-South accents she was accustomed to hearing. "No wonder rich boys grow up to be selfish, arrogant bas—snakes in the grass. They never have to apologize, never have to make amends, and they never get the piss and vinegar thrashed out of them."

Suddenly Diamond was scrambling to defend herself as much as Robbie.

"Look to your own conduct and language, sir!" She was outraged. "No amount of annoyance or inconvenience can excuse such crude language and infamous behavior."

Standing her ground, returning him stare for stare, she couldn't help but see that the vest he wore was actually a coat in progress, with padding sticking out of the armholes and no sleeves, and that his shirt was minus studs and hanging open, baring the entire length of his chest. Shock struck as she realized she was glimpsing naked male flesh . . . that she had just entered a private male sanctum, a place where men routinely disrobed and bared themselves.

Jerking her gaze from him, she felt herself reddening from her breasts up.

"You have behaved reprehensibly toward a child who—"

"*I've* behaved—Look, lady, I came here to be fitted for a suit of clothes, and your precious 'child' brought the damned walls down on my head!" He lowered his head and sifted through his dark hair to expose a burgeoning goose egg. "How's *this* for 'inconvenience' . . . and this . . . ?" He held up a dangling lapel and pulled out the thigh of his trousers. "How's this for 'annoyance'?" There was a sizable rip where a seam used to be, and his demonstration parted the fabric and bared a shocking piece of thigh. *A hairy, naked male thigh.*

"Tell me I didn't have reason to drop him right on his annoying little—"

"We fix, monsieur." Monsieur Martene intervened, gesturing frantically as if trying to smooth a disturbed nap. "We fix all . . . *tout de suite!* We finish the clothes with our compliments."

"No, no, Monsieur Martene." Diamond glanced at the little tailor squirming at the edge of her vision. "You will put this 'gentleman's' garments on *my* bill. I insist."

She straightened her shoulders and turned for one last salvo, and discovered that the man had closed the volatile inches between them and now towered over her . . . big and dark and disheveled, with eyes like molten copper. Waves of heat radiated from him; she could almost feel his pulse beating on the air around her. Her only rational thought was that she had never encountered a man like him before . . . so rude and opinionated . . . so physically overwhelming.

Her gaze dropped to his bare chest and fixed on smooth, hard mounds of flesh tipped with dark flat nipples and supported by smoothly defined ribs. Stunned, she slid her gaze still lower. His midsection was a tautly sculptured rectangle and as he shifted some of his weight from one leg to another, the thick, ropelike muscle over his stomach contracted sinuously. She swallowed hard. It was as if she were seeing beneath that sun-bronzed skin . . . witnessing a body working within a body. Then it registered that his chest and stomach were just as tanned as his face. He must have gone shirtless. Outside. Frequently.

She couldn't move or look away. Awareness of him seeped through her every pore. His eyes narrowed slightly. His lips parted. His chest—that mesmerizing expanse of flesh—seemed to be rising and falling faster.

Say something, she thought, *anything!*

"I believe"—she swallowed hard—"an apology is in order."

"Very well. I accept." His voice was so low and resonant that it caused sundry unmentionable parts of her body to hum.

Her physical response temporarily eclipsed the meaning framed within those vibrations. His words registered only when his provocative smile appeared. He seemed to know what was happening inside her and he—he *accepted*?

"I didn't mean—" She saw the glint in his eyes deepen. "Ohhhh!"

She managed to turn on her heel and made it to the door without colliding with either Monsieur Martene or his insulting customer. The little tailor followed, showering her with apologies until she turned to him at the street door.

"If you would be so good as to deliver the rest of Robbie's riding clothes, Monsieur Martene . . ." She shot a withering glance at the curtained rear door. "And be certain to include the cost of that awful man's garments on *my* bill."

In the coach she found Robbie perched on the edge of the seat, braced as if he might make a dash for the door at any minute, with Hardwell scowling fiercely at him over tightly crossed arms.

"What did he do this time?" Hardwell demanded as she slid onto the seat beside Robbie. She looked at her young cousin, and under their combined regard, Robbie reddened and pushed his damp hair up off his forehead.

"What?" he said, looking alarmed. "I didn't do nothin'—"

"*Anything*," Diamond corrected.

"—on *purpose*."

"It wasn't the danged 'telephone' again, was it?" Hardwell sat abruptly forward. "If he's rung up the mayor again, or the clerks down at the bank—"

"It wasn't the telephone," Diamond said, watching Robbie squirm and seeing in his clear blue eyes, beneath his boyish bravado and mischievous energy, unmistakable traces of anxiety. Why was she the only one who seemed to see that in him . . . who understood how desperately he needed security and love? "It was just a little matter of some screens in the fitting rooms toppling."

"I—I didn't mean to." Robbie peered defensively up at her. "I just give one a bump and it fell over an' hit another one . . . and that one hit another one . . ."

Hardwell shut his eyes and groaned. "Ye gods. I won't be able to show my face at Martene and Savoy for months. First the bank, then the mayor's office, then the mercantile, and now my tailor's. Soon I'll be a pariah in every blessed precinct of Baltimore."

"It was a mess, Robbie," she said, ignoring Hardwell's lamentations. "That man was hit on the head and could have been badly hurt."

"I didn't mean ta," Robbie said, huddling back. "Anyway . . . ye should have heard th' son of a gun cuss—"

"This isn't about *his* behavior, it's about *yours*." She leaned closer to him. "When we get home, you're to go straight to your room and think about what happened. I believe you'll have a few things to say to me before dinner."

Robbie glanced at Hardwell, who looked as if he had a torrent of opinion dammed up behind tightly pursed lips. Then his gaze wound its way reluctantly back to Diamond. After a moment, he gave a huff of surrender and nodded.

She watched him draw his feet up on the tufted velvet seat and cross them Indian style, then looked up to find Hardwell regarding her with a combination of worry and frustration.

"You've got too soft a heart, Diamond girl," he said. "Mark my words. One of these days it's goin' to get you into real trouble."

Diamond tucked her chin defensively and transferred her attention out the window. The city landmarks of Baltimore had receded, replaced by lush emerald fields of young wheat and maturing oats. As she watched the familiar countryside approaching her home, Gracemont, dark, aromatic fields of crops alternated with orchards of blossoming apple, plum, and pear trees. It was her favorite time of year, filled with promise and with . . . approaching hoofbeats.

Someone on horseback was hailing their driver, and from the way Old Ned slowed the horses, it had to be an acquaintance. Hardwell and Robbie leaned immediately to the windows.

"Hello!" A top hat tipped in greeting soon became visible through the window and a moment later a man in formal riding clothes appeared at the coach window. "I've had a devil of a time tracking you down this afternoon."

"Morgan Kenwood!" Hardwell's face lighted. "You're back."

"Mr. Humphreys." The tall, handsome figure tipped his hat. "Diamond."

"Morgan!" Diamond forced a smile and slid her purse and the three letters it contained beneath her skirt. "I didn't expect you back for *weeks*."

"How was Ireland? Did you get some good breeding stock?" Hardwell demanded eagerly, flinging the door open in invitation.

"I surely did." Without hesitation, Morgan Kenwood dismounted, tied his horse to the coach, and climbed aboard. Halfway inside, he encountered an unexpected obstacle. Robbie sat with his arms and legs crossed, glowering at him, asserting a tenacious claim on the seat beside Diamond.

"Well, well. Who is this?" Morgan said with a frown.

"Diamond's cousin," Hardwell answered, waving a wordless order at Robbie to vacate the seat and come sit by him. "He came to live with us just after you left." When the boy didn't move, Morgan aimed past him, for the space beside Diamond.

She abruptly seized her cousin's arm and dragged him to her side, placing him between her and Morgan. "Remember your manners, Robbie. Mr. Kenwood has just returned from a long journey." She looked up at Morgan, thinking that he looked oddly colorless . . . from his impeccable charcoal riding coat to his cool gray eyes and determined smile. "When did you arrive?"

"Yesterday evening." He turned to her. "And my very first thoughts upon arriving were of Gracemont. And *you*."

"About Ireland . . ." Hardwell fidgeted. "Find any prizes over there?"

Morgan smiled. "Ireland is full of prize Thoroughbreds, to hear the Irish tell it. The problem is, they price the beasts accordingly. Even so, I managed to acquire a half-dozen animals that together will make quite a contribution to our bloodlines."

"When will they arrive?" Hardwell rubbed his hands together eagerly.

"I brought them back with me," Morgan declared. "A crossing is always difficult this time of year and I decided to take no chances with these beauties. And, of course, I was eager to get back"—he sat back and looked intently at her—"for Diamond's birthday."

The way his voice softened around those words caused her stomach to contract and she lowered her gaze, hoping the feeling didn't show in her face.

Her birthday. In four short weeks, she would reach the age of twenty-three and would receive the final installment of the inheritance left to her by her father. Unfortunately, Morgan and everyone else in Baltimore knew what the arrival of her twenty-third birthday meant. She would have an even more fantastic fortune at her fingertips. Massive sums. Huge, vulgar piles of money. It meant the maneuvering for favor and funding which already plagued her would intensify. And, of course, there was the little matter of a few promises that would come due . . . including one she had made to Morgan.

As she looked at Morgan's elegant frame and read his intention to redeem her promise in his eyes, she knew beyond the shadow of a doubt that the "real trouble" Hardwell had just predicted was on its way.

THE TINKLE OF the bell on the shop door was soft, but somehow managed to penetrate the swirl of emotion that had kept Bear McQuaid immobile since the boy's mother frosted him with a look as frigid as a Montana stream in January. He blinked, looked down at his dusty, half-finished evening coat, and blinked again, having trouble focusing on it. Burned into his vision was the image of a pair of lightning-blue eyes set in a flushed oval face. He had just stood there, staring at her . . . feeling reason and will abandoning him . . . caught hard in the grip of . . .

He shook his head to clear it and was alarmed by the way the woman's striking figure and fiery blue eyes lingered in his starved senses. He felt the lump on his head again, took a purging breath, and told himself the blow must have addled him more than he realized. He was probably lucky he wasn't out cold. Rotten kid. A flash of lightning-blue streaked through his awareness one last time before settling into memory. Infernal female.

Still smoldering from her stare, he actually felt for his eyebrows . . . then growled with disgust when he found them intact.

Moments later Martene ushered him out of the devastation, into the front room, and anxiously began to wield a brush over his still sleeveless coat.

"A thousand pardons, monsieur." The little Frenchman clapped irritably for his apprentices, who had made themselves scarce after two hours of coping with Robbie's rambunctious behavior. "We finish the clothes for you straightaway . . . no charge. Mademoiselle Wingate insists upon having ze bill."

Bear froze in the middle of drawing a breath.

"Mad-moi-selle who?"

"Wingate, monsieur." The tailor's brush continued its rhythmic strokes. *"Très riche. Très jolie."* There was a sigh and the brush halted. *"Très difficile."*

"Wingate." Every nerve in Bear's body suddenly came alive. "Is she related to Diamond Wingate?" When Martene shook his head, Bear felt a brief surge of relief that evaporated a moment later.

"Not related, monsieur. That *is* Mademoiselle Diamond Wingate."

The wall that had fallen on Bear minutes ago hadn't

stunned him as much as that bit of news. "Her? She's the one? B-but she's—she's—"

Too damned young, he thought.

"But what about the boy?"

Martene shook his head. "Her cousin, monsieur. She 'as taken him to live with her. He will give her the ache in the head, that one." He looked up and caught Bear's expression of horror as he stood before the mirror, interpreting it as a comment on the clothes. "Do not be alarmed, monsieur. It is only a little dust. By the time of the party, we will repair all. You will be dashing, indeed."

Bear stood stock-still, feeling as if his insides had collapsed and were sliding toward his feet. By the time of the party he wouldn't be dashing, he would be *dead.* Halt would lay him out flat when he learned what had happened. And he would damned well deserve it. Diamond Wingate was his best hope for financing his railroad, and he had just dropped her cousin smack on his arse and insulted her six ways from Sunday. There was no way he could go to a society party in two days, face her, and ask her for a few hundred thousand dollars to build their railroad.

''WELL?'' HALT WAS waiting when Bear exited the tailor shop, clad once again in the business suit on which he had already spent most of their traveling money. "Will yer clothes be ready in time?"

"I have to come around and collect them Saturday morning." Without so much as a pause, Bear struck off down the street.

"And?" Halt fell into step beside him, puzzling over his mood. "What about th' payment? Is he willin' to take half and let us pay the rest later?"

A hitch occurred in his stride. "Didn't mention it.

Didn't have to. A kid was climbing around all over the dressing screens and knocked one over on my head." He removed his hat and ducked his head, parting his hair in demonstration. Halt issued a low whistle.

"That's a beaut."

Bear jammed his hat back onto his head. "Yeah, well, the kid's 'mother' seemed to think so. She insisted on paying for my new suit by way of apology."

"She what?" Halt stopped at the edge of the pavement and his ruddy face fairly split with a broad grin. "That's wonderful, lad." Catching the discrepancy between Bear's news and mood, he scowled. "You didn't by any chance do somethin' stupid, did ye? Like tellin' her you couldn't accept?"

Something stupid? Bear groaned silently. "No."

"Excellent!" Halt's grin reappeared. "That's the first bit o' good fortune we've had in weeks. To celebrate, we'll go out an' have us a steak dinner."

Bear scowled. "We can't afford that."

"Who says? Things are finally lookin' up for us, lad. We got *bankers* befriendin' us and women buyin' us suits o' clothes." He clapped Bear on the shoulder with a laugh and pulled him along. "Ye know . . . I got a good feelin' about you an' ol' Miss Wingate. A real good feelin'."

Through the evening, every time Bear started to reveal the true nature of the event that Halt had pronounced their "good fortune," Halt would say something that showed his faith in Bear and his unflagging optimism about their long-held dream of building a railroad, and Bear would again stop short of telling him the identity of the woman who had insisted on paying for his evening clothes. How could he confess that he had already met, insulted, and infuriated their potential investor such that she would probably spit in his eye the moment they were introduced?

By the time they settled onto sagging canvas cots in their rooming house that night, Bear realized that he didn't have a choice. Just a week ago, he had lectured Halt on doing his part and being willing to make sacrifices in the name of their dream. He could do no less himself. He would have to go to Vassar's party, brazen it out, and hope he could persuade Miss Wingate to overlook their inauspicious beginning . . . in the interest of profit and the march of "Progress."

FOUR

SATURDAY EVENING ARRIVED unseasonably warm and rich with the scents of the maturing spring. The Wingate carriage wound its way through the darkening countryside toward Pennyworth, the Vassars' estate, carrying only Diamond and Hardwell. Hannah Humphrey had insisted on staying at home with Robbie, who had refused a third dessert at dinner and sent everyone into a state of alarm.

Weathering the bounce and sway of the coach, Diamond adjusted and readjusted her posture to keep from wrinkling her long, snug-fitting satin bodice and arranged and rearranged her skirts to keep from flattening the ribbons and flounces on her elaborate bustle. When she achieved a suitable arrangement for her skirts, she turned her attention to the lace that rimmed her princess neckline, fluffing, smoothing, and tugging. Hardwell chuckled, and she looked up.

"You look lovely, Diamond. You'll charm Morgan's socks off."

Morgan could jolly well keep his socks *on,* she responded silently, trying not to let her thoughts show in her face. The very last thing she needed was Morgan Kenwood hovering over her all evening. Why couldn't he have kept to his original schedule and arrived home from Ireland only days before her wretched birthday?

Her dread of seeing him was compounded by feelings of guilt. She had allowed him to extract a promise from her to announce her marriage plans on her birthday . . . knowing full well that he interpreted that promise to mean she would be announcing plans to marry *him*.

It wasn't entirely dishonest of her. At the time she made the promise, she had not yet eliminated marriage as a possibility and, if she were to marry, she honestly considered Morgan Kenwood to be one of her leading matrimonial candidates. His family's home, Kensington, bordered Gracemont; she had known him all of her life; and his breeding and appearance were perfectly—

A sudden lurch of the carriage caused her to grab for the strap hanging beside the door, to steady herself. "Why are we speeding up?"

Hardwell was already heading for the window and squinting out into the gathering darkness to see what was happening. "It's another vehicle—a wagon." He pointed out the window, to the rear, and Diamond looked back to glimpse a pair of horses in harness struggling to overtake their landau. The billowing dust made it difficult to see who was trying to pass their carriage on such a narrow and rutted road and in such abysmal light.

But as they neared Pennyworth, the road widened enough to permit the wagon to draw abreast of them and it became clear that the driver did not intend to pass. In the dissolving daylight, they could see the man driving the wagon begin to yell and wave his hat. His words were obscured by the rumble of the wheels, but he seemed to be calling to them to stop their carriage.

"Perhaps he's in trouble," Diamond said, glancing at Hardwell.

"No doubt. Lunatics usually are." He stuck his arm out and waved the driver off. "Drop back, man!" he shouted. "Have you no sense a'tall?"

He thumped the roof of the coach to signal Ned, and upon a crack from the whip and a snap of the reins, the horses broke into a gallop. The heavy coach lurched again. Diamond braced her feet against the opposite seat, tightened her hold on the hanging strap with one hand, and gripped the opening of her evening wrap with the other. She had never known Ned to push the horses like this . . . especially with darkness coming on. Her heart began to pound.

Their pursuer drove his horses with shocking recklessness, trying to keep pace. Then, just as they rounded a curve and the gates of Pennyworth came into view, one of the wagon's wheels hit a deep rut, broke several spokes, and sent the vehicle bouncing and careening off the road. Diamond and Hardwell strained to see if it overturned and were able to catch a glimpse of the man climbing up on the footboard of the wagon to survey the damage.

Soon Ned slowed the horses, pulled into the drive leading to the Vassars' handsome English Tudor house, and settled into the line of carriages inching toward the front doors. Inside, they began to collect themselves.

"What do you suppose he wanted?" Diamond ran a hand over her hair.

"What do you think?" Hardwell said, giving her a meaningful look.

Money was the first thing that came to her mind. It was what everyone else wanted from her.

Hardwell grew impatient and suggested that they disembark on the spot and walk the rest of the way. Their arrival wouldn't have quite the flare of a grand society entrance, but at least she wouldn't have to cool her heels and further crease her satin in a stuffy coach.

No sooner had Diamond set both feet on the ground than she heard footsteps in the gravel behind her and turned to find a man running toward them.

"Please, Miss Wingate—" A tall, lanky fellow in a rumpled gray suit and steamed-up spectacles loomed out of the darkness and stumbled to a halt in front of them. He was so winded that he could scarcely speak, and in the moment it took him to catch his breath, Diamond recognized the paleness of his coat and his bowler hat. He was the driver of the buggy that had just chased their coach.

"You—have to"—he panted—"come with me—"

"See here, man, whatever you're about, we're having none of it." Hardwell extended a protective elbow in her direction and she slid her hand through it—just as the man seized her other arm.

"I have to show you. It's not far . . . a demonstration . . . my moving steps . . ."

The mention of "moving steps" brought another flash of recognition. This was the same man who had raced their carriage on foot a few days ago.

"Really, Mister . . ."

"Ellsworth. Nigel Ellsworth."

"Really, Mr. Ellsworth"—she tugged against his grasp—"this is not the time or the place for such a proposal."

"But it's *never* the time or the place. I've been trying to see you for weeks now, and I always get turned away at the gates or at your company offices," the inventor blurted out and then gasped another breath. "If you'll just come with me, it will only take a few minutes. And you'll see what a wonderful idea—"

"I cannot come with you." She watched the feverish light in the fellow's eyes. "But if you'll come by Gracemont on Monday, I promise I will—"

"She most certainly will not," Hardwell declared, deciding to take matters into his own hands. "How dare you accost us like this? Are you mad?"

"I'm not mad, I'm desperate." Ellsworth tightened his grip.

"Let go, or I shall be forced to call for help," Hardwell ordered, tightening his hold on Diamond and bracing to resist any effort to move her.

"I'll let go"—Ellsworth began to pull—"*after* she's seen my moving steps."

"Please, you're hurting my arm," Diamond said, trying to wrest free.

"Release her this instant." Hardwell abruptly changed tactics, lunging at Ellsworth to push him away. But the inventor simply took advantage of the additional momentum to pull Diamond farther along.

The next moments were something of a blur for Diamond as she found herself pulled steadily down the darkened drive. She was vaguely aware of shocked faces peering down from the coaches they passed, and she finally managed to wrestle Ellsworth to a halt. "You cannot honestly believe that such behavior will enhance my opinion of your invention."

"My invention shall speak for itsel—*oof*—"

The tussling pair slammed unexpectedly into what felt like a wall. She took advantage of the pause to shove back and look up at the dark form towering over them . . . following a pair of satin lapels up to a proper black tie and crisp white collar.

"I don't believe the lady wants to go," came a low, menacing rumble.

The mad stair-maker must not be seeing what she was seeing, Diamond thought, or he would release her on the spot. A square, sun-bronzed chin jutted over that pristine

collar and above that she spotted two dark-rimmed eyes
that glowed like candle flames. Familiar flames.

"Out of the way!" Ellsworth tried to shove aside the
form blocking their path. "She has to see my-i-e-eee—"

Ellsworth was seized by the back of the neck and the
seat of the trousers and hoisted off the ground. Freed, she
caught only a glimpse of the ensuing scuffle as she
whirled, lifted her skirts, and ran back up the drive. But in
that glimpse, she recognized familiar elements . . . motions which, joined to the man's voice and face and eyes,
piqued a memory.

"Are you all right?" Hardwell engulfed her in a hug a
moment later.

"I'm fine, really," she murmured, feeling a bit wobbly in
the knees as she paused to look over her shoulder. Her
rescuer had wrestled the crazed inventor down the line of
carriages and disappeared from sight. The receding sounds
of their struggle were drowned out by the rush of men
approaching from the direction of the house.

"Deepest apologies, my dear—are you all right?" Their
host, Philip Vassar, reached them and waved the
housemen behind him to proceed down the drive. "I swear
to you, I shall see the wretch is prosecuted to the full-
est—"

"No, please, Mr. Vassar," Diamond said, summoning a
smile and hoping it looked more convincing than it felt.
"He's just a poor, desperate man—"

"A *lunatic*, you mean," Hardwell declared fervently.
"We were just fortunate that other gentleman arrived when
he did."

"Other gentleman?" Vassar asked. "What other gentleman?"

• • •

BY THE TIME Bear had wrestled the flailing, protesting gatecrasher down the drive and sent him sprawling into the road, he was roundly regretting his impulsive action. He stood in the gate opening, spread his feet, and glared, hoping it would be enough to dissuade the fellow from getting up and charging back through the gates.

The interloper fumbled to right his spectacles and bowler hat, and Bear reddened from the neck up as he watched. There was something to be proud of, he told himself; he had just trounced a bespectacled bookworm. He was relieved to leave the little wretch to the three beefy fellows in servant dress who came running down the drive behind him. When they started for the uninvited guest, the man scrambled to his feet and ran as if the hounds of hell were upon him.

Bear dusted himself off and started back to his rented buggy. He had been stuck in that row of grand carriages, watching the other guests disembarking and scrutinizing their garments to reassure himself he was rigged out properly, when he heard the crunch of approaching footsteps in the gravel beside him. A fellow in a bowler hat ran by, and Bear couldn't help the surly thought that if the fellow was hurrying to the party, he was dressed all wrong. Seconds later, the runner accosted a man and woman exiting a coach.

There was a shout and some shoving and tugging, and the runner tried to drag the woman off with him. Bear had bounded from the buggy, knowing that he would probably regret giving in to that urge to action. After weeks of being cooped up in crowded trains, flophouses, and bankers' offices, it felt just too damn good to have his blood pounding in his veins again.

That primal and exhilarating exertion, however, had proved all too brief. Now he found himself feeling hot and sweaty and a little foolish. Checking his coat, vest, and tie, he found them all in good order. His relief was short-lived.

What the hell was he doing, involving himself in something he knew nothing about and putting himself and his business of the evening at risk? He should be trying to think of something clever and conciliatory to say to Diamond Wingate when Vassar introduced them.

Sorry about that cousin of yours, a few days back. I don't usually go around dropping children on their . . . heads.

I hope you didn't take my irritation personally. I always get a bit testy when a wall falls on me.

Thanks for the new clothes, Miss Wingate. Now, how about a few hundred thousand in cash to line the pockets?

He winced at the sardonic edge of his thoughts. He'd rather chase strays in a four-day rain than face that woman again and eat the crow that he knew would be on the menu between them.

"Oh, yeah, McQuaid," he muttered. "You're in for a real good time."

Twice he paused to dust the toe of a shoe on the back of his trouser leg as he stalked back up the drive. Then he looked up and found none other than Philip Vassar hurrying down the drive toward him.

"If you're looking for your gatecrasher, he's probably half a mile away by now," Bear called, jerking a thumb over his shoulder. "I tossed him out on his ars—posterior, and when he got a look at your men, he took to his heels."

"You? You're the gentleman?" Vassar halted for a moment, then broke into a huge grin. "In the right place at the right time . . . eh, McQuaid?" He clasped Bear's hand and clapped a hand on his shoulder, urging him toward the house. "Not quite the sort of introduction I had in mind, but it should prove memorable, nonetheless."

"Introduction?" Bear felt his stomach tightening.

"Charging in to her rescue . . . chivalry makes a damn

fine reference," Vassar said with a ghost of a smile that became more substantial as Bear shook his head and seemed confused. "You mean you honestly don't know who you rescued?" He chuckled at the irony. "That was Diamond Wingate."

Bear felt himself walking and heard himself speaking, but it seemed to be happening to another man as Vassar led him up the drive. All he had seen in the flurry and the darkness was a fancy female dress, the top of a light head, and a twisting, thrashing form. That was Diamond Wingate?

A small knot of gentlemen standing near the front steps parted as they approached, revealing a frilly bustle, shining red-gold curls, and a curvaceous figure wrapped in embroidered peach-colored satin. Diamond Wingate turned as he approached, and he halted . . . might have decamped altogether if Vassar hadn't had him by the arm.

"Here he is, Miss Wingate," Vassar said with suppressed excitement. "Your very own paladin. May I present Mr. Barton McQuaid of Montana."

Bear scrambled to recall both his manners and his fevered impressions from the tailor shop. Damn. Had she looked like this at Martene's place? Most of what he recalled from that encounter was the feel of his blood pounding in his veins, the preparatory tightening of the muscles over his belly, and the humiliating rush of unwelcome heat into his lips.

He had been so wrought up—caught between the ache in his head and the urge to throttle her precious "cousin"—that he had neglected to capture the details of that strawberry-blond hair, silky skin, and full, ripe-for-mischief mouth. It was all coming back to him now, however, including the memory of her noteworthy curves. He summoned the nerve to meet her gaze and recognition pelted him like cold rain.

It was her, all right. He'd know those lightning-blue eyes anywhere. Especially the *lightning* part.

"I believe I owe you a debt, sir," she said coolly, offering her gloved hand, and he tried not to seem reluctant to take it.

"Pleased to have been of service," he heard himself say. The very next moment his throat filled with raw, elemental heat and he couldn't have uttered another word if his life depended on it.

For a long moment they stood hand in hand, eyeing each other, confronting each other both in memory and in present fact. Scarcely a breath was taken around them as the others tried to discern what was happening.

A throat-clearing rumble finally intruded. Diamond recognized Hardwell's general-purpose reminder and came to her senses, jerking her hand away.

"Truly grateful for your assistance, sir," Hardwell declared, stepping in to offer his own hand. "I am Diamond's guardian, Hardwell Humphrey. If there is anything I can do for you . . . anything at all . . ."

"You seem a bit flushed, my dear," Vassar observed. "Perhaps you'd like a quiet place to rest and collect yourself."

Diamond Wingate lifted her skirts and, with her guardian's help, made her way up the steps. Watching the sway of her elaborate bustle, Bear scarcely noticed Vassar's chuckle or the way he was being propelled toward the steps and the arched entry of the house. His wits had withdrawn to hold a tactical summit and the result was a frantic urge to abandon this whole idiotic scheme. He remembered her all too well. Clearly, she remembered him, too. There was no way he could approach her without getting his proposal tossed back in his face.

As they mounted the steps along with the arriving

guests, Vassar was drawn into conversation by an acquaintance and grabbed Bear by the arm.

"This is the fellow I wanted you to meet," his host was saying with obvious pleasure. "Just in from Montana. A railroad man. Barton McQuaid, I want you to meet Mason Purnell, owner of our local dry-goods empire."

"I haven't even taken off my hat, and already I've heard how you set Miss Wingate's pursuer out on his ear," Purnell told him, offering his hand.

Bear could do nothing but accept that handshake and nod in a way that he hoped looked more modest than mortified. Over the next half hour, he gradually perfected that equivocal nod as he repeated it, again and again, over the firm handshakes of men, and the oddly clinging handclasps of women. Vassar steered him around the center hall, the drawing room, and the conservatory with proprietary pride, introducing him to everyone and answering discreetly the veiled queries about the "rescue" of Diamond Wingate.

Rescue. It took a few repetitions of the word for the reality of it to penetrate Bear's defensive haze. He had indeed rescued her. It occurred to him that after such an "heroic" effort on his part, she could scarcely have spit in his eye and denounced him as a child beater. In point of fact, except for the heat in her eyes—more sparks than lightning, now that he thought about it—she had greeted him much as she might have anyone upon a first meeting.

A wave of relief sluiced through him. Then the hard part was over! He had not only met her, he had actually managed to even the score between them. He smiled and drew a deep, steadying breath. Now, all he had to do was be unfailingly polite and reasonable and accommodating . . . and get her alone somewhere for a quarter of an hour . . .

FIVE

SOON EVERYONE AT Evelyn Stanhope Vassar's spring party knew the identity of the tall, dark stranger Vassar was squiring around like a proud papa. Evelyn filled them in on the details.

"He is a railroad entrepreneur who has spent most of his time out West," she told a group of local information brokers, while wearing an expression of the sort cats wear when fishbowls are found empty. "He is unmarried and, to the best of my knowledge, unattached. And it's plain to see, as my Philip says, that he has a number of . . . *assets.*"

The women gathered around Evelyn in the upper hall smiled at the way she rolled her eyes as she said it. One glimpse of the tall Westerner was all the matrons of Baltimore needed to appreciate the delicious versatility of the term their commerce-minded husbands used so matter-of-factly: "assets."

Diamond Wingate, recovered and rounding the corner in the upstairs hallway, heard her hostess's words but was not privy to the expression that accompanied them. Even if she had seen it, she lacked the experience needed to understand the sort of attributes that more mature women might consider "tangible assets" in a man.

Evelyn read in the others' faces that someone was approaching and turned to greet Diamond.

"Here she is." Evelyn wrapped an arm around her shoulders and lowered her eyes and voice. "No one would blame you, dear, if you decided to retire for the evening."

"And miss the delights you have in store for us?" Diamond said determinedly, eliciting a relieved look from her hostess. "I cannot allow one poor, demented man to send me scurrying into seclusion."

Two, however, had created a significant temptation to do just that. The first man, that poor inventor, had merely unsettled her. His rash demands were just another variation on what had become the central theme of her life: requests and propositions for money. It was the second, her tall, dark rescuer, who had sent her trembling into the house. That rude, irritating man from the tailor shop . . . for a second time she had found herself rattled by his overwhelming presence.

In the days since their encounter, she had systematically examined her response to him at Martene and Savoy's. Her reaction had obviously been part shock at his high-handed treatment of Robbie, and part embarrassment at her unexpected encounter with a man in dishabille. Comforted by that analysis, she had used reason to defuse the volatile incident in her memory.

Occasionally, however, as she lay in her bed at night, she suffered a spontaneous recall of the sight of his hard, naked chest and felt again the confusion and guilty fascination she had experienced when looking at it. The stubborn persistence of that memory—and of her intensely physical reaction to it—hinted at a whole side of her and a whole range of experiences that she had never imagined existed. And she would have been quite content to have continued on in blissful ignorance of them.

But, this evening, the gentlemen around her had parted and there he was again . . . looming big and dark, his eyes glowing, and his insufferable self-possession rolling over her like a sultry southern breeze. Suddenly she was all nerves and goose bumps again, caught between their current encounter and the potent memory of his naked chest in all of its voluptuous glory.

It took a while in the privacy of an upstairs bedroom for her to reassemble her poise. However gentlemanly he appeared, she told herself, she knew the truth of his character. She had seen him at his barest—literally—and knew that he was hot tempered, easily provoked, and alarmingly prone to physical violence. And while he might appear to make his baser impulses serve a noble purpose in public, and might even have managed to ingratiate himself with Philip Vassar, he would find her made of altogether sterner and more skeptical stuff.

As the ladies joined the guests collecting outside the doors to the dining room, she scanned the group for a glimpse of the big Montanan, telling herself it was simply that she was determined not to be caught unprepared again. When she didn't see him, she heaved a quiet sigh.

Her relief was short-lived, however. She looked up a moment later to find the newly arrived Morgan Kenwood bearing down on her from the front hall. He was outraged at the news that she had been accosted on the Vassars' front drive and vowed to be her protective shadow for the rest of the evening.

EVELYN STANHOPE VASSAR, always an unparalleled hostess, had truly outdone herself tonight. When the doors to the mirrored dining hall were thrown open, she led her guests among long dining tables draped with snowy linen and adorned with cleverly crafted islands of fresh-cut flowers, silver candelabra, and sparkling crystal. Liveried waiters lined the walls, waiting patiently for the guests to file in and find their seats, and in the background, a string trio provided spirited baroque music to set a lively mood. It was enough to make everyone forget the talk of the evening and her tall, dark rescuer . . .

. . . until Morgan escorted Diamond to her seat and she looked up from the script on her place card to find a pair of tawny gold eyes staring at her from across the table. Word of their pairing flew, and every guest filing into the dining room strained for a glimpse of Diamond Wingate and the big Westerner together.

Diamond scarcely noticed Morgan's annoyance that he was not seated by her or that he located his place across the dining room, beside doe-eyed Clarice Vassar. She was too busy being utterly disinterested in the sun-bronzed face and broad-shouldered form that would be her unavoidable scenery throughout dinner.

"Diamond dear, I believe you've already met Mr. McQuaid," Evelyn Vassar crooned as she swept by on her rounds as hostess. "He is from the Montana Territory, you know. A railroad man . . . a close business acquaintance of Philip's."

"Yes." Diamond felt betraying heat flooding her face. "We've met."

"We have, indeed." Barton McQuaid responded with a knowing smile and a deep rumble that set her fingertips vibrating. "Glad to see you're none the worse for wear, Miss Wingate."

"There you are," Hardwell broke in as he located his place, just down the table from them. "Nothin' short of remarkable . . . the way you handled that lunatic, Mr. McQuaid." He declared to the other guests around him:

"Picked him right up and shook him like a dog does a bone—never seen anything like it!"

Diamond, on the other hand, had seen something appallingly like it, only three days ago.

"Habit, I guess," McQuaid said, reddening genially under the scrutiny aimed at him. "One of the first things you learn, out in Montana, is to stick up for women and children."

"Well, you certainly seem to have mastered *half* of that lesson," Diamond said with a pleasantness that cloaked the barb in it for everyone but him. When the comment struck a spark in his eyes, she smiled.

As their hostess took her place and the serving began, Diamond was acutely aware of the many pairs of eyes turned in their direction. Annoying as that scrutiny was, it didn't begin to compare with the irritation she felt at the knowledge that *his* eyes were on her, roaming her with impunity. What on earth was Evelyn Vassar thinking, putting them opposite each other for dinner?

Minutes later, as the guests turned their attention to Evelyn's marvelous menu, she was able to make distracting conversation with Mason Purnell and Mrs. Orville Lancombe, who were seated on either side of her. Barton McQuaid was mostly silent, answering politely when questioned, but volunteering nothing. After a time, however, even his silence began to grate on her.

Had the man no social graces at all? Not that she wasn't grateful to be spared that unnerving vibration that occurred in her fingertips whenever he spoke . . . but honestly, one would think he could manage to put forth a comment here or there as a social obligation.

Then, halfway through the braised pheasant, Philip Vassar raised his voice to include everyone seated at the long table. "My friend Mr. McQuaid is a railroad man, you know. He's currently working to build a railroad line in the

Montana Territory. A most promising venture. Tell us about your valley in Montana, McQuaid. The one you intend to open to wheat farming."

The Westerner looked less than thrilled to be quizzed on his business involvements in so public a forum.

"I hold the rights to a little valley containing some of the best wheat land in the territory. Good soil. Plenty of water. Right now it's short-grass prairie and range land, but someday it will make farmers and ranchers a healthy living."

"And you a healthy profit," she said, not realizing she had spoken aloud until he responded.

"Profit is the usual goal of business ventures, I believe," he murmured, so quietly as to be meant primarily for her.

"And the sky . . . tell them about the sky," Vassar prodded.

He shifted and turned a taut smile to Vassar and his end of the table. "The sky. A mere telling can't do it justice. It's so big and so close . . . you feel like you're about to be swallowed up in it. In the winter, when the snow covers the ground, the blue is so intense it makes your eyes ache. And on the hills at night, when you look up, the moon seems so close that you could just pick it from the sky and put it in your pocket."

"An *ambitious* bit of larceny," she murmured. He flicked another taut look her way and she took a certain satisfaction in the way his jaw flexed.

"Well, as a friend of mine always says," he responded, "a man should always make the sin worth the penance."

"And the wind," Vassar persisted. "What is it they say about the wind?"

McQuaid gave a wry smile. "The Indians and the old-timers say the wind talks. They say it whispers through the hills and canyons, speaking wisdom and warnings to all who will listen. I don't know if that's true, but I do know there are nights out under the stars, on the wide-open range, when a man surely can believe the wind is talkin' to him."

The temptation was just too great.

"And when the wind talks to you, Mr. McQuaid, what does it warn you against?" she asked with excessive politeness.

There was instant silence up and down the table.

He leveled that molten copper gaze on her, picked up his goblet, and downed the rest of his wine before responding. "I get the same message the wind gives every other man willing to listen: beware of watered whiskey, horses with blankets on, and"—he smiled as he delivered the thrust—"women who talk too much."

Laughter broke out along the table and she straightened, meeting his gaze squarely and refusing to look away. A battle, she sensed, had just been joined. Very well. She wasted no time in launching an offensive.

"Tell us about this railroad you are building, Mr. McQuaid," she said. "Is your right-of-way through the mountains? What gauge of track will you use? How do you intend to deal with the labor problem? Who is building your engines—or are you buying older ones to start? What natural obstacles do you face? How many trestles and tunnels will you have to build? Who have you hired to do your engineering work?"

"You're in for it now, McQuaid," Vassar said with a wicked laugh. "I must warn you, Miss Wingate has a keen interest in railroads."

McQuaid seemed surprised and leveled a penetrating look on her.

"The terrain is mostly moderate," he said evenly. "No tunnels or trestles will be necessary . . . though blasting will be required in some quarters to level and widen the track bed. I intend to use I rails, and since we have plenty of space there is no need to consider a narrow gauge. The railroad industry has to work toward using standard track and cars wherever possible. Labor won't be a problem . . . there are plenty of men between here and Montana willing to do hard work for a decent wage. And as for obstacles"—his voice lowered a step—"I don't intend to let any develop."

He was so utterly, insufferably sure of himself, she couldn't resist.

"Then I take it you don't anticipate any difficulty from James J. Hill and his Chicago, Milwaukee and St. Paul Railroad."

Bear McQuaid saw a smile curling the corners of those satiny lips and fought the surprise that threatened to derail his determination.

"I intend to leave Mr. Hill to his business and expect that he will have the good sense to leave me to mine," he said matter-of-factly.

Her laughter was downright deflating.

"I'm certain he would be relieved to hear that."

HE DESERVED A horselaugh, Bear told himself later as he retired with a group of gentlemen to Vassar's library for cigars, brandy, and ruminations on the latest business news. He had acted like a pure jackass, declaring that the immensely wealthy and powerful James J. Hill—the man who had single-handedly opened much of the Northwest to transportation and settlement—would do well to avoid any trouble with *him*.

He had brazened through the rest of the meal with grit and a smile. A decade of facing down bunkhouse bullies and cocky young kids with guns strapped to their hips had taught him the value of a good bluff. And there was no better bluff than smiling as if you knew something some-body else didn't.

As the men spread out across the library, loosened vest buttons, and reached for goblets of brandy, Bear found himself scrambling for mental footing.

Why did his best hope for an investor have to be a woman? He never did well with women. Recalling the vision she made across the table, at dinner, he amended his thoughts; she wasn't just a woman, she was a bona fide beauty. She had spun-gold hair that glowed in the candle-light. *Glowed.* Her skin was damn near flawless, her eyes were wide and blue as the Montana sky, and her dewy lips looked downright edible—until she opened them and re-minded him that while he might have changed his ap-proach to her, she certainly hadn't changed her opinion of him.

He took a deep breath, hoping to force some air to his brain. When the steam in his senses cleared, his thoughts had worked their way down his memory to her liberally bared shoulders and lusciously displayed—

Cleavage. Diamond Wingate had cleavage.

Loan or no loan, he had to get the hell out of here.

He headed for the door, only to have Philip Vassar in-tercept him and thrust a cigar into his hands. "Treat her with respect, boy," the banker cautioned. "Acquiring her took more damned effort than acquiring my wife."

"Beg pardon?" Bear blinked at him.

"The cigar." Vassar laughed and gestured to the tobacco Bear held. "It's a Caruba Imperial. Come on. Light her up and I'll introduce you around."

As Bear finished all he could stand of Vassar's fancy cigar, he listened to the men he had just met talk about their business ventures. At some point or other, nearly every one of them mentioned the name Wingate in connection with a business dealing. When he had a chance to ask about it, Philip Vassar pulled him aside.

"Oh, she's *that* Wingate, all right. Provides the venture capital for half of what gets done in Baltimore these days." Vassar chuckled. "She held a lottery at her quarterly board meeting and gave away a hundred thousand dollars to inventors and business people." He leaned in and gave Bear a conspiratorial thump on the chest. "A real soft touch."

Bear tried to reconcile Vassar's assessment with the woman who had jousted verbally with him during dinner. Soft? He thought of the determined glint in her eyes as she bombarded him with questions about his railroad.

About as "soft" as a Baldwin Ten Wheeler.

"What about railroads? Does she honestly know something about them?"

Vassar took a puff from his cigar and blew a ring of blue smoke. "About as much as any man I know. And not just balance sheets and operations . . . she knows construction, too. She owns a smart piece of both the B and O and the New York Central, and votes her own shares. She was one of the ones who set up that fund to give railroad workers a pension when they get too old to work." Vassar gave a huff of a laugh. "I told you . . . a regular soft touch."

As he strode from the library with the rest of Vassar's inner circle, Bear found his thoughts in turmoil yet again. Diamond Wingate was not merely a headstrong beauty with a troublesome abundance of charms; she was a smart, opinionated woman who knew just too damn much about railroads to suit him.

Imagine having her constantly looking over his shoulder . . . constantly . . . He spotted the pale peach silk of her dress across the drawing room, and realized she was being squired about by a tall, aristocratic-looking gent with a faintly proprietary air. As he watched her move and realized he was following the irresistible sway of her bustle, he caught himself and forced himself to imagine it full of cash. She wasn't going to do anything with that wad of cash, he told himself, but sit on it. Whereas he and Halt could put it—and with it, a lot of good men—to work.

Whatever her irritating personal quirks, Diamond Wingate knew about railroads, believed in them, and under the right circumstances, *invested* in them.

Vassar was right. She was his best hope. He had to find a way to deal with Diamond Wingate as if she were an investor, pure and simple. He had to take his proposal to her and make her a clean, aboveboard proposition. Strictly business. Because, after all, it *was* business. He would be offering her a profitable opportunity. And if all went as planned, she stood to gain handsomely from her investment in his rail line.

There was the truth of it, he told himself, rolling his shoulders, and missing the widened eyes and fluttering fans that his casual movement caused in the matrons' corner. By soliciting her participation in his venture, he was actually doing *her* a favor.

Get in, sell your idea, and get the hell out.

With his new outlook firmly in place, he took a deep breath while tugging his vest into place—sending an audible sigh through that same appreciative population—and began to stroll around the drawing room, working his way toward her.

DIAMOND WATCHED TALL, broad-shouldered Barton McQuaid prowling around the drawing room and felt roundly irritated that she couldn't take her eyes from him. Annoying man. It was little comfort that her difficulty seemed to be shared by virtually every other woman present, or that he was oblivious to the fact that they were staring at him. He was preoccupied and appeared to be less than pleased to be here.

That insight spawned another. His garments—no doubt the very ones she had been forced to pay for—were tailored to perfection. There wasn't an erratic seam or an excess inch of goods anywhere on his striking frame, and yet he still seemed to be stuffed into his clothes. Or trapped in them. His visible discomfort and pensive manner presented a stark contrast to the ease and pleasure he had displayed at dinner when he spoke of Montana. It was suddenly as clear as if he had said it aloud: he would give anything to be there instead of—

"Join me for a turn about the garden," came a whisper at her ear. She looked up to find Morgan Kenwood leaning close with a wine-induced glow of warmth on his patrician face. "I'll be waiting."

His hand slid deliberately up the inside of her bare upper arm. Her stomach contracted and didn't relax, even after he released her and casually made his way toward the terrace doors. Passing a pair of admiring females on his way out, he gave them a regal nod, as if their admiration were his due. She knew if she joined him on the darkened terrace, he would alternately pressure and cajole her to announce their engagement and set a wedding date.

She would rather have a tooth pulled.

Several teeth.

The next moment, however, dealing with Morgan-in-the-dark became the least of her worries. She spotted a slender male form, dressed in an oversized frock coat and white neck band that mimicked a cleric's collar, standing in the drawing room doorway. The unrelenting black of his clothing posed a stark contrast to the pale hair that hung to his shoulders and had been caught back in an old-fashioned queue. She would know that dark clothing and pale hair anywhere. Her breath caught as his fair head turned this way and that, searching the guests.

Her first impulse was to hide . . . to find a curtain, a planter, a sofa, anything. But, unaccustomed to such cowardly urges, she waffled and hesitated a moment too long to make a successful escape.

"Diamond!" Louis Pierpont bore down on her with a look of such rapture on his delicate features that she groaned silently.

"Louis!" She had to make the best of it. "What are you doing here?"

He seized her gloved hands, held them up reverently before his gaze, and gave a dramatic sigh. "I could not bear to be away from you another day, my dearest jewel. I took the fleetest packet from Barbados and flew straight to Gracemont the moment we docked. I was devastated to find you not at home. Your Mrs. Humphrey said you had come here."

He glanced around at the people eyeing him and developed a slightly pained expression. But it was not chagrin at his lack of proper dress or embarrassment at the disapproving stares of Baltimore's elite that caused him such discomfort. Louis Pierpont, the sole survivor of what was once one of Baltimore's most influential families, cared little for such things.

"I simply had to come to you. I knew the Vassars would not mind if I arrived uninvited. They are good and charitable people." He tossed a glance around them at the grandeur of Pennyworth's drawing room. "Despite their regrettable materialism."

Clearly, it was finding her in such a worldly setting that caused the aggrieved expression he wore. She knew full well his attitudes toward elegant society and lavish entertaining. He had long ago forsworn accepting invitations to such events, as a witness to the world that he pursued a higher, "nobler" path.

"But you said in your letter you wouldn't be home for weeks," she said, hoping her distress wasn't visible. "What about the new mission?"

"The mission staff arrived from Boston earlier than expected, and things went so well with the new doctor and reverend that I decided the mission could get along without me." He smiled as if indulging her. "You didn't think I would miss your *birthday*, did you?"

"No, of course not." It was all she could do to return even a portion of his smile; her face felt frozen.

The flicker of longing in his eyes was painful to witness . . . until his gaze dipped lower and slid down her fashionably bared shoulders. The pallor of his cheeks disappeared as he flushed and dragged his wandering attention under control. Conscious of his dismay—she also knew his views on the decadence of clothing from "heathen" Paris—she glanced down at the neckline of her gown.

"My heavens, Louis," she said, abruptly turning the focus back to him. "You seem so much thinner. Have you been ill?"

"The heat in Barbados is so difficult. I'm afraid I dwindled a bit." He took out a handkerchief and dabbed at his forehead and throat. "But I'm certain that will change, now that I'm home." He fastened his gaze on her eyes and made so bold as to brush her cheek with his fingertips. "I must gather my strength"—he lowered his voice—"for our future together."

Panic seized her.

"Oh, my!" She snapped open the fan dangling from her wrist. "It must be the surprise—I'm suddenly feeling light-headed."

Louis looked around them and quickly ushered her to one of a number of deserted chairs along the nearby wall.

Sinking onto a seat, she swayed, closed her eyes, and pressed the back of a hand artfully to her temple.

"Perhaps a glass of punch . . ." she said, gazing up with what she hoped would pass for appealing frailty.

"I shall get you one straightaway," he declared.

The minute Louis disappeared through the rear salon door, following a trail of goblet-carrying guests toward the refreshment tables, she straightened, waited an extra heartbeat to be certain he was gone, and then bounded off the chair in the opposite direction. And ran straight into a wall of black wool.

Six

BARTON MCQUAID, APPROACHING from the other side, caught and steadied her. After a pause, he jerked his hands from her bare shoulders and cleared his throat. "Miss Wingate."

"Mr. McQuaid. I was just . . . ummm . . ." She reddened and again lifted a wrist to her forehead.

"In need of a breath of fresh air?" he prompted.

She frowned, then realized he must have seen her attack of the vapors. "Not at all." She straightened. "I was just on my way . . ."

Glancing past him, hoping to see someone or something to help her complete that response, she glimpsed trouble brewing instead. Morgan Kenwood was coming through the French doors that led to the terrace, looking anything but pleased. She stifled a moan and glanced frantically toward the rear salon doorway. There, Louis Pierpont, punch cup in hand, was being detained briefly in the doorway by people who recognized him and offered him greetings.

What was intended to be a private groan escaped her.

On her left was Morgan Kenwood . . . horse czar, country squire, neighbor, and self-appointed fiancé. On her right was Louis Pierpont III . . . philanthropist, sometime missionary, childhood friend . . . and self-anointed betrothed.

There was no time to develop a plan. She was about to be caught between contradictory and onrushing futures—a matrimonial squeeze—and the last thing she needed was to have them collide in front of Baltimore's elite.

She needed an obstacle, something big enough to hide behind and mobile enough to drag from the room with her. The only thing at hand was one large and largely annoying Westerner. She regarded her other dreaded options a moment longer . . . then slid to McQuaid's side, shoved her arm through his, and steered for the door.

"I was just on my way out, Mr. McQuaid."

He scowled and looked off in the direction of whatever—whoever—had set her fleeing. He must have caught sight of Louis returning. "Where are you leading me? Besides away from your parson?"

"He's not a parson. He's a missionary. And he definitely is not *mine.*"

"Does he know that?" he asked.

He must have seen the look Louis gave her, she realized. In addition to McQuaid's more obvious faults, he was a bit too perceptive to suit her.

Eager to be out of both his company and his debt, she released his sleeve as soon as they cleared the doorway and entered the main hall. But Morgan's distinctive baritone drifted through the doorway behind her—"Wait, is that her?"—and she realized that while she might be out of the salon, she wasn't out of danger. McQuaid's company and the strains of music floating down the staircase from the ballroom on the second floor seemed her best hope of avoiding both Morgan and Louis until she could think of a way to leave the party early.

"Upstairs"—she seized his arm again, scrambling for an explanation of why she was pulling him up the steps with her—"the Vassars have a most marvelous fresco on the ceiling of their ballroom. You simply must see it."

"A fresco." He took the steps, beside her, with long, sure strides. "Heck, yes. Can't wait to see that. Never miss a *fresco* if I can help it."

She glanced up at him through severely narrowed eyes. One corner of his broad, expressive mouth was curled slightly. Insufferable man. He probably didn't even know what a fresco was. As soon as this interminable evening was over, she was going to see to it that she never crossed paths with him again.

A spirited country dance was under way in the gaslit ballroom and the music had enlivened conversation as well as feet. It was no surprise to her that heads turned and fans came up to hide whispers as they paused in the doorway. She could just imagine what was being said. He'd rescued her as she arrived, been paired with her at dinner, and now sported her on his arm . . . it was nothing short of a scandal in the making.

Anxious at the delay caused by people socializing and blocking the way just inside the door, she gave a quick glance over her shoulder and received yet another jolt. Morgan had started up the steps to the ballroom, but it was the sight of the person behind him that caused her hands to turn to ice in her gloves.

In growing horror, she stared at another all-too-familiar figure climbing the stairs, dressed in a regal set of men's evening clothes, negligently donned and worn. One of his cuffs was unfastened, some of his vest buttons and shirt studs were not done, and his silk tie was carelessly lopsided. Reckless dishevelment only seemed to add to rakish, raven-eyed Paine Webster's magnetic appeal. He could have worn a burlap bag and still have been the most attractive man in four counties.

Her fingers must have clamped on McQuaid's arm, for he glanced down at it, then at her with a frown. "Do leave some flesh on. I may have a use for that arm some—"

"Quick, this way." She pulled him discreetly along through the groups of guests, toward the dance floor.

"Beg pardon?" He balked, when he sensed her intent, and stared at her.

"Just come with me!" she whispered through a rigid counterfeit of a smile.

He glanced over his shoulder to see what had set her to flight and apparently spotted the familiar Morgan Kenwood bearing down on them.

"Who . . . that guy? First the missionary, and now him. Don't tell me they're trying to sell you inventions too."

"Not exactly," she muttered, halting at the edge of the dance floor and scanning the couples forming twosomes for the next dance. She looked up at him, taking in the light in his eyes, the fierce cast of his features, and the physicality that surrounded him like a cloak. She could be asking for trouble. But in this instance, she just might be better off with the devil she *didn't* know. Her decision made, she opened her arms and did the unthinkable.

"Dance with me."

Even having been absent from polite society for ten years, Bear McQuaid knew that a woman asking a man to dance at a party like this was a stunning breach of etiquette. He stepped in front of her to block the other guests' view.

"You know, you ought to take it easy on that punch," he declared, alarmed by the sight of her offering him such personal access to her.

"Dance with me." She glanced around him and whatever—whoever—she saw caused her eyes to widen. *"Now."* In desperation, she met his gaze and lowered her voice and pride. "I'll make it worth your while."

The offer startled him and he scrambled for a response. "My rates, I should warn you, are fairly steep."

"My pockets, I assure you, are fairly *deep*," she said in an impatient whisper. When he still hesitated, she reached for his hands, placed one at her waist, and stretched the other out in hers . . . just as the music began to play. She took a step backward, but he didn't move.

"One problem." His voice lowered. "I haven't danced in years."

"Why doesn't that surprise me?" she said sharply, again glancing past his shoulder. "All right—I'll lead and we'll keep to the edge."

He didn't know which was worse: the torture of having to follow her around the dance floor like an ill-trained bear, or the torture of having to hold and look at her warm, fragrant form without allowing that contact to have its logical, predictable effect. His only solace was the resounding echo in the back of his mind: *She would make it worth his while.*

Damn straight, she would.

"Your feet should alternate with mine," she said with a wince.

"My feet do damned well if they can alternate with each other," he said testily. "If it becomes too much for your delicate constitution, we can always stop and let your friend over there take my place." As they turned, he caught a glimpse of her prime pursuer watching, red-faced, from the far edge of the dance floor. "Who is he, anyway?"

"He is Morgan Kenwood . . . the owner of Kensington Farms and Stables. We've been friends for years. His family's land borders mine and he thinks—" She abruptly changed courses, both in conversation and footwork, bumping into him and stepping hard on his toes.

"Hey!" His eyes bulged briefly. Concentrating with desperate new intensity, he seized control of their movement.

"What do you think you're doing?" she demanded.

"I just remembered how to dance," he said, grimly turning her in a graceful arc. "The pain brought it all back."

They moved in less-than-voluntary harmony for a few moments before he recalled where he had been aiming his attempts at conversation. Anything, he thought, would be preferable to staring in stony silence at that damned golden hair of hers . . . those big blue eyes . . . those smooth, naked shoulders. Why did women have to cinch themselves up like that . . . make themselves nothing but treacherously irresistible curves and crevices?

"So, what does he want?" he asked shortly. "This Kenwood fellow."

"What does everyone want?" she said through a forced smile.

Without thinking, he quoted Halt Finnegan's definition of the "good life": "A warm bed, a full stomach, and a good five-cent cigar?"

When she looked up at him and blinked in confusion, he reddened.

"Money," she supplied after a moment, averting her gaze.

"Money?" A pricking sensation occurred in the region of his conscience. "You think he's after your money?"

"It usually comes down to that."

"You don't think he might have at least *one* other motive?" he asked, thinking that with a woman who looked like her, any red-blooded man should be able to come up with at least a dozen possibilities more interesting than government greenbacks. He caught himself peering raptly at the plunging neckline of her gown and jerked his gaze away. Any man except him, of course. All he wanted was . . .

A straightforward, by-the-book business loan. He felt another twinge of conscience that said it wasn't quite that simple. Every time he came within ten feet of her, his honorable financial intentions got tangled up with long-dormant physical needs. The worst part was, he didn't know which of his two desires—for her money or her person—was causing this uneasiness.

The music ended, just then, and they were forced to disengage and applaud the music and their own duplicitous performance.

When he stepped back, she seized his arm. "Don't leave!"

"Well, actually, Miss Wingate"—he swallowed his misgivings and forced himself to seize the moment—"I was hoping to speak to you—"

"There you are!" came a booming voice that to Bear's ear had a forced joviality to it. They turned together and found Morgan Kenwood approaching with a determined stride and a brusque urgency to his manner.

"Diamond, my dear!" A higher-pitched and disagreeably nasal voice came from the side a moment later. Diamond turned to find her "missionary" coming across the dance floor with a look of distress on his sallow face.

Bear watched her stiffen and melt back a step toward him. Her hands fluttered frantically behind her back, searching for his arm or hand—anything to hold onto—as a third voice assailed her.

"*Diamond mine!* You stunning creature, you—I've been looking everywhere for you!" A darkly handsome and carelessly dressed fellow was drawing attention from around the room as he approached with a half-empty champagne glass and a sensual swagger.

She was being descended upon from three different directions at once. Bear heard her whimper of distress and allowed her to find his hand. She grabbed it as if it were a life preserver. From his position behind her, he could both feel her terror and see the reason for it. The looks in those three male faces were nothing short of predatory. He'd seen circling wolves with less hunger in their eyes.

One by one, they stopped before her, and she huddled back a bit more each time, until she was virtually standing on his feet. Scowling at the way she was crowding him, he caught sight of the panicky flutter of her pulse at the side of her throat. She glanced up at him with a sickly smile and he experienced an insane urge to grab her up by the waist and run from the damned room.

"Why, Paine, you're home already? How wonderful," she said, her voice reedy and oddly constricted. "And you, Louis . . . And of course, Morgan . . . Why, you're all so . . . dashing and so . . . so very . . . very . . ."

She sank toward the floor.

It was a brilliantly executed swoon. A sway, some blinking, a wrist to the forehead, a vaporous flutter of eyelashes . . . then her legs folded and she surrendered to gravity and the mercy of someone else's reflexes. It fell to Bear to catch her before she hit the floor, since he was the closest to her.

Galvanized by her unexpected collapse, he tried to collect and concentrate her weight into a manageable bundle. The more he grappled with her unwieldy form, the more furious he became . . . with those three grasping vultures for stalking her like a defenseless stray . . . with her for dropping her blessed problems at his feet, literally . . . and with himself for being willing to pick them up.

He scarcely heard the commotion that followed, the squeals of the ladies, the gasps of the men, and the conflicting orders from her three gentlemen "friends" regarding what to do and where to carry her. He ignored most of it, until Evelyn Vassar appeared, ashen and frantic, before him, clearing a path through the gawking guests and directing him to the nearest bedchamber.

He swept her down the hallway, in their hostess's wake, with his back and shoulders straining and his heart pounding as if it would jump out of his chest. She wasn't a tiny woman . . . not exactly what he would call a fragile flower of—Oh, hell, she weighed a blue ton!

It was in the grip of such ungentlemanly thoughts that he was caught staring at her face . . . when first one of her eyes opened . . . and then the other. He stumbled and damn near dropped her on her conniving little—*not* so little—bottom. In the next heartbeat, both of her eyes squeezed tightly shut and he was forced to watch in outraged silence as her lips curled in a smile of relief.

By the time Evelyn Vassar reached the bedroom door and threw it open, he had worked up a full head of steam. He carried Diamond to the four-poster bed, swung her over it, and while Evelyn was busy shooing onlookers away and closing the door, he dropped her onto the counterpane. She gave a surprised gurgle of protest as she hit, but after parting her eyes just enough to shoot him a murderous glare, she went instantly limp and silent once more.

Through a haze of chagrin, he backed away from the bed, from the room, and from the knot of curious people gathered in the hall outside. He retreated, in fact, to the main floor, where he found himself the object of intense stares and whispers. He was eyeing the front doors, contemplating making use of them and not stopping until he reached the comparative sanity of the brawling waterfront, when Philip Vassar called to him from the stairs.

"McQuaid! Well, well . . . you've created quite a stir this evening," the banker said, joining him in the hall, clapping a hand on his shoulder, and steering him toward the empty library. "Every tongue in the place is wagging. You and Miss Wingate have made Evelyn's party. Party, hell, you've made her whole season." He closed the library door in a stealthy manner and savored the resulting silence for a moment before going to pour them both a brandy.

"So"—he handed Bear a draught of his best French stock and waved him into one of the tufted leather chairs—"did you talk with her about your proposal?"

"No." Bear couldn't help the edge in his voice. "First she was busy fending off your local wolf pack. Then she was unconscious."

Vassar nearly choked on his brandy. "Our local wolf pack?"

"Your horse baron, Kenwood, and that missionary . . . I believe she called him Louis. Then there was some other fellow . . . dark, rumpled, half-drunk . . ." He snorted contemptuously. "He called her 'Diamond Mine.'"

"Ye gods." Vassar frowned. "Don't tell me Kenwood's still after her. He seems to think he has 'first rights' with her, since they grew up together. The missionary—that has to be Louis Pierpont III. There's a piece of work. His family left him a small fortune and he promptly gave it all away . . . hoping to buy his way into Heaven, I suppose. Moralizing little sop. He'd love nothing more than to give Diamond's fortune away, too." He chuckled. "Though, in truth, she doesn't need much help in that department."

"And the third one?" Bear prompted, strangely intent on hearing it all. "Dark . . . pretty-boy face . . . three sheets to the wind . . ."

Vassar nodded. "Ah, yes. That has to be Paine Webster. I caught a glimpse of him earlier, as he arrived." He cocked his head. "Odd . . . I thought he was out of the country. The family sent him to the Orient . . . ostensibly on business, but in reality to get him out of the way for a while. They're garment people. They own a couple of mills here in Baltimore and manufacture ready-to-wear. Good people. He's the bad seed they keep trying to grow into something worthwhile. 'Paine-in-the-Butt Webster.' There's a man aptly named."

Vassar finished his brandy and set his glass aside on the nearby humidor.

"The three of them descending on her at once." Vassar shook his head. "No wonder she fainted." He cast a speculative eye over Bear as he rose. "And you to the rescue again. Dammit, McQuaid, if you haven't already *earned* your blessed loan!"

As Vassar left the library, Bear sat staring into his dwindling brandy and felt an irrational burst of relief that those three vultures were doomed to merely circle her. Laying a hand on his midsection, he came alert and began searching for other worrisome feelings and reactions connected to his intended investor. They weren't hard to find.

Whenever she was near, he found himself staring at the lights in her hair and her Montana-sky eyes. The mounds bared by her daring neckline and the prominent curves of her waist and hips made his palms itch. And he felt an alarming compulsion to intervene between her and lunatic inventors, pushy suitors, and even the damnable local gossips.

This preoccupation with her was exactly what he had been dead set on avoiding. What the hell difference did it make to him whether she was being hounded and pursued by money-hungry men or not? She was an investor, nothing more. A signature on a dotted line. A letter of credit on the hoof. A bank account with a bustle.

Bounding from the chair, he paced back and forth, then reached into the closest humidor for one of Vassar's fancy cigars.

In the midst of lighting it, he paused to stare at the rolled tobacco.

He hated cigars.

What the hell was the matter with him?

THE NOISE FROM the dockside tavern was loud as Bear climbed the rickety rear stairs leading to the room they had rented. He could usually count on the snores of the lodgers on the other side of the partitioning blanket, as well as Halt's own "night music," to drown out the din from downstairs. But tonight as he paused to let his eyes adjust to the moonlight coming through the crusty window, the snoring and tavern noise only seemed to amplify each other. Determined not to be the only one who got no sleep tonight, he shook Halt, who bolted upright in an instant and jammed a revolver to his middle.

Bear froze.

"It's me!" When the Irishman blinked and focused and finally withdrew the gun, Bear felt a flash of heat rush through him. "What the hell's the matter with you?" he demanded as Halt swung his legs gingerly over the side of the cot. "Pulling a gun on—"

Then he caught a glimpse of Halt's face in the dim light and sucked in a breath. It looked like someone had broken a board over his head. One eye was swollen nearly shut and his jaw and lips were puffy and discolored on one side.

"What happened?" Bear dropped to one knee beside him.

"I was comin' back from a bite o' supper . . . that place on Alehouse Street." Halt's voice sounded strained, almost hoarse. "I heard somebody comin' up behind me, but didn't think nothin' of it. City livin's made me careless, I guess. They clouted me on the head, dragged me down an alley, and pounded me like I was a tough cut o' bully beef."

"They?" Bear lit the tallow lamp and held it up to inspect Halt's injuries.

"It takes more'n one set of fists to do this much damage to a hardheaded Irishman." Halt grinned and then groaned at the pain it caused. "Can't say if there was more than two of 'em. I was a bit too busy for countin'."

"Damnation." Bear noticed the way Halt was holding his side, and pushed Halt's hand away to feel for broken ribs.

"Naw, nothing broken," Halt declared, inhaling sharply when Bear touched a bruised spot. "I'll mend quick enough. Th' worst is"—his voice lowered to a pained hush—"they got our money, lad. Ever' last cent we had."

"Every last cent?" The news hit Bear hard. He sat back on his heel. "Did you get a look at them? Any idea who they were?"

"Street toughs, most likely. Never seen 'em before."

Bear drew a bottle of brandy from his pocket and thrust it into Halt's hand. "Here. Use some of this to dull the pain. Compliments of our favorite banker." He watched Halt work the cork free, put the bottle to his nose, and breathe deeply of the rich vapors.

"Yer a good man, Bear McQuaid," Halt said, flashing Bear a pained grin that widened with astonishment when Bear produced a handful of fancy Cuban cigars from his other pocket. Halt passed one of the cigars under his nose, inhaling the rich tobacco, then took a drink of the brandy. The sigh of pleasure that issued from his battered form sent a sliver of guilt through Bear.

"Well, what about your evenin'? Our old Miss Wingate?" Halt slid to one side to make room for Bear on the cot beside him. "What did she say? Did ye get her to agree to a loan?"

"I . . . couldn't get her alone to ask about it. But I did manage to meet her. They say she makes a lot of loans to new businesses . . . some with a helluva lot less potential than the Montana Central and Mountain."

Halt deflated. "Ye didn't even get to ask 'er?"

"She always had people hangin' around. And she's not exactly how we pictured her," Bear said, taking a drink from the bottle when Halt offered it.

"What do you mean 'not how we pictured 'er'?"

"Kindly. Like your old grandma. A real soft touch."

Halt took the bottle back and drank again. "So, what's she like, then?"

"Younger." Bear squirmed inside, deciding how much to reveal. "A damned tough nut. Knows railroads front to back and left to right. And she's not one to be fooled by fancy manners or to go all goosey over a handsome face."

"That's good." Halt gave a muted chuckle and took another drink. " 'Cause right now, the best o' both of us put together wouldn't make a decent curtsy or a handsome face." Bear scowled until he saw the flash of teeth in Halt's battered visage. He began to relax at the realization that Halt's humor was back, and he grinned.

"We wouldn't at that."

After the bottle had passed back and forth a few more times, the seriousness of their situation surfaced again, counteracting the effects of the brandy to sober them both.

"No loan. No way to exercise them land options. Plum out o' money. And runnin' out o' time," Halt mused. "It don't look good for us, Bear, me lad."

They sat in silence for a few more minutes, each considering the ramifications of their latest loss. Then as their hopes sounded the depths of despair, their determination only had one way to go.

"Not good. But not impossible," Bear said, glancing overhead and around them, at their meager lodgings. "At least we got a roof over our heads."

"True enough. Th' rent's paid three more days."

"We each got two strong arms and willing hands." Bear sat straighter.

"We can find work enough to keep our bellies filled." Halt squared his aching shoulders. "And we still got old Miss Wingate. She's a right old gal. Tough, but fair. She'll do right by us."

Bear's rising spirits were momentarily hobbled by Halt's enthusiasm for Diamond Wingate . . . until her words came back to him. *I'll make it worth your while.* He seized and held on to that promise, while stubbornly blocking the rest of his memories of her.

"I'll pay her a visit, first thing Monday morning," Bear declared. "I'll take the maps and charts and lay it all out in front of her . . . make her a straight-up business proposition. No pussyfootin' around."

Halt grinned, affirming his faith in Bear's powers of persuasion.

"She'll write ye out a bank draft, and our worries'll be over."

SEVEN

THE SUN STOOD high overhead by the time Bear Mc-
Quaid drove his rented buggy down the road leading to
Diamond Wingate's home. He was already hours behind
his self-appointed schedule of "first thing Monday morning" . . . the result of having to haggle over unpaid buggy
rental fees at the livery stable. Worse still, he had been
forced to use his very last resource, his lucky twenty-dollar
gold piece, to settle the mounting debt and couldn't help
feeling that it was a bad omen for the day's business.

He spotted the sprawling estate—"Gracemont," the stableman had said—as he crested a gentle rise and had a
fleeting urge to turn the horse around and head straight
back to the city. Only the memory of Halt's stubborn
cheerfulness as he wolfed down a couple of stale biscuits
and headed off in search of manual labor to put food in
their bellies, kept him from calling the whole thing off.

He had spent the last two nights tossing and turning on
his narrow cot, plagued by the tactile memory of Diamond
Wingate's voluptuous body lying limp and pliant in his
arms. Worse, with the slightest bend of thought he was

revisited by certain untenable urges toward her . . . a sort of emptiness in the middle of him, a gripping desire to step in front of her and . . .

And what? Take on all comers? Her problems were none of his concern, he had told himself so often that it now droned like a chant in his head.

Still, he couldn't help thinking about her reaction to those three local fortune hunters. She knew what they wanted from her and wasn't having any part of it. On one level he had to respect that. And on another level . . . he had to pray she'd forget all about those scruples when it came to *his* need for cash.

He reined up, pulled off his hat, and wiped his damp forehead as he stared at the huge set of iron gates that marked the entrance to Gracemont. There were at least a score of people milling about in front of those brick pillars and that iron scrollwork. Uneasy at the prospect of stepping into the middle of something he knew nothing about, he scowled, flicked the reins, and drove on.

The people outside her gates were nothing short of destitute, he realized as he drove into the stares of ragged men, women, and children. They carried their possessions with them in worn satchels and old gunny sacks, and he could see that down the road, they had built fires and made a crude camp.

As he looked past them, through the gates, he spotted a fellow sitting in a chair that was tilted against the side of a stone gatehouse. The man's hat was propped over his face; he appeared to be having a nap. Bear called to him, but succeeded only in rousing the attention of the people waiting outside the gates. They collected around him, watching keenly for the gatekeeper's response. From their comments and behavior, he realized that these people were waiting for something from Diamond Wingate. A handout.

He climbed down from the buggy and made his way through the expectant crowd. "Hey! Gatekeeper!" he called.

The man looked up, gave the gate a passing glance, and lowered his chair as he spotted Bear in the forefront of the crowd. He rose and sauntered over.

"I'm here to see Miss Wingate," Bear said uncomfortably.

"Yeah—us, too!" came a voice from the crowd, touching off a din of shouted demands and pleas.

"You got an appointment?" the gatekeeper demanded, ignoring the others.

"No," Bear said, humiliated by the realization that no matter how much better clothed he was, he was truly just one of the needy throng at her gates.

"I am a social acquaintance of Miss Wingate's." He glanced at the others pressing around him. "I had no idea I would have to ask for an appointment to call upon her at home."

The gatekeeper appraised Bear's gentlemanly clothes and craned his neck to inspect his buggy, then nodded. "A'right. Ye can come in." He addressed the others, who began clamoring for admittance, too. "Only him, ye hear? I'm only openin' the gates for him. You lot—stand back. They'll bring out yer dinner soon enough."

Being admitted to the place was almost as unsettling as being denied admittance. Leaving the other supplicants to her good graces behind, he felt like a damned fraud. So much for his determination to make this visit professional and purely business.

The house at the center of the sweeping circular drive was a sprawling brick Georgian Revival structure that centered around a large white portico and a formidable pair of black lacquered doors. The road leading to those doors was lined with beautifully groomed lawn and arcs of neatly trimmed hedges. Every part of the place, from beds of tulips and newly planted roses to the shining brass work of the coaching lamps on either side of the door, was lovingly tended. It was an estate, an heiress's home, a place wrapped in an aura of money and privilege. It brought back such a wave of memories that he had to summon every ounce of his nerve in order to climb out of the buggy.

The door swung open before him as if by magic, and he was welcomed into a spacious entry hall appointed in black-and-white marble and richly polished mahogany. He had just given his name to the butler, when a voice hailed him from the top of the stairs. "McQuaid? Is that you?" He looked up and recognized Diamond's guardian, Hardwell Humphrey.

"Why, it is McQuaid! As I live and breathe." Humphrey and the genteel-looking older lady at his side hurried down the steps toward Bear. "My dear"—he patted the hand nestled in the crook of his arm—"this is the fellow I told you about from the Vassars' party. The one who rescued Diamond. McQuaid, this is my wife, Hannah."

"What a pleasure to meet you, Mr. McQuaid," Hannah Humphrey said, offering him her hand. "Hardwell told me all about you and your heroic deeds. Unfortunately, we are just on our way out . . . a standing engagement . . ."

"But Diamond is here," Hardwell declared with a wave toward the rear of the house. "Out in the stables, givin' Robbie his first ridin' lesson. I'm sure she'd love to see you." He turned to the butler, who stood close by waiting to receive Bear's hat and the roll of maps under his arm. "Jeffreys, take Mr. McQuaid out to see Miss Diamond." He turned back and extended his hand. "Good to see you again, McQuaid. You'll have to come to dinner with us soon."

That was all there was to it? Bear thought incredulously, as he watched the pair exit and climb into a large, elegant coach. He just walked in, was recognized, and was shown straight into her presence? Relief rolled through him. Maybe this wouldn't be so difficult, after all.

The butler took Bear's big black Western hat and roll of maps, but then returned the hat to him, saying that he might wish to keep it if he were going out to the stables. Bear nodded, took it back, and handled it a bit awkwardly as he fell in behind the dapper little servant.

On the way out, they passed through a series of rooms that surpassed what he had seen at the Vassars.' The colors were richer and more subdued and the furnishings were mostly gracious mahogany pieces . . . a very restful and pleasing sort of environment that he sensed few were privileged to enter.

The grounds and handsome brick stables were equally well appointed and kept in immaculate condition. They traversed the length of the stable alley, between rows of box stalls, in which he glimpsed a number of fine-looking horses. As they reached the doors at the far end, he heard Diamond's voice.

"No, no," she was calling to someone. "Just stand there and let him get used to you. Keep your eye on where he is, but don't move. Let him come to you. He's just as curious about you as you are about him."

He paused in the stable door.

Diamond Wingate, clad simply in a forest-green riding skirt, boots, and a white blouse, was standing on the bottom board of a whitewashed corral fence . . . looking as fresh as mountain laurel in morning dew. He forced his gaze to move along and observed that her ten-year-old cousin was standing in the enclosure with a small, untethered horse. The boy held an empty lead rope and looked as stiff as shirt board.

"But what if he bites or kicks me?" Robbie's voice was thin and anxious.

"You're not made of carrots or sugar," Bear called out to him. "As long as you don't make any wild or sudden moves, you're plenty safe."

Diamond turned abruptly, grabbing the nearest fence post to steady herself. "Mr. McQuaid."

The sight of him in the doorway carried an all-too-predictable impact on Diamond. Her eyes widened, her cheeks reddened, and her breath stopped. For the past two nights she had tossed and turned and pounded down innocent pillows, trying in vain to banish the sight of him from her mind and telling herself that her reaction to him on the night of the Vassars' party was simply a result of her predicament and his unexpected chivalry.

But gratitude, she knew all too well, did not account for the guilty excitement that seeped through her at the memory of his hand on her waist and the scandalous pleasure of being caught up in his powerful arms . . . held tight against his chest . . . his lushly muscled, hauntingly memorable chest. With the slightest slip of her vigilant sense of decency, the image of his naked torso crept into her thoughts.

Even now her gaze had migrated and fixed on the front of his shirt.

"Miss Wingate." He tugged the brim of his hat and strolled over to her. "Mr. Humphreys said you were teaching Master Robert, there, to ride."

"I am." Two words were all she could manage as she forced her gaze up.

He leaned a shoulder against the fence post and glanced between the boards at the boy and horse. Why did he have to do that, she grumbled mentally . . . that insolent slouch that seemed to challenge the rest of the world to find something interesting enough to bring him upright?

"Interesting approach . . . teaching him to ride by having him just stand there."

"He's never been around horses." She scowled, reminding herself that there was a good bit more inside those well-tailored garments than a naked chest and a scrap of chivalry. He was arrogant and abominably prone to— "I want him to get used to being around them before climbing aboard one."

Watching Robbie, he lowered his voice. "He might feel better if he had more control . . . say . . . if he put the lead on the horse and walked him around."

"I had planned to have him do that next," she informed him shortly, then turned to her cousin. "Hook the lead on him, Robbie, and walk him around the fence. Go right up to him. Be businesslike and make sure he sees you coming."

With a glance at Bear, Robbie squared his shoulders and made himself approach the horse. He fixed the hook in the ring at the bottom of the halter, and in moments was leading the little horse around the corral. He seemed more confident with each step, pausing now and then to give the horse's neck a pat.

She flicked a look at Bear from the corner of her eye and couldn't help noticing his tanned skin . . . the prominent line of his jaw . . . the tilt of his hat over his eyes. From his head, her gaze wandered down his shoulders, to where his big hands had pushed his coat back and were propped on his hips. Even in ordinary clothes, he still possessed a lithe, casual grace. . . .

"When the lesson is over"—he turned to her with another bit of advice and caught her looking—"you ought to have him brush down his horse and give it water. Make him responsible for the animal's care. That's a big part of—"

"I know what he needs to do," she said, glaring, reddening at her own thoughts. "I have been riding and caring for horses since I was a young girl."

"Oh? And how much do you know about boys?"

"Children are children, Mr. McQuaid."

"Well, that could be your problem, Miss Wingate."

"My problem?"

"In my experience, boys are more like horses than children. Training them right requires a strong hand and a strong stomach."

"Just what sort of experience produced this fascinating insight on *boys*?" she demanded, crossing her arms.

He smiled. A smug, male, trump-card sort of smile.

"I was one once, myself."

Diamond drew her chin back, feeling as if she'd been sucker-punched. The next instant she found herself visited by a spontaneous image of him as a young boy . . . shoulder high with cowlicks and missing teeth . . . dirt everywhere . . . probably an endless sweet tooth . . . big, lively copper eyes that would melt pure granite. He had probably wormed his way around and into the heart of his poor old mother. And every other female he ever met. No doubt he had left a trail of broken hearts from here all the way to Montana.

The sound of a horse fast approaching caused Robbie's mount to jerk its head up and prance nervously. Diamond looked up, past Robbie and around the corner of the stables. "Hold on to him," she called. "He needs you to be steady and in control. Show him it's nothing to be alarmed about."

Bear followed her gaze and they spotted the rider in the same moment. The same thought registered in both of their minds: *Oh, no.*

"There you are!" Morgan Kenwood called as he reined up by the corral and dismounted. She climbed down from the fence and turned, clamping her hands securely on a fence board behind her. "Well, I certainly didn't expect to see you out and about, my dear." Then he spotted Bear, looked questioningly at Diamond, and then nodded at Bear. "McQuaid, isn't it? What are you doing here?"

"The same as you, I imagine." Bear gave him an equivocal smile.

"As you can see, we're in the middle of a riding lesson," she said.

"You are? Excellent." Morgan tied up his horse and came to stand by Diamond, watching Robbie fingering the lead rope and looking uncertain. He frowned. "What's the boy doing?"

"He's leading the horse around the ring, getting accustomed to it before he has to climb aboard it," she answered in clipped tones.

Morgan laughed. "Getting accustomed to it? There's only one way to do that. Put the boy on the horse and take him out into the orchards. That's the way *you* learned to ride, if memory serves correctly. Or have you forgotten everything I taught you?"

Before Diamond could react, Morgan was striding through the gate. "Here, boy." He reached for the saddle perched on the fence rail near the stable door. "It's time you learned to handle your own tack."

With equal parts effort and frustration, Robbie managed to saddle the horse and then, at Morgan's insistence, used the fence to climb aboard. Diamond watched from nearby, her mouth taut and her eyes bright with irritation. Every instruction she gave Robbie was quickly countermanded by Morgan, until she finally intervened and declared that was enough for one lesson.

"Enough?" Morgan laughed. "Don't be silly. The boy is just coming to the fun part." He looked up at Robbie. "He needs to take the horse out . . . get the feel of the reins and saddle . . . use his heels a bit."

"Really, Morgan, I think we've had quite e—"

But Morgan had brushed aside her protest and was striding to the door and bellowing for a groom to saddle her horse. She gave him a furious look and headed to the stable door herself.

"Saddle Blackjack for Mr. McQuaid," she told the groom when he appeared. Then she turned to Bear. "You will join us, won't you?"

"Mr. McQuaid is dressed for business," Morgan declared, glaring at Bear. "He no doubt has pressing concerns elsewhere." It wasn't an observation so much as an order, and orders of that sort always grated on Bear's independent nature.

"Oh, I've ridden in worse gear." McQuaid unfolded his arms and pushed off from the post. A wry smile played at the corners of his mouth as he removed his coat and hung it on a fence. Then he unknotted his tie and started on the buttons of his vest. "I wouldn't miss this for the world."

As they rode out along the paddock road, heading for the orchards, Kenwood maneuvered his horse between Diamond and Robbie, forcing novice Robbie to ride ahead of them on the narrow path.

"Really, Morgan." She reined aside, mentally consigning him to perdition for insisting the boy take the horse out on a trail and then abandoning him. "Someone should—*I* should ride beside Robbie." Without waiting for his reply, she called, "Wait for me, Robbie!"

But at that same instant, McQuaid's horse shot by hers and took up the post beside Robbie on the path ahead.

"It's okay, I'll ride with him," McQuaid called back to her.

Short of making a scene, she was stuck beside Morgan, who began droning on about some horse's fancy pedigree. She took refuge in her own thoughts and in the contrast posed by Barton McQuaid's broad back and ease in the

saddle and Robbie's small shoulders and tense perch on
the horse.

BEAR WAS UNDER no illusion as to why Diamond invited him to ride along with them. It was her way of retali-
ating for Morgan's high-handed takeover of Robbie's riding
lesson. And, remembering Saturday night, it was very
likely her way of keeping Kenwood at a distance, as well.
Clearly, it was going to be a while before he would find an
opportunity to broach the subject of his railroad loan. He
decided to use the time to think of a way to raise the topic
of railroads and the expense of building them.

*Riding horseback across the country takes weeks, but
trains make it in only a few days. Trains don't give you saddle
sores. Ever notice the way the cost of steel rail just keeps
going up?* Maybe he should just jump right in with: *From
the sound of things, you've invested in crazier things than my
railroad.*

Oh, yes. Very smooth. He stifled a groan.

It was going to be a very long afternoon.

AS THEY RODE, he caught Robbie stealing glances at
the way he sat in the saddle and trying to copy the way he
held his reins. After a while, the boy's curiosity got the
best of him.

"What kind of hat is that?" he asked, scowling up at
Bear in the brightness.

Bear took off his hat and looked at its slightly worn
black felt before putting it back on. "It's a Montana hat.
Out West, we have to wear real hats . . . the kind that
protect a man from sun and wind and rain and snow."

"You're from out West?" Robbie asked, looking down at

his city shoes and shirt, then at his hat again. "You don't look like a cowboy."

He gave a short laugh at Robbie's assumption. "Well, I have been. When I first went out West I lived on a ranch and worked cattle."

Robbie turned to get a better look at him, and almost slid off his saddle. Morgan barked an order for him to sit straight and keep looking forward. Robbie shot a dark look over his shoulder, but complied.

"I seen cowboys in books," he continued, examining Bear. "If you're a real cowboy, do you have a gun, too?"

Diamond, riding well behind them, listened in vain for his reply as Morgan launched into another dissertation on the differences in horseshoeing, and she had to settle for just looking at Barton McQuaid.

His immaculately cut trousers were stretched taut over his muscular legs. His white shirt now hung open at the top, baring his muscular neck, and clung to the squared contours of his shoulders. He had removed his cuff links and rolled up his sleeves, revealing dark hair on sinewy forearms. Whenever he took a breath she could swear she saw the outline of the muscles in his chest and upper arms through the fabric.

She had never seen anyone quite like him, so absorbingly . . . Western. *Cowboy.* Whether he had ever been one or not, it was the perfect word to describe him. She realized she was being a bit obvious with her stare and jerked her gaze away. It landed on Morgan's heated face. He had asked something and she hadn't a clue what. Smiling blandly, she transferred her attention to her cousin's riding form.

"You're doing well, Robbie!" she called out. To her relief, he grinned and waved, seeming pleased to be on horseback.

• • •

AS THE SUN grew stronger, Bear noticed Robbie digging under his collar and shrinking from his scratchy new wool jacket and breeches.

"Fancy clothes," he observed.

Robbie looked down at his pearl-buttoned vest and flaring jodhpurs, reddened, and gave his collar a resentful tug. "I—I'm just wearin' these to keep *her* happy. She thinks she's gonna make a gent outta me."

"I'd say she has her work cut out for her."

"Does she ever." Bear's sarcasm was lost on Robbie. "I ain't gonna be no candy ankle." Then the boy's vehemence faded and he grew more thoughtful. "But livin' with her ain't—*isn't*—half bad. She gives me whatever I want. All I have to do is ask for somethin' and I get it."

"Whatever you want?" Bear said, raising an eyebrow.

Robbie nodded. "My very own spyglass . . . three desserts at supper . . . a wind-up train engine . . . stories every night. She bought me two of them dime Western stories once when we were in town, an' she even read 'em to me, a little each night. That's where I learned so much about cowboys." He slackened the reins and turned in his saddle, leaving his mount to direct itself.

"Hardwell and Hannah, they say she ought to learn how to say no, but she can't. Not to me, not to anybody. That's why those folks come to the house every day and follow her to church and all around town. They know she'll feed 'em and give 'em jobs and buy stuff from 'em."

"Well, just because she gives things away, doesn't mean she never says no to people," Bear said, mulling over Robbie's point of view.

"But she *don't* say no. Never. Hardwell an' Hannah, they say she ought to get a man to say it for her. But she don't want no man around. I tell you what I think." He looked oddly adult as he pronounced his assessment. "I think she just likes givin' stuff away." He shrugged with youthful acceptance. "She just *likes* it. She's a soft touch."

A soft touch. Saturday night he had scoffed when Vassar used those same words to describe her. It unsettled him now that her mercenary little cousin had the same take on her. She gave money and food and help to whoever asked. He had seen the proof himself, lined up outside her gates. A soft touch. But it didn't fit somehow with her testy behavior toward him or her edgy observation of the other night. What does everyone want from her, she had asked, and supplied the answer. *Money.*

"Say, mister—"

Bear frowned. "Out in Montana, everybody calls me Bear."

Robbie stared at him. "How come they call you that?"

"Could be because I outran a bear once," he said with a menacing look. "Or because I always wake up like a grizzly bear in spring . . . slow and surly."

"Keep your back straight, Robert," Kenwood called from behind them.

Robbie groaned and glanced over his shoulder. "Can't we go any faster?"

Bear considered the boy and his eagerness. "So you think you're ready to try a gallop, do you? We'll see about that." Then he turned in the saddle and called to Diamond and Kenwood, "We're going to ride ahead."

Diamond was alarmed. "I don't think—"

"Just stay on the path and we'll catch up," Kenwood called.

"Let's go." Bear and Robbie rode off along the path across the fields and through a stand of trees. Bear set a brisk but reasonable canter and, with advice from Bear,

Robbie was able to maintain a surprisingly natural seat on the horse.

"You're doing okay, for a first time out. Now for some fun." He gave his mount the knee and led Robbie into a light gallop.

Soon the boy and the gelding were working together in a fluid motion that was a joy for a seasoned horseman to behold. By the time they reached the edge of the orchards and slowed to a walk, Robbie was breathless and grinning from ear to ear.

"That was great!" he cried, petting his mount. "Now, let's go faster!"

"Give your horse a chance to catch his breath first. You should always remember . . . your horse is doing twice the work you are. If you're short of breath or tired or thirsty, that goes double for your mount. Out in Montana, the country is pretty rugged and you don't survive if your horse doesn't. You learn pretty quick to take care of your horse. He becomes your partner."

"Oh, I'll take good care of *my* horse, all right," Robbie said adamantly. "Diamond . . . she said she'll get me one as soon as I learn to ride. A big old stallion . . . black as jet and quick as a snake bite."

"A *stallion?*" Bear wagged his head, thinking of what Diamond would say to that news. The next minute he became aware of a familiar sound and paused to listen. "Is that water I hear?"

"Yeah. There's a creek down there." Robbie pointed to a string of trees growing along a slight depression, then apparently had an idea.

"Race you!"

Robbie dug his heels hard into the horse's sides and jerked back hard on the reins at the same time. The startled horse reared, then exploded beneath him and headed

off across the intervening hay field at a dead run. The boy
let out a yelp, flailed, and finally succeeded in grabbing the
front of the saddle.

Bear raced after him, calling to him to hang on. The
field blurred by as Bear concentrated on the horse's panicky movements and the boy's frantic cries. He could see
the reins dangling well out of Robbie's reach and realized
he would have to use his own mount to slow Robbie's
. . . a solution that carried some risk. He raced just
ahead, so that Robbie's horse could see his and then
leaned in to seize the runaway's bridle. As he reined up,
both horses gradually slowed.

"You all right?" Bear demanded, panting.

Robbie was as pale as parchment all the way to his
fingers, which were clamped around the edge of the saddle. "I—I—los-st the reins an' he jus-st started runnin'
wild . . ." His blue eyes were huge with fright and Bear
had the oddest feeling that he was looking at Diamond.
Frowning, he recovered the reins and handed them to
Robbie, who shrank back. "Awww, no—I'm gettin' off!"

"No you're not," Bear declared, grabbing his arm and
holding him in place. The boy was trembling. "You made a
big mistake back there, but you lived to tell the tale. If you
get off that horse now, you're making an even bigger one.
A man has to learn to conquer his fears. He has to learn to
admit his mistakes, learn from them, and go on from
there."

Robbie's eyes filled with tears, and he lowered both
them and his head in shame. After a moment, Bear loosened his grip. His voice became as low and compelling as
thunder.

"Take the reins. We'll ride down to the creek and you
can practice your dismount."

By the time they reached the creek and Robbie had
dismounted, much of Bear's annoyance had drained. He

watched Robbie's shame-stained face and remembered too well how it felt to disappoint someone you wanted desperately to please . . . worse, to disappoint yourself. He waited for Robbie to look up.

"In time, I think you'll make a damn fine rider," he said with a wry smile. "But you can already hang on to a runaway horse with the best of 'em."

EIGHT

THAT WAS WHERE Diamond and Morgan Kenwood found them, some minutes later, standing at the edge of the grass-lined stream, giving their horses a drink. Neither Diamond nor Morgan Kenwood mentioned Robbie's narrow scrape, which could only mean that they hadn't seen it. More than once, Robbie cast a pleading look at Bear to persuade him to keep silent about what had happened. But he needn't have worried; Bear sensed that keeping the incident between the two of them would drive the lesson deeper into the boy's conscience. For some reason, that seemed more important than the fleeting satisfaction he might have gotten from Diamond's reaction to her charge's reckless behavior.

Diamond noticed Robbie's subdued behavior. "Robbie, are you all right?"

"Sure," Robbie said with a scowl. Then he glanced at Bear and gave his head a serious scratching. "Just wanna get back on that horse and ride, is all."

When they started off again, she didn't wait for Morgan to dictate riding arrangements. As soon as she was in the saddle, she insisted that Robbie ride beside her. Bear was left to contend with Morgan Kenwood's visible irritation.

The men rode in silence, neither tempted to indulge in a conversation that could easily slide past civility. It was only when the stable came in sight that Kenwood turned to him.

"I think you should know, McQuaid, and I would save you the ignominy of discovering it in a more embarrassing manner . . . Miss Wingate and I have something of an *understanding*. She has given me to know that a certain 'announcement' will be made in a few weeks, on her birthday."

"She has, has she?" Bear studied the aristocratic Kenwood, whose exaggerated posture on horseback made him look continually like he belonged in the middle of a park with pigeons perched on his head. In a pig's eye, he thought. Women didn't do their best to escape being in the same room with men they intended to marry. And Kenwood must be desperate indeed to perceive a threat to his matrimonial aspirations in *him*.

"I'll be the first to congratulate you," he said in deadly earnest, "when the announcement is made."

BY THE TIME they returned to Gracemont's stables that afternoon, Robbie was sagging badly. Diamond watched him squirming inside his new clothes and scratching himself as if they were an unbearable torment. She was wearing wool herself; it wasn't *that* warm. She focused more closely on his reddened face and dispirited manner, wondering what was wrong with him. Then when he was halfway through his dismount, he got his foot tangled in the stirrup and fell the rest of the way to the ground. He didn't rise.

"Robbie!" She rushed to him and pulled him upright,

cradling him. "What's the matter? Are you all right?" He was limp in her arms. "Robbie?" She steadied his shoulders and felt his forehead. He was hot and sweaty and his eyes had a watery, faraway look that boded ill. "Robbie—look at me. Do you hurt anywhere?"

"S-so hot." He raked a hand listlessly through his damp hair, standing it on end. Then he reached under his collar to scratch. "And I itch . . . all over . . ."

She looked up to find Morgan and McQuaid standing over them.

"Something's wrong. Help me get him inside."

Instantly, Morgan took charge, muscling McQuaid aside and gathering Robbie into his arms. He strode for the house and, once inside, insisted on personally carrying the boy to his room. Diamond trotted along beside him, stroking Robbie's head and reassuring him that all would be well. At the bottom of the main stairs, Morgan turned to Barton McQuaid with a manner that could only be described as arrogant.

"I shall stay here with Diamond and the boy. Be a good fellow, McQuaid, and fetch Dr. McGowan. He has an office on Charles Street."

Diamond was so worried that she seconded Morgan's request with a pleading look. McQuaid searched her face for a moment, frowned, and nodded. As they hurried up the step, she looked back over her shoulder and saw him putting on his hat and striding for the front doors. An unreasoning sense of relief poured through her at the thought that he was again riding to the rescue and would soon return with Doc McGowan.

The next hour was almost unbearable for her. With Mrs. Cullen's help, she put Robbie immediately to bed. In removing his clothes, they discovered a rash of red bumps on his neck and stomach and even in the edge of his hair. But, as Mrs. Cullen said, it was hard to tell quite what they meant, because of a general redness caused by what appeared to have been a frenzy of scratching.

Diamond settled on the bed beside Robbie, holding his hands to keep him from scratching. At her slightest movement, his hands tightened on hers as if he were afraid she might abandon him. He seemed so small and frail in the midst of that big bed, and his fever-brightened eyes seemed alarmingly vulnerable.

"Why didn't you say something, Robbie?" she asked, stroking his hair.

"I . . . didn't wanna miss ridin' a real horse."

It was all he had talked about for days: learning to ride and getting a horse of his own. "There will be plenty of time for that after you're well," she said with more confidence than she felt.

Calling for a basin of cold water and cloths, she began to bathe his face and arms, trying to make him more comfortable. He rested fitfully, tormented at regular intervals by itching that caused him to squirm and whine.

Morgan alternately hovered and paced, doing his best to look distressed. Several times he paused by the bed to set a hand to Diamond's shoulder or stroke her back, and each time she felt like smacking him. After a time, he leaned down to whisper that he was concerned that her caring for the boy personally might put her own "dear health" in jeopardy. She looked up at him, speechless, and he smiled with what she supposed passed for affectionate concern in his repertoire of responses.

"I would protect you at all costs . . . even from your own soft heart, my precious Diamond," he added, giving her cheek a possessive stroke.

How dare he imply her judgment was faulty or that she was incapable of deciding for herself what was and was not prudent? They weren't even engaged and he was trying to enforce his ideas of what was and was not good for her!

She had struggled her whole life to assert some control over her own destiny, to battle back the forces that overwhelmed her will and her choices . . . her overprotective father, her suffocating wealth, the ever-present expectations and demands of others. Now that she was finally on the brink of receiving full control of her fortune and setting things straight in her life, she was determined that no one was going to interfere. She certainly didn't need anyone trying to protect her from the workings of her own heart!

By the time old Dr. McGowan arrived, puffing heavily from being rushed up the stairs, Diamond was beside herself. Robbie's spots and itching seemed to be getting worse. The good doctor examined him thoroughly, issuing a goodly number of "um-hm's" in the process. Diamond was so intent on Robbie that she scarcely realized that Morgan's arm had found its way around her waist or that he was staring smugly over the top of her head at Barton McQuaid.

When the doctor turned and removed his spectacles, she held her breath.

"I do believe," he said, "that what we have here is a plain old, ordinary case of the chicken pox."

"Chicken pox?" She felt a surge of relief. "Not smallpox or diphtheria?"

"Heavens, no." The doctor smiled. "Just garden-variety chicken pox. Most children get 'em. They recover after a few days with no more than a few scars . . . which can be avoided, too, if you can keep him from scratching. A little calamine or a paste of soda and water on the bumps will help the itch. He'll be up and around in . . . oh, a few days." He chuckled, removing his spectacles. "Just be glad he's getting them out of the way while he's young."

"Getting them out of the way?" Morgan asked, coming alert. "Why?"

"Because kids get right through 'em," Doc McGowan said. "Whereas if you get 'em as an adult, it's another story. They can be downright serious."

Morgan peeled his arm from Diamond and staggered back a step.

"It's all right, Morgan," she said, a bit annoyed by his reaction. "You can't get them more than once." The doctor's agreement didn't seem to reassure him. "And I've already had them."

"Well, *I* haven't," Morgan said, stiffening. "I've never had chicken pox or mumps or—" His hands flew to his neck and chest, feeling for signs of disease.

"I, on the other hand," McQuaid said from the doorway, where he was leaning one shoulder against the frame, "had them in spades." He smiled at Morgan without the slightest trace of sympathy. "Spots and bumps everywhere." He pushed off with his shoulder and strolled forward. "In my hair, in my ears, inside my mouth. I knew a fellow in Carson City—thirty years old—who got them all over the soles of his feet and up his legs and all over his—Well, let's just say he couldn't perform the 'necessary function' without a good bit of pain. Nearly drove him crazy. Couldn't walk, couldn't eat . . ."

"In your ears? Your *mouth*?" Morgan's eyes widened. "You get them all over your—" His gaze flew to the front of his trousers and his hands twitched with a suppressed urge.

"Big, ugly sores. Like boils. They head out and break open. Ooze and itch and burn like the very devil." McQuaid shook his head. "And then after they've crusted over and dried up, some fellows come down with the shingles. Their skin turns scaly and red and cracks open and sloughs off . . ."

A groan escaped Morgan. He looked at Diamond with blanched dignity and backed hastily toward the door. "I must go home. I've just remembered . . . I promised Mother I would take her into the city." He rushed from the room.

Doc McGowan exited next, shaking his head over Morgan's reaction and telling Diamond to call him if she needed him. Mrs. Cullen showed the doctor out and, at Diamond's request, sent word of Robbie's condition to Hardwell and Hannah, who were at the Masseys' for their regular canasta game. When the room had cleared she turned to Barton McQuaid with an accusing look.

"You laid it on a bit thick, didn't you?" she said, crossing her arms trying to hide the vindictive pleasure she had felt watching Morgan deflate.

"Just told the truth, Miss Wingate." He was entirely too pleased with himself.

"Diamond?" Robbie's raspy voice came from the bed, and she hurried to his side. "Is he right? Am I gonna get boils so bad I can't pee?"

"No, you are not." She shot a see-what-you've-done look at McQuaid. "You heard what Dr. McGowan said. Boys your age always have it easier."

"But I itch so much." His eyes filled with tears of misery.

She settled on the edge of the bed and stroked his face. "I know you're uncomfortable, Robbie, but you'll get through it. I did, when I was a little girl."

"And I did." McQuaid's voice came from the other side of the bed. She looked up and found him standing with his hands on his waist, staring down at the boy. He had a reckless, not-to-be-trifled-with glint in his eyes.

"Besides, you're too ornery to die. You've got trouble written all over you, Wingate. Me, too." McQuaid jerked a thumb toward his shoulder. "That's how I know. And guys like us . . . we don't die of kid stuff like chicken pox. We die with our boots on . . . in a hail of bullets . . .

comin' out of a pair of swingin' saloon doors . . . down by the OK Corral."

"McQuaid . . ." She glared at him and he laughed and settled on the side of the bed, his brows upended in the wickedest look imaginable.

"Your lady cousin, here . . . she would be in big trouble if she got 'em now. Sweet young things like her . . . they usually just curl up and die." He flicked her a look that sent a flush of heat all through her. "A good thing she had 'em earlier, while she was still ornery enough to survive."

"McQuaid!" She balled her fists in her lap and sat straighter, trying to look more formidable. "That is quite en—"

"Now, the trick to survivin' this chicken pox thing is to choose where to scratch and where not to. Scratching is what causes the scars . . . so you want to pick places to scratch that you don't mind lookin' a bit rough . . . like your legs and sides and belly. You'll want to avoid scratching your face and arms and chest—because you'll want to grow up to be a handsome dog. Like me." He winked on the side turned away from Diamond and Robbie broke into a grin. "Women, for some reason or other, don't seem to take to a scarred-up face. And while you probably don't have much use for females now, believe me, they'll come in handy in the future."

"Mr. McQuaid, really!" she scowled, though with alarmingly less heat. Robbie was entranced.

"*Really,* Miss Wingate," he said, looking directly at her. "I'm just doing my Christian duty by Master Robert here . . . comforting him and such." He gave Robbie an outrageously earnest look. "How am I doing? You feeling comforted?"

Robbie nodded, sensing that he and McQuaid were in on something together . . . something that was all the more fun because Diamond was excluded and didn't seem to like it a bit.

"Drink your water," McQuaid said, motioning to the glass of water on the nightstand by the bed. "All this talking can make a man thirsty. And speakin' of thirsty . . . you know, there's nothing like a good cold glass of water. Some men swear by beer or whiskey. But me? I'm a water man. Good clear, cold water right out of a mountain stream. Ever been in the mountains, Robert?" When the boy said no, he wagged his head. "I figured not. You don't look like the got-snowed-in-in-a-mountain-pass-and-had-to-eat-my-shoe-leather-to-survive type. Well, you haven't been in real mountains until you've been in the Rockies. And the streams up in the Rockies are as clear as crystal and cold and sweet. . . ."

Diamond watched Barton McQuaid charming her cousin and knew on some level that he was sweetening her vinegar, as well. Curse his handsome hide. Who would have guessed that he possessed such a gift of gab? Or that he would be willing to use it to such humane ends . . . entertaining and distracting her rambunctious young cousin so thoroughly that he hadn't remembered to scratch in more than five minutes.

The problem was: Robbie wasn't the only one being distracted.

She should be outraged by the crass way McQuaid was entertaining her impressionable cousin. But for the life of her she could not bring herself to put an end to it. It pained her to admit it, even to herself . . . but she rather liked playing the horrified lady guardian. It gave her a perfect excuse to watch McQuaid's expressive face and frame work their magic. And, Lord—he did have some sort of magic. It made her fingertips tingle when he spoke. It made her pulse beat faster when he came into view. It made her stare at him when no one else was looking and want to stare at him when everybody in the world was looking.

"Tell me about Montana, Bear," Robbie said, snuggling into the pillows.

"Bear?" Diamond looked at him, then at McQuaid.

"Yeah. Out West they call him 'Bear' . . . on account of he outran a bear once," Robbie said. When McQuaid held up a finger, he remembered the rest. "Also 'cause he's mean as a grizzly when he gets up in the mornin.'"

"Close enough," McQuaid said.

"You seem to know quite a bit about Mr. McQuaid," she said, turning a burning, suspicious look on the tall Westerner.

"He doesn't know the half of it," McQuaid said, folding his arms across his chest and looking thoughtful. "I've been on Texas cattle drives and been trapped in mountain snow squalls and I've smoked a peace pipe with Indian chiefs—"

"Really?" Robbie's eyes widened. "Did they capture you?"

Bear McQuaid laughed. "Not exactly. We did some trading and I—I'm ashamed to say—came out on the short end. That pipe of tobacco cost me dearly." He punched a finger at Robbie. "Which is a good lesson for you, Wingate. Stay away from tobacco."

"Wow." Robbie drank it in. "Tell me about the cowboy stuff . . . and about your gun. I wanna hear about your gun."

Before long, McQuaid was sitting back against the foot post with his long legs stretched out before him and his feet crossed, telling Robbie about some of the places he had been and the characters he'd met in his travels over the length and breadth of the West. Diamond listened, too, reining him in when his stories became a bit too explicit, acting suitably shocked and disapproving.

"Really, Mr. McQuaid—"

"Bear," Robbie reminded her. "Call him 'Bear.'"

"Really, Mr. Bear," she said with a perfectly straight face, "I don't think Robbie is going to be in any situation requiring him to skin a buffalo anytime soon. I believe we can skip the gory details."

"Oh, no," Robbie said, with a bloodthirsty grin, "I want to hear ever'thing . . . all about the guts an' what you do with the eyeballs. . . ."

"Fine." Diamond stood and straightened her riding skirt. "But if you have horrible dreams tonight, Robert Wingate, don't come crying to me." Then she turned to "Bear" McQuaid. "I can see I'm not needed here. I may as well arrange dinner. You will stay?"

"You're inviting me to dinner?" he asked with mock surprise.

"I believe that's what I just did." She folded her arms.

"Well, that's quite generous of you," he drawled, eyeing her in a way that made her blush. "What are you having?"

Insolent man, she thought as she tromped down the steps to the center hall and headed for the service stairs leading to the kitchen. As if he wouldn't stay to dinner unless they were having buffalo steaks and shoe-leather pie.

IT WAS A light supper . . . only four courses . . . a simple white wine, no heavy beef dishes, and a raspberry fruit creme for dessert. Diamond—who had given in to her ingrained habit of changing for dinner and sat in her usual chair at the head of the table wearing a soft blue challis dress trimmed with French cutwork lace—directed the servants to offer McQuaid—seated at the foot of the table in his vest and shirtsleeves—seconds and then thirds.

He ate like a starving army. Though, in truth, it wasn't

unpleasant watching his appreciative appetite. It probably took a goodly amount of food to fuel that large, powerful—

Dragging those thoughts under control, she realized that he hadn't bothered to put on his coat for dinner. That should have roused her proper indignation. But when he sat back in his chair and closed his eyes, savoring the wine, she felt nothing even approaching disapproval.

His head popped up and he frowned. "Do I hear a bell ringing?" he said, glancing at the door.

"It's the telephone."

"The what?"

"Telephone. Surely you've seen them. The wired boxes you speak into and talk to people miles away. Philip Vassar has them at his bank."

"I've heard of them," he said. "Never seen one, though."

Jeffreys entered the dining room. "Beg pardon, miss. Mr. and Mrs. Humphrey are experiencing some difficulty with the carriage. They say they can borrow the Masseys' carriage if they are needed home right away. Otherwise, they shall have to wait until the Masseys' stableman fixes the wheel."

"I'll speak to them," she said, rising and heading for the door. She paused as Bear McQuaid rose from his chair. "You can come and see, if you like."

He followed her out into the center hall and around the curved staircase to a shadow-laden library. She paused just inside the door to touch something on the wall, there was a faint "click," and light bloomed instantly around them. It was a strong, brilliant white that had none of the whoosh or smell or yellow tinge of gaslight. He looked up at the crystal fixture overhead. Above each of the former gas jets was a clear glass dome containing a glowing golden filament that looked similar to the ones he had seen in the electrified street lamps of some of the better sections of Baltimore.

While he was staring in fascination at the electrical light, she went to the large desk in the center of the library and raised the telephone to her ear. The sound of her voice drew his attention back to her and he joined her, scrutinizing the device in her hand. It was a wooden handle fitted with two black cones, one flattened and one bent slightly, that she held to her ear and mouth. The device was attached by a cord to a polished cherry box fitted with a crank that looked like a coffee-grinder handle.

"No need to rush," she said, speaking succinctly into one of the cones. "We're keeping Robbie cool with baths and using calamine and soda poultices for the itching. The doctor said it's something he'll just have to suffer through." Her eyes narrowed and she held the listening part away from her ear. Bear could have sworn he heard the sound of raspy laughter from the earpiece. After a moment she returned it to her ear and said tersely, "Good-bye, Hardwell." As she returned the telephone to its metal cradle, he stared at the polished box and receiver on the desk.

"You can honestly talk to people through that box and wires." He rubbed his chin. "I read about these things in the newspapers on the train. I had no idea you had 'telephones' here."

"Baltimore is a very progressive city. We can reach any one of more than two thousand people, and new lines are being strung all the time. We have just added service to Cumberland, Frostburg, Annapolis, and Frederick—"

"We?"

"I . . . invested. Our Chesapeake and Potomac Telephone stock is soaring." She lowered her gaze to the contraption. "Would you like to talk to someone?"

The only person he wanted—needed—to talk to was standing across the corner of a desk from him. But distance wasn't the only difficulty to be overcome in communication. With all that he had to say to her, he found himself staring speechlessly at the golden highlights in her hair.

He straightened abruptly.

"How about calling your friend Kenwood? We could ask if he's broken out in spots yet."

When she looked up he could tell she was trying desperately not to smile. "He doesn't have a telephone . . . or 'spots' . . . yet."

Turning away, he strolled around the cluttered library. The floor-to-ceiling shelves were stocked with expensive leather-bound volumes, some of which had been displaced to stacks on the floor by mechanical objects that defied easy identification. He skirted the paper-strewn desk in the center of the room and passed a leather sofa piled with rolled-up documents and legal folios, on his way to a set of makeshift shelves below the windows.

He stared at the bewildering assortment of gadgets and materials, then picked up something that looked like a rug beater with a metal cup on the handle end. Then he peered into a pair of glass cylinders filled with red liquid and connected by a coil of copper pipe and studied what looked like a small metal horn projecting from a tin box to which bare copper wires were attached.

"What is this stuff?"

"Progress." She strolled closer, smiling at his skeptical expression. "Or steps on the way to it. They're inventions I've purchased . . . that is, I've bought the rights to manufacture."

He thought of the inventor who had accosted her at the Vassars' party. Scowling, he held up the "rug beater." "You actually intend to produce this?"

"I consider it more an investment in the inven*tor* than the inven*tion*."

As he mulled that over, something off to the side caught his eye. He turned and found himself facing a full-sized pair of locomotive wheels set back into the wall by the door. They were attached by a driving rod and rested on a piece of steel rail.

"What the devil are these doing here?" He strode over to them and ran his hands over their polished curves. "They look like Baldwin wheels."

"They are," she said, coming to stand beside him. "Mr. Baldwin sent me this pair of wheels when I—"

"Don't tell me. You *invested* in his engine company." His stomach tightened as she nodded. Baldwin Engine Company, for God's sake. Was there anything she didn't own a piece of? He stared at them, his heart pounding.

Just beside that massive set of driving wheels, on the ledge of the nearest bookshelf, was a miniature passenger car sitting on a bit of simulated track. He leaned to get a better look, traced the outline of the roof, and bent to peer into the windows. The interior was elegantly rendered in lush green velvet and highly polished mahogany; everything was perfectly to scale, including a tiny brass spittoon and sleeping berths complete with miniature sheets and pillows. He glanced at the gilt lettering above the side windows.

"A Pullman car." He frowned, studying it.

"Mr. Pullman was nice enough to send us a model of our own personal car. My father ordered one just before he died." She bent beside him to look in the windows. "This was my favorite thing in the whole world when I was a little girl. I took a thousand trips in this little car . . . London, France, India, China . . ."

Her eyes and voice softened as she pointed to a curtain-draped berth at the rear of the little car and smiled. "That was always my bed. At night I always refused to draw the shades because I wanted to imagine lying on my bed and watching the moon chase the car along the tracks. Then every morning I had breakfast in a different country and read books about—" She halted and straightened abruptly, staring at that little car with a tumultuous look.

She struggled internally for a moment and when she spoke again her words were clipped and efficient. "How many Pullman cars have you ordered for your new railroad?"

Bear was still focused on that miniature train car and the jarring contrast it posed to a pair of five-foot driving wheels. One spoke of an investor's power and determination and the other was an unexpected glimpse into the dreams of a little girl's heart. He had to shake his head as he straightened, to make himself register the question. She had asked about his railroad . . . his . . .

"None," he answered. "It's a short line. Mostly freight. Beef and grain. We won't usually have passengers."

She pounced on that statement. "Over two hundred miles of track that opens up new land to settlement? You'll have people coming and going constantly. People have to move themselves and their households and their stock and equipment. You'll have to have at least one or two sleepers, and Mr. Pullman's cars are by far the best."

He scrambled to meet her gaze and assessment, caught off guard by her changed mood.

"They're overpriced," he said shortly. "Farmers don't need down pillows and velvet seats. The line's not long enough for anybody to use it for a bed."

"But it would be foolish not to add that capacity," she said with equal terseness, "when you have to buy a few passenger cars anyway."

A few passenger cars here, a few Pullman cars there . . . he could see her waving a privileged hand and making them appear instantly on the track. She had no idea what it took for a struggling railroad to come up with the cash for something as luxurious as a Pullman Sleeping

Car. Or something as basic as steel and timber. Or cranes and equipment. Or a serviceable old engine or two.

Irritably, he turned away and spotted on a nearby shelf a pair of metal cylinders with shafts, attached to rubber hoses and a curved metal contraption fitted with what could only be called a piston. Reaching for the curved part, turning it over and over, he examined the workmanship and interplay of parts. A brake shoe . . . with a pressure line and cylinder attached. Recognition flooded him. He'd never seen the working parts of a Westinghouse air brake outside of a rail car. How the heck did she get hold of—

"That was sent to me by—"

"George Westinghouse," he supplied.

"That's right." She seemed pleased that he recognized it. "Soon the whole railroad industry will be using them. They're so much safer that there is talk that the government in Washington may soon require them on all train cars."

"Just what railroaders need," he muttered, replacing the brake shoe on the shelf, "more government interference."

"I hardly think it's interference. They're simply trying to use new ideas and equipment to make the rails safer."

"Safer?" He reached for and held up one of the hoses. "These things can be a menace. The pressure holds fine in the engine and first few cars, but in anything over five cars, the pressure drops and the rear cars don't brake at all. And since there aren't enough brakemen to turn the hand brakes, the cars go runaway and overtake the front cars on the slightest downward grade. There isn't a curve in Colorado or Wyoming that hasn't seen cars hop rails because of these damned things."

She seemed indignant. "That's absurd. They're ten times safer than the old hand brakes. They've saved hundreds of brakemen's lives." She stalked closer and pulled the main pressure cylinders from the shelf. "And anyway, these are the new and improved brakes."

"New and improved?" He gave a skeptical huff.

"Mr. Westinghouse has added a new valve system to maintain pressure, so the rear cars will have just as much braking power as the engine and tender. By the time they're installed in all new cars and engines and refitted into existing cars—"

"Mr. Westinghouse will be a damn sight richer than he already is," he declared. "Look . . . every requirement those bean heads in Washington dream up just drives up costs for railroaders."

"Who make plenty of profit as it is," she responded firmly.

He caught his four-letter rebuttal before it escaped. Purging the blue from his thoughts, he glowered at her ladylike appearance and her privileged surroundings. For all her knowledge of railroads, her *experience* was sorely limited. She might have seen the mighty B&O laying track along an existing Maryland road or across gently rolling Tidewater countryside, but she had absolutely no idea what it took to build a railroad under less-than-civilized conditions.

"Tell me, Miss Wingate"—his voice carried a fierce edge—"how much profit does a man deserve when he sinks his life's savings into land and equipment and works night and day to lay track . . . under a searing sun in summer and through life-threatening cold in winter . . . over loose, stony terrain that refuses to hold a proper grade or through hostile hills that make you chisel one out of a wall of granite . . . despite shortages of men and equipment and raids by Indians who don't like what the Iron Horse does to their land and their buffalo . . . without proper sleep and decent food for weeks at a time . . . battling foul weather, black flies, and bad water . . . us-

ing tools so cold your skin freezes to them . . . and steel
so hot it burns your hands to blisters?" He halted long
enough to draw breath and his voice lowered to a raw,
mesmerizing vibration.

"Just how much profit compensates a man for pouring
his guts and dreams out in a long steel ribbon that helps to
bind a nation and build a country?"

The heat and conviction in his words left no doubt in
Diamond's mind that every image he conjured had been
drawn from his personal experience. He wasn't talking
about just any railroad entrepreneur; he was talking about
his own battles with stubborn nature, hostile populations
and elements, and brutal working conditions. She thought
of the rail construction she had seen and made herself
imagine it a thousand miles from anywhere . . . crews of
tough, independent men . . . impossible terrain . . .
storms, shortages, and prolonged isolation.

The copper eyes poised above her suddenly seemed as
clear as Baltic amber. Through them she glimpsed the
workings of the inner man. He was the proud, stubborn,
powerful sort of man who made big things like railroads
happen . . . one of that unique breed who poured out
their dreams along with their blood and sweat and souls
into the steel ribbons of Progress that spanned a continent.

In that moment, she sensed that she had touched the
essence of him, that she now knew him in ways she could
spend a lifetime trying to describe.

"A man who pours his body and soul into building a
railroad, who drives railroad crews with his own grit and
determination, who braves both the elements and the odds
. . . such a man doesn't expect to be paid in mere coin."
She watched in dismay as her words struck sparks.

"Oh, no?" He gave an irritable laugh. "So you think the
country's builders ought to unselfishly spend their last dol-

lar for the greater good, do you? What about Cornelius Vanderbilt, Jay Gould, J. P. Morgan, and John Work Garrett and James J. Hill? Do you honestly think they would have lifted a finger toward building a railroad without the expectation of profit? It takes money to make money, Miss Wingate." He leaned closer. "You of all people should know that. Progress is a very expensive commodity."

A shiver raced up her spine as his words echoed down through every layer of her awareness, all the way to her well-guarded core. Warmth welled up unexpectedly in her, softening her posture and pooling in her eyes.

"My exact words on a number of occasions," she said quietly, searching him. "This is a rare moment, Mr. McQuaid. We actually agree on something."

Her softening momentarily disarmed him. He was primed for a battle royal and, instead, found himself facing no discernible opposition.

They agreed.

He was drawn to her eyes for confirmation and had the curious sensation of stepping into a rushing Montana stream. That warm, swirling blue drew the heat from his temper, leaving only a steamy, lingering glow of anticipation.

Suddenly the fact that they had come toe to toe and eye to eye while making their points took on an entirely different potential. His head filled with the faint scent of strawberries. Her scent. Every square inch of his skin was suddenly hot and tingling with awareness of her.

"And just what is it that we agree on? Progress or railroads or profit or . . . something else?"

She tilted her head up, maintaining the visual bridge between them, along which all sorts of breathtaking commerce was passing.

"Progress, Mr. McQuaid. I'm a great believer in progress."

"Bear," he reminded her.

"Bear." Her breath quickened. "And in the men who make progress happen."

"Men who make progress." A wicked grin curled one side of his mouth as it lowered toward hers. "Does that include me? Am I making progress?"

"Progress?" Her gaze sought his as she felt his breath bathing her lips. "I believe you're one of the most *progressive* men I've ever met."

Shameless hussy, some small prune-proper part of her whispered. But the pounding of her heart and the stark new sensitivity of her skin inured her to it.

He dragged his lips lightly across hers, back and forth, mesmerizing her with the "almost" of the kiss that was coming. If she raised her chin just a fraction of an inch, she would fulfill that luscious promise of contact, but she would also end this delectable suspension in time and desire. And it was so entrancing to hover just at the threshold of pleasure, experiencing new sensations of wonder and longing.

Then, with a soft rushing sound that might have been her breath escaping—or his—he ended the suspense and joined their mouths.

It was like being enveloped in a warm cloud, she thought. His lips were surprisingly soft and deliciously expressive against hers. Pleasure radiated through her, beginning at that delicious point of contact and spreading slowly down her throat and through her breast, just under her skin. His hand on the nape of her neck gently guided her closer and she tilted her head to fit her mouth more fully to his.

That soft, caressing motion, that endlessly pleasurable contact, was dizzying. She felt her world spinning, her breath shortening, and her knees going weak.

His free arm slid around her waist and pulled her

against him so that her breasts rested against his chest
. . . that taut, hard-muscled, sun-bronzed expanse that
lately had disrupted her sleep but enlivened her dreams.
Her hands came up his sides and slid haltingly over him,
savoring his hidden shape, relishing the private memory
that guided her exploration.

Joy rose in her like a bright bubble. His mouth on hers
was soft and hard . . . commanding and yet entreating
. . . giving as well as taking pleasure. . . .

NINE

VOICES AND COMMOTION from the front hall broke through her narrowing concentration. Hardwell and Hannah flashed into her mind, then Morgan, then the servants, then the people at the front gates.

He must have heard it, too, for he released her the instant she began to pull away and he jerked back in the same instant. She whirled, caught her balance, fixed her gaze on the door, and walked straight into the arm of the sofa.

"Ohhh." The impact righted her vision and jolted her mental faculties back into operation. Her bare lips felt slightly swollen and unbearably conspicuous. Her cheeks were hot—probably crimson. Trembling noticeably, she paused to compose herself at the edge of the stairs, just out of sight of whoever was in the center hall.

The sound of her pet name being crowed at the top of a familiar male voice sent a wave of guilty recognition through her.

"Diaaamond Miiine! Where aaare you?"

She stepped out from behind the newel posts and there

in the middle of the entry stood none other than Paine Webster. He was dressed in evening clothes that clearly belonged to a bygone evening, his coat was rumpled, his collar stood open, his shirt was stained, and his tie was missing altogether. He stood with his feet well apart and his legs braced to keep him upright. Behind him, poor Jeffreys and one of the stable hands were trying valiantly to wrestle a huge streamer trunk through the open front doors.

"Paine?" She hurried toward him, but stopped several feet away as she encountered overpowering smells of drink and sweat and stale tobacco smoke.

"There you are!" His voice muted to a low roar at the sight of her. "My li'l Diamond mine. God—you look good enough to eat. Damn good thing we Webs-s-sters aren't given to gout!" He lunged at her.

"Paine!" She tried to evade him, but even in his inebriated state he had reflexes like a cat. He grabbed her up by the waist and swung her around and around until they both nearly toppled over. She pushed back enough to get her feet on the ground and stop them, but he refused to release her.

"Diamond mine . . . you haven't changed a bit." Paine panted, staring at her with eyes that were dark-centered and struggling to focus. Holding her breath, she pushed back further.

"You haven't changed, either." She had to turn her head to breathe something besides alcohol fumes. "It's all right, Jeffreys." She spotted the glowering butler. "I'll see to Mr. Webster myself." As Jeffreys and the stable hand withdrew, she realized Bear was standing by the staircase, looking as if he might intervene at any second. She worked to remove Paine's hands from her person. "Please, Paine, I have company."

The sense of what she said must have penetrated. He

looked up, spotted Bear's formidable frame, and released her.

"Sorry, sweet th-thing . . . had no idea." He pulled down his waistcoat and squared his shoulders, staggering toward Bear with his hand outstretched. "Look f-famil-i-ar, ol' man. Have we met?" Bear hesitated, glancing at her, before taking it.

"Barton McQuaid," he said.

"Paine Webs-ster. At your s-service." Paine bowed so extravagantly over their joined hands that he was in danger of toppling over.

Diamond rushed to put her arm through his and steady him. "Why don't we go into the drawing room and have a seat." With a wince of apology in Bear's direction, she steered Paine toward the drawing room. But halfway to the door he remembered something and reversed course, dragging her with him.

"Almos-st forgot. This is-s for you, Diamond mine." He pulled her back to the trunk, fumbled with the latch, and finally threw back the lid.

Inside was fabric, a veritable king's ransom in exotic and remarkable textiles. Embroidered satins, brocades, lush moirés, and sheer silk veiling. Most of it was cream or ivory, and she watched with mounting dread as he reached into the trunk and pulled out one bolt after another, holding them up to her and sending the sheer fabrics billowing and the heavier ones unrolling like a priceless carpet on the floor around her. By the time he reached the halfway point in the trunk, she knew exactly what was happening and tried to stop him.

"It's all beautiful, Paine. But please"—she reached for his arm—"you're in no condition—"

It was too late.

"For your wedding gown and trous-s-seau. Spent weeks

s-searching the markets of Singapore. Th' finest s-silks money can buy. Nothing but the bes-st for my bride."

He reeled to his feet and took her by the shoulders. His face was naked with need, but not the sort of need a man feels for a woman. This was a starved-child look, a boyish plea for approval and affection. Diamond's distress at witnessing it must have been disastrously visible, for he quickly loosened his grip on her and resumed his devil-may-care manner.

"Talk makes me thirs-sty," he declared, heading for the liquor cabinet in the drawing room.

She looked at the lush array of fabrics spread at her feet, at the back of the man who had brought them half-way around the world to her, then at the man who had only moments ago held her in his arms. Flushing with confusion, she headed for the drawing room and stopped just inside the door. Paine had invaded their little-used liquor cabinet and was pouring a huge tumbler of brandy.

"Have you had anything to eat?" she asked. "We just finished dinner and it would be no trouble to—"

"No, no . . . wouldn't put you out. Not hungry, really. Just thirs-sty." He flashed her a wicked grin and raised his glass in salute as he sauntered drunkenly to the sofa, perched on the arm, and slid down it to a seat.

"Have you been home lately? When was the last time you ate?"

"What day is-s-it?" he asked with an unfocused grin.

She decided to take the glass from him, but he read her intention, downed the rest in a few gulps, and surrendered it to her empty.

"So, who's your friend over there—whas-s his name again?" Paine asked, squinting at Bear, who was leaning a shoulder against the door frame and glowering. "Anyone your future hus-sband should know about?"

"Paine Webster," she said, glaring at him. "As soon as

you pass out, I'm going to scoop you up, pour you into your carriage, and send you straight home."

"Heartles-s-s creature." He grinned as he felt the numbing effect of the brandy creeping over him. "You'd never d-do that to me, sweetness. You love me too much." When she forcefully folded her arms, he smiled. "Do me a favor, Diamond Mine. S-see my clothes are cleaned and p-pressed? Think what a shock it will be to th' family to see me hauling home after a three-day b-bender, looking as neat as a new p-penny." He smiled and closed his eyes as if relishing the image. His eyes didn't reopen.

A moment later his head drooped and he sagged sideways against the arm of the sofa. She called his name and lifted his head. It rolled off her hand.

"You would do this to me," she muttered, "with Hardwell and Hannah due home anytime and—" *With Bear McQuaid standing in the doorway, watching . . . with his kisses still warm on my lips.*

She looked up and found Bear observing her reaction through narrowed eyes. The heat that bloomed in her face when she turned back to Paine was as much resentment as it was chagrin. The moment between her and Bear McQuaid was gone and she had dissolute, loose-lipped Paine Webster to thank for it.

"I have to get him upstairs." Taking refuge in activity, she discarded the empty glass and reached for one of Paine's arms. "If Hardwell and Hannah find him here they will be furious."

"I vote you put him back on the horse he rode in on and send him home."

"I'm afraid you don't get a vote," she said, stooping to drape Paine's arm around her neck. When Bear didn't move, she screwed up her courage and looked up at him. The darkness in his expression settled on her heart like a stone. She resorted to her standard offer.

"If you'll help, I can make it worth your while."

He straightened, his scowl deepening. "I get to name my price, again?"

She refused to think about what had just happened in the library or the alarming sense of loss she felt. She was up to her eyeballs in promises she couldn't keep now. What was one more?

"Fine. Name your price. Now will you come and take his other arm?"

As they struggled up the stairs with Paine's limp, un-wieldy form, Bear observed the effectiveness of Diamond's technique: Paine's arm around the neck and a solid hold of the back of his trouser waist. Not exactly the sort of thing taught in debutante training.

"I take it you've done this before."

"Once or twice," she said breathlessly.

"You let men come to your house to pass out from three-day drunks?" He was breathing hard, as well. "How accommodating of you."

"Not *men*. Just him. He needs help, and I can't—"

"*Say no,*" he finished for her.

"Can't turn him away in his hour of need," she finished for herself, scowling over at him. "We have been friends . . . for as long as I can recall. We grew up together. His family did business with my father."

There was a brief, charged silence.

"Those people at the gates . . . you grew up with them, too?"

She experienced a confusing sense of embarrassment that had to do with the fact that he had seen not only the people at her gates, but Paine's outrageous imposition on her. *She* was helping *them,* she told herself. What did she have to be embarrassed about?

"Don't be ridiculous," she said.

"Ridiculous is doing whatever anybody asks of you," he

said, wrapping both arms around Paine to hold him up while she opened a bedroom door.

"I don't do whatever anybody asks of me." She tried to resume her place under Paine's arm, but he warned her off.

"I've got him," he said on a growl. "Just lead the way."

A moment later, he dumped Paine on the bed in the darkened guest room and turned to stare at her with his fists propped on his waist.

"You trot out food to whoever shows up at your door. You buy worthless inventions just because people ask you to. You put up drunks in your guest room. Robbie was right about you. You just can't say no."

"Robbie said that to you?" She paused for a second, stung by the fact that Robbie, whom she had welcomed into both her home and her heart, would say such a thing about her to a total stranger. Biting her lip, she turned to the bed, surveyed the messy figure sprawled across the counterpane, then rolled him up onto his side to peel his coat from him. "That's absurd. I can refuse anything I wish, any time I wish."

"What do you think you're doing?" His gaze fastened on her grip on Paine's coat.

"Removing his blasted coat and shirt. They'll need to be cleaned and—" When he gave a sharp laugh, she straightened. "What is so amusing?"

"There's your proof. He comes to your house, dead drunk, passes out, and instructs you to have his clothes cleaned for him while he sleeps it off." The molten heat of his gaze caused her face to catch fire. "And you actually do it."

"He was teasing," she said, caught between chagrin at seeing her actions in another, insightful light and a need to defend her right to help Paine.

"Was he?" He paused, searching her face in the dim

light coming from the hallway and delivered the *coup de grâce*. "Judging by how seriously you take his 'teasing' . . . let me be the first to offer congratulations on your upcoming nuptials."

Her face burned. "I do not intend to marry Paine Webster."

"He thinks you do."

"He's wrong."

He studied her for a moment. "Kenwood would be relieved to hear that."

"Morgan? What does he have to do with—"

"He informed me this afternoon that you and *he* are promised."

"He said that to you?" She froze.

"He did. And by my count, that gives you one fiancé too many."

She looked up and met his eyes, unable to move or to speak. Her knees suddenly went weak.

"You really can't say no, can you?" he charged quietly.

"You don't understand," she said, around the panic collected in her throat.

"I understand all too well." He took a step closer.

She took a step back.

He took another step toward her and brought a hand up to cradle her chin.

She couldn't make herself resist. The horror of being discovered in bigamous engagements was dissolving in a surge of complex, contradictory feelings . . . about her way of doing things . . . about her newly emerged sensual feelings . . . about her fascination with him. Things got more complicated still when he closed the remaining distance between them and slipped one arm around her waist.

"All you have to do is tell me no."

She couldn't. She was riveted by the glimmer of light in

his eyes. Her arms hung at her sides as he pulled her fully against him.

"Say no and I'll stop," he murmured, releasing her face and running his hand down the side of her neck.

She sucked in a sharp breath as his touch drifted down her side, grazing the side of her breast. When his hand curled possessively around her waist, confusion boiled up in her. She told herself she remained silent because she refused to be bullied into responding to his demand. But she knew full well that her silence also had to do with the fact that she didn't want to say no to him.

"It's not hard. Two little letters. N-O." He lowered his mouth and said it against her lips. "No." Poured it over her mouth. *"No."*

The moist furls of his breath caused her lips to tingle, and her head filled with the hot tang of musk spiced by a hint of wine. When her lips parted, she could taste him on every breath: winelike and salty sweet. Her whole body began to tremble.

The stroke of his tongue across her lips was so warm and gentle that she could feel it melting her cool, protective edges. He seemed to be tasting her, exploring her even as she was him, and the sensations—so similar to those earlier pleasures—were somehow sweeter for their unlikeliness. Moments ago she had despaired of ever experiencing such pleasure again. Now she felt his presence saturating her senses, reviving her delight in the sensual, confirming the sensations that earlier had called forth deeply instinctive responses in her.

She met his kiss fully, sinking into the softness of his mouth and against the enthralling hardness of his body. Her body warmed and became pliant, her skin felt sensitive and hungry for sensation. As her lips parted under his tongue, she returned its provocative strokes, examining herself and her responses even as she explored him. Long-sealed parts of her were opening to perception and aware-ness.

She slid her arms around his waist and up his back, splaying her fingers over the thick fans of muscle that arched from his spine. Deep in her mind she welcomed and preserved each sensation, shivering at the way his moist lips drifted down the side of her neck and his tongue probed the notch at the base of her throat.

Suddenly her fingers were sliding through his dark hair, memorizing its texture even as she cradled his head against her. When his hands cleared buttons and lace from the downward path of his kisses, she held her breath and then arched slightly to give him access.

Pleasure spiraled downward through her, rousing her body . . . setting her breasts tingling and settling a sweet ache in her lower abdomen. Closer, she wanted to be closer to him . . . to feel him against her skin, to have him touch the rest of her as he was her waist and shoulders.

Kiss after hungry kiss, his embrace tightened. Caress after caress, she felt his body hardening against hers, curling over and around hers. She molded to his frame, merging her shape with his, joining him in a seamless interplay of sensation and response. Following his example, she began to direct her kisses along a wider arc . . . nuzzling and tasting him, savoring the salty heat of his skin, and experiencing against her nose the faint tickle of his chest hair.

Then, as she moaned softly and rubbed the burning tips of her breasts against him, he tugged down the rim of her corset and lowered his mouth to her nipple. Sharp flashes of pleasure raced along an undiscovered network of nerves that somehow linked all the sensitive peaks and hollows of her body. She gasped and held her breath, her eyes closed, seeing with her mind his bronzed head at her pale breast . . .

Then somewhere in her recesses the sounds of voices registered, parting the fog of sensuality that shrouded her senses. She froze, listening and slowly broadening her awareness to include her location and condition.

Sliding her head to the side, she ended another deep, soul-bending kiss. A moment later, she found herself on her back on the bed . . . inches away from Paine's snoring form . . . wedged beneath Bear's big, hard body . . . with her dress unfastened and her corset tucked to reveal the tip of one breast. Braced above her was Bear McQuaid, his vest and shirt unbuttoned, his eyes black with hunger and his lips swollen with the effects of a dozen shameless kisses.

Horror struck as she recognized those voices and realized that they were growing louder. "Hardwell and Hannah," she muttered hoarsely, staggering from the bed and groping frantically for buttons. "They're home!"

He buttoned only the top of his shirt, then jammed the rest into his trousers and pulled his vest together. She was still struggling with her garments, when he brushed her hands aside and finished for her, freeing her trembling hands to smooth and right her hair. The instant she was presentable, she headed for the hall, then turned back and grabbed him by the arm to pull him along.

They were just past Robbie's door, when her erstwhile guardians appeared at the top of the steps. Hardwell, still carrying his walking stick, and Hannah, just removing her gloves and reaching for her hat pin, hurried down the hall toward them.

"Is he all right?" Hannah asked, looking past them, toward Robbie's room.

Robbie. Diamond flushed with horror. She hadn't given her stricken charge a thought in over an hour. Turning back immediately, she opened the door to her cousin's room and held her breath.

In the dimly lit room they found Robbie sleeping, albeit somewhat fitfully. After a reassuring moment around the bed, they tiptoed out in silence.

"Poor little thing," Hannah said when the door closed behind them. "He must have been scared out of his wits."

"Actually"—Diamond looked at Bear and found him watching her with virtually every emotion known to humankind blended into one tumultuous look—"he was frightened. But Mr. McQuaid was good enough to talk him out of it."

Hardwell turned to him, beaming. "What a useful fellow you're turnin' out to be, McQuaid. It seems we owe you yet another debt. How will we ever repay you?"

THE NIGHT BREEZE blew the fog from Bear's senses as he drove his rented buggy back to Baltimore. He had weathered winters so cold that his whiskers froze and snapped off, without so much as a shiver. But the contrast of the unspent heat of his body and the chilled night air now set him quaking as if he had a raging fever. He could barely hold on to the reins.

What in God's name had he done back there? The sequence of events replayed in his mind, starting with the library. He groaned. Railroads—they had been talking about railroads. And investing. It had been the perfect opportunity to raise the possibility of her *investing* in *his railroad*. But then they began to argue and somehow he went from lecturing her on the realities of laying track out West to kissing her. Then that idiot Webster showed up . . . and he got furious with her and her inability to say no and decided to make her say it.

And the rest of the night went to hell in a handcar!

Or to heaven.

Dammit. It was a golden opportunity to fund his life-long dream and he had just kissed it good-bye. Literally.

By the time he reached the outer limits of Baltimore, his temperature and his passions had cooled, leaving him with a sober new view of his predicament.

He had gone to see her with the best of intentions and had found himself wading through throngs of beggars at her gates, coping with arrogant horse breeders, rescuing reckless ten-year-old hellions on horseback, dealing with chicken pox and doctors and telephones, helping her put habitual drunks to bed, and being warned off by two men who both claimed to be marrying her. But the worst of it was that after tonight, his vow to keep his dealings with her strictly business was forfeit.

From this evening on, everything that passed between them would transpire over the memory of an intimate encounter that had set them both reeling. How could he face her without thinking of the softness of her lips, the sweet hesitation of her tongue against his, the voluptuous yielding of her body beneath him? How the hell was he going to separate his need for her money from his desire for her?

There was an aged yellow gaslight burning outside the livery stable when he arrived to return the horse and buggy. He swung down from the seat and called to the stable hand, who appeared after a few minutes with a just-wakened look. Bear reminded him they were owed two more days on their rental, and the fellow grumbled an acknowledgment and led the horse into the stable to unhitch the buggy.

Shoving his hands into his trouser pockets, Bear struck off down the dusty side street that led to St. Charles. For once he wouldn't mind the long walk to the waterfront tavern where they were staying. It would give him time to think of a way to break the news of his failure to Halt as well as a way to pay for breakfast tomorrow. And dinner.

He strolled onto St. Charles, past Vassar's Mercantile Bank, the Oystermen's Fraternal Building, several prosperous shops, and the elegant La Maison Restaurant without looking up from his feet. But as he strode under one of the electric street lamps he became aware of a loud hum, saw specks and dots swirling before his eyes, and jerked his head up. A thick swarm of insects of every size and description was buzzing around him. Batting them away with both hands, he bolted for the unlighted part of the street and stopped only when the hum faded.

Scowling, he looked back at the street lamp and realized the light looked as if it were alive and undulating. Thousands—hundreds of thousands—of insects had been attracted by the brightness. He glanced farther along, at the next street lamp, and witnessed a similar teeming. To avoid the swarms he would have to keep to the dark side of the streets until he was out of the electrified area.

Crossing the street toward the front of the Exeter Hotel, he spotted a man coming down the steps, waving his hands and swatting at insects that had been drawn across the street by the hotel's carriage lamps. He might not have noticed the man if he hadn't been battling the same menace. He glanced at the fellow and away—then instinctively looked back with attention piqued and focused. The fellow had been looking at him, too, but now turned quickly and entered a waiting cab.

Bear halted in his tracks, trying to be certain of what he had seen. Then as the cab rumbled past, he caught a brief glimpse of the man in a shaft of light from that infested street lamp. Lionel Beecher . . . he would stake money on it. He watched the cab racing out of sight and was hit by a cold drenching of reality.

Beecher was here, in Baltimore, and staying in the business district. He started to walk, and as he thought of reasons for Beecher's presence, his step quickened.

Lionel Beecher was a hired gun, a professional thug . . . a man whose nefarious skills and talents were available to the highest bidder. And railroad tycoon Jay Gould was always the highest bidder. Except when it came to buying land options and right-of-way through central Montana. Gould had sent Beecher to make offers to some of the ranchers around Billings, intending to get the jump on Bear and Halt's proposed rail line. Gould wanted nothing more than to get a foothold in Jim Hill's rail empire: the newly completed Chicago, Milwaukee and St. Paul line, which would soon stretch from Chicago all the way to the Pacific. But Beecher's arrogance and heavy-handed approach offended local ranchers and they were only too pleased to accept marginally better offers from Bear and Halt.

Now Beecher was here in Baltimore.

With senses heightened, he hurried on, zigzagging to avoid the streetlights. As he left the electrified district, he heard footsteps behind him and looked over his shoulder. Seeing no one, he strode on, and the footsteps returned, growing closer . . . then suddenly running . . . straight for him. He started to run, but was hit from behind and stumbled.

An instant later, as he scrambled to his feet, fists came flying out of the dimness, connecting with his midsection and chin, knocking him back against a wall. Pain galvanized his responses. Crouching and weaving, he dodged the next blow and the one after that, buying time. Then he burst upward, connecting with his fists and sending one of his attackers sprawling back into the street. Taking advantage of their surprise, he lowered a shoulder and rammed it into the other's stomach, slamming him back against that same wall. Trading blows in quick succession, he managed to get in a lucky punch that caused the thug to double over. The first attacker was already on his feet, angry as a gored ox and charging again. They joined and wrestled, each struggling to free an arm and land a punch. Bear ended the stalemate with a well-aimed kick to his opponent's knee, and in the split second it took for the wretch to recover, Bear drove home a blow that sent him sprawling back onto the street.

Bear's primary urge was to finish the fight they had started. But there were times when flight was more prudent than fight. These two dock rats fought with dispassionate precision as if they were used to such encounters and were pacing themselves. Wheeling, he took off down the street at a dead run.

Grunts of surprise and muffled curses reached him and he heard them coming after him. But they had obviously been hired for their fists, not their speed. After a few minutes, they gave up their pursuit, and Bear was left running alone down the narrow, ill-lit streets of the waterfront district.

Minutes later, he ducked inside the noisy waterfront tavern that was their temporary home, and spotted Halt in a far corner, brooding over the dregs of a tankard of watery ale. He made his way through the tables of sailors and longshoremen spending their hard-earned pay on marked cards and bad liquor.

"Where the hell have you been?" Halt rose irritably at the sight of him. Then his eyes widened at the blood on Bear's lip. "What happened to ye, lad?"

"Beecher's in town," Bear declared, panting and wiping his damaged lip. Beckoning Halt to come with him, he swept the tavern with a wary look and headed for the rear door.

In the alley Halt turned to him. "Are ye all right, lad?"

"Nothing busted. Two of them . . . like what happened to you." Bear pushed his coat back and jammed his fists on his waist, sucking air. "Happened just after I saw Beecher, down at the hotel across from Vassar's bank."

"Yer certain it was him?" Halt said, disturbed.

"It was him, all right. I'd know his face anywhere. It was probably his two hounds that worked you over the other night."

"Damn an' blast his scurvy hide," Halt swore softly, touching his still-swollen eye. "He's here to see we don't get a loan to exercise them options." Then he looked up at Bear. "Well, he's too late, right, lad?"

Bear straightened and took a deep breath, trying to overcome the sick, light-headed feeling caused by his run and by the bad news he had to deliver.

Reading the truth in the way Bear turned a defensive shoulder, Halt groaned. "Ye didn' get the money?"

Bear clenched his jaw. "Her cousin came down ill and then there was a slew of people around. And then when I finally got her alone for a few minutes . . . it wasn't possible to—"

"Did ye even ask her?"

They regarded each other tautly for a moment, then Halt heaved a harsh breath of resignation.

"Look, I know ye don't want to ask the woman. It chafes a man's pride, havin' to toady up to a stubborn bit of skirt. But our options only run till end of summer, and with Beecher slinkin' around again and makin' trouble . . . If we haven't laid two hundred miles of track by th' end of September, we're finished."

"Don't you think I know that?"

Bear turned away and climbed up the stairs to their rented room.

By the light of the sooty lantern, he stripped his coat, vest and shirt, preparing for sleep. Halt watched him for a moment, then reached into his bag and pulled out the bottle of Vassar's brandy. "Here . . . take a bit of th' edge off'n yer sore head."

Bear took a swig and held it in his mouth, against his injured jaw and lip, shuddering as it burned. Then, as usual, Halt's spirits stubbornly began to rise.

"Well, it ain't all bad, Bear, me lad," he said with determination. "I found work today, down on the docks, unloadin' cargo. The foreman's a sentimental ol' Paddy from County Cork. Took me on straightaway. We'll have coin enough to keep a roof over our heads for a while. And I found a place where we can get a free meal once a day. A mission, over on Hale street." He grinned in that indomitable Irish way of his. "All we have to do is listen to a bit o' biblical persuasion. . . ."

TEN

"I'M SO SORRY, Mr. McQuaid," cherub-like Mrs. Humphrey told Bear when he was shown into the drawing room of Gracemont first thing the next morning. "She and Hardwell just left. She always does volunteer work at the Eastside Settlement House on Tuesday mornings. Then she and Hardwell had business of some sort." Her eyes twinkled. "We never know when Diamond goes out what sort of business she will find herself involved in . . . when she will be home . . . or *who* or *what* she will have with her when she returns." She lowered her voice. "She is prone to surprising us."

"She certainly is." Bear smiled tightly. "I have pressing business to attend to in town, myself. I'll call another time."

By the time he climbed up into his rented buggy and slapped the reins, his mood was dark indeed. He had to have money soon, to make good on his land options. And of course there was the little matter of the tons of steel rail he had spent his life savings to purchase. He had to come up with the rest of the money for it soon or watch it go elsewhere to the highest bidder. Then there was the wood for the ties, steel pins, tools of all shapes and descriptions, cranes and hoists, freight wagons and horses and mules, flatcars, tents and supplies for the workers . . . and of course, the workers themselves, who had to have transportation out to the middle of nowhere . . .

It all added up to one massive ache building between his shoulder blades. He rolled his shoulders, but instead of sliding off, the tension migrated down his arms and his legs. He flexed his arms and hands, trying in vain to relax them.

What he needed was some good, hard physical labor. Maybe Halt's sentimental foreman would see his way clear to hire a half-Irish railroader from North Carolina. His stomach rumbled and he massaged it.

Most of all, what he needed was a good hot meal.

THE MERCANTILE BANK was busy that afternoon, when Diamond arrived with Hardwell. But Philip Vassar had issued a long-standing order that she, as one of his largest depositors, was to be shown immediately into his office whenever she arrived, and she was quickly ushered into his presence and offered a bit of refreshment. After inquiries about the dispersal of the funds she had obligated in the lottery following her quarterly board meeting and a number of other small matters, she finally came to the real purpose of her visit.

"Robbie has the chicken pox, you know," she said toying with the clasp of her beaded purse. "He's been quite miserable and has asked if he might have another visit from your friend—that fellow from Montana—what was his name again?"

"Barton McQuaid." Vassar leaned forward with heightened interest. "He visited your sick cousin, did he?"

"He happened to be calling on us when we discovered Robbie's illness. He was good enough to tell Robbie a few stories about Montana. You wouldn't happen to know where I might contact him?"

Vassar blinked, paused for a minute, then sat back with a broad smile. "As a matter of fact, I would . . . or at least I will. He is scheduled to be our house guest for several days, starting—umm—tomorrow. Evelyn has been hounding me to get him to come for a visit, but he has been so busy—"

"I can imagine," she said, trying not to do anything of the sort. In fact, she had put a total ban on imaginings of all kinds, hoping to prevent the replay of the previous evening's events in her mind. She had enough to cope with as it was; she didn't need wild, passionate lapses of sanity visiting themselves upon her at random.

"Why don't you join us for dinner on Saturday?" Vassar said.

"Really, I only wanted to see if he might visit Robbie and—"

"I won't take no for an answer," Vassar said genially. "Evelyn would be so delighted." He must have read in her face her impending refusal, for he pulled out the lowest card in the social deck. "You know . . . Evelyn was just saying the other day how seldom we see you . . . how much Clarice misses you . . . how much they both miss all the excitement of the balls and parties we gave when you and Clarice made your debut."

Guilt crept up her spine like a hunchbacked bell-ringer.

"I suppose Robbie could do without me for—" she muttered, then brightened as she remembered. "Oh, but the Charity Society Ball is Saturday night." She smiled sweetly. "If it were anything but the Charity Ball, I would certainly beg off, but . . . perhaps another time."

"I had forgotten about the charity do." Vassar forced a

smile. "McQuaid will be attending with us, I'm sure. No doubt we'll see you there."

With her thoughts in turmoil, she took her leave and made her way out into the marble-pillared lobby of the bank.

Now what was she to do? It wasn't until after Bear left her house last night that she could think clearly enough to realize what had happened. Lord, he must think her the most debauched and unprincipled female in existence . . . engaged to two men at the same time and indulging in wild, licentious delights with a third at the drop of a hat. She needed to explain, to assure him that she intended to clarify things with Morgan and Paine as soon as possible, and to pray he would believe her and keep her secret.

With her thoughts fully occupied, she spotted Hardwell chatting with one of his friends and started across the lobby. The lofty, polished surfaces and cathedral-like echoes of the bank made everyone who entered that vast temple of commerce feel a need to speak in reverent whispers. Everyone, that is, except a man determined to spurn the grandeur of material wealth in favor of nobler and more enduring riches.

A strident, slightly nasal male voice rang out over the papery swish and metallic chink of money being counted and the drone of financial whispers. Diamond stood frozen in the middle of the wooden gate that marked the entrance to the bank offices, filled with dread at the sound of that voice and the sight of the man who owned it. The massive lobby suddenly seemed to shrink, bringing her face to face with none other than Louis Pierpont III.

"Diamond! My dear!" He descended on her, grabbing the hands she extended to fend him off and pressing them to his heart. His sallow face melted into such a soppy look of longing that she felt dampened from head to toe. "How wonderful to see you up and about. I called on Sunday afternoon, but Mrs. Humphrey said you were still indisposed."

"I'm feeling fine now, thank you." She tried in vain to withdraw her hands from his. "Hardwell and Hannah insisted that I get out for a bit of— Louis, what are you doing here? At Philip Vassar's bank?"

"I accompanied dear Mrs. Shoregrove here to help her make certain 'fiduciary' arrangements." He directed her glance with his toward a teller window where a sadly bent old lady stood watching them. He nodded with a huge smile and the old woman smiled back and daintily waved her handkerchief. Louis squeezed Diamond's hands with excitement.

"She is making a sizable contribution to my city mission. And"—he grew visibly excited—"she has decided to change her will to benefit our combined Baltimore Charity Board." He looked at her as if he expected her to find the news as enthralling as he did.

"How . . . good of her," Diamond said, glancing at the doddering old woman, who was just completing her business and turning toward them.

"I was just about to take Mrs. Shoregrove down to the Harborside Mission to show her the multitude of good works her contribution will make possible," Louis said, loudly enough for his aged contributor to hear. He dragged Diamond with him as he hurried to offer the little old widow his arm. "Diamond, *you've* never been down to the Harborside Mission, either, and you're one of our most generous sponsors." He clasped his hands in philanthropic glee. "Oh, what an opportunity . . . to show you both the great work you've made possible. You must come with us, Diamond." He looked over Diamond's shoulder and enlarged the invitation. "And you, Mr. Humphrey, you must come, too!"

Before Diamond could think of a plausible excuse, her

arm was captive in Louis's free hand and she was being pulled discreetly toward the door. Once on the street, it was clear that their only choices for transport were the Wingate coach or a serious test of their shoe leather. Hardwell insisted they use the coach and Louis, citing their courtesy and thoughtfulness to dear old Mrs. Shoregrove, eagerly climbed aboard.

THE HARBORSIDE MISSION provided one free meal per day to whoever lined up at the door, entered, and stayed for a brief edifying "message." The staff opened a dormitory of beds upstairs each night for "clean" indigents and provided used clothing when it was made available by donors.

As the coach rattled along, Louis launched into a list of patrons and sponsors of the mission, pausing after each name to detail each donor's charitable record. Diamond squirmed as she listened to Louis's explicit and unmistakably judgmental accounting of Baltimore's philanthropists. And she couldn't help noticing that Louis's sallow face and pious gray eyes took on surprising color and animation as he spoke of the sizable sums he had raised to support the mission and various other charities.

When they entered the bumpy, irregular streets of the waterfront, Diamond and Mrs. Shoregrove reached for their scented handkerchiefs. Dampness, the stench of wood corrupted by brine, the aromas of old fish, burned oil, and stale beer hung over the waterfront district like a pall.

"Only imagine," Louis said woefully, "having to constantly abide in this foul and corrupting atmosphere."

They didn't have to imagine for long. The coach stopped on Hale Street, a broad thoroughfare created by the merging of several narrower streets. They disembarked in front of a large brick building, before a pair of neatly painted white doors. Above the entrance hung a signboard proclaiming the name of the mission and the biblical quote: "The poor you will have with you always."

Extending from the open door and well along the fronts of the neighboring buildings was a line of ragged and ill-kempt men, many in knitted caps and battered seamen's clothes. They watched with scowls and mutters as Louis led Diamond and the others to the head of the line and inside. The austere hall was whitewashed and hung with sayings meant to inspire the mission's clientele to remedy their dismal situations. At one end of the hall were rows of planking tables and benches and a long window counter through which food was being served. The other end was set with chairs facing a small wooden podium beneath a banner stating: "The Lord helps those who help them-selves."

Deadly aware of her buttercup-yellow dress and elabo-rately feathered hat, Diamond was ready to head straight back to the coach when Louis took her by the arm and pulled her toward a lean, imperious-looking matron in a black dress and a severely sensible hair net. He introduced the woman to Diamond and Mrs. Shoregrove as the head of the kitchens and a cornerstone of the mission's pro-gram. The woman looked Diamond over with a sniff, folded her hands over her waist, and announced that she hadn't planned dinner for more than the mission's "regular trade."

"We didn't intend to stay for a meal," Diamond said in clipped tones. She swept the room with a look. "Well, Louis, I believe I have seen all I need—"

Her gaze snagged on a figure in the food line. It was his hat that caught her eye. Big and black with a tall, neatly creased crown . . . it looked as though it came straight off the front of one of her penny dreadfuls . . . or off the head of a certain heart-stopping Westerner. Her eyes widened as they traveled down a familiar pair of broad shoulders, a lean, muscular body, and long, powerful legs. Their owner looked up and met her gaze with a jolt of recognition.

Behind her, Hardwell gave a grunt of surprise, raised his arm and called out: "McQuaid! As I live and breathe—what the devil are you doing here?"

Standing in line, smelling like a sweated-up steer, and waiting for a turn at the trough, Bear answered as he stared across the room. He wanted to run for his life but could only stand frozen, trapped in two shocked beacons of memorable blue. Every muscle in his work-sore body tensed and contracted with embarrassment at the sight of her . . . standing there in her perfect yellow lady dress and feathered hat . . . looking like a daisy in a damned hog wallow.

What in hell was *she* doing here? It took a moment for him to pull his gaze from her and register the sight of Hardwell Humphrey striding along through the rows of tables with a hand extended to him. He glanced down at his chambray shirt, work pants, and worn boots, then stifled a groan and stepped out of line to meet that handshake.

"What are *you* doing here?" Bear parroted his question, while shaking his hand and scrambling for an explanation for his presence in the soup kitchen.

"Came down with Diamond," Hardwell said, gesturing to her with one hand while adding in a mutter, "and that damned fool Pierpont." Then he looked Bear up and down and seemed a little puzzled. "Blame me, if you aren't the veriest cowboy I've ever seen." He turned to Diamond. "Look here, missy . . . your friend McQuaid, in his out-West gear."

"Hello, Mr. McQuaid," she said joining them, offering

him her hand, and reddening noticeably. "I confess, you're the last person I expected to find here."

"Here?" He reddened under her shocked regard, thinking fast as he looked around. "Why, this is the perfect place for me."

"It is?" She blinked.

"You bet it is." As he looked around at the mission, his gaze fell on the row of stringy, hardened male faces watching them and a mercifully plausible explanation popped into his head. He jerked a nod at the men shuffling forward in line. "Where better to find workers eager for a fresh start out West?"

Even after he'd said it aloud, it still sounded fairly plausible and he plunged ahead, turning to Halt . . . who was standing by with narrowed eyes, taking in his familiarity with these nattily dressed society folk and drawing who knew what conclusions. What mattered most, however, was convincing Diamond and her party that he was doing what he had just claimed.

"As a matter of fact . . . I was just talking with a fellow I found here the other night." He beckoned to Halt. "Come on over, Finnegan."

With a rueful glance at the serving window, Halt abandoned his place in line and strode over to join them. Bear now was forced to introduce Halt to a much younger and prettier Diamond Wingate than he had been led to expect.

"Miss Wingate, may I present Halt Finnegan, formerly of Boston . . . a railroader from way back." Halt gave him an ominously restrained smile, wiped his hand on his shirt and extended it to meet hers. In the introductions that followed, Bear found himself called upon to elaborate. "A real stroke of luck, finding Finnegan here. He worked on the Union Pacific when they were racing across the country, back in sixty-seven. Since then, he's been all over the West laying down steel."

"I am not at all certain it is proper for you to use these premises for recruiting railroad laborers," Louis Pierpont said to Bear, inserting himself determinedly between Diamond and Bear.

"Not proper?" Bear shifted his weight back onto one leg and leveled a controlled look on the pasty little wretch. "What could be more proper than offering these men a chance for decent work?"

Pierpont reddened. "Decent work? On the railroads? I have long been of the opinion that railroads have bred an unseemly impatience in the populace . . . everything moves so quickly, they come to expect that everything should move so quickly. And the workers themselves"—he leveled a quick, faintly judgmental look on Halt—"are widely considered to be rowdy and undisciplined and given to a number of unsavory vices."

"Vices?" Bear said with a sardonic laugh, watching Louis's hand move possessively to the small of Diamond's back. "I'll grant that railroaders do like a bit of drink now and then. But you'll not find a harder-working or more charitable bunch of men than a railroad crew. Right, Mr. Finnegan?"

"Right as rain, *Mis-s-ster McQuaid,*" Halt replied.

He was going to hear about this, Bear realized.

"Come, my dear." Louis took Diamond by the elbow and turned her toward the kitchen doors. "You must see the rest of our mission."

Diamond was so overwhelmed by her reaction to seeing Bear that it took a moment for her to recover her self-possession. Never in her life had she felt such joy at the sight of someone . . . not even her father, when he came home after one of his long business trips. Pleasure had welled up in her, carrying with it a flush of heat and an unladylike urge to rush to him . . . to touch him . . . to absorb every line and angle of him.

When Louis grabbed her elbow to usher her along, she was too absorbed in containing those startling impulses to protest. And unless she was mistaken, the sight of her had produced a strong reaction in him, as well. She could feel it on the air between them; a resonance, a special tension, a palpable sense of connection.

It was only as they stood in the middle of the smelly, bustling kitchen that she tore her attention from Bear long enough to realize that she was someplace she didn't want to be. And that Louis was crowding her such that he was practically standing on her feet.

". . . piped-in gas, to run the stoves and ovens . . ." He was droning on.

Hardwell was leaning down to old Mrs. Shoregrove, repeating everything Louis said at a slightly higher volume: "Gas . . . he says he has *gas*!" The kitchen matron was watching from nearby with her hands propped at her waist. Bear stood with his legs braced apart and his arms folded, watching Louis hover over her. And Bear's find, Mr. Finnegan, had tagged along and was grinning rather effectively at the woman serving the soup of the day, while she provided him with samples of fresh-baked bread.

Diamond let her gaze and her mind wander toward Bear and he caught her gaze, looked at Louis, and rolled his eyes. It was hard to be too indignant on Louis's behalf when she was an inch away from slapping him silly, herself. To her credit, she did manage to bite her lip to keep from smiling back.

When Louis had made a sufficient virtue of peeled cabbages, donated potatoes, and greasy ham bones, he led them through the odoriferous storage rooms and up a back set of steps to the dormitory on the second floor. Louis instructed Bear and Halt Finnegan to go first, it being considered ungentlemanly to climb stairs behind a lady. Diamond had never quite appreciated that custom until she watched Bear's long, muscular legs working just ahead of her.

She told herself it was the surprise of seeing him in such worn and simple clothing that caused her to stare so intently at him. In truth, it was more the fit of those clothes than the condition of them that absorbed her. His trousers were molded to his big frame, shaped by long wear and numerous washings into a glovelike fit. And his boots, slightly worn at the substantial heels and scuffed at the toes, lent a fascinating air of rough history to his lower half . . . not to mention a sensual roll to his gait.

By the time they reached the top of the stairs she had made a thorough inventory of his buttocks, thighs, and calves and experienced—curiously—not one drop of shame in the process. Proof that she was corrupted beyond repair. If Louis, clutching her arm so tightly against him, had the faintest notion of what was going on inside her, he would be disillusioned in the extreme.

When they all arrived on the second floor, Louis's hovering became intolerable. "Diamond, my dearest . . ." He planted himself directly before her as if trying to harness her wandering attention. It didn't work.

She saw Bear's head move and glanced at him.

"My dearest?" He mouthed silently.

"Here"—Louis gestured grandly to a sea of wood and canvas cots—"we permit those with no shelter to sleep . . . providing they adhere to our rules. We permit no smoking, no chewing, no profanity or vulgarity, no liquor— not even the scent of it—and absolutely no talking after lights out. I monitor conduct here myself, most nights . . . in there." He indicated a small room a few feet away, furnished in Spartan style, with a bed, a table and straight chair, and a shelf of books.

"You sleep here?" she asked, tearing her gaze from Bear to look at Louis in dismay.

"I do now." He sacrificed a smile for her. "You know, of course, that I sold the family house some time ago. The apartments I have occupied since seemed such an extravagance, when I spend several nights a week here. I thought the money could best be used for more charitable purposes." He seized both of her hands, his passion for philanthropy now aflame.

"This is the first such shelter here in Baltimore. I plan several more in the indigent parts of the city. And if things go well, before the year is out I shall have a splendid, big house to make into an orphanage, along with gardens and stables and orchards." His eyes gleamed with visionary delight. "It will be out in the healthful countryside, north of the city. I am learning a great deal from this work, which will be put to good use after—"

She tensed, sensing what was coming and unable to stop it.

"—our vows."

God in Heaven! Whatever possessed him to blurt it out in front of Hardwell and Mrs. Shoregrove and—she moaned privately—*Bear McQuaid*?

"Our vows?" Bear's casual posture changed instantly. He leveled a look on Diamond that made her want to sink through the cracks between the floorboards. "Congratulations, Pierpont. I had no idea you were engaged." He sounded anything but felicitous. "And who is the lucky lady?"

Diamond squeezed Louis's hands savagely, causing him to start and stare at her. She hoped her expression conveyed even one quarter of the fury she felt at the moment. It must have had some impact, for Louis stopped short of a direct announcement and settled instead for a cryptic:

"I should think that would be obvious."

"Not to most of us," Diamond said through clenched teeth.

She jerked her hands from Louis's and the depth of her irritation finally began to penetrate his rashly possessive frame of mind. Her face was crimson as old Mrs. Shoregrove yanked on Hardwell's arm and demanded to know what was being said. Hardwell closed his sagging jaw and responded.

"That's where Pierpont sleeps," Hardwell said loudly, pointing. And something made him add: "Alone."

"I believe I've seen quite enough," Diamond said angrily, avoiding Bear's gaze. "We really must be going. Mrs. Shoregrove, we shall be happy to see you home." As they all headed for the stairs, Bear caught her eye.

With eyes like molten copper, he held up three sun-bronzed fingers.

Three, he knew there were *three*.

Her face flamed as she hurried down the stairs. By the time she reached the dining hall below, the others were hard-pressed to keep up . . . except Bear, who strode determinedly around the others to reach her.

"Well, Miss Wingate," he declared tautly, pushing open one of the front doors for her, "you certainly are a busy woman."

She made herself meet his glower and felt as if she'd been punched in the chest. "I am, indeed," she said, sounding winded. "Not too busy, however, to see my poor young cousin diverted from his illness." She halted at the carriage. "Will you come and visit him? *Now*."

"Now?" He glanced at Halt Finnegan, who was leaning a shoulder against the door frame, scowling darkly at him. "*Now* would be fine."

Diamond refused Louis a farewell handclasp as she turned to the coach step and lifted her skirts. Bear helped her inside, then stood aside as Hardwell assisted old Mrs. Shoregrove and climbed in himself. When it was Bear's turn, he gave a glance back over his shoulder at Louis, who was babbling on about calling on Diamond tomorrow, and then at Halt, whose narrow-eyed smile promised retribution.

By the time they delivered Mrs. Shoregrove to her house, the atmosphere in the coach was icy enough to threaten frostbite. Bear self-consciously shifted his long legs and tried to make room for his hat . . . which he stubbornly refused to remove; Diamond's lips, like her folded arms, were tightly clamped; and all of Hardwell's attempts at conversation met a quick and nasty end.

Eventually, Diamond stole a look at Bear. He caught the slight motion of her head and looked at her in the same instant. Their gazes met in a glancing blow that caused each to recoil sharply and stare out opposite sides of the coach.

Hardwell scratched his head, blew on his hands, and turned up his coat collar against the chill for the rest of the ride home.

WHEN THEY ARRIVED at Gracemont, Diamond strode briskly past Jeffreys in the main hall, dropped her gloves and hat on the center table, and headed for the stairs with a curt: "This way, Mr. McQuaid."

Halfway down the upstairs corridor, well out of hearing, Bear gave in to the anger he had been nursing for the better part of an hour, grabbed her by the arm, and pulled her to a stop.

She whirled, her eyes flashing and her chin raised. An instinct for self-preservation made him choke back some of the anger in his opening volley.

"Do you know what they call a woman who marries three men?"

ELEVEN

"NO," SHE SAID furiously, refusing to be intimidated by his size and proximity. She tucked her arms into a defensive knot. "Suppose you tell me."

He searched her simmering blue gaze, seeing in it turbulent swirls of humiliation and an expanding roil of anxiety. But in her jutting, fiercely set chin he read nothing but combat readiness.

"Greedy," he declared.

Clearly that was not what she expected to hear. She drew her chin back.

"I am *not* greed—"

"Ambitious," he added, watching closely the shifting weather in her eyes.

"I have *never* been ambitious!"

"Or just damned optimistic."

She blinked, drew a hot breath to rebut that, as well, then closed her mouth without speaking. A moment later, she jerked her arm from his grasp.

"What do you mean *optimistic*?"

"Most women have enough trouble riding herd on one

man," he declared, propping his hands on his waist as he leaned over her. "Imagine the effort that would be involved in wrangling *three*."

"I don't intend to 'wrangle' anybody," she said, taking a step backward.

"Yeah? Then how come there are three men out there panting in expectation of enjoying nuptial bliss with you?" There was a bit too much heat in that to suit him. He reined back, but only for a second. "Or is it just three?" He shoved his face down into hers and she took another step back. "Maybe there are four or five—hell, there could be half a dozen!"

"Three," she said furiously. "There are only three."

"Congratulations on your restraint."

She scrambled for footing and found it in righteous anger.

"For your information, it could have been *dozens*!"

That set him back a moment. He experienced a swift, unexpected stab of jealousy.

Dozens, hell—he thought—it could have been *thousands*. Every man in Baltimore, married or single, had probably asked himself at one time or other what it would be like to have a wife as rich as Croesus . . . or Diamond Wingate. And even the most amicably wedded of men, upon seeing her sparkling blue eyes and striking figure, had probably gone home to their beds imagining what it would be like to have Diamond Wingate sharing their pillows with them. She could have had any man she wanted. Why the devil had she picked those three?

In the lengthening silence, her shoulders sagged.

"You don't understand," she said tightly.

"Damned straight, I don't."

"There is an explanation."

"I'm all ears."

She took a deep breath. "I've known each of them for

years . . . since I was a little girl." She lowered her gaze. "When I came out in society, suitors began to show up everywhere. I couldn't go to the bank or into the city shopping, or to a party without being set upon—sometimes physically. Then Morgan stepped in. He was so—"

"Eager to help?" he supplied.

She didn't contradict him.

"He began to escort me and that meant the others had to keep a distance. It was such a relief that I . . . well . . . when he began to talk about the future . . . I—"

"Couldn't say no."

"I am perfectly capable of finishing my own sentences." Her head came up with defiance, but after a look at his face, she paused and once again lowered her eyes to her clasped hands. "Then Morgan began to talk more and more about making money. He became obsessed with rescuing his stables and restoring Kensington to its former glory. He was so single-minded and driven that I began to spend time with Paine Webster.

"Paine was a great relief. Despite his failings, he is really a very dear man . . . gentle and witty and compassionate. He's been pursued by females since he was in short pants, so he understood exactly what was happening to me. Then, when his family saw that we were keeping company, they began to pressure him to propose. I believe they hoped I would rescue him from the clutches of debauchery. Dutifully, he began to talk about the future, and I—"

"Couldn't say no." It was becoming an intolerable refrain. "And Louis the Missionary . . . what's your excuse for the 'righteous' Brother Pierpont?"

"I'll have you know, Louis is not self-righteous. He has a strong and high-minded set of convictions and a noble soul. He understood my need to give money away and my desire to make the world a better place. More importantly, he understood the dangers the world can pose for a person left with too much of a good thing. He too was the heir to a sizable fortune."

"Who is now living above a soup kitchen," Bear said testily.

"By his own choice," she said, looking away. "And while it may be true that he's gone a bit beyond the pale with his hatred of money and—"

"You think he hates money?" He gave a sardonic smile. "He likes it well enough when he's milking it out of little old widow ladies." She stiffened, but the uneasiness in her face said that she wasn't entirely comfortable with Louis's behavior in that regard, either.

"Louis spent a great deal of time with me, advising me," she continued. "He helped me find places where my money would do some good. He's devoted to protecting me from the onslaughts of the world. So, when he began to mention marriage and all the 'good works' we could do together, I—"

"Couldn't say no."

He studied her face, seeing more of her point of view than was probably prudent. Rich girl. Young. Alone. Besieged on every side. She had three fiancés because she had needed them . . . each in his own way and time. Heaven help him, he could almost understand how it could have happened. He felt a tightness settling over his chest and had to battle it in order to hold on to his anger with her.

"So now you have to decide, is that it?"

"I've already decided," she answered.

"You have?" He felt his skin contract. "Which one is the lucky man?"

Diamond looked up and found his eyes glowing with that molten-copper heat that always seemed to dissolve

the strength in her knees. It was a good thing she was
supported by the wall at her—

Looking about, she realized she had been slowly backed
against the wall and corralled between Bear McQuaid's
arms, which were braced on each side of her head. His
long, muscular frame was bent over her and their faces
were barely an inch apart. She could barely breathe, much
less think. Only the most basic of survival instincts provided her the strength to give him a push and step away.

Even then, her senses were still captive. She couldn't
look away, couldn't hear anything but the ragged sound of
his breathing, couldn't feel anything but the warmth he
had radiated into her body. The way he was looking at
her—from beneath the brim of his big Western hat, a chaotic mix of discernment, accusation, and desire in his
eyes—sent her defenses into chaos.

"Well," he prompted, "what did you decide?"

"I'm not marrying any of them," she said. "I'm not going
to marry at all."

He blinked, stared at her for a minute, then erupted.

"Those three have been planning their futures and fortunes around you!" He stabbed the air furiously with a
finger. "What the hell makes you think they'll just turn tail
and slink away when you tell them you don't want to be
bothered with a husband?"

Her face and conscience both burned. The moment she
had dreaded was here. She had to face up to the mess she
had made and declare her course in resolving it. But,
somehow, the worst thing about it was that it was upright,
forthright, indomitable Bear McQuaid who had discovered
her shameful secret and confronted her with it.

"They'll accept my decision . . . because . . . I'll
make it worth their while."

"Make it worth their—" He gave a short, hard laugh.
"What could you possibly offer them that would make

them forget a breach of promise by the richest, most eligible woman in the city?"

"I should think that would be obvious," she said, tucking her arms and paring her answer to its core. "Money."

When he stared disbelievingly at her, she defended her strategy. "If you give people enough money, they'll go away. They always have."

"You just hand over cash and they bow out of your life? Very tidy, Miss Wingate." But her statement continued to unfold in his mind, and every perceptive instinct he possessed came alert and focused on her. "What do you mean, 'they always have'?"

The containment in her expression and posture heightened.

"I've had a lifetime of experience at giving money to people," she said tautly. "Charitable people, stingy people, brilliant people, simple people, honest people, conniving people . . . it doesn't matter who or what they are. If you give them enough, they'll go away."

He probed her gaze, seeing deeper into her than either of them wished . . . far enough to glimpse the surprisingly steely assumptions about human nature that had framed a well-disguised set of defenses in her.

Everyone wanted money.

Everyone wanted her money.

When she gave money to people, they went away.

That was it? That was why she gave away money by buckets and barrels? So people would leave her alone?

"And just how much of your fortune do you think those three will require as compensation for losing the richest woman in Baltimore?" he continued, still grappling with that unsettling insight. "Thousands? Hundreds of thousands? A million?"

"It will undoubtedly be expensive." Her chin set with defiance. "But money has never held the fascination for me that it seems to inspire in others. Money is a means, a tool. It's a means to an end, a way of making things happen. Over the years, I've learned to make its power and potential work for me as well as against me."

The nuances packed into her statement and determined expression caught him flatfooted. Meanings nested inside meanings. A damned pile of layers. This was why he never did well with women. There was always more to what they said and did than met the eye, and he hated the feeling that half of what transpired between him and females generally slipped through his fingers.

"So, whether you want to admit it or not, you've made money your answer to everything," he charged, distilling her words and scrambling to hang on to insights that were sliding unexplored over the edge of his awareness. "If your cousin gets into trouble, you just buy his victim a new suit. If you need a dancing partner to get you out of an awkward situation, or a fourth for riding, or a shill in your romantic intrigues, you just make it worth someone's while. You're used to buying your way through life."

Her eyes became the color of polished steel.

"One has to make do with what one has, Mr. McQuaid."

That glint of steel was visible in more than just her eyes, he realized. Everyone in Baltimore thought she was a soft touch because she gave away heaps of money. No one ventured close enough or lingered long enough to see what—or who—existed behind those piles of ready cash.

As he stood turning that chilly deduction over in his mind, trying to square it with the warmth of the woman who had responded so generously to his kisses, she turned to her cousin's door and flung it back with a bang.

"Well, my troublesome little patient . . . look who's come to see you!"

•   •   •

SHE HAD HONESTLY meant it when she said she didn't intend to marry.

It sounded right in her head. It had always sounded right in her innermost thoughts. But as she stood by the door of Robbie's room, stopped in mid-escape by the stories Bear was spinning about life out West, she found her determined words produced a hollow echo inside her . . . one that had nothing to do with a longing for children and a sense of family. She had a child now, or a reasonable approximation of one. She could always find another child to take in—a whole house full of children if she wanted them. It definitely was not a "motherly" lack she was feeling.

It was the prospect of spending the rest of her life as the spinsterly heiress, the doting elder cousin, and Baltimore's resident "soft touch" that produced this gnawing sense of emptiness inside her. Combined with the memory of Bear McQuaid's kisses and of recent nights spent tossing and burning in her solitary bed, that potential future sounded every bit as bad as being stripped of power and personhood by some high-handed, money-hungry man. And she knew exactly where to lay the blame for this disturbance in her once serene view of her future.

She turned back, still gripping the door handle, to watch Bear demonstrating throwing a rope around a calf's neck.

Hardwell was right. Bear McQuaid did look like the veriest cowboy she could imagine. Straight out of Dodge or Carson City or Tombstone. Tautly sculptured face . . . whipcord-lean body . . . movements like a lithe, powerful mountain cat. The very terms in which she described him revealed how much her susceptibility to him was influenced by an unhealthy indulgence in dime novels. He was trouble on the hoof . . . danger in a black Stetson hat . . . an emotional stampede just waiting to run her down. And no matter what lurid Western metaphor she chose, the final chapter seemed to be that he was under her skin and headed straight for her heart.

No. Her eyes widened as she felt a breathtaking warmth spreading through her chest. He wasn't just headed for her heart; he was already there.

Drawing a sharp breath, she turned the handle and fled into the hall.

"Jeffreys . . ." She caught the butler on his way up-stairs with Robbie's afternoon snack. "Have Ned bring the coach around and wait until Mr. McQuaid is ready to leave."

"Yes, miss." Jeffreys nodded. "And you, miss?"

"I'll be in the library. Working." She turned toward the stairs, avoiding the little butler's gaze. "And I needn't be disturbed."

IT WAS APPROACHING dusk when Bear had Diamond's driver drop him off in front of Vassar's bank, reasoning that there were at least two respectable hotels within walking distance and he could say he needed a stretch of the legs.

What he really needed, he knew, was time to prepare to face Halt. In their six-year association, Bear and Halt had kept little from each other. A wealth of shared experience had bred both truth and trust between them, and Bear had violated both from the first moment he set eyes on Diamond Wingate.

He slouched his shoulders and tilted his hat over his eyes as he set off for the waterfront, hoping to make himself less recognizable and possibly less of a target. Remembering the last time he had walked to the tavern, he took care to check alleys and fences and the corners of buildings for lumps and shadows.

As he continued on, undisturbed, his thoughts again turned to his partner and his predicament. He dreaded facing Halt with his failures with Diamond Wingate. Infernal female. Every time he left her, he vowed not to go near her again except to ask for a straightforward business loan. And every time he approached her, with nothing but businesslike intentions, he got dragged into her personal problems again.

He thought of the pride and desperation burning in her as she whirled away from him in the hall. There was a woman, he mumbled to himself, who had far too much of everything. Too much money, too much pride . . . independence, generosity, wit. If only she were a mousy little thing with protruding teeth and beady eyes. If she only had a few hundred instead of a few million. If only she weren't quite so bright and feisty and desirable and enjoyable and . . .

And if only he weren't a bigger fraud than all three of her panting, sticky-fingered fiancés combined.

When he turned the corner beside the Cork & Bottle, he spotted a carriage in front of it . . . a fine black carriage with white wheels drawn by a set of matched grays. It gave him a bad feeling. He thought of Beecher and considered avoiding the tavern in favor of the back stairs. But, on second thought, he concluded that if Beecher had found them and was waiting, it wouldn't do any good to put off the confrontation. Sooner or later, they would come face to face.

Steeling himself, he ducked inside the main door.

Halt was sitting near the dingy main window with his feet propped up on a table and his arms folded over his barrel of a chest. "An' just where 'ave you been?" he demanded, lowering his feet and lurching to the edge of his chair.

"She asked me to come visit the boy. In fact, she insisted." Taking a page from Halt's book, he quickly changed the subject. "Who belongs to that carriage outside?" He looked around the busy tavern, trying to spot its owner.

"It's ours, lad," Halt said with a fierce little smile. "Yours an' mine."

"Come again?" Bear stared out the door at the glowing carriage lamps.

"Yer friendly banker sent it for us." Halt stood and rolled his shoulders. "It seems we're invited to be his house guests, you an' me. Startin' tonight."

"Both of us?" Bear stared at him.

"Mr. McQuaid *and* Mr. Finnegan." Halt reached for his hat with a wicked look. "High time I sampled a bit o' the sweet life ye been enjoyin' of late." When Bear scowled and started upstairs, Halt grabbed his arm. "I already got yer gear, lad. An' I found a bloke over at the mission—down on 'is luck and needin' a place to sleep—t' hold our place upstairs."

Halt turned to the next table where a man in a rumpled gray suit lay face down beside a half empty tankard of ale. "Come on, Ellsworth, hie yerself upstairs. A cot will feel a sight better than that table." He jerked his head in the fellow's direction and explained: "Ain't much of a drinkin' man. A half-pint 'o grog an' he's out like a light."

Halt gave him a nudge and the fellow raised a long face and unfocused gaze to Bear, who started with recognition.

"I know him—he's that crazed inventor—" Bear said, scowling.

"What *inventor*?" Halt demanded.

"The one I rescued Diamond Wingate from at Vassar's party," Bear said, watching the fellow fumbling to right his spectacles on his face and feeling a resurrected pang of guilt that annoyed him. "He's a raving lunatic."

The fellow squinted at Bear and raised a wobbly finger of exception.

"An en-gin-nnneeeer . . . ak-tually."

Halt stuck his thumbs in his belt and regarded Bear soberly. "He's got nowhere else t' go, lad."

The gaunt face, the impossibly smudged spectacles, the soiled gray suit that looked as if it had come through the battle of Vicksburg . . . everything about the poor wretch spoke of hitting rock bottom . . . of the death of a cherished dream. When the fellow looked up, over his spectacles, with the tatters of a dream in his eyes, Bear couldn't help feeling somehow responsible. The poor wretch needed help. And Bear just couldn't bring himself to say *no*.

"How much trouble could a lunatic get into on a cot?" Bear reached for one of the fellow's arms.

As they dragged him toward the stairs at the rear, Ellsworth raised that precise finger yet again: "En-gin-nn-neeeer . . . ack-tually . . ."

A short while later they were in Vassar's coach and underway. Bear could feel Halt's stare.

"Well?" the Irishman demanded and Bear knew exactly what he wanted.

"It's a long story."

"I got time, lad." Halt settled back in the plush upholstered seat with a grandiose sigh. "Now that I'm a man o' leisure. Like you."

Bear saw no reason to confess that he had first met and angered Diamond in the tailor shop, and so began his story with his arrival at Vassar's party and his fortuitous intervention with the crazed inventor who was now occupying their sleeping quarters. He proceeded to their dinner conversation, to Vassar's description of her, their dance, and her timely swoon.

"All truly fascinatin' stuff, lad," Halt said dryly, sitting forward. "But what I want to know is why ye didn't tell me what was goin' on. Why didn' ye just say ye wrapped yer tongue 'round yer tonsils every time ye laid eyes on 'er? I'd 'ave understood right enough. She's a beauty, she is."

"It had nothing to do with her being a beauty," Bear said, with more heat than was prudent. "Nor with my tongue wrapping around— Where the hell do you get these damnable sayings of yours?" His voice rose. "What I told you is God's honest truth. She's one tough nut."

His insight from earlier that afternoon swept unexpectedly through his mind, insinuating itself into yet another level of his awareness. He had had no idea of how fitting a description that was until a few hours ago.

"Ask Vassar, if you don't believe me," he declared. "She knows a damn sight more than she ought to about the railroad business and—"

"An' ye go all tiddly in th' knees whenever she turns them big blue eyes on ye."

"I do *not*."

When Halt chuckled wickedly, Bear realized just how vehement he sounded and how ridiculous it was to deny that he was susceptible to Diamond's attractions. A man would have to be made of stone not to react to her sky-blue eyes and elegant curves. He was grateful that the shadows in the carriage hid some of the heat in his face.

"Aw, lad . . . one look at th' woman an' I knew why ye had trouble askin' for th' money. What irks me is that ye had so little faith in yer partner that ye wouldn't tell me about it."

Bear closed his eyes, afflicted by the knowledge that he still hadn't told Halt the half of it. He had rescued her three . . . four . . . hell, he'd lost count of how many

times. She was indebted to him up to her enchanting earlobes, but he didn't seem to be any closer to securing a
loan from her than he was the first day he met her. Dammit.

His guilt was alleviated somewhat when they arrived at
Pennyworth and were greeted like old friends and shown
to guest rooms that Halt declared to be grander than a St.
Louis cathouse.

After bathing and changing clothes, they were shown
into the drawing room. There they joined Philip and Evelyn Vassar in a glass of sherry and were introduced to their
daughter, Clarice. Bear held her hand for a moment,
studying her and wondering how such a sweet-faced plum
of a girl could have issued from a union of squat, bulldog-
ish Vassar and his tall, wasp-waisted wife.

Evelyn Vassar came to immediate attention, put down
her glass of sherry, and flew to her daughter's side. "Clarice, dear, you're flushed."

"Surely not, Mamma. I feel perfectly—"

Evelyn pressed a determined hand to the girl's forehead
and pronounced her: "Warm. As I suspected. You'll forgive
us, gentlemen . . . my daughter isn't feeling well."

"Well, gentlemen . . ." Vassar watched his wife spiriting his daughter out of temptation's way, then broke into a
grin. "It seems as if we've been abandoned."

Moments later, Vassar settled with a sigh of pleasure
into his chair at the head of the table, loosened his tie, and
gestured that Bear and Halt—seating themselves at his
left and right—should do the same. After instructing the
butler to trade the delicate white wine for a robust red
wine, he proceeded to light up a cigar right there at the
table.

"Almost forgot, McQuaid," he declared through a haze
of pungent blue smoke. "Give your evening clothes to the
servants to freshen. The Charity Society Ball is this Satur-

day. Should be quite a do. The registered charities get everybody sauced proper and slip a hand into their pockets. Wine and money flow free and everybody tries to appear more charitable than their neighbors."

He took a drink of wine and peered over the rim of his glass at Bear. "And of course, Diamond Wingate will be there. . . ."

TWELVE

IN THE SHADOWS collected by the trees and hedges lining the entrance to the Vassars' Pennyworth, three figures watched the family's driver bring their coach around from the stables. When it stopped directly in their line of sight, the leader of the three muttered an oath and made a sharp hand motion. Moving with restricted impatience, they shifted in the bushes to better view the area between the front doors and carriage. Twigs snapped underfoot.

"Watch where you put your damned feet!" Lionel Beecher snarled at his sinewy companions. "You sound like a herd of buffalo." The others glowered irritably at each other, then followed on with considerably more stealth.

When they once again had a clear view of the front doors, the tall, rangy Beecher bent and gingerly pushed branches aside to observe the doors. "You're sure this is where he came?"

"Seen 'im with our own two eyes," one whispered back.

"Him and that other one got in that fancy rig wi' the white wheels." The other pointed to the distinctive carriage. "When we seen it agin in town, we follered it here."

"They're stayin' 'ere, all right. Pay up."

"Not until I've seen them with *my* own two eyes,"
Beecher said, focusing his gaze on the arched entrance.

He hadn't long to wait. Shortly a black-clad manservant
emerged from the door and stood in readiness at the top of
the steps. A short, thick man in evening dress appeared,
then turned to urge a tall, rail-straight woman and a
shorter, younger female to hurry along.

"That's Vassar, of the Mercantile Bank." Beecher
ground his teeth. "What the hell would they be doing at *his*
house?"

As the Vassars descended the steps, two more figures
appeared in the doorway; one in evening dress, the other
in more ordinary clothing. Squinting across the distance,
Beecher recognized Bear McQuaid and Halt Finnegan.

"Damnation." He pulled away from the sight, but an
instant later reapplied his eye to the gap in the branches
and watched Bear McQuaid join the Vassars in the coach.
As the vehicle rumbled off around the circular drive,
toward the main road, Beecher reacted.

"How the hell did he manage this? The bastard's not
only in Vassar's company—he's moved into Vassar's
house!" He swung his burning gaze to his henchmen, his
voice rising. "Two dozen fat bankers in Baltimore, and he
finds the *one* we didn't visit. Vassar's known to be tight
with a buck—I didn't think he'd give McQuaid the time of
day, much less—"

Just then the carriage neared their hiding place.
Beecher silenced abruptly and dropped to a crouch, pulling the others down with him. As soon as the vehicle was
safely out of range he stood and headed back through the
trees for the main road. By the time they reached the
horses, hidden a quarter of a mile away, he had already
formulated a plan.

"He's got the damned money—or soon will have it.

That means he'll be heading back to Montana to make good on his land options. They'll start shipping his steel and ties . . . he could be laying track by . . ." He squinted, doing mental calculations. "Damnation. Gould will have my guts for garters if—"

Beecher realized that the others were watching him and returned their stare, visibly assessing their possible uses.

"Hard to say how long McQuaid will be here." He rubbed his chin thoughtfully. "Nobody in Montana could know he's got the money yet. If I can get back there first, maybe I can pick up a few of his options *for* him." He seemed to like the picture forming in his mind. "And you two . . ." A humorless smile spread over his long, sallow face. "He's going to need men . . . with strong backs . . . used to bad food and meager pay."

"What?" One of his henchmen scowled at the other as Beecher's meaning dawned. "You mean, hire on wi' him?"

"The hell I will," the other declared, crossing his beefy arms and pulling his head into his thick neck. "I ain't bustin' my back breakin' rock day after day in th' hot sun." He received a vigorous second from his companion. Beecher studied them for a moment with a broadening smile.

"Of course you won't. And how would you like to 'not work' for double whatever he'll be paying you?"

THE CHARITY SOCIETY Ball was one of the highlights of the social season. The Baltimore Charity Organization Society had been formed in the early eighties to bring a semblance of order and accountability to the chaotic and sometimes shady dealings of the city's charitable concerns. In the five years of its existence the organization had managed to review, inspect, and register most of the organizations that dealt with the city's poor, sick, and needy.

Inspired to do their part in charitable reform, some of the leading ladies of the city had developed a plan to assist legitimate charities with fund-raising.

Thus the Charity Ball was born . . . a curious and not always comfortable pairing of the wealthy and the zealous for an evening of flattery, influence-peddling, and conscience-pricking. This year, as in each of the two years past, it was hosted by Charles J. Bonaparte . . . grandson of Napolean Bonaparte's youngest brother, and a prominent social and civic reformer. This year, as in each of the last two years, one of the main attractions of the event was the presence of Baltimore's resident soft touch.

From the moment she arrived, Diamond was besieged by money-seekers and, as on other occasions, took refuge on the dance floor. There, at least, she could be subjected to only one wheedler at a time.

"Oh, Miss Wingate, if you could but see the tears of gratitude streaming down our urchins' hunger-wasted faces . . . *two, three, four* . . . if you could but hear their plaintive, motherless cries as they . . . *two, three, four* . . . settle into their lonely beds each night . . ."

"Of course we have added two operating theaters to the hospital since you last— *Oh, dear—was that your foot?* Where was I? Oh, remember the problem of blood making the floors slippery? Well, we installed concrete and put a sink with running water in both of the new operating—*Are you certain your foot is all right?* Also, you'll be pleased to know that we finally found the source of that foul odor in the rear wing, near the cisterns. It seems some of the cleaners were emptying the slop pans into—*Oh, no—your hem! I hope it can be repaired. . . ."*

"Last year we had a fourteen point three percent increase in the utilization of our services, but had revenue increases of only—*isn't that Senator Gorman over there?*—ten point seven percent last year. We expect to need at least twenty percent more this—*hello, Governor Lloyd! You're looking fit as a fiddle!*—year. That's ten thousand additional dollars, with costs still rising. Our projections are that—*Mrs. Bonaparte! My, aren't you stunning this evening!*"

"It's a shame we've haven't met before, Miss Wingate. We have things in common, you and me. We'd both give our last ounce of flesh, our last shred of virtue, and our last drop of blood for others. We'd strip the pride of possession from our souls and the very shirts from our backs, our chests, our breasts . . . You know . . . a healthy young woman like you must get lonely out there in that big old house. . . ."

In the first half hour, Diamond had been fawned over, stepped on, leered at, banged into, tripped up, sweated on . . . suffocated, overpowered, dampened, propositioned, and importuned by one too many of Baltimore's fervent fund-seekers. When she looked up from torn lace at her hem and smudged satin pumps to find Morgan Kenwood bearing down on her, her first thought was, *Thank God.* At least Morgan knew how to dance on his own feet.

Her relief evaporated moments later when he swept her onto the dance floor and promptly began to lecture her.

"Honestly, Diamond, you cannot allow these people to abuse you so. Why some of them"—he cast a sneer around him at the motley assortment of clothing and manners on display—"are little more than riffraff. Not a decent set of manners in the bunch. And three of them combined wouldn't make a normal ration of wits. Charity has its place, but, as the saying goes, charity begins in the home. And that's where you should be: *home* preparing for—"

"There you are!"

That irritating nasal voice sounded like the horns of the U.S. Cavalry, riding to the rescue. Searching the crowd as Morgan turned her smoothly past a bank of onlookers, she spotted him at the edge of the dance floor, dressed in his customary "parson" garb and looking decidedly out of place. "Louis!" She gave him a smile of gratitude for his timely appearance . . . which dimmed as she caught his scowl and realized it was caused by the sight of her in Morgan's arms. Turning her head irritably, she spotted a dark, rakish face and a pair of mesmerizing blue eyes trained on her from across the room and surprise caused her to miss a step.

Oh, Lord, she groaned silently. Louis she had expected; he was newly elected to the board of the Charity Organization Society and the director of the Harborside Mission. And Morgan she could understand being here . . . for, despite his distaste for charities, he liked to be wherever people of power and importance gathered. But what the devil was Paine Webster doing here? She just had time to notice that his clothing was immaculate and his face had an oddly taut and angular appearance. There was something different about him, she thought. As Morgan led her into a series of graceful turns that gave her a succession of glimpses of Paine, she realized what it was. He was sober.

She looked up at Morgan's superior expression, over at Louis's unabashed disapproval, and back at Paine's serious new demeanor. There was one thing they all shared: determination. Clearly, each of them had come to do business.

And it wasn't hard to figure out what sort of business they had in mind.

BEAR WOULD HAVE offered Clarice Vassar his arm as they exited the coach in the warm spring evening, but Evelyn intervened, commandeering his arm and spiriting him toward the entrance. While they waited in line to be announced, Bear scrutinized the elegant Louis XIV furnishings in the entry hall and peered casually over the heads of the other attendees, looking for Diamond.

Tonight, he had told himself, was the night. Tonight, he was going to get her alone and put forth his proposal, no matter what she thought of him afterward. No more hemming and hawing. No more getting sucked into her self-incurred disasters. No more looking into those huge blue eyes and going all "twiddly in th' knees." In the grip of that grim determination he sailed through a series of introductions and straight into the cavernous ballroom.

The guests had sorted themselves into groups on much the same principle that water seeks its own level. Scions and debutantes clustered in opposite corners eyeing each other; middle-class matrons huddled in awe near the walls while society ladies arrayed themselves prominently in the chairs under the musicians' gallery; men of substance were closeted in the library or out on the terrace puffing cigars, while men seeking substance flocked to the refreshment table, stuffing their mouths and pockets with foods they'd never tasted before.

Then he spotted her, swirling around the dance floor in elegant circles with Morgan Kenwood. For a moment he was too stunned to move. Her skirts were a deep, Montana-winter-sky-blue that paled as they wrapped up over her waist, to become a white tinged with blue in the bodice. Small lapis beads and seed pearls were appliquéd around her neckline and extended into lacework that formed a seductive sort of sleeves. The train of her gown, looped over her wrist for dancing, created a broad, lustrous curve as she whirled around the floor to the strains of a waltz.

She looked like a princess.

And he felt like a frog . . . until he made his way to the edge of the dance floor and spotted Louis Pierpont at the edge of the crowd, waiting for a chance to pounce. His jaw clenched and his hands contracted involuntarily into fists.

It was none of his damned business, he told himself, forcing his hands to open and his jaw to unlock. He looked at the guests ringing the dance floor and realized that many of them were watching Diamond with an acquisitive eye. He looked back at her graceful form and cameolike features and felt a startling urge to give every last one of the vultures a good trouncing . . . especially Pierpont.

"Lovely music, eh?" came a cultured male voice from beside him. "And the scenery's not half bad."

Nudged by memory, Bear looked over to find Paine Webster tracking the direction of his gaze with a knowing smile. He stifled his first reaction, dismay, in favor of a echo: "Not half bad."

Webster laughed. "Never met a woman as consistent as Diamond."

Bear scowled. "'Consistent' is not a word *I* would choose to describe her."

"But the perfect description nonetheless." Webster's smile had a bittersweet tinge as he watched her sweeping around the floor. "She is the same both inside and out. Rare for a woman. She is precisely what she appears to be."

"Is she?" Bear said, irritated by Webster's oblique boast of an intimate knowledge of her.

"She is beautiful, generous, passionately tender-hearted—"

Bear snorted. "And stubborn, changeable, and ridiculously independent."

"Then you haven't known her long enough. Or well enough," Webster said, searching Bear in a way that made him feel uncomfortable and annoyed.

"Lucky me," Bear shot back.

Webster's meaning-laden smile unsettled him.

"Yes. Lucky you."

The music ended just then and, as Kenwood escorted her from the floor, they were set upon by a dozen other guests who all apparently deemed it their right to have a turn about the room with her. Webster hurried over and together with Kenwood and Pierpont fended them off to procure her a bit of room.

Bear watched her with her three fiancés and felt an unsettling spurt of anger. Her troubles with those three, he reminded himself, were of her own doing. He was about to turn on his heel when she looked up, spotted him, and went motionless. Against his better judgment, almost against his will, he allowed himself to meet her gaze.

The distance between them and the crowd around them both momentarily disappeared. In the space of a heartbeat, he was once again in the guest room of her house, his body pressed hard against hers, exploring the sensual connection that seemed to have been forged between them the moment they met. It was a brief but steamy visitation of desire that condensed moments later into agitation.

"Miss Wingate," he said, taking her offered hand, chagrined to find that he had crossed the middle of the busy dance floor to reach her side.

"How good to see you, Mr. McQuaid." The relief in her eyes approached worship. Then she turned to the others with her hand still in his. "You remember Mr. McQuaid. The railroad builder from Montana."

Out West, looks as sullen and challenging as the ones they gave him would have likely resulted in the sound of steel clearing leather. Here, however, they resulted in a doggedly civil tension that caused each man to stand taller, inflate his chest, and lower his voice half an octave.

The jockeying for position as the four accompanied her

to the punch table was nothing short of intolerable. Money or no money, Bear thought, he should have headed for the door at the first sight of her trio of fiancés. Instead, he had allowed himself to meet her eyes and now felt her furtive glances of entreaty twining irresistibly around his better sense. She was doing it again—pulling him into the tangled web she had woven for herself. And—dammit—he didn't seem to be able to resist.

Ellen Channing Day Bonaparte, the hostess of the evening's festivities, and William Fisher, the first chairman of the Charity Organization Society, positioned themselves on the musician's gallery in the ballroom, calling the guests together for the first of what would be several donation reports made throughout the evening. These announcements of major contributions were, in reality, cannily timed prods to the pride of less forthcoming donors. It was considered something of a measure of one's importance on the economic and social ladder to be included in these lists of social benefactors.

Fisher clapped his hands and called for attention so that Mrs. Bonaparte could announce: "We are off to a wonderful start this evening. The Children's Home Society is grateful to announce a gift of fifteen thousand dollars from Miss Diamond Wingate." Whatever was announced afterward was largely lost in the reaction of the crowd to such a princely sum. Exclamations of surprise and awe swept the room as eyes widened and necks craned for a glimpse of her.

"There she is!" Evelyn Vassar had just threaded her way into the ballroom with some of her lady friends to hear the announcements. Catching sight of Diamond at the side of the crowd and pointing her out to the others, she applauded and nodded to Diamond enthusiastically.

"Did they say what I thought they said?" Morgan demanded of Diamond. "Fifteen thousand dollars? My God, giving them that much money only encourages them to be wasteful and inefficient. It only fosters pauperism."

"A laudable contribution," Louis intoned, ignoring Morgan. "But one must not put all of one's charitable eggs in one basket. There are other charities—fine organizations that also deserve attention and patronage, my dear."

"Oh, I have plans to donate to others," she said. "Including the mission."

"You do?" Louis relaxed visibly. "Well, of course, I know you are quite devoted to our cause. And just how much, may I ask, do you intend to donate?"

"Well, I believe that depends," she said, flicking a glance at Bear.

"On what, my dearest angel?" Louis was poised on the edge of his nerves, body taut, eyes shining, hands wringing in anticipation. But a burst of applause from the crowd drew her attention back to the gallery.

Her response was eclipsed by yet another announcement: "And a wonderful donation to the Firemen's Fund of ten thousand dollars, which they can surely use after the Hampden fires. A gift from Miss Diamond Wingate."

"Ten thousand?" Louis's face developed unbecoming red blotches.

"For fighting fires?" Morgan whispered furiously. "That's the city's responsibility, not yours!"

"They had no funds for equipment or the new station they needed in Hampden and the east end," she said, stepping backward and looking about for an avenue of escape. There were people on their left, people on their right, and a wall directly behind them. She cast a longing glance toward the doors.

"But, ten thousand dollars," Paine said, wetting his dry lips. "All because a few ramshackle buildings burned? You could burn down half of the east end and rebuild it for that kind of money."

Bear watched her weathering their collective scolding and was torn between his anger at them and his anger at her. The conflict produced opposing impulses to step in and set the self-serving bastards back on their heels and to stay out of it and let her sink into the hole she had so willfully dug for herself.

Diamond Wingate was far from helpless, he told himself. She had more than enough resources, determination, and internal steel to deal with the constant demands of her fortune and other people's reaction to it. She didn't need his help. Then she looked up, and he glimpsed the struggle visible in her irresistible blue eyes. He sucked in a breath and couldn't seem to expel it.

". . . have chosen this fortuitous evening to announce a major gift to the new Johns Hopkins Hospital," William Fisher was proclaiming in a booming voice that Bear would have ignored, if dread hadn't been so visible on Diamond's face. "Miss Diamond Wingate has pledged the magnificent sum of *one hundred thousand dollars* to establish a wing devoted to the needs of children!"

"One hun—" Morgan's mouth worked silently and he grabbed his chest.

"A hundred thousand?" Louis looked as if he'd been poleaxed. "Why that is beyond generosity—beyond the bounds of charity—beyond all reason!"

"Hoping to buy yourself a bigger halo, Diamond Mine?" Paine said sharply. "I have it on good authority that they only come in one size."

"I—I hadn't realized they would announce the hospital donation tonight," she stammered, shrinking visibly from the boisterous reaction of the crowd and the unprecedented hostility of her three fiancés. "I had only just decided to donate it . . . to celebrate my birthday."

At the mention of her birthday, veins appeared in Morgan's temples. "You might have spoken with me about this,

Diamond. I cannot believe you would be so irresponsible as to give that much money to a *hospital*."

"How could you take it upon yourself"—Louis demanded, his countenance aflame—"to dispose of such a vast sum without consulting me?"

"What are you trying to do, Diamond Mine?" Paine put in, hovering irritably over her shoulder. "Give my father a heart attack?"

Bear watched people turning to congratulate or gawk at Diamond and spotted Evelyn Vassar, nearby, applauding decorously and mouthing the words: "Bravo, my dear!" When he looked back, Diamond was registering the curiosity and judgment in the looks turned their way and growing ever more frantic.

"What I am *trying* to do is help the children of Baltimore live healthier lives," she declared quietly, glancing about and praying no one outside that circle of five could hear. But her defense of what they clearly considered to be an "excess" only spurred them on to greater outrage.

"I insist, Diamond, that you cease making donations of this magnitude." Morgan's words were all too audible. Heads turned and necks craned. "In fact, I believe you should cease making donations of *any* magnitude!"

She gasped, recoiled physically, and banged into Louis.

"Don't be absurd, Kenwood," the little missionary snapped, then turned on her himself. "Diamond, you know how I feel about the university's exorbitant spending on that 'hospital.' The wretched, smelly thing will get built with or without your help. There are far more worthy endeavors for your money than—"

"Spare us the holy harangue, Pierpont," Paine said irritably, reaching in to claim her hands. "Diamond, you know how my father despises universities—those peacocks at Johns Hopkins most of all. He will be furious. You'll have to take it all back."

"You're over the line, Webster," Morgan declared angrily. "This is none of your precious family's concern."

"It certainly isn't," Louis interrupted, stinging visibly from Paine's remark. "A family ought to pluck the beam from their own eye before telling others how to behave. And you, Morgan—what do you think you're doing, telling her what to do with her money?"

Bear saw the guests around them drinking in the tension and the reasons for it. His fists clenched. The fiancés' gentlemanly truce had dissolved into a verbal combat that revealed their basest motives toward Diamond. After tonight she should have no illusions about how callously they had abused her friendship and no qualms about squashing their matrimonial expectations.

Then, just as it seemed that things couldn't get much worse . . .

"I have every right," Morgan declared recklessly, "to insist that my future wife consult me in the disposition of our soon-to-be marital assets."

The pronouncement had the impact of a small dynamite discharge at close range. Diamond grabbed her throat with a strangling sound; Louis pressed his handkerchief to his mouth in horror; and Paine reached for the hip flask hidden in his trouser pocket.

"Your future wife?" Louis's blotches returned with a vengeance. "How dare you say such a thing in public without—"

"It's time, Diamond," Morgan declared, seizing her free hand. "We've waited long enough. Your birthday is only a few days away."

"Birthday?" Paine said with alarm, pulling her around to face him. "Tell him, Diamond Mine, who will be announcing an engagement on your birthday."

She opened her mouth but it was Louis's voice that issued forth.

"Diamond and I, of course." Louis tried to claim her arm from Paine, but had to settle for hooking her elbow. "We intend to announce our upcoming vows on my dearest's birthday."

"You? Marry Diamond?" Disbelief briefly outstripped Morgan's outrage.

Louis turned to her. "Tell them, dearest. Tell them we intend to marry before the summer is out and to turn Gracemont into our first orphan asylum."

Her eyes filled with horror. "Orphan asylum?"

"Diamond," Morgan prodded, "tell them!"

"Speak up, dearest!" Louis demanded.

"Set them straight, Diamond Mine, or I shall have to," Paine threatened.

The humiliation of being made the object of a public quarrel by men she once counted as dear friends had reduced her to anguished silence. Bear had seen sheep caught by wolves that were shown more mercy. His blood pounded in his head, his hands ached from being clenched, his arms burned with the need for action. Then Morgan reached for her wrist, intending to assert his claim physically, and the last rational restraints inside Bear snapped.

"Sorry to disappoint you, gentlemen," he heard his own voice, harsh with anger, booming over the scene. "But she's not marrying any of you!"

Diamond's contentious fiancés froze, then slowly turned their glares from each other to him.

"She is marrying *me*."

The silence that followed his pronouncement was deafening. Hardly a breath was taken in or released in the ballroom as the echoes of his words reached the distant corners.

"You?" Morgan said in a rasp.

"Me." he affirmed loudly. "As soon as is humanly possible."

What the hell was he doing? part of him protested. He must be crazy—she had driven him right around the bend. Then he lowered his gaze to her upraised face and felt a convulsive thud in his chest. Those blue eyes . . . so irresistibly clear and deceptively deep—an incomprehensible urge to possess and protect them gripped him.

It hit him like a thunderbolt: he wanted her. Signed and sealed. Lock, stock, and barrel. He didn't want just an option, he wanted ownership. With his next heartbeat, he understood that his impulsive claim was not just the answer to her problems, it was also the answer to *his.*

Around them, Baltimore society stood in shock, absorbing the reality of a confrontation four long years in the making. Passions, pride, and matrimonial ambition had driven many a young man to the brink of open conflict, but until now none had ever plunged over the edge.

Mindful of Diamond's generosity and having seen over the years her passion for discretion and decorum, the doyens of local society didn't know whether to view it as a scandal that should be laid at her own feet, or as outrage perpetrated against her by men who knew better than to air such matrimonial grievances in public.

"My goodness!" came a familiar female voice. "What a surprise—a truly wonderful surprise! Our dear Diamond is *finally* engaged to marry!" When Diamond tore her gaze from Bear McQuaid, she came eye to eye with a beaming Evelyn Stanhope Vassar, who began applauding for all she was worth.

Society's direction was decided as Evelyn was joined by a few perceptive friends, and was soon followed by every woman in the room who was the anxious mother of an eligible female.

"Diamond," Morgan was saying feverishly, "tell them it's not true!"

Bear reached for her and her gaze lowered to his big, work-hardened palm. It looked like the Promised Land.

An engagement—a public and unquestionably authentic betrothal—was her only hope of escaping this debacle with any sort of reputation left. Her mind raced. Who better than an outsider . . . a handsome, memorable Westerner who was eager to leave Baltimore and return to his home out West? A long engagement . . . McQuaid would return to Montana . . . she could be the pining fiancée . . . eventually the jilted female . . . who never quite recovered from the heartbreak of her one true "love" . . .

"It's true," she said breathlessly. "We do intend to marry."

It was only when he had drawn her from her failed fiancés' clutches and put an arm around her waist, that she looked up and saw a small, fierce flame in his eyes. She was going to pay dearly this time. Her knees weakened and she sagged slightly against him. Whatever the price, she would gladly pay it.

As the opportunity-emboldened mothers of Baltimore flocked to wish her and her new fiancé well, her three contentious jilts were forced aside and withdrew, deflated by their sudden and disastrous change of fortunes. In the ensuing confusion, she caught glimpses of them fleeing the room in high dudgeon and felt conflicting pangs of loss and relief.

Hardwell and Hannah came rushing upstairs from the drawing room, their faces flushed and their eyes shining. They peeled her from Bear's grasp long enough for congratulatory hugs.

"Can't say I'm surprised," Hardwell announced, sticking

out his chest and beaming. "These two had eyes for each other from the minute they met!"

Hannah dabbed at her eyes and sniffed a little, but her response was immensely practical. "We'll have a wedding to prepare—how exciting!"

"Feel free to call on me," Evelyn Vassar said, putting an arm around Hannah. "I'd love nothing better than to help with the dear girl's nuptials." She turned to Bear and Diamond. "And when may we expect the happy event?"

Without a heartbeat's pause, Bear declared: "Next week."

Diamond, who had been moving and responding in a haze of relief at her deliverance, was jolted forcefully back to the present.

"What?"

"The end of the week. Saturday sounds good." He clamped an arm around the back of her waist as if afraid she might bolt for the door. "You know I have to be back in Montana shortly—and I won't be able to return for some time."

"I'm willing to wait," she said a bit too hastily, praying that he would read the message in her eyes.

"But *I'm* not." His determined smile said he read her objection well enough, but intended to ignore it. "I can't wait to make you Mrs. McQuaid."

Before she could sputter a protest, he grabbed her around the waist, hoisted her up, and swung her around and around. The laughter his impulsive behavior caused was entirely good-natured . . . which was the only thing that kept her from slapping him silly the minute her feet touched the floor.

"I suppose"—she put a hand to her reeling head—"we can *discuss* it."

THIRTEEN

"WHAT THE DEVIL got into you in there, McQuaid?" she demanded raggedly, pulling him toward the darkest corner of the moonlit garden.

It had been more than an hour since their surprise announcement in the ballroom and she was still reeling from the excitement it had unleashed. Her feet were killing her, her hands had been squeezed, pressed, patted, and drooled on by half of Baltimore, and her face ached from besotted smiling at a man who took perverse pleasure in taunting her with his new "husbandly" authority.

"Telling everyone that we're to be married next Saturday . . . have you gone stark raving mad?"

"Is that any way to talk to the man who just saved your matrimonial hide?" he responded, pulling her off the secluded garden path and planting himself in front of her.

He was so close that she had to bend backward to glare at him. His face was cast in shadows by the overhead branches, but she could see his eyes clearly enough to make out the glint in them. Something—his sensual presence or the intimacy of the darkness around them or the

memory of having been alone with him in the dark before—caused a softening in her response.

"I owe you for that. And I intend to see you amply paid,
but—"

"I intend to see me amply paid, too," he said with an
intensity that brooked no interruptions. "I have saved your
rosy butt for the last time, Diamond Wingate. I'm calling
in my markers. All of them."

The time she had dreaded had come. "Fine." She swallowed hard. "Name your price."

"I believe I already have." Though she couldn't quite
see, she had the worrisome sense that he was smiling.
"You're marrying me next Saturday."

"That's not the least bit funny, McQuaid," she said with
a tinge of panic. As she pulled away, his hands closed on
her shoulders to prevent her escape. Her heart thudded.
"See here . . . I appreciate what you did in there . . .
more than I can say. You saved my reputation, my social
standing, and just possibly my entire future. But I've told
you . . . I don't intend to marry . . . on Saturday or
ever."

"They say the road to hell is paved with failed intentions," he said with alarming calm. "You just agreed to
marry me in front of half of Baltimore."

"I was desperate. And coerced. Rather rudely, I might
add."

"Coerced?" He gave a short, sardonic laugh. "I offered
you a way out, an honorable escape from an intolerable
situation. And you took it. You agreed of your own free
will." He took her by the shoulders and she could feel his
stare penetrating her, invading her thoughts and feelings.
"Can you honestly say that you find the prospect of marriage with me disgusting?"

She didn't answer, except in her thoughts. *Not fair.*

"Revolting?"

Still no response. *He knew better.*

"Intolerable?"

The heat of his hands and the warmth of his body began to invade her garments, setting her skin tingling. *Marriage with sun-bronzed, smooth-talking, sweet-kissing Bear McQuaid. Looking at him across the breakfast table each morning, listening to his outrageous stories, watching him walk up stairs in his tight-fitting trousers and Western boots . . . lying in bed at night beside him . . .* For one brief instant the prospect held as many intriguing possibilities as potential hazards. Then the drift of her thoughts alarmed her, as did the softening of her objections.

"Perhaps you'd rather I'd send for Kenwood or Pierpont or Webster . . . let them know that you never intended to marry me . . . that you're a free woman once more." She couldn't hide the anxiety that generated in her and when he saw that his words had reached their mark, he eased and drew back slightly. "You know of course that the moment their pride quits smarting, they'll start thinking. And it will occur to them that you owe them something for all their 'services' to you. Miss Wingate will still be fair game. Mrs. McQuaid will be out of their reach."

He was probably right. Curse his hide. It set her thinking and when she looked up at him in the moonlight her glare and her irritation were both fading.

"Don't you see, Diamond?" The taunt was gone from his tone. "This is the answer to everything."

She wrung her hands as she struggled to think, to reason it all out, to search out the ramifications of the step she would be taking. Was he right? Was this her best course . . . the answer to her problems . . . the answer to *everything*?

Then she looked up, searching for answers in his face and his certainty. And she found her answer in her own desire, reflected in his eyes. He was the one man in her life who had seen her as she really was, weaknesses and all, and still accepted her. He had been her confidant, partner, and sometime accomplice. He had rescued her again and again, with no thought of himself. He was the one man in her life who had never mentioned her money or approached her as if she were a bank account with a bustle.

More importantly, he was the only man who had invaded her thoughts and dreams and desires . . . who made her laugh, made her furious, made her think . . . who made her hope.

He was the only man she had ever *wanted*.

Reading in her physical softening her acceptance of his logic, he lifted her chin and looked into her eyes.

"That's my price, Miss Wingate."

"It's a great deal higher than I bargained for." She felt her skin tingling where he touched her.

" 'No' is not in your vocabulary," he reminded her.

"But, perhaps—"

" 'Perhaps' isn't an option, either. I'm leaving a week from Monday."

"Then . . . I suppose . . . the only thing left is 'yes.' "

He expelled a deep breath, betraying just how much her answer had meant to him. Whatever doubts and questions remained in her mind were swept aside by that small but telling action. It was the ultimate persuasion. It meant he wanted her, too.

He proved it with his next breath, as he slid his hand around the nape of her neck and lowered his head.

The soft resilience of his lips against hers, the warmth and intimacy of his tongue caressing her . . . she remembered it all the instant his lips touched hers. The taste of him and the scent of his soap and starch and wine-sweetened breath was familiar and felt instantly right. A faint hum began in her blood and grew steadily louder, as if her body itself were approving her decision.

She melted against him, feeling as she did that her body's contours were reshaping, adapting . . . that she was somehow being changed by the decision she had just made. Then he wrapped both arms around her, pulled her hard against him, and deepened his tantalizing explorations of her mouth. She felt a sudden and searing rush of heat that all but melted her rational apparatus.

Alive now with a new and mesmerizing awareness of her body and her physical response to the man in her arms, she wrapped her arms around him, pressed her aching body against him, and opened eagerly to his kiss.

By the time they heard people strolling on the nearby garden path and broke apart, it was all she could do to remain upright. Her very bones seemed to have been softened by the heat of their joined desire. Her lips felt swollen and conspicuous and her face and breasts were flushed. When they stepped through the terrace doors and into the limelight again, she seemed every inch the blushing bride. No one doubted for a minute that the glow in her eyes and the radiance of her smile were caused by her pleasure in the prospect of becoming Mrs. Barton McQuaid.

THERE WERE A thousand things to do between the Charity Ball and the following Saturday, the first of which was giving Robbie the news that his favorite cowboy would soon be a member of the family. He bounced on the bed, whooped, and shouted hallelujah . . . then wanted to know when they were "lightin' out" for Montana. It took four helpings of dessert at supper—his first meal outside his room in ten days—to salve his disappointment at learning that he and Diamond weren't going anywhere.

Bear called only once during that week . . . a short
visit to consult on arrangements for the wedding, during
which they were interrupted repeatedly by unexpected
guests, deliveries of unsolicited wedding gifts and, of
course, Robbie. Diamond had no chance to mention the
score of questions and issues that had occurred to her
since she agreed to make good her acceptance of his very
public proposal. He was heavily occupied with arrangements for shipping men and materials west and was
pleased to leave the wedding preparations to her.

The balance of the week was a blur of people and planning. Evelyn Vassar insisted on holding a bridal tea in Diamond's honor, and Diamond was deluged daily by more
acquaintances paying calls and by more unneeded wedding gifts. By the time she caught her breath, it was Saturday afternoon and she was seated beside Bear in a halo of
warm sunlight, hearing toast after toast being proposed to
their nuptial happiness.

The haze of unreality that had muffled the events of the
frantic week began to settle out, freeing her perceptions
and responses. Uppermost in her clearing thoughts were
the details of their vows, exchanged not long ago in the
drawing room, before a score of guests. There had been a
progression of weighty promises, he had put a simple gold
ring on her finger, and the minister declared them to be
man and wife. Bear then kissed her with a bit more enthusiasm than was strictly necessary, and she was introduced
to all as "the new Mrs. Barton McQuaid."

Everyone had gathered around to kiss the bride and
shake the groom's hand. Champagne was brought out and
Diamond managed to intercept three glasses of the wine
before Robbie downed them. Lord knew how many she
didn't catch, for when they went in to dinner her charge
sat at the table with his knees drawn up, giggling and
making annoying horse noises.

Up and down the rest of the blossom-laden table, faces were glowing. Talk was lively and emotions ranged from relief to exhilaration.

"This is all so lovely," Evelyn Vassar said, gazing at Diamond with genuine fondness. "A pity you couldn't have shared the occasion with more of your friends. Oh, I nearly forgot . . . Did you hear? Alice Taylor is engaged to marry. Richard Elkhart of the East Bay Elkharts. And Emma Harding received a call Thursday from none other than Paine Webster. And"—she glanced at her daughter—"our own dear Clarice is beginning a new career. She'll be tending the sick . . . starting tomorrow."

"Mamma!" Clarice scolded, though she didn't seem truly displeased.

"Oh?" Diamond made herself ignore the mention of Paine's abrupt new interest in Emma Harding to focus on Clarice's news. She puzzled over Clarice's apparent pleasure in what was usually considered an odious task. "You're going to care for someone who is ill?"

"I am." The girl's dark eyes danced. "It's Morgan. He's come down with the chicken pox."

"How . . . awful for him. And how . . . wonderful of you to volunteer to help, Clarice." Diamond didn't know whether to feel wounded or to laugh. Clarice had had eyes for Morgan Kenwood since she and Diamond made their debut, four years ago. Now, with Diamond out of the way . . .

"Mrs. McQuaid . . . Mrs. McQuaid!" Hardwell called down the table. When she didn't answer, Bear leaned down and gave her a nudge.

"I think he means you."

Good-natured laughter broke out along the length of the table and she blushed. More toasts were offered, and as she listened to the good wishes of family friends and heard herself referred to again and again as "Diamond Mc-

Quaid," the impact of what she had just done came crashing down on her.

Diamond Wingate no longer existed. Someone named Diamond McQuaid was taking her place and Diamond had no idea who that was.

"And where will you be going after the wedding? Montana?" someone asked.

"Yes."

"No."

They answered at the same moment, then looked at each other, surprised. Bear explained: "Actually, I'll be leaving for Montana soon . . . I have to start laying track right away. Diamond will be staying here."

"*Tsk, tsk.* Abandoning your bride after so short a while," someone else declared teasingly. "How soon will you be coming back, Mr. McQuaid?"

"A few weeks."

"A few months."

They responded together, then smiled tautly at each other, both annoyed and both praying it didn't show. "Barton has a good bit of work to do." She explained the discrepancy in their estimates with determined pleasantness. "I could never deprive his railroad of its most important asset."

"Ahhh, you can see who'll wear the pants in this family," Hardwell said.

"Who?" Diamond and Bear demanded together.

Robbie giggled. "Kiss 'er again, Bear. An' steal her pants when she ain't lookin'."

A heartbeat of shocked silence preceded a roar of laughter. Evelyn Vassar picked up her spoon and tapped her goblet and was joined instantly by others. Hannah took pity on Bear's confusion.

"It's a custom. You're supposed to kiss the bride every

time someone calls for it with a ringing glass," she told him.

He leaned over to Diamond and gave her a smacking kiss on the cheek.

"Aw, you can do better than that, my boy!" Hardwell laughed.

With a deep breath, Bear took her head between his hands and planted a scorcher of a kiss on her lips. Applause approved both his effort and its results.

Dazed and chagrined, Diamond looked up and saw for the first time a sizable, age-whitened scar at the edge of his jaw. Her gaze fastened on it as he traded quips with Philip Vassar, and she realized that she had no earthly idea how he got that scar.

What did she know about this man? He was born in North Carolina but had spent much of his life in the West . . . had been a cowboy and had run a ranch for a while before settling on building railroads. And he didn't have any family. She had learned that when she suggested delaying the wedding to allow time for his family to attend.

Looking at his plate, she saw the braised squash and glazed carrot fans pushed to the side. He apparently didn't like vegetables. She saw him signal for a refill of his glass. He apparently did like wine. When he downed half the glass in one swallow, her eyes widened. What if he liked it too much?

Her thoughts were interrupted when someone made a joke about Bear's fortunes no longer riding just on rails. It was a pointed reminder that as the last "I do" was said, moments ago, he had assumed legal possession of all that was hers. Under the law, he was entitled to control and dispose of her property at will. Her anxiety bloomed. This was one of the issues she had had no time . . . or presence of mind . . . to discuss with him.

"No doubt you'll want to make a few changes in the way the companies are run," Mason Purnell, a longtime friend of the family, suggested.

"No more lotteries at board meetings, I imagine," the secretary of her board of directors said, clearly relieved by the prospect.

"No more handing out money to every Tom, Dick, and Harry who thinks he's found a way to turn lead into gold," Vassar put in with a sly grin.

"There'll be a sight fewer sad-faced orphans doggin' her steps, each time she goes to town," Hardwell said, beaming.

Even Hannah spoke up. "I suppose we'll have fewer people at the gates, waiting for—"

"Not at all," Diamond declared, sitting beet-red and rail-straight on the edge of her chair. "Things will go on just as before. Won't they, *Barton?*"

"I believe we'll have to see about that, *Mrs. McQuaid,*" he said, toying with his fork and pointedly avoiding her stare. He addressed the others. "My wife has done a fine job with the Wingate holdings. I don't intend to interfere in her management of them"—just as her outrage began to wilt, he continued—"unless she refuses to learn the lesson I have been trying to teach her."

There was a rustle of surprised amusement around the room, and all eyes focused on her reaction.

She turned to him with her fists at her waist and a haughty look on her face, hoping it would pass for teasing.

"Just what lesson is it you've been trying to teach me, Mr. McQuaid?"

"You still don't know?" He gave a long-suffering sigh for effect, then raised a wicked smile to her and the others around the table. *"How to say no."*

The laughter this time felt altogether too pointed and

too personal . . . like pins pricking her sensitive pride. She thought seriously of strangling him. Here. In front of God and everybody. But then, she decided darkly, to be wedded, widowed, and arrested for murder all on the same day might cause something of a stir.

FOURTEEN

IT WAS WELL past dusk when the last of the guests departed. Hardwell and Hannah dragged Robbie off to his room and then tottered off to theirs in search of bicarbonate of soda and a pair of comfy slippers. As the light purpled and faded into the darkness of the warm spring night, Diamond was left alone to face Bear and the aftermath of her wedding.

Her fortune wasn't all Bear McQuaid now controlled, she thought as she sank onto the bench in front of the stately vanity in the master suite. Peering into the shield-shaped mirror, she tugged her fashionable dressing gown so that its broad, scooped neckline lay centered, exposing each shoulder equally. With the slightest movement, one side slid downward, drawing the other side up and revealing altogether too much of her. She righted the blessed thing, only to watch it creep down her other arm and reveal a good portion of her breast.

Chewing the corner of her lip, she jerked the neckline all the way to one side and surveyed the damage. Her nipple, crinkled taut and erect, jutted out like a flag on the top of a hill. With a gasp, she jerked the fabric up to her chin.

The door to the adjoining bedroom swung open, startling her. She whirled and came face to face with Bear, clothed in trousers and a half-open shirt. His feet were bare, his beard shadow was gone, and his hair was wet; he had just come from bathing. In his hands were a bottle of wine and a pair of long-stemmed glasses. Her gaze slid to his bare chest . . . the same tanned, sculptured physique she'd seen that day at Martene and Savoy . . . and in her dreams since.

Both her face and that one shameless nipple burned.

"I see you found your room," she said, turning the heat of that erotic combustion outward.

"It's purple," he said. "A washed-out, sickly kind of purple."

"Lilac Dream," she informed him. "It was very popular on the Continent."

"Sounds French." He pulled his attention from her long enough to look around the great, domed bedchamber. The postered and draped bed was massive and the hand-carved chests, chairs, and paintings were crafted on an equally impressive scale. "I take it this isn't your room."

"It was my father's. My mother died when I was very small, but when he built the house he put in a room for her, beside his," she said, folding her arms over her chest and gripping them. "That's the one you were just in." She focused on the bottle of wine. "I hope you don't intend to drink all that"—she was distracted by his movement as he shifted—"u-until a-after—"

"We've sealed our vows?" he supplied with a suggestive grin.

"A-after we've had a chance to *talk*," she stammered, feeling her face redden. He was going to kiss her again, she knew, and pull her hard against that mesmerizing expanse of living bronze. And take her to his bed. And take her to his . . .

She squeezed her bare knees together under her gown. How hard could it be, this "wifely duty?" Other women—women far less capable and determined than she—had lived through it. And from servant whispers and giggles, she surmised that some women actually came to enjoy a husband's marital services.

"Talk?" he said with a hint of distraction. "About what?"

Transfixed by the sight of her seated before her mirror, her hair down around her half-bare shoulders and her eyes huge and dark centered, Bear couldn't move. The light from the candles behind her spun strands of gold through her hair and highlighted her curves through the folds of her thin, light-colored gown. When she stood up, he felt heat sluicing downward through his body and pooling in his loins. The last thing he wanted to do was *talk*.

"About financial matters. I'm sure you'll have to sign papers so that I can continue to vote the stock, and we ought to come to some sort of agreement—"

"We will," he responded, strolling forward.

"I mean now. I believe it's best to get it out of the—" She shrank from his approach, shooting to her feet and backing toward the massive window. "I am hereby serving notice that I intend to go on investing in inventions and ideas and making charitable donations as I see fit." He could have sworn she was trembling. "And just what was that nonsense at dinner? Teaching me a lesson. As if I were a ten-year-old child. You have some nerve, Bear Mc-Quaid."

"Fortunately for you." She was picking a fight with him, he realized, hoping to delay the inevitable. He hadn't expected that. It betrayed a carnal innocence and uncertainty that added to the burden on his already strained scruples. "Otherwise, I'd be six feet under in some dusty

Boot Hill out West. And you'd be facing three very unhappy men and social ruination."

All day he had been keeping his conscience at bay with a determined litany of "the ends justify the means." Clearly, he had convinced himself, the ends of this marriage were positive on all fronts. In marrying him she was saved from three untenable engagements, public scandal and disgrace, and the solitary life she had claimed to prefer to marriage with any of her fiancés. In marrying her, he got his railroad loan and access to a stable financial base without having to reveal and humiliate himself by asking her for it.

When you got right down to brass tacks, their goals weren't all that different. She wanted independence and so did he. He could give her the freedom she wanted while maintaining his own. Clearly, this marriage was the logical and reasonable solution to absolutely *everything*.

And all he had to do was continue to deceive her.

Shaking off his thoughts, he set the glasses on a nearby table, uncorked the wine, and poured.

"I'm not an unreasonable man. I'm willing to negotiate."

She ignored the glass he offered her.

"Negotiate? I'll do nothing of the sort."

"Well, I'm not exactly keen on the notion, myself." He thrust the glass into her hand and she had to accept it to keep it from spilling. "But it was your idea to talk and to come to some agreement. Sounds like 'negotiations' to me."

When he sat down on the window seat she stiffened and edged back, thus declaring her intention to resist both husbandly edicts and advances. He exhaled patiently.

"All right, I'll open," he declared. "No more free meals at the front gates."

"What?"

"That's my first demand."

"Demand?" Her eyes narrowed. "What gives you the right to—"

"Setting aside for the moment the fact that I'm your husband before God and humankind *and* the legal head of your household . . . I have rescued your rosy backside enough to have a major claim on it, and a stake in the way things run around here." When she backed into the window seat and sat down with a plop on the pillows, he smiled. "No more free meals at the front gates."

"But those poor people—"

"Can damn well line up for food elsewhere. They camp on your doorstep to make you feel guilty. And it works." He narrowed his eyes. "Doesn't it?"

"I suppose that's not entirely unreasonable." Her gaze slid to his chest and he saw she had difficulty swallowing. "But only if I get to donate to—"

"To any mission or shelter except Brother Pierpont's," he said, sipping wine and finding his attention stubbornly sliding down her lace-rimmed gown. It was hanging askew on her shoulders and he caught a tantalizing glimpse of the swell of one breast. His trousers began to feel a little snug.

"Demand number two: you'll announce publicly that all requests for money—whether they're business proposals or charity requests—must go through your company offices."

"But that's absurd, a waste of time and energy, since I'm the one who—"

"It's not wasteful, it's sensible. It's also a sort of protection for you. I won't always be around to toss crazed inventors and scheming cheapjacks out in the street." He finished his wine and set the glass on the window ledge. "People will come to realize that there's no point in mobbing you in the streets. And without their pitiful harangues and long-faced pleas, you'll be able to make clearer-headed decisions about the inventions you do buy. Agreed?"

"Well . . . I suppose . . ."

Leaning over to catch her glass on a finger, he lifted it toward her lips, urging her to drink. She took one sip, then sensing the support it could provide, quickly finished the entire glass.

"Good." He took her goblet and set it aside with his. "And one more point." He slid toward her and noted with some satisfaction that she didn't flee.

"Yes?" She looked up with a jumble of emotions swirling in her eyes, not the least of which was fear. It stunned him momentarily. He'd never seen her quail at anything. She was always stubborn and self-possessed and quick with a smart retort. But just now, in those arresting blue orbs he glimpsed a weakness in her internal fortress, a vulnerability in those impenetrable walls.

She didn't know what to expect from him, from any man. She was about to surrender a part of her self she hadn't known existed until recently. She was about to put her body as well as her fortunes in his hands. Something softened in the center of his chest. Whatever the future brought them, whatever happened between them after this, he vowed to see that she would have nothing to regret in this night.

"Robbie." He ran a single finger along her shoulder.

"Robbie?" Her voice was small and distracted. A positive sign.

"Only one dessert. And only if he's earned it." He watched goose bumps rise under her skin and he leaned close enough to inhale her warmth and roselike scent on every breath. "And no more of those lacy collars, or fat-legged riding breeches, or velvet knee pants."

"But he looks so—"

"Silly. He looks like a damned sissy in-n—" His voice split and after a moment proceeded in a much lower register. "I have to say . . . you have much better taste in nightgowns than in boys' riding gear. This one's nothing short of spectacular." When she grabbed up the drooping neckline, he gathered her anxious gaze into his, took hold of the fabric below her hands, and slowly pulled it back down.

"Very nice goods," he said softly. "Wouldn't want to rumple it."

Her grip on the gown loosened, and after a moment, she released it. Still holding her gaze in his, he continued pulling downward. On the lower periphery of his vision he watched the fabric slide down her chest and expose the top of one of her breasts. Sliding his fingers over that silky mound with its crinkled velvet tip, he watched the shock of his touch register in her eyes.

When she raised her hand, he intercepted it, thinking that she would try to push his hand away. To his surprise, she directed it instead to his bare chest. The feel of her cool fingers gliding along his overheated skin carried a galvanic shock that slowly damped into tingles of pleasure. For a time they sat touching, caressing each other in the same way, reading in each other's eyes the sensual charge building between them.

"You are so beautiful," he said, lowering his gaze.

"Please, Bear—"

When he looked up again, her eyes were filled with renewed tension.

"Don't look," she whispered.

"But there's nothing to be—"

"Please—" She pressed her fingers to his lips. "Not that."

He frowned, but nodded and released her. She caught his hand and directed it back to her breast, where hers closed over it, forcing it tighter around that warm resilient mound. Her lashes fluttered in response. When his fingers tightened on her nipple, he both heard and felt her breath catch in her throat.

Her fingers explored his breast the same way and he experienced the same heart-stopping jolt of pleasure. It was all he needed. He felt for the ties of her dressing gown and soon her night clothes lay in a pool around her waist.

She forced his shirt up over his shoulders and then down his arms, mirroring his action and his touch. Embracing, chest to chest, sensitive tips pressed against sensitive mounds . . . each watched excitement building in the other's eyes. Then he lowered his head and brushed her lips with his.

The flames those glancing kisses ignited in her depths were visible through her passion-darkened eyes. Again and again, from every conceivable orientation, they touched lips lightly to lips and savored the reward of restraint, lingering in delicious expectation on the edge of pleasure. His hands slid down her sides to her waist, tracing her curves. Her hands slid down his back and dipped beneath the waist of his trousers, tracing the pillars of muscle that supported his frame.

The erotic taboo she had established between them seemed to heighten his other senses. His hands registered every inch of her skin as his eyes could not, giving him a new appreciation of the sensuality of texture and shape. In some places she was pure silk, in others fine new down, in still others she felt like the richest cream. He breathed in the fragrance of her hair and moistening skin and groaned softly as those scents went straight into his blood.

Unable to wait any longer, she wrapped her arms around his neck and joined their mouths. He pulled her half-naked form against him, unleashing the desire he had held in check. Deeper and deeper they sank in an intimate whirl of pleasure. As they sank back into the pillows, he banged his shoulder on the window frame and roused enough to pull her upright and onto her knees. Her garments fell away as he lifted her in his arms and carried her to the waiting bed. In seconds, his trousers joined them on the floor and he was sinking onto the bed and into her welcoming arms.

As his kisses began to wander, she reminded him of her request by closing his eyes with her fingertips. Quivering, she felt his mouth at her breast and his tongue laving her with slow, wet velvet strokes. It was as if his kisses were dissolving her skin, baring her nerves and sinews to him. She writhed softly, yielding to the gentle invasion of her thighs and accepting his weight with a moan that seemed to come from beyond herself . . . somewhere in the purest feminine, somewhere in the depths of existence itself.

He threaded his fingers through hers and dragged their hands above her head, looking only into her eyes as he flexed his body above hers and raked her most sensitive flesh with his own. When she began to meet his thrusts with instinctive motions, he pulled back and began the joining of their bodies.

Her heart seemed to stop as her flesh yielded to him. The stinging quickly subsided, muting into a delicious heat and fullness in a part of her she had never experienced as empty until now. And when they lay fully joined, the joy she felt in claiming this part of him—this part of herself—was beyond anything she had experienced.

He began to move rhythmically, slowly at first and carefully, gauging his effect by her expressions. As she grew more accustomed to his presence, his movement pushed her through a succession of new intensities . . . deepened, heightened, and broadened perception. She felt as if she were rising and expanding through endless new realms of pleasure. The wonder of it was that he seemed to be there, as well, mingled with her awareness of self, joined and yet somehow still joining with her.

Then, just as she felt herself approaching some unknown limit, some new and significant portal of sensation, she felt him stiffen, arch, and shudder, his face a mask of pleasure so intense it mimicked pain. Moments later, he collapsed over her, panting for breath, nuzzling and kissing her, his skin damp and his face hot with satisfaction.

Through the steam cooling in her head, she managed to realize that what had happened between them was "it." The act of procreation. The way of married love. Her wifely "duty." It was perfectly wonderful. She looked over at him and saw nothing but pleasure and wonder in his handsome features. With a smile, she surrendered to exhaustion.

Some time later she awakened to a feeling of warmth and closeness. When she opened her eyes, Bear was lying beside her, propped up on his arm, looking at her with a softness that warmed her all the way to her toes. But as she turned to better view him, his gaze dipped to her bare breasts and hers followed.

"Oh!" She sprang up, reaching for a sheet to cover herself, but he held her by the waist to prevent it.

"I've already seen all there is to see, sweetheart. Taken a detailed inventory." Chuckling, he overcame her resistance and drew her back down into his arms. "I'm one very lucky man."

She felt herself going crimson, from the roots of her hair to the tips of her toes. "Really, McQuaid—"

"Bear." He grinned at her desperate attempts at propriety.

"Really, Bear, I'm not at all accustomed to—"

"Lying buck naked with a man after hot and heavy loving? I would think not." His copper eyes heated with a rekindled flame. "You're probably even less accustomed to a man nibbling your skin"—he demonstrated on the side of her neck, heedless of her gasp—"and caressing your breasts"—he did that, too—"and wrapping his legs around you." She should probably have been appalled by the weight of his thigh across her abdomen, but it recalled the delicious heaviness of his body on hers in the hours just past and served as prelude to a stream of shocking but irresistible memories.

"Ple-e-ease . . ." She seized his hand and held it still.

"Please what? Continue? Stop?" A twinkle appeared in his eye. "It's simple, sweetheart. If you want me to stop, all you have to do is say the word."

"What word?"

" 'No.' " He leaned over her and gently squeezed the corners of her mouth, making her lips move. "Come on, you can say it. *No-o-o.*"

She remained stubbornly silent for a minute, glaring up at him. "I don't respond well to brute force," she said through her puckered lips.

"Then what do you respond to?" Craftiness crept into his expression as he released her. "Ah, yes, it's coming back to me." He lowered his head and tongued and nibbled the tip of her breast, bringing it to aching prominence.

"Ohhh—" Her breath caught and she pushed at his shoulders, struggling against both his determination and her own debilitating pleasure. When she ceased pushing, he raised his head. She had caught her lower lip between her teeth and her eyes were dark and luminous.

"Just say no."

"What a beast you are," she said, fighting back an embarrassed smile.

"A hungry beast." He grinned. "A beast who knows only one word. And it's not 'don't,' or 'stop,' or 'whoa.' " He nuzzled her nipple again and then blazed a trail of hot, moist breath down the center of her stomach.

"What are you—ohhhh . . ."

"Such delicious curves."

She watched as long as she dared, stunned equally by the sight of him making free with her naked body and by the pleasure it gave her. When he veered to the crest of her hip, she jerked her gaze away and grabbed the sheet.

"And hips. And legs—long, cool thighs. Such shapely knees," he murmured . . . kissing, tickling, and nuzzling his way down her body.

"Ohhh, Bear—"

"Just say no," he said with a laugh.

"Strong, smooth calves. Small ankles. Pretty little feet."

"My feet are not little," she said through a half-stifled whimper of delight, curling her toes and twisting her ankles to evade his shocking adoration. Every nerve in her body seemed to be crying out with either pleasure or need. Pushed beyond modesty and decorum and half past sanity as well, she finally sat up, seized him by the shoulders, and pulled him up onto the bed on top of her.

"Enough," she commanded in low, provocative tones.

"But you haven't learned to say no, yet." He grinned and brushed her hair back, stroking her face in the same motion.

"If you really want to teach me that blasted word, you'll have better luck if you try something that I *don't* want you to do."

She absorbed his laugh in her kiss, and together they tumbled into a sensual exploration that was by turns fiery and playful. This loving was so different from the last—so direct and frankly experimental—that she could scarcely believe it was the same act.

He rolled onto his back carrying her with him and she found herself nestled between his legs and exploring his body much the same as he had hers. When she had memorized his long legs and sculptured belly and muscular shoulders, she sat up, astride him, to study the way his dark hair, tanned skin, and molten copper eyes looked against the white of the sheets. Even relaxed and wearing a suggestive grin, there was no missing the physical power and personal force latent in every angle and attitude of his body. He was leashed potential. A being of infinite complexity and capacity. Beautiful. Enthralling.

"Love me, Bear," she whispered, voicing the desire filling her being.

He arched his back and dumped her over onto the bed.

"I will," he whispered into her hair. "I do."

In seconds, he was sliding into that seductive wedge between her thighs. From there it was only a few long, sweet strokes before he was sinking into the lush welcome of her body.

Once again she felt herself expanding and escaping the limitations of experience and expectation. In this place, she felt no rules, no obstacles, no boundaries. They joined without reserve, sharing self, sensations, and pleasure . . . obeying only their desires . . . content to let the flow of passion carry them ever higher.

She arrived again at a now familiar but uncrossed threshold where time slowed and existence expanded infinitely. For a moment she floated, suspended and breathless. Then she crashed through that fragile sensory boundary, into a maelstrom of pleasure and release. For the second time that night, she felt in the depths of her being old patterns and old desires being swept away, replaced by a new sense of order, new hope for the future, and a heart full of newborn love.

•   •   •

EARLY THE NEXT afternoon, Bear sat propped against a thick tree trunk on a blanket placed to overlook Gracemont's picturesque orchards. The air was still sweet with the remnants of apple blossoms and the linen cloth at his feet was littered with the remnants of a sumptuous picnic meal. Diamond lay beside him on the blanket, warm and openly content in the dappled sunlight pouring through the tree limbs. Her face was alluring in its softness and as he watched he felt that curious ache spreading through his chest again.

It had started last night when he entered the bedroom and saw her on the bench before her mirror clutching her nightgown under her chin, her eyes huge and uncertain. And it had continued through a steamy night and into the cool of dawn . . . through the pleasure of watching her rise and dress and share with him the endearing intimacies of the ordinary. He had never really watched a woman brushing her hair or selecting a dress for the day or slipping stockings over her toes and up her legs. And he had certainly never seen a woman as beautiful as Diamond walking naked across a room toward him . . . her arms open and her eyes glowing with invitation.

He marveled at the astonishing transformation in her as she came through their wedding night. And he was still more in awe of the way she had placed her trust in him, and the serious way he had responded to that trust.

"Well, Mrs. McQuaid, what do you think of married life?" he asked.

"Well, Mr. McQuaid, I think it's a lot like being rich." She rolled onto her stomach, propped her head on her palm, and regarded him with a twinkle in her eye. "For every problem it creates, it also creates an opportunity. The best way to get along in such a situation is to concentrate on the opportunities. And I have to say"—she rolled her eyes—"the kind of currency involved in marriage is a lot more interesting."

He laughed and shook his head as he reached for her, drawing her against his side and into his arms. "Who but you would think of marriage in such terms: 'the currency involved in marriage.' You sound like a real tycoon."

"Heaven forbid." She feigned horror. "Anything but a tycoon or a magnate or a shipping baron. Just plain heiress is bad enough."

"You bear the burdens of wealth and privilege well," he said dryly.

"When wealth becomes this large, it *is* a burden," she said, nuzzling her cheek against his chest and hearing his heartbeat in the brief silence.

"And so you decided simply to give it all away," he said, teasing her.

"Exactly," she responded.

In the next silence, Diamond marveled at the ease with which she'd just admitted her deepest, darkest secret. Everything seemed so easy with Bear, even confessions long in the making.

"Funny. I've never told anyone that before," she said quietly.

"What? That you—" He frowned, unsure of what he was hearing.

"Tried to give all my money away," she finished for him, unable to look up at him just now. "It all started when I was thirteen. My father had just died and Hardwell and Hannah came to take care of me. They were afraid I would grow up spoiled and vain, and so tried to instill in me a sense of responsibility toward others. I simply saw it as a chance to get rid of the money.

"The cursed stuff made my life miserable. I couldn't go to school, seldom got to play with other children, and at first they wouldn't even let me learn to ride for fear something would happen to me. I reasoned that if I gave the money away . . . I could have a normal life and do the things other children did."

"Clearly, your plan didn't work."

She nodded ruefully. "I gave away what I could, then after a while, I realized I could get rid of even more by investing in businesses. I began to make loans and buy impossible-sounding inventions and ideas. People heard of my 'generosity' and began to plague me every time I appeared in public. I ended up more limited than ever. Worse yet—several of my lunatic investments began to make money. Lots of money. In fact, the more I gave away, the more I seemed to make. I became known as the local soft touch." She looked up and found him staring at her with the strangest expression.

"You can't tell me you don't like giving money away," he charged. "I've seen you do it. You enjoy it."

"I admit that as I grew older I began to focus more on 'giving' than 'giving away.' I saw and liked the results of my donations and purchases. I saw the way people's lives and conditions changed and realized that my money could be a route to making life better for people. Progress. And I had the power to make Progress happen. After a while, my heart and my head finally caught up with my actions. I learned what it was to truly give."

After a moment, he touched her face and looked deep into her heart . . . then closed his eyes.

"You're a wonder, Diamond Wingate."

"Diamond Wingate *McQuaid*," she reminded him, with a playful jab in the ribs. "And I'm not a wonder . . . just a bit of a soft touch."

FIFTEEN

HANNAH HAD REFRESHMENTS waiting in the drawing room when they returned to the house, walking hand in hand, swinging the picnic basket, looking somewhat disheveled and thoroughly enchanted. Robbie, who had complained loudly about being barred from their picnic, came bounding in to see them and attack the cookies and finger sandwiches on the tea cart.

Bear watched him stuffing his mouth until his cheeks bulged and then climbing up onto the settee to sit cross-legged, dirty shoes and all. When he looked up and spotted Bear's narrowed eyes, Robbie froze. With the motion of one lone finger, Bear both ordered his feet down from the upholstery and warned him against another raid on the refreshments.

"Smart fellow," Bear said in a quiet voice. "Got to keep your feet off the furniture if you want to get along with the ladies." Then he winked.

Eager to stay on Bear's good side, Robbie posted himself beside his new cousin and watched and imitated every move Bear made. Diamond watched the pair for a time, thinking about that astonishing demonstration of power. Looking from Bear's magical index finger to her own, she wondered if the ability were bred in the bone or if a body could somehow learn to do it.

"Oh, I almost forgot, Bear," she said rising from the tea table and setting her cup on the tray. "I have something for you."

He watched her disappear through the doorway into the hall and return shortly with a ribbon-bound pasteboard box. When she held it out to him, he made no move to take it.

"What is this?" he asked, dread tensing his shoulders and mood.

"A gift." She thrust it closer to him and he recoiled. "A wedding gift." He seemed so shocked that she felt compelled to assure him: "It's commonly done between a bride and a groom."

A gift. A *wedding* gift. Coming from her lips, those words sank straight to the core of his conscience. His self-serving logic and the self-interest it was constructed on began a slow, mortifying crumble. Red crept up his neck and brightened his ears.

"I have everything I need."

Now, his conscience added. Since he had married the richest girl in Baltimore. Since he and Vassar had sat down five days ago and hammered out documents that would allow him to take three hundred thousand dollars on loan from the combined Wingate assets. Since Halt had left for Montana the following day with letters of credit and cash money orders that would allow him to close the deals for their right-of-way land.

"I'm fairly sure you don't have one of these," she said with a tentative smile. "Go on. Open it."

"I can't accept a gift from you, Diamond." He set the

box down on the seat beside him and rose to deposit his cup on the tea table. His hand shook.

"Don't be silly. This is something you'll like. Something you'll use. Something you need." Seeing that her words made no dent in his determination, she picked up the box and carried it to him at the table. Holding it out, she delivered an ultimatum. "I'm not going to sleep tonight until you open this."

"What makes you think I want you to sleep tonight?" he said, raising one eyebrow, hoping to divert her.

She blushed, just as he planned. But in truth, he was the one who felt embarrassed. How could he have known that she expected a gift from him? When he met her gaze for a moment, the anxiousness in her blue eyes struck him as oddly girlish. Standing there with her hair wind-teased and her cheeks glowing from an afternoon with him in the sun, she was the embodiment of every boyhood dream he'd ever harbored.

"I can't accept anything from you, Diamond."

"And why not?"

With his conscience groaning and his pride burning under Hardwell's and Hannah's eyes, he determined to be honest with her, at least in this.

"I had no idea you would expect to exchange gifts." His face began to blaze. "I didn't get you anything."

"Exchange? As in 'trade gifts'?" She smiled and wagged her head with exaggerated patience, and looked to Hardwell and Hannah for sympathy. They smiled back. "A real gift is given to enlarge the heart of the giver and to gladden the heart of the receiver, not because a gift is expected in return." She thrust the box against his chest. "Open it." When he didn't move, she added: "It's all right. Really. I give things to people all the time without expecting anything."

If those words were meant to reassure him, they failed

miserably. They merely reminded him of how she gave and gave to others and got nothing in return except the "satisfaction of giving." And he was forced to choose between denying her that lone satisfaction and refusing to take further advantage of her.

Then she looked up at him with her angel-blue eyes and he took the box from her and carried it to the tea table.

Inside the bows, pasteboard, and layers of tissue, he found a miniature railroad passenger car, painted black and green, with burgundy trim, complete with interior furnishings and external coupling equipment. It was perfectly authentic, down to the last bolt and rivet. Lifting it out, he held it up to the light. The glass of the windows glinted golden, like the gilt lettering on the side. Pullman. He swallowed hard, recognizing it. This was her little car—from the library.

"But this is yours." He frowned as he saw the expectation in her eyes turning to pleasure.

"Not anymore. I thought it would be the perfect gift for a railroad man. His own private railroad car." Her shrug had a self-conscious air about it. "I never use it. It just sits there in the roundhouse, collecting dust. And it can make your work in Montana so much more bearable . . . since you may have to work under difficult conditions." She paused, searching his turbulent expression. "Sometimes the difference between success and failure can be as simple as a good night's sleep."

"Wait a minute—you mean—" He looked between her and the miniature Pullman car in his hands, then at Hardwell and Hannah, who were beaming. "You mean this is—you're actually—"

"Giving you the Wingate private car, for you to take to Montana." She laughed. "You didn't think I meant for you to sleep in *that*, did you?" Feeling more assured, she drew closer and ran her fingers over the little car, brushing his in the process. "It's not big enough to hold anything but a few dreams."

The scent of her, the warmth of her tone, the incidental touch of her fingers . . . he was suddenly reeling from her presence and from the unthinkable generosity of it. She was giving him his own private Pullman car, velvet drapes, brass spittoons, and all. He felt his blood draining toward his knees.

"Diamond, I don't know what to say," he murmured, unable to take his eyes from that miniature representation of the massive turn of fortune he was experiencing.

"How about 'I like it'?" she prompted. "Or 'It's perfect.' "

"I do and it is," he said. He looked up to find her loveliness enhanced by her delight. He felt his throat constricting.

"Robert, I believe it's time for your chores in the stable," Hannah said.

"Oh, I got plenty o' time for—" He was staring raptly at the newlyweds, sensing something juicy was about to take place. "Hey!"

Hardwell had seized him by the ear and was ushering him toward the door. "Do as Hannah says, boy, and save yourself a night of bread and water."

Diamond and Bear were vaguely aware of the others' exit and of the closing of the great double doors behind them.

"I'm not very good at saying thanks," Bear confessed, grateful for the privacy. "I haven't had much practice."

"Me, either." She beamed up at him, her eyes glistening.

He touched her cheek and ran his hand down her neck, summoning words.

"Thank you, Diamond McQuaid."

"You're welcome, Bear McQuaid."

Desire erupted out of the core of him, setting his hands quaking. Afraid he might drop the little car, he set it on the table. Then he reached for her with both hands and a wide-open heart. From the moment their lips touched, there were no more thoughts of weddings and fortunes and marital duty. There were only Bear and Diamond. Man and woman. Lovers.

Minutes later they emerged from the drawing room, ruddy-faced and glowing, to announce that they were going down to the train yard to see Bear's gift. Bear suggested Hardwell and Hannah not wait dinner on them, saying that they might not be back in time, and as she climbed into the coach, Diamond gave Bear a puzzled frown.

"I had the car brought out and cleaned and prepared to move days ago. It's not that far to the siding in the train yard. We could make it back in time for dinner."

He rolled his eyes, then gave her the most deliciously wicked grin.

"It's a Pullman car, right?"

"Yes." She still didn't quite get the point.

"That means it has *beds*."

HARDWELL, HANNAH, AND Robbie had already retired when Diamond and Bear arrived home late that evening. She asked Jeffreys to bring them up a tray of food and a bottle of wine while they bathed. Neither of them wanted to think about the fact that these would be their last hours together for perhaps months to come.

Diamond bathed quickly and slipped into her dressing gown. She was just coming out of the bathing room when Jeffreys arrived with the linen-draped cart laden with savory cold dishes and breads, wine, and Cook's special pound cake with chocolate sauce. The efficient little butler set the table with linen and china, then lighted a candelabra and laid roses from the garden around the base of it.

"Thank you, Jeffreys," she said, her eyes sparkling at his thoughtfulness.

"My pleasure, miss . . . I mean, ma'am." Shaking his head at his mistake, he started to withdraw, but spotted a roll of paper sticking out from under the linen drape on the cart. "Oh, I nearly forgot, ma'am. Mr. McQuaid's papers. He left them here on the day Master Robert took ill . . . and they got stuck in the butler's pantry by mistake. He may—"

The door to the other bedroom opened and Bear stood in the opening, smiling. "There you are. And food—Jeffreys, you're a prince. I'm half starve—" His gaze fell on the roll of documents in the butler's hands and, after a moment's pause, he strode straight for them.

"My deepest apologies, sir," Jeffreys said, handing them over. "I thought you might need these on your trip. I'm afraid I had mislaid them. I hope it hasn't caused any—"

"No, no." Bear waved off the apology. "No harm done. Glad to have them back, though." He tucked them away on the window seat, then as the door clicked softly behind Jeffreys, he turned with a determined smile on his face. "You, my Diamond, look good enough to eat." He swept her up against him, whirled her around, and set her back on her feet in one fluid motion. "But right now I have to know what it is on this cart that smells like Virginia ham."

In the wee, dark hours of the morning, Diamond awakened to the feel of Bear's arm beneath her head, his chest at her back, and his legs molded against hers spoon fashion. She lay in that sweet cocoon for a time, hearing his breathing and feeling his pulse beating beneath her cheek. Their coming parting crept into her thoughts and soon every beat of his heart seemed to be like the clack of the train wheels that would soon carry him away from her.

How could he have, in so short a time, become so vital a part of her? A month ago she hadn't even known Barton McQuaid, and now she couldn't imagine how she would get through the next two or three months without him.

His smile made her feel as if the sun were rising inside her, illuminating every dark corner, dispelling every dark thought and dubious secret. In their short time together, he had come to know her better than anyone and to accept her complex and sometimes contradictory inner qualities. Early on, he had gathered both her secrets and passions into his keeping and guarded them well. He had kept her confidences and treated her failings with honesty and respect.

With each revelation, each encounter, he had challenged her to be stronger and more honest, had insisted she take control of her life and do the right thing. Yet, he didn't condemn her when she behaved in less than admirable ways. He seemed to know instinctively that the root of her greatest weakness was also the source of her greatest strength.

What a marvelous gift, she thought: to be known thoroughly and to still be valued and cherished. Who but Bear McQuaid—with his unflinching honesty combined with surprising compassion—could have opened the doors to her innermost self? Who but Bear McQuaid could have touched and changed the shape of her personal depths?

Gingerly, she moved his arm and peeled her skin from his to slide to the edge of the bed. With a tender smile, she studied the softened angles of his face, his boyishly tousled hair, and the vulnerability of his big, sprawled frame.

"I love you, Bear McQuaid," she whispered. "Hurry back to me."

The air from the open window was surprisingly cool as
she slipped from the bed. Shivering, she donned her dressing gown and went to close the window. As she perched
on one knee on the window seat, turning the handle, she
caught sight of the moon-brightened roll of papers that
Jeffreys had just returned to Bear, lying amongst the pillows at her knees.

Papers. What sort of papers would he have brought to
her house on the day Robbie came down with chicken
pox?

Lighting an oil lamp on the desk, so as not to disturb
Bear, she undid the cord binding and unrolled the dog-
eared documents. On top were several letters, then a stack
of ledger sheets filled with numbers and figures—clearly
financial reports. What claimed her attention was below
all of that: maps . . . several of them, each detailing different aspects of some location . . . slope, effective
drainage, and soil and bedrock composition. Below was a
map clearly marked "Montana Territory" . . . with Billings, Great Falls, Helena, the falls of the Missouri River,
and the routes of the Utah and Northern Railroad and
James Hill's Chicago Milwaukee and St. Paul highlighted
with ink. There also, sketched in red, was the route representing the two-hundred-plus miles of Bear's Montana
Central and Mountain Railroad.

Warmth rose in her as she traced that route with her
finger and realized from the discoloration of the paper
along that route, that she was not the first to do so. How
many times had Bear studied this map . . . run his fingers along that line, trying to read the future in it? Beginning just outside Great Falls and continuing south and
east . . . the Montana Central and Mountain was intended to connect Billings to the Chicago Milwaukee and
St. Paul.

She rolled aside that map and studied the next one

down . . . a detailed rendering of the MCM's route, which identified the former owners of the parcels of land he had purchased for right-of-way. Various ranch and individual names were penned along the route, and plat designations and legal descriptions were written off to the side. Finally she came to the huge, folded engineering map of the route, which detailed with concentric dotted lines the elevations they would encounter and with varying penciled patterns the soils and substrates present in each segment.

They had a few creeks and the headwaters of the Musselshell River to cross, but the route slipped between the Big Snowy and Little Belt Mountains. She felt a twinge of longing in her chest as she conjured images of snow-capped mountains in the distance . . . blue, blue sky . . . great rolling plains.

Coming out of her reverie, she realized Bear was stirring in the bed and began to replace and reroll the documents. But as he settled into a more comfortable position and continued to sleep, she felt relieved not to have to explain her snooping and stole a look at some of the documents themselves.

The sums of money on the balance sheets were considerable; every expense in railroad building had been anticipated and included. She smiled. She'd seen thousands of such lists in proposals people brought her for funding. It was interesting seeing them from another perspective. Then a letter caught her eye. It was from the territorial governor of Montana, supporting Bear's proposal and recommending him and his partner Halt Finnegan without reservation to possible lenders and investors.

Partner? She scowled. He had never mentioned a . . . She read the name again and thought it sounded oddly familiar. But where would she have heard his partner's name, when she didn't even know he had one?

There were other letters of support—also encouraging

investors to lend Barton McQuaid the required capital—along with confirmed orders for steel rail and equipment. The invoices were all marked: "to be paid upon delivery."

Something slowly knotted in her middle and she dropped the papers onto the stack and turned aside. She shouldn't be looking at this; it was none of her business. But her heart began to thud and she couldn't help stealing another look at those letters and invoices.

Strangely, there was nothing in the documents and papers to indicate who besides him was funding his railroad. No list of stockholders, no mention of loans or other financial agreements. This was merely a proposal. And a well-worn one from the looks of it.

Hurriedly, she tucked the letters and invoices back inside the maps and rolled them up, eager to get them out of her hands. When she had carried the roll to the window seat and tucked it back among the pillows, where she had found it, a faint sound from the bed caused her to start. It was only Bear shifting in his sleep again.

Uneasy now for no reason she was willing to admit, she climbed onto the window seat and pulled a pillow into her arms, hugging it for comfort. There was no sense dwelling on it. Or worrying. They were clearly *old* papers and maps. Everything must be finalized; Bear was heading for Montana to begin construction. He'd been working all week to make arrangements for materials and equipment. Nothing had changed. Everything was perfectly fine.

If only she could get her racing heart to agree.

THE HOUSEHOLD WAS in a flurry late the next morning as Diamond and Hannah prepared hampers of food and linens and a dozen other little necessities of civilized life for Bear's new home away from home. A stack of willow baskets, hampers, and trunks grew quickly in the front hall. While Diamond was making an inventory of it all, a clerk from Philip Vassar's bank arrived asking for Bear. Papers for signing, he announced apologetically. Mr. Vassar had to have them before Mr. McQuaid left for Montana.

"Papers?" Diamond reached for the leather folio herself, but the clerk gave her a strained smile and tucked them under his arm.

"If I might see *Mister* McQuaid, ma'am."

Annoyed, Diamond went personally to fetch Bear from the stables, where he was overseeing Robbie's chores and having a few "manly" words with him.

"*Mister* McQuaid," she said breathlessly. "Philip Vassar has sent someone with some papers for you."

He froze for a moment, then handed Robbie the bridle he was holding. His jaw set and his boot heels pounded into the gravel path on the way to the house. He made no attempt to explain. But when he spotted Vassar's clerk, he made a nearly convincing effort to relax and seem offhand.

"I had planned to stop by the bank on my way out of the city this evening," he said. "Just leave the papers with me and I'll look them over."

"Mr. Vassar thought you were leaving earlier and didn't want to miss you." When Bear reached for the folder, the clerk seemed uncomfortable. "Sorry, Mr. McQuaid, but these require signatures that have to be witnessed."

"All right. Fine." Bear nodded at him and then gave Diamond a perfunctory smile. "I'll have it done in two shakes." He glanced around, spotted the empty drawing room, and waved the courier toward it. When Diamond started in after them, he stopped her at the door with an emphatic smile. "I can take care of this, Diamond. Why don't you go ahead with"—he looked past her to the mound of things assembled in the entrance hall—"packing. Good Lord—that's enough supplies for me to open a dry-goods store." He waggled his brows, turned her around, and gave her bustle a pat.

Diamond had never been dismissed in her life. Wheedled, lectured, harangued, leered at, begged, and propositioned . . . but never *dismissed*. The tension and abrupt swings in Bear's mood and behavior confirmed her intuition that something wasn't right. When the drawing room doors thudded together, she whirled to look at them and felt the vague uneasiness she had lived with since last night become instantly focused.

He closed her out so he could sign a few papers?

When she sailed into the drawing room, he was just settling at the writing table near the windows, where the clerk was laying out an array of documents.

"Diamond?" He halted halfway into the seat and rose again, dismayed. As she approached, he stepped between her and the table.

She glanced up at his face, and she knew.

"What sort of papers do you have to sign?" she asked, fierce with control.

"Financial details. N-nothing you would be interest—" He halted and reddened around the ears as he realized how absurd that reasoning sounded.

"Financial 'details' have been my life," she said, feeling her blood withdrawing from her limbs, leaving them cold and heavy. Her stomach, now inundated, began to sink. "What makes you think I wouldn't be interested in whatever business dealings you have with Philip Vassar?" Those words carried a weight of foreboding. Philip Vassar was *her* banker.

"Nothing really. It's just that you're already busy and I have all of this under control."

She looked into his eyes and, after a second, his gaze fled hers. Steeling herself, she darted around him and picked up a set of the papers before the clerk could snatch them away.

"The Mercantile Bank of Baltimore," she read aloud, "acting as agent on behalf of the Wingate Companies enters into this agreement with the Montana Central and Mountain Railroad and its principal, Barton H. McQuaid . . ."

Blinking, not wanting to believe what she had just read, she read it again.

The Wingate Companies—her companies—were providing the funding for Bear's railroad. And the deal had been brokered and approved by Philip Vassar . . . her advisor, her banker. All without her knowledge or approval.

How could he . . . how could they possibly . . . without asking her? She looked up, remembering the comments made at the wedding. She was a married woman. They didn't have to have *her* approval. They had *her husband's.*

A cannonball blowing through the chest couldn't have stunned her any more. She couldn't exhale, couldn't move except to lower her eyes along that typewritten page filled with legal terms and definitions that set forth with dry precision a bone-deep betrayal of her trust. She managed to lift the page and uncovered at the top of the next sheet the amount he was taking from her companies: three hundred thousand dollars.

Dear heaven—it was a fortune! *Her* fortune.

The papers made a swooshing sound as they slipped from her hand, hit the desk, and scattered. She looked up, caught in a maelstrom of conflicting images and memories, seeing their unusual history in an ugly new light. Bear roaring at her during their first meeting, then becoming the gentleman when he learned who she was; Bear worming his way into Robbie's confidence with his stories; Bear conveniently rescuing her . . . carrying her when she fainted, lecturing her, kissing her, keeping her shameful secrets, and then stepping in to save her from three grasping fiancés. The more she recalled, the worse it seemed. The evidence was irrefutable. Bear had gone through the motions of marriage vows with her . . . used his considerable carnal skill to lure her to put her trust in him . . . pretended to treat her with care and tenderness . . . even refused the wedding gift she offered him . . . all the while planning and maneuvering to finance his railroad with her affections.

"Did you think I wouldn't find out?" she asked, her voice choked. "Or did you expect that by the time I learned of this, you'd have your precious railroad and it wouldn't matter?"

"If you'll let me explain—"

"Explain?" she said, trembling all the way to her knees, feeling as if she'd been broadsided by a Baldwin Ten Wheeler. "I believe those papers say it all, McQuaid. You needed money for your railroad and you were clever enough to marry yourself a fortune. A bank account with a bustle. A damned *soft touch*." She started for the door, but he grabbed her by the arm and held her.

"I meant to talk to you—to make you a businesslike proposal—"

"When?" she demanded bitterly, refusing to look at him. "Before or after your lecture on how my fiancés would steal me blind?" Tears welled, burning her eyes. "Before or after you 'rescued' me and then demanded that I marry you in payment? Before or after you made certain I couldn't say the word 'no'?"

Pain-spurred anger billowed beneath her shock, bringing with it a surge of energy. She managed to jerk her arm from his grip and headed for the door.

"Diamond—" He recovered in time to make it to the doorway ahead of her and plant himself in her way. "Look,

I was an idiot and a coward for not facing you with it," he said, blanching as if the admission were ground from his very bones. "But I'm not a thief. If you'll just listen to—"

She looked up with her eyes blazing and tears burning down her cheeks and he stopped dead.

"Don't you have some papers to sign?" she said, her voice raw with pain.

Scorched, he released her.

As she reached the center of the hall, she shouted for Hannah, Hardwell, and Jeffreys. Within seconds, her lady guardian and butler were rushing down the stairs and in from the front portico in a frantic state.

"Have Ned bring the coach around *now*. And help him load this mess into it," she ordered furiously, swiping tears from her red-streaked cheeks. "Bring a wagon around, too, if you have to—I want all of this out of here—as soon as possible. Hannah"—she turned to the startled elder lady—"please . . . would you clear McQuaid's things out of the master suite?" She halted and stiffened, struggling to keep from breaking down. "Be sure to get everything. I don't want *anything* of his left behind."

"Just what in blazes do you think you're doing?" Bear demanded, towering like a thundercloud in the doorway behind her.

"Helping you leave. That was what you were planning to do, wasn't it? Leave?" She started for the library, but he intercepted her at the stairs.

"We have to talk, Diamond." Seared pride filled his voice with compelling smoke. "I know this must seem low-down and conniving, but I swear, I never meant it to be. I never wanted to take anything from you. I'm going to pay back every penny. This is a business loan, pure and simple."

"There is nothing pure *or* simple about what you have done, Barton McQuaid," she said, swallowing back the sob rising in her throat. "I want you out of my house and out of my life." She wrenched free and stabbed a finger toward the front doors. "Go back to your precious Montana and build your damned railroad . . . if there is such a thing as the Montana Central and Mountain. Go!" She poured her pain and anger into one final command before she stalked into the library. *"And don't come back."*

Hardwell came running from the morning room just in time to see Diamond storm into the library and slam the door with enough force to rattle the walls three floors up.

Bear looked around and found Hannah, Hardwell, Jeffreys, Mrs. Cullen, and several parlor maids staring at him in alarm. Into that charged scene bounded Robbie, his face ruddy and his eyes alight and searching.

"What happened?" he asked with his usual artlessness. "Somebody die or somethin'?"

Jolted from his shock, Bear barreled down the hall to the library and banged on the door with his fist. "Come out of there, Diamond. Let's discuss this . . . at least listen to me." There was no response, so he banged again. Harder. "Open up, dammit!" he shouted. "You can't stay in there forever!"

But the silence on the other side of the door said she intended to give it a try. He stalked back to the dumb-founded Jeffreys.

"Get me a hammer and a steel chisel." When the butler hesitated, Bear specified: *"Now!"*

Minutes later, everything was in tumult. Bear was taking a hammer and cold chisel to the hinges of the library door; Hannah was clearing out the master suite while wringing her hands; Hardwell was trying in vain to catch Robbie and haul him to his room; and Jeffreys and the servants were scurrying to pack the coach while craning necks and straining to catch a glimpse of what was happening between the newlyweds.

Then the last hinge was yanked out and tossed aside. Bear half lifted, half dragged the massive oak door from the opening and slammed it against the wall.

"Have you gone mad? Tearing the house apart?" Diamond was standing in the middle of the room, her arms clamped around her waist as if she were holding herself together. Her eyes were red and her chest was heaving with spasms left by dying sobs.

Bear had never felt such volcanic fury, despair, or guilt in his entire life—much less all in the same moment. Half an hour ago he had had everything he had ever wanted and more: the money, material, and equipment to build his railroad . . . his own private railroad car . . . a beautiful and loving wife to come home to when his railroad was done. But now, seeing her standing there with her heart breaking . . . believing that none of what he had said to her or done with her was real . . . that he had used and was now discarding her . . . he felt as naked and resourceless as he had at sixteen when he was banished from the only home he'd ever known.

She had trusted him . . . taken him into her home and her bed and her well-guarded heart. In these last three days he had managed to penetrate her defenses enough to glimpse the passionate, loving woman at the core of her. He had seen her, known her, as no one else ever had. It didn't matter that he hadn't intended her harm . . . that he had honestly believed he was helping her as well as himself. *She* didn't believe any of that. Hell—she didn't even believe he was building a railroad! If he walked out that door and stepped onto that train by himself, she would never believe it.

He stared at her beautiful Montana-sky eyes, now reddened and filled with pain. He saw her chin quiver and dropped his gaze. It fell on something near her feet. There, on the Persian carpet, lay the little green and gold Pullman car . . . the one she had given to him as a wedding gift. One corner was crumpled and the top had broken open, spilling the miniature contents across the rug.

He closed his eyes, and when he opened them again, it was to one simple and desperate possibility.

"So, you think I gulled you into marriage just to do you out of some money," he declared hoarsely. "You don't believe there is a Montana Central and Mountain Railroad. Fine. Then you'll have to come with me to Montana and watch me build it." He moved toward her. "Get your things."

"I'll do no such thing." She stiffened and stepped backward.

"You're coming with me, even if I have to carry you kicking and screaming." He advanced again. "Now get your things."

Anger boiled up inside her. He wasn't content to just take her fortune and play her for forty kinds of a fool—he had to personally control and humiliate her. For the first time in years, she used the word she had worked diligently to cull from both her life and lexicon.

"*No.*"

All movement stopped in the hall. A murmur went through the servants at that monumental occurrence, and Hardwell and Hannah stared in shock at one another, wondering if they had heard correctly. She repeated it.

"*No.* I'm not going anywhere. *Non,* nay, *nein,* and just plain *NO!*" He just stared at her, and she snapped, "Are you having trouble with the concept?"

Of all the damned times for her to begin saying no! The lines were drawn in the sand and there was nothing for him to do but to enforce his manly edict.

"I said, I'm going to prove to you that I'm not a thief, a huckster, or a common crook. Get your things. You're coming with me."

"No." She huddled back, her resolve growing and hardening with each repetition. It was getting easier for her to say no; he had no time to waste.

On impulse he lunged forward, planted his shoulder in her midsection, and hoisted her up onto his shoulder. She screeched and flailed for balance and began a tirade composed of one word.

"No-no-no-no-no-no-no-no-nooooooo!"

He headed with her for the front doors and managed to trundle her outside, despite her kicking and pounding on his back and grabbing the door frame as they passed. Desperately, she called to Hardwell, Hannah, and even Jeffreys—none of whom were equipped to challenge the towering Westerner's actions. In mounting panic, she called to Robbie to go for help.

Instead, her young charge came running after them, yelling, "Can I come, too, Bear? Let me come, too!"

"Some time out West might do you a world of good," Bear said vehemently. "What do you say, Diamond?" He halted at the carriage door and gave her upturned rear a resounding swat. "Shall we take him with us?"

"Nooooo!"

Bear glanced at the boy with a fierce grin.

"Climb aboard."

SIXTEEN

LOCKED IN THE small but lavishly appointed "necessarium" of what was once her own private railroad car, Diamond pounded on the door until her hands were sore and demanded release in every language known to her.

"If I let you out, will you behave like a reasonable person?" Bear called through the thick mahogany door panels.

"No!"

When they were under way, he tried again. "Ready to cooperate, yet?"

"No!"

"Aren't you getting a bit warm in there?" he asked still later.

"No!" She opened her blouse, raised her skirts, removed her petticoats, and rolled down her stockings. She'd rather cook than capitulate.

"How about some food? Hungry?" he called to her later.

"No!" She wrapped her arms tightly around her growling middle.

Late in the afternoon he was back again. "We just bought some lemonade at the last stop. Aren't you thirsty?"

"No."

Neither did she want a chair, a blanket, a pillow, or any supper. And no, she *still* wouldn't promise not to try to escape and return to Gracemont if he let her out.

After dinner the quiet settled in and for the rest of the day all she could hear was the clank of cars coupling, the monotonous clack of wheels against the rails, and the occasional screech of brakes as they slowed for stations.

The necessary was large enough to permit her to pace a step or two, had a small window high on the outside wall for ventilation, and was supplied with fresh water in the form of an ornate brass and copper cistern hanging in one corner. But the only places to sit were the stool and the floor, and the only thing to do was listen to the world going by as she counted the *fleur de lis* on the wallpaper. Seven hundred thirty-two. She counted them six times.

As night fell, she piled her petticoats on the tiled floor and propped herself in the corner, too exhausted even to cry. Her last glimpse of herself in the small mirror over the washbasin had revealed that her eyes were swollen, she had lost half of her hairpins, and her skin was red from the brine of her tears.

Why was he doing this? He already had a small fortune in hand, and he could plunder a good many more of her assets before she could get the wretched law courts to move against him. What was the point of hauling her out to Montana against her will? What more did he want from her?

BEAR SAT IN the elegant central parlor of the private car, the next morning, staring at the door to the necessary. Despite the full-sized brass bed in the sleeping compartment, despite the damask sheets and down pillows and the lulling sway of the car, he had hardly slept a wink in the night just past. More than once he had gone to the door, put his hand on the key, and stopped just short of opening it. His dread of now having to face her must have shown in his face, for Robbie looked over from his seat by the windows and shook his head.

"Just open the danged door. You'll have to sooner or later."

"I will." Bear shrugged off his uneasiness. "I was just waiting until we reached a stretch where we wouldn't be stopping any time soon." She'd never try to jump from a moving train, he told himself, hoping he was right.

When he went to the door and turned the key in the lock, nothing happened. A full minute later, he opened the door himself.

She was standing on the pile of her petticoats with her skirt raised and tucked into her waist and her stockings rolled down around her ankles. Her hair was a shambles, her face was blotchy, and her eyes were slightly puffy. But she radiated a dignity and resolve that defied all suggestion of surrender. Without uttering a word, she untucked and lowered her skirts and stepped past him into the comparative freedom of the parlor.

"Where are we?" she asked as she paused by Robbie's plush upholstered chair and looked over his shoulder out the window. They were passing through hilly, mostly wooded terrain, punctuated by occasional sharp valleys containing modest farmsteads.

"Nearing Pittsburgh . . . headed for Chicago," Bear said when Robbie looked to him for the answer. "Still on B and O track. Are you hungry?"

"No."

He expelled a patient breath. "Then I think we should talk."

"No."

She spotted the door to the sleeping compartment at

the rear of the car and headed for it. He followed her in and she flattened back against the wall in the narrow compartment, glaring at him.

"Look, I know that you're angry and not thinking straight," he declared, realizing what a poor choice of words that was the instant it was out of his mouth. "You have no money and no baggage, and you're too far away from Baltimore now to get home without either of those. So you may as well settle in and make up your mind to cooperate."

She studied him briefly and then responded with determination.

"No."

Taking no chances that she would escape and somehow talk her way onto the next eastbound headed to Baltimore, Bear locked the car as he left it at the siding in Pittsburgh later that morning. He said he had to check on the allotment of rails and the construction crane they were taking on and to check on a second dormitory car he had learned was for sale here. Robbie begged to go with him and Bear allowed it, leaving Diamond to suffer through three hours of the clangs and jolts from coupling cars and the growing midday heat by herself.

By the time they returned, she had washed up and brushed her hair and made herself reasonably presentable. She had also explored the papers littering the desk in the office area of the car and spent some time poring over the financial agreements Bear had signed with her companies. For providing the capital to build, Wingate received a one-third share of stock and profits as well as title to one-third of the land granted to the MCM by the government.

She was loath to admit it, but it seemed a fair and potentially profitable arrangement for Wingate—provided there really was a railroad called the Montana Central and Mountain—and that it actually issued stock, made profits, and received federal land grants—all of which she seriously doubted.

When they returned late that afternoon, Robbie was full of the sights and sounds of the train yard, roundhouse, and switching station. He eagerly described two tall dormitory cars, a string of flatcars filled with steel rail, and three boxcars filled with tools and equipment.

"And that crane—you should see it, Diamond. It's tall as a house an' has big ol' pulleys an' steel gears—Bear says he'll let me sit in the driver's seat sometime." His face glowed with excitement.

"I wouldn't get my hopes up, Robbie," she said, keenly aware Bear was watching her reaction. "There may be a crane in the train yard, but that doesn't mean it belongs to McQuaid or that it's coming with us. And judging by my experience, McQuaid doesn't usually let anyone but himself sit in a driver's seat."

"No, Diamond, honest . . . it's Bear's . . . I swear," Robbie said earnestly. "I heard him tell th' switcher to shunt it over here."

"That's low, McQuaid," she said, rising irritably to face him. "Using me, taking me for a fortune, is one thing . . . but using my ten-year-old cousin to vouchsafe your stories is intolerable." She turned to her cousin. "Robbie, from now on, we'll occupy you with lessons . . . starting tomorrow."

When the door to the sleeping compartment slammed behind her, Robbie looked at Bear with horror dawning. "She's gonna make me do *lessons*. Ya got to do something."

"Any suggestions?" Bear said irritably.

Robbie scratched his head and thought for a moment, searching back through his vast experience in observing man-woman relationships.

"Buy 'er somethin.' " he declared. "That usu'lly works."

By the time they reached the main rail yard on the

south side of Chicago, Bear was desperate enough to take Robbie's suggestion and try a bit of bribery.

"Diamond," he addressed her after breakfast that morning, "I have a number of things to do here, and we won't be leaving until tomorrow evening. If you promise that you won't—"

"No." She rose and began stacking the dishes into the basket they came in.

"But you haven't heard my proposal," he said, scowling.

"I don't need to hear it to know that the answer is *no*."

"So you don't want to go shopping for some clothing, then," he declared, rising and throwing his napkin onto the table. "Stupid me . . . I could have sworn you'd be sick of wearing the same things for three straight days. Or maybe it takes you a while longer to 'ripen' . . . say, the seven more days it will take us to get to Montana."

He stalked out the door, telling himself that that was what he got for taking marital advice from a ten-year-old.

Diamond stood with her face burning, watching the glass rattle in the door he slammed, realizing that she had just doomed herself to wearing these same wretched clothes for at least the next week. Her annoyance soon mellowed into surprise that he would think of such a thing . . . buying clothing for her.

The hope that gesture stirred in her was painful in the extreme. It took some time for her to quell it and convince herself that whatever concessions he made toward her didn't change the kind of man he was or the facts of what he had done. He still had lied to her at every turn, married her to finance his mythical railroad, taken advantage of her deepest feelings, and taken her from her home against her will. She'd be an idiot to fall for his cozening a second time.

"I've found a book we can use to begin your lessons," she informed her cousin, causing him to freeze with one leg out the small sleeping-compartment window. *"The Geography of North America."*

"Jesus H. Christ."

"You're going to recite sums and multiplication tables, young man"—she snatched him by the ear and dragged him out of that opening—"until you forget all about giving Jesus a middle name."

When Bear returned, some time later, things were tense in the extreme. Overriding her objection, he ordered Robbie to accompany him as he paid a call on the station-master and transacted some business. She was clearly furious, but instead of railing at him, she folded her arms and sat down forcefully, refusing to look at him. For some reason, that was more disturbing than if she had yelled or belted him one. He was so agitated when he shoved Robbie out the door and exited himself, that he forgot to lock the outer door of the car.

It took a few moments for Diamond's thoughts to clear and register that she hadn't heard the click of a key. Watching the pair disappear across the tracks toward the main platform and station house, she quickly tried the door, hurried down the steps, and struck off for the station platform herself.

The sun shone through a thin gray haze created by the collection of large, coal-burning engines staying warm while loading and unloading. It felt wonderful to be out in the open, even if the air did have an acrid, oil-and-metal tang . . . even if she did look like a drudge . . . and even if she soon was being jostled by passengers, freight haulers, and porters, and half deafened by conductors shouting out boarding calls. Above it all, she could hear the shouts of hotel hawkers and food vendors and the intermittent shrieks of train whistles. After two days of strained quiet, the noise of station life was music to her ears.

When she reached the far end of the wooden siding outside the station, she stood looking down at the cinder-laden tracks that led east.

Pittsburgh was a long way from Baltimore. Assuming she could inveigle tickets home for herself and Robbie, what would she do once she was there? Her directors had been all too pleased to turn over control to her husband; they'd probably be no help in her bid to reclaim control of her fortune. And if she called her lawyers together and demanded they sue for an annulment? Social suicide. Everyone was shocked by her hasty nuptials as it was. To have to go back and admit that she had made a terrible mistake . . .

Then there was the house itself, empty of pride and pleasure and joy and purpose . . . at the same time, perversely full of memories. She would have long years ahead to regret whatever hasty decision she might make now.

As she stood contemplating her course, she looked up and across the open tracks. There, some distance behind her distinctive green and burgundy private Pullman—on the same track—were two double-story wooden cars with small windows inset at irregular intervals in two rows along the sides. A face appeared briefly at one of the windows and she realized with a start that those two cars must be the dormitories that Robbie had described with such enthusiasm. She felt a twinge of guilt for having been so adamant in negating both his news and his excitement.

While she was concluding that the cars needed painting, her eye strayed to the string of flatbed cars coupled just ahead of them. There were at least a dozen cars heavily loaded . . . with steel rail. At the head of the train, almost out of sight—behind the engine and tender, but ahead of their private car—sat a construction crane with its huge arm fitted with pulleys and a massive metal bucket. The sort of construction Bear had once described to her would certainly require that sort of heavy equipment. Her heart began to pound.

Then she noticed some lettering on one of the boxcars near the end of the train. Squinting, she made out the letters *M, C,* and *M.* The full impact of all she was seeing struck her like a hammer hitting an anvil. This was the Montana Central and Mountain in the making. He really was building a railroad!

She looked at the empty eastbound track, then back at the Montana-bound train carrying a future railroad on its back.

"God help me," she muttered, meaning it as a prayer, and headed for the steps at the end of the platform. She darted across the empty tracks to investigate and came first to one of the dormitory cars. It was empty except for the scent of stale sweat and tobacco and two burly hardbitten fellows lolling on the bunks.

"Whadda *you* want?" one demanded, popping up and staring at her.

"I'm Diamond Wingate . . . McQuaid. Just making sure everything is . . . suitable."

She could feel their heated gazes on her as she made her way down the center aisle and out the door. Relieved to be out in the open again, she settled for a peek into the other dormitory. Between the two cars, there was space here for forty or fifty men.

Next, she investigated the steel on the flatbed cars. Standard gauge. Probably "ninety pound" . . . heavy enough to ship cattle, wheat, or even coal over. She couldn't resist climbing up onto one of the cars and running her hand over the sun-warmed metal. It was oddly reassuring. She had heard endless talleys of rail laid during B&O stockholder meetings, but she had never truly understood what creating those numbers involved. Until now. A kernel of excitement opened deep inside her.

When she finally reached the crane, she climbed up the steps and tried the door to the enclosed metal platform overlooking the boom of the crane and the balancing weight. Inside, she found massive levers in the center of the floor connected to gears, chains, and cables clearly visible through the floor grating. Behind her was the boiler that provided the power to run the crane and in the center was one leather-covered metal seat. The driver's seat. As she stood looking out over the crane, she felt some of her anger melting away.

Here was incontrovertible proof that the Montana Central and Mountain was real somewhere besides on paper. The solidity of those oiled steel rails . . . the dormitory cars . . . the power sleeping in that giant of a crane . . .

"Miss Wingate!"

The sound of her name startled her and she looked down to find a long, lanky fellow in a disheveled suit climbing up the steps. When he looked up, she spotted a pair of spectacles on his nose and a moment later recalled where she had seen him before. She closed her eyes. *The moving-steps man.* Good Lord—a thousand miles from Baltimore, he was still pursuing her!

"No, no—don't come up!" she called, heading for the ladderlike steps. "I'll come down!"

He backed down the steps and stood on the ground by the tracks, waiting for her with a faintly hopeful expression. The instant her feet touched the gravel he was hovering over her.

"Why, Mr.—"

"Ellsworth—Nigel Ellsworth," he said, righting his battered spectacles, which promptly slid askew again. "Do you remember me, Miss Wingate? My invention—my—"

"Moving steps," she said, looking around for help. "Of course. But I must tell you, I am no longer in a position to fund proposals such as yours."

"Oh." He smiled ruefully. "That's all right. I'm out of the inventing business. It didn't pay enough to keep body and soul together, so I've gone back to my former profession."

"You did? And what profession was that?"

"He's an engineer," came Bear's voice from over her shoulder. She turned and found him and Robbie hurrying up the siding toward her.

"You're a train engineer?" she said, frowning. Ellsworth was lean to the point of being gaunt and had an aesthetic, "bookish" air. She had never seen anyone who looked less like a locomotive driver.

"No, a construction engineer," Bear said. "He doesn't drive trains, he builds tracks." He clamped a possessive hand on her elbow. "I've hired him to work on the Montana Central and Mountain. He used to work for the B and O."

"You did?" she said, trying to wrest her arm from Bear's grip.

"Well, yes, actually—" Ellsworth said, reddening.

"We'd better get back to the coach," Bear said sharply, refusing to release her. "I have work to do yet this afternoon and I've arranged for some dinner."

By the time they reached their car, Diamond couldn't keep silent another minute. "Have you gone mad?" She faced him in the middle of the parlor, her hands on her waist. "Hiring that poor demented fellow as your engineer?"

"He's been around trains—he helped the B and O lay track," Bear said, caught off guard by having to defend his business decisions. "Besides . . . the surveying is finished and the route is already platted out . . . most of the real engineering is already done." When she still stared at him he put his hands on his waist, unintentionally mim-

icking her posture. "The poor wretch was so down and out
. . . he needed a job . . . and when he asked . . ."

"Don't tell me. Let me guess," she said, narrowing her
eyes. "You just couldn't say no."

He reddened . . . ears first, then face.

It was at that moment that she knew no matter how
deep the wound of his betrayal or how many tears he had
caused her to shed . . . she was still in love with Bear
McQuaid. And probably always would be.

AFTER THE DINNER dishes were cleared away, Bear
announced that he would be back in a few hours and
Robbie popped up to accompany him. He stood for a moment, fingering the key, then suggested that Robbie stay
with Diamond.

"Now that *is* insulting. A ten-year-old jailer," she said,
folding her arms. "If I had wanted to escape, you know, I
would be well down the tracks by now."

"But you aren't. You're still here." Bear studied her as if
he were trying to figure out why.

"I have an investment to protect," she declared. "I intend to see the building of the Montana Central and
Mountain with my own two eyes."

He shifted from one foot to the other, realizing that she
was laying down a challenge. His future with her depended on him proving himself . . . on him building the
railroad that had brought them together and then had torn
them apart. Bringing her, even against her will, had been
the right thing to do. The deepest tension inside him
eased. When she saw the last bit of track go into place,
when she saw the first run and understood that he was a
man of his word, she would have to believe him.

"I have to get back to work."

He grabbed his hat off the rack beside the door and

ducked outside. When he reached the ground and struck off down the tracks, he heard the door open behind him and looked back. Diamond, wearing the figured tablecloth as a shawl, and Robbie were hurrying down the steps.

"Where do you think you're going?"

"To watch you do business," she said, bustling toward him. "If I'm going to go bankrupt, I intend to see it happening firsthand."

Muttering, Bear turned on his heel and left her and Robbie to follow him across several tracks to a siding that didn't see frequent use. The rails were rusty and the wooden shacks nearby looked hastily assembled. Small groups of disheveled-looking men were standing around smoking and talking. They silenced as Bear approached and then settled curious looks on Diamond.

Bear climbed up on an overturned crate and announced: "I've got work and plenty of it. A fair day's wage for a fair day's work. Bonus pay if you stay till the job is done."

"Yeah?" someone called as a number of the men came over to stand before him. "Where is this work?"

"Montana. We'll be laying over two hundred miles of track . . . the new Montana Central and Mountain." The mutters and comments were far from positive. "The steel lies right over there—on that string of flatcars," he continued. "You can see the top of the crane from here. And if you sign on now, you'll get first choice of the bunks—two cars' worth of them." Enthusiasm was still low.

"You gonna charge for the ride out there?" someone in the group asked.

"You must've worked on the B and O." Bear gave a short laugh. "No charge. Transportation is provided . . . on that very train."

"What about food? You got a cook? Or do we have to buy local?"

Clearly, these were men who had laid track before and knew the pitfalls of working this sort of job. Violent strikes had rocked Baltimore's railroads a few years back, over just such issues: requirements that workers shop at company stores and eat at company-owned dining halls, requirements that workers pay for their own tickets to return home after working outbound runs. Some workers were lucky to be able to bring any money at all home to their families.

Bear paused, thinking, then declared: "We got a cook. And a kitchen. We'll have all the food you need . . . first plate free."

"Oh, yeah?" The skeptic pointed at Diamond. "That yer cook, over there?"

A tense moment followed, in which she watched Bear struggle with temptation. She kept silent, wondering just how desperate or greedy he truly was. Would she be "the cook" if it suited his purpose?

"No." He looked intently at her as if sensing her thoughts. "That, gentlemen, is Mrs. McQuaid, my wife."

Everywhere Bear went recruiting men that afternoon, he had similar problems. Despite his offer of a decent wage and transportation, many of the men were wary to sign on without proof of Bear's claim that food and lodging would be provided.

"Well, just get a kitchen, then," Robbie suggested as they walked along.

"I can't afford a kitchen," he said, glowering.

Then Diamond, who had been awaiting an opportunity, spoke up.

"Of course, I'm just a *former* owner and a mere woman . . . but it seems to me, you can't afford not to have one . . . unless, of course, you've built time into your schedule for your workers to go out each morning and hunt prairie chickens for breakfast."

He studied the light in her eyes, then turned his glare on Robbie.

"I think I liked it better when all she said was no."

That afternoon another car was added to the row of cars headed for Montana: a kitchen car, complete with stoves, pots, griddles, and utensils. As soon as it was coupled onto the other cars, Bear stalked over to that first makeshift camp, grabbed the head scoffer by the collar, and dragged him over to see it. With such direct persuasion, the fellow signed up on the spot, and soon half a dozen others had joined him.

By the time they pulled out of the station the next afternoon, they had filled one dormitory and part of the next. At every stop, Bear made his pitch and hired one or two additional workers. When they reached Milwaukee, he located and hired a cook and heaved a sigh of relief.

Diamond watched him recruiting workers, making promises, and sharing his dream with these men, and recalled the way she herself had been swept up by his conviction and desire to be a part of Progress. With each recruiting talk she witnessed, she found it a bit harder to maintain her cynicism about his motives.

He not only wanted to build this railroad, she had to admit, he was passionate about it. It was the most important thing in the world to him, more important than, say, telling the truth to her. The thought produced a twinge of pain in her chest. It was thin comfort to learn that, although his integrity didn't extend to his relationship with her, he did at least have some.

By the time they stopped in Wisconsin to take on cars loaded with lumber and began to inch toward St. Paul, Diamond was heartily regretting her stubbornness over the clothing in Chicago. Washing each morning in a small basin and wringing out her smalls and stockings each night were just not sufficient. When she broached the prickly subject, couching her interest in shopping in terms of Robbie's need for clothing, Bear's knowing look rasped her still-tender pride.

"So, are you saying you made a mistake back in Chicago?" he asked.

"No."

"But you say now that you need clothes . . . so it's really the same thing."

"No, it is not."

"Oh, then you stick by your claim that you don't need clothes." He smiled as she struggled silently with his conclusion. "Fine. Then I'll just take Robbie into town and get him a few things." As he donned his hat and started out the door, he looked back at her red face and clenched fists and smiled. "Want to come?"

"No!"

That evening, after they returned from a trackside restaurant, Bear winked at Robbie and sent him out to "check on the crane." Then he carried his cup of coffee to the settee and watched Diamond settle into a chair with the lap desk over her knees to write Hannah and Hardwell a letter. As she inked her pen and began to write, he cleared his throat.

"Are you still angry with me?" he asked.

"Why should I be angry?" she said, refusing to look up. "Other than the fact that I was tricked into marriage by a man who only wanted my money and within two days was already looting my assets. A man who then abducted me from my home and hauled me halfway across the country locked in a privy—"

"It wasn't my fault you slept in the necessary that first night," he said.

"A man who is too arrogant or too stingy and cheap to allow me to buy a change of clothes," she continued irritably, "unless I abase myself before him."

"Ouch." He sat up straight. "You think I'm cheap and stingy?"

"If the shoe fits . . ."

He rose, headed out the door, and a moment later returned.

"Well, then, I suppose I should take back these boots. Cheap, stingy bastards don't buy top-quality boots. Or French linen underclothes. Or belts with silver buckles. Or lady hats with egret feathers . . ."

When she looked up, he was standing not far away with his arms piled high with packages and boots and a hatbox and a number of garments draped over his shoulders. She set the desk aside and rose staring at the things and clasping her hands together tightly to hide their sudden trembling.

"For me?" she asked, her throat tight.

"Well, I doubt I'd ever get my big feet into these." He thrust the sleek black boots into her hands. "And I'd look downright silly in this headgear." He flipped open the top of the hatbox with his nose and managed to pull out a black broad-brimmed hat. It was a feminized, stylish version of the one he generally wore. And there was indeed a small white egret feather stuck in the band.

She couldn't help smiling, no matter how much she would probably regret it. She would just have to worry some other time about this thrilling lightness in her chest.

"If they don't fit," he said with a hint of uncertainty, "we'll just have to fatten you up or starve you down until they do. We have to pull out at first light tomorrow, and we'll be high-ballin' it all the way to Great Fa—"

A rumble and ringing metallic crash burst through the car, shaking walls and floor and windows to the breaking point. When the quaking stopped Bear wheeled, dumping the clothes on the floor, and bolted outside.

"What's happened?" Diamond called, rushing after him.

In the lowering evening light, they could see tons of steel rail lying like scattered pickup sticks on the ground. A glance at the car they had fallen from told the story; the supports on one of the flatcars were dangling . . . seemingly had given way. Bear rushed to survey the damage, then planted himself on top of the fallen rails as the men came pouring out of the dormitories.

"Anybody get in the way of this? Anybody hurt?" he demanded.

There seemed to be no injuries, until one grizzled-looking old railroader came forward with: "The kid's shook up a bit." He was ushering a limping, wide-eyed Robbie forward.

"Robbie!" Diamond flew to him and dropped to her knees. "Where are you hurt? What happened—what were you doing out here?"

"Just knocked me down, is all," Robbie said, still winded and gasping for breath. "Hit my arm . . ." When asked to do so, he could move it and, though it was sore, it didn't seem broken. Bear turned to the men gathered around.

"Anybody see what happened?" He looked from face to face. "Anybody see anything?" After a fruitless wait, he expelled a heavy breath. "All right. We got work to do if we're pulling out at first light." He glanced at Diamond. "Can you get him back inside?" When she nodded and moved Robbie toward their car, he turned to his men. "The rest of you . . . it looks like your work starts early. Get some ropes out of the equipment car to haul these rails back up and secure them."

It was some time before Bear returned to the car. Diamond had tucked Robbie into the big bed in the sleeping compartment, so that she could check on him during the night, and was sitting at the table.

"Is everything all right?" she asked, seeing the rust and

grease on his shirt and the grim look on his face. He nodded.

"Checked all the lashings and supports on the other
cars. They seem to be okay. Robbie?" he asked, sinking
into a chair.

"Nothing is broken. He'll be fine." She rose and came
near his chair. "Would you like something to drink?"

Preoccupied, he shook his head. "I'll get it. Go on to
bed."

As she lay on the bed beside Robbie, wearing her new
cotton nightdress and staring up at the moon shadows
dancing on the decorative tin ceiling, she listened to Bear
moving around in the parlor of the car and didn't know
which bothered her most, the fact that he was worried
about something or that he didn't think enough of her to
tell her why.

SEVENTEEN

IT WAS CLEAR, as Diamond looked out the windows of the train, that they weren't in the civilized East anymore. The dense white pine forests of Wisconsin and oaks of eastern Minnesota gave way to short-grass prairie that seemed to roll on to eternity, unbroken except for the occasional tops of trees jutting up from dry creek beds and clustered along muddy, meandering rivers. And as they pushed farther west, the land grew even more forbidding, studded with rocky buttes, wind-carved escarpments, and deep ravines.

But the terrain was not all that was changing.

Beginning with their last night in St. Paul, Bear had begun to "walk" the cars regularly, climbing up the ladders and over roofs and cargoes, traveling the length of the train and back. Diamond watched in horror as he jumped between platforms or bounded from a ladder up onto the roof of a car, and wondered if he were that desperate to escape her and the tension that sometimes crackled like static electricity between them. When she saw Robbie raptly watching Bear's acrobatics, she dragged him away from the window and declared that if he ever tried something like that and survived, she would happily strangle him afterward.

By the time they reached the Dakotas she discovered that several men bearing rifles had quietly appeared in the engine cab, on top of the coal tender, and on strategically placed platforms and flatcars.

"Is this gun business really necessary?" Diamond demanded irritably of Bear, when Robbie announced that one of the men had let him hold a rifle.

"Rough country," Bear said, scowling. "Have to be prepared for anything."

Just what sort of "anything" was made clear the next afternoon when she heard the rifles firing and felt the train slowing down. Rushing to the windows, she and Robbie spotted a number of bison running from the sound, vacating the tracks up ahead. She slid weak-kneed into a chair with her hand clutching her racing heart, while Robbie jumped around the car and whooped with excitement.

THEY PULLED INTO Great Falls in the early hours of the morning and had to wait until after sunup for the tracks to clear so they could reach the station. By the time they came to a full stop, the wooden platform was crowded with people who had heard their whistle and come running to meet the train.

"About time ye got here!" Halt Finnegan shouted as he worked his way through a motley crowd of cowhands, railroad clerks and porters, and barkers hawking everything from land tracts to gold claims to hot meals. The Irishman's voice boomed and his grin was filled with relief as he clamped a thick arm around Bear and all but lifted him off the ground. "So how was it—yer first ride behind yer own engine?"

"Not bad, Finnegan." Bear's grin was tempered by the fatigue and strain he glimpsed in his partner's face. "You ought to try it sometime."

"That I will. And th' rails?" Halt craned his neck for a glimpse of them.

"All present and accounted for," Bear said. "Got the crane and picked up thirty or so men. I took on a kitchen and hired a cook back in Milwaukee. It wasn't in our plan, but I figured it would save time and money in the long run."

"A cook?" Halt frowned, but seemed more distracted than disapproving. "I hope he makes good biscuits. A man can't get a decent biscuit to save 'is soul, in this infernal place." He lowered his voice and pulled something out from under his coat. "Here, lad. Ye might be needin' this."

Bear looked down at his revolver and holster and felt his skin contract.

"What's happened?" He stood straighter and instinctively began to scan the people on the platform for signs of threat.

"Not much." Halt looked around them and flashed Bear a look at the gun inside his own coat. "But Beecher's in town. Was here when I got here . . . payin' calls on th' ranchers we bought land from, tellin' 'em we didn't get loans and our contracts with 'em weren't worth a spit in a windstorm. Offered 'em twenty cents on the dollar—"

"They didn't sell to him?"

"No, but it's just the luck o' the Irish I wasn't one day later," Halt said, "else we'd 'ave lost the McGregor land. Once the ranchers got word I was back, they quit listenin' to Beecher, and I made good on our options an' registered th' deeds." He gave a wicked laugh.

"I could get used to this . . . having a jingle in my pockets. When we drive th' last spike in th' Central an' Mountain, I may have to find meself a rich wife!"

Wife. Bear remembered suddenly and turned back toward the car. Diamond was standing not far behind them, holding Robbie's hand. Her cheeks were red and her eyes were dark. Clearly, she had heard Halt's comment.

"Well, I'll be . . ." Halt recovered quickly. "If it ain't the little lady herself." He removed his hat and headed for her with his hand outstretched. "Welcome!"

She didn't release Robbie or abandon her grip on her satchel.

"And you are?" she asked evenly.

"Halt Finnegan." Bear inserted himself between them. "My partner."

"Ahhh." She gave Bear an accusing look. "Your *partner.*" Then she turned a polite smile on Halt. "You look strangely familiar, Mr. Finnegan. But I can't imagine where we would have met . . . so I must be recalling someone else."

"There's but one o' me, ma'am," Halt said with a twinkle in his eye, glancing between Bear and Bear's frosty wife. "And this must be the young lad I heard about . . . the one who took sick a while back."

"The very same," Bear said, knowing he had to make some explanation. "I insisted Diamond come and see the Montana Central and Mountain being constructed. That way she'll know she's getting her money's worth." Those words, combined with her presence, spoke volumes about the state of their marriage and her chilly air.

"Ye'll get good value for yer dollar here, miss, er— ma'am." He looked to Bear. "I got ye a room at th' hotel. A good thing, I reckon."

"Robbie and I won't be needing a hotel, Mr. Finnegan," she declared.

"Halt, ma'am." He grinned his Irish best and reached for the satchel. "Let me take that for ye." To Bear's surprise, she relinquished it to him.

"I cannot speak for Mr. McQuaid, but Robbie and I will be staying in our rail car." She cast a glance over her shoulder at their private rail coach and Halt's eyes widened as he took it in. "What we *could* use is a place to bathe."

"I believe we can accommodate ye, ma'am," Halt responded.

As they neared the station house, Bear slowed suddenly.

Leaning back against the wall, with their feet propped beneath them on the siding were three tough-looking men wearing dusty hats, worn boots, and revolvers slung around their hips. One was smoking a cigarette, one appeared to be napping while standing up, and the third was whittling a small piece of wood. When the smoker spotted Bear, his sun-creased eyes contracted to slits. He nudged the others and nodded toward Bear and Halt.

"Some new boys in town," Bear observed quietly, feeling every muscle in his body—even his scalp—go tense.

"More than just them." Halt too was moving with deliberate casualness.

"They've got Beecher written all over them," Bear mused and Halt nodded in confirmation.

"What or who is Beecher?" Diamond asked, looking to Bear, then to Halt.

"Nobody," Bear said, stopping when they were directly opposite the glaring threesome. He produced the gun he'd been keeping out of Diamond's sight and heard her take a sharp breath. Releasing her arm and tucking back the sides of his coat, he proceeded to strap the Colt revolver on his hip and tie it down. His movements were brisk and practiced and, as intended, they sent an unmistakable message to the three hired gunmen.

He pulled Diamond's hand back through the crook of his elbow and led her and Robbie down onto the main street. All the way, they could still feel the men's gazes boring into their backs.

"You see that, Diamond? Bear's wearing a six-gun!" Robbie said, staring eagerly over his shoulder at the surly threesome, who peeled themselves from the wall and struck off down the main street, in the opposite direction. "An' them other men—they had guns, too!"

"Don't stare, Robbie," Diamond said through her teeth, pulling him back around. "It's not polite."

GREAT FALLS WAS a typical end-of-the-line railroad stop. At its center were wood-framed buildings that fronted along a broad, dusty street. The permanent buildings were mostly commercial properties: sundry stores and shops, a bank, a boarding house or two, a saloon, a land and assay office, and a rambling, hastily constructed hotel.

Around that stable core had collected a shifting, changeable society of tents. Like their insubstantial shelters, the enterprises housed in these tent cities tended to be short-lived and not always wholesome: saloons and dance halls, cheap eateries, bathhouses, sleeping tents, gambling dens, and peddlers' stalls.

Halt led them through the more permanent part of town to a street of tent buildings that had been covered in the front with wood, to give them a more respectable appearance. There, he showed them the temporary offices of the Montana Central and Mountain Railroad . . . an impressive wooden front with a gold-lettered sign that, like the others, opened into a sizable canvas tent. Inside were a few tables, a desk, and a number of displayed maps marking the route of the railroad and the parcels of land that would be for sale along it.

"Welcome to th' office of the Montana Central and Mountain Railroad," Halt said proudly. "As soon as th' track is laid an' we've built up a store of revenue, we'll decide on a place and build a real building."

Diamond felt Bear's gaze on her and decided to withhold judgment for a while. She had seen new businesses begin in far worse circumstances and become quite successful. She didn't want to discount the Montana Central and Mountain unfairly because of the underhanded way its owner had raised its capital.

"Any questions, Miss—Mrs. McQuaid?" Halt asked.

"Only one, Mr. Finnegan." When he raised a finger and produced his best Irish smile, she softened. "*Halt*. Where can I find that bath?"

Mrs. Goodbody's Bathing Emporium was a few doors down, identified by a hastily painted sign that promised hot water and towels for a modest fee and declared soap to be available at an additional cost.

Diamond handed the protesting Robbie over to Bear, with the suggestion that someone take a scrub brush to him, and then she entered the door marked Women. For a dollar she was shown to a tall wooden stall in the open air, provided with a large copper tub, a crude stool, and a series of pegs for her clothes. The attendant handed her a sliver of coarse soap and a stiff piece of toweling, then returned shortly with a boy carrying buckets of water.

Closing her eyes so that she wouldn't see the scum on the tub or what might be floating in the water, she settled into the warmth with a groan. If only she could keep her eyes closed all the time she was here . . . she wouldn't have to see things like Bear strapping on a gun in front of three men who looked like they chewed nine-penny nails for breakfast.

What the devil was he trying to do? Get himself shot? Her stomach was only now coming out of a knot. He had an appalling penchant for responding to any sort of threat with physical force. Back in Baltimore it had been disconcerting and somewhat embarrassing; out here it could be downright deadly.

Those men at the station had glared openly at him, unconcerned—perhaps even hoping—that their behavior might provoke a response. Bear had certainly obliged them with one: halting right in front of them to strap on his revolver. Her heart had stopped as she watched his big supple fingers fastening holster ties around his thigh, just above his knee. She had read enough books to know that out West a man didn't usually tie down his side arm unless he assumed he'd have to draw it fast.

This was the *West*, she realized with a jolt. *Her* West. It unnerved her that it was proving to be every bit as woolly and untamed as it was in her books. Here society and the law were what people of conscience made them. It was up to strong, decent, forward-thinking men to bring civilized behavior to these parts, not to strap on a gun and swagger around pretending to be Cactus Jack or Black Bart. If this was Bear McQuaid's idea of progress, it was little wonder he had trouble getting loans for his precious railroad. At any given moment, he was just half a step away from out-and-out barbarism.

As she soaked and steeped, she remembered the way he had muscled poor Ellsworth at the Vassars' party, the way he had carried her when she fainted, and the way he had slung her across his shoulder and carried her off with him to Montana, and she felt a warmth rising in her that had nothing to do with the heat of the water. She groaned and abruptly sat up to scrub. What did it say about her, that she seemed to find his powerful, physical, volatile nature so fascinating?

It was the better part of an hour later, after toweling her hair and pinning it up, that she pulled on her new knickers and camisole, then donned new stockings, a petticoat, and her sturdy new boots. She found herself stroking the fine cotton of her new blouse and fingering the demure lace at the collar. It was perfect. Just the sort of thing she would have chosen for herself . . . if, of course, she had been allowed to go shopping and choose for herself.

Quickly, she donned the rest of her clothes and packed her others in her satchel. With her resistance once more in place, she threaded her way out of the maze of bathing stalls to the front entrance of Mrs. Goodbody's.

There, leaning against the wall, just outside the doorway to the men's side, stood Bear. Tall, muscular, and heart-stoppingly Western . . . he was wearing those glove-fitting blue trousers of his, Western boots, a simple cotton shirt with the sleeves rolled up, a leather vest that appeared aged to butter softness, and of course, his hat . . . which was pulled low over his eyes. She stopped inside the doorway, staring, feeling as if she were looking at a stranger . . . a handsome, dangerous foreigner . . . denizen of a hazardous but enthralling land. Something hot and restless and deliciously defiant stirred in her as she looked at him and remembered—

A woman's voice cut through the air like a rusty knife.

"Beaaarr McQuaaaaid! You han'some devil, you—come on an' give your fav'rite filly a big ol' kiss!"

Diamond watched him jerk his head up to locate the source of that grating voice and, an instant later, saw him flattened against the wall by a typhoon of femininity. A blur of frizzed red hair and even redder silk taffeta engulfed him and kissed him as if she were claiming territory for the King of Spain.

"Jesus, Mary, an' Joseph—I've missed you!" It was difficult to tell whether Bear had pushed her away or she had simply come up for air.

"How are you, Silky?" Bear said with a husky laugh.

"Right as rain, now that you're back, you handsome dog."

Something—a pang of conscience or perhaps the heat of her stare—caused him to glance toward the women's door, where he spotted her. Silky followed his gaze to her, then pulled back to allow him to stand upright.

"Don't let me interrupt," Diamond said, her face on fire as she started past the pair. "I just need to collect Robbie and I'll be on my way."

"Diamond." Bear lurched around Silky to grab her arm, but once he had it he seemed unsure just what to say to her. "This is . . . an old friend of mine, Silky Sutherland." He turned to the flamboyant creature in the gaudy red dress. "Silky, this is my wife, Diamond Wingate . . . McQuaid."

"Wife? Finnegan said you got hitched. Didn't believe a word of it." Silky gave a wicked laugh. "Till I heard she was rich."

Silky swayed toward Diamond with her hands on her hips. Diamond stood her ground as she was circled and examined with insulting thoroughness. She was a heartbeat away from yanking out handfuls of frizzy red hair, when Silky stopped directly in front of her and looked her right in the eye.

"She's pretty as a picture," she continued, speaking to Bear. "No mystery here, McQuaid. Rich and beautiful— hell, *I'd* have married her, if I could!"

Diamond tucked her chin, staring in shock at the most brazen female she had ever met. From the corner of her eye she could see Bear squirming and looking pained. When she refocused on Silky, the creature smiled at her . . . a beguiling expression that was honest and open and utterly fearless.

"You treatin' my friend McQuaid right, Diamond Lady?"

It was a demand for a decision: would they be friends or foes? Diamond's first thought was that she had never seen that much kohl on a woman's eyes before and her second was that if Evelyn Vassar were here, she would most certainly be sinking into a ladylike swoon and expecting Diamond to do the same. But Evelyn wasn't here, and Silky's forthright manner had a defiant sense of freedom about it that Diamond was shocked to find she rather admired.

"I intend to wait until he falls asleep tonight," Diamond said calmly, "before I kill him."

Silky's laughter was cut short by a male voice from behind Bear.

"Now, there's a rousing endorsement of married life, if I ever heard one."

A tall, rail-slender man in a dark, Western-style suit was standing on the wooden walk behind Bear . . . holding a cheroot in one hand and wearing a smile that had nothing to do with pleasure. The recognition on Bear's face was not at all reassuring.

"Beecher," he said as if the name fouled his mouth.

"McQuaid." The man gave an exaggerated nod of acknowledgment, then turned his gaze full force on Diamond. "I believe congratulations are in order."

"I don't want anything from you, Beecher—not even congratulations."

"Hardly a civilized response, McQuaid," Beecher said with a wave of his smoking cigar, still staring too intently at Diamond. "But I suppose your lovely bride must learn the truth about you sooner or later. Lionel Beecher, ma'am." He doffed his hat, then replaced it. "An old acquaintance of your husband's. I pray you don't measure all Montanans in his half-bushel."

Bear rolled his right shoulder back and drew his arm aside to call Beecher's attention to his side arm. Beecher glanced down at Bear's revolver and with taunting deliberateness flicked back the side of his coat, revealing that he was unarmed.

"Oh, and just so you know," Beecher continued with an

unpleasant smile. "I've filed an exception with the land office in Washington. I've told them there is only one way a spur line will be built between here and Billings . . . that's if Mr. Gould, Mr. Harriman, and the Northern Pacific build it. You had your chance, McQuaid. It's been more than twelve months, and you haven't laid a single mile of track. No doubt you'll be hearing from them soon."

Diamond couldn't swallow, could barely breathe. The air between the men crackled with animosity, lacking only the smallest spark to set it off.

"Hey—lemeeggo!" Robbie's voice preceded him out the bathhouse door. An instant later he came flying out into the middle of the standoff with his wet hair standing on end and his shirt only half on. "Crazy bast—" He spotted Diamond and bit off the rest, substituting a scowl of indignation. "They poured scaldin' water all over me in there— tried to cook me proper!"

The tension cracked and Diamond stepped through it to claim Bear's arm.

"You'll have to finish this conversation another time. Good day, Mr. Beecher." She collected Robbie in her free hand and gave Silky Sutherland a fierce nod. "We should have tea someday, Miss Sutherland. I'm certain there is a lot you can tell me about . . . Montana."

"DON'T *EVER* DO that again," Bear said furiously as he trundled her up the steps of their private car.

"Or what?" She turned around, halfway up the steps, to face him. "You'll pull your gun on me, too?"

"You don't know who or what you're dealing with." He grabbed both railings and vaulted up onto the first step, expecting her to back up onto the platform. But she held her ground and they came suddenly chest to chest and eye to eye.

"Then you tell me what all that was about," she challenged, caught unexpectedly in the molten copper of his gaze. "Who is this Beecher fellow and why in heaven's name did you threaten to pull a gun on him?"

"It's none of your concern." He tried to turn her but she refused to move and his hands on her shoulders unleashed the heat that had simmered between them for the last ten days. He stared at her lips; she stared at his. She felt his chest moving as he breathed; he felt her breasts surge against his chest.

"Wouldn't you rather know about Silky?" His voice thickened.

"No." Her mouth was going dry.

"Liar. Silky is a damn fine woman. And an even better friend."

"I don't want to hear about her, I want to hear about Beecher."

His jaw clenched and the heat in his eyes cooled. "He's Jay Gould's handpicked henchman. A swindler. A cheat. A coward and a bully."

"Who doesn't wear a gun," she charged.

"Who hires other scum to do his beating and shooting for him."

"What did he mean . . . he's filed an exception with the land office in Washington? What does that mean to the Montana Central and Mountain?"

"Nothing. We put up the money for the right-of-way and as long as we lay the track, the grants are ours. When we sell the land, we'll recoup most of the loan money. Don't worry, you'll get your blessed money back . . . every damned penny of it."

The words rumbled through her. *Your money.* The stubborn heat in his eyes and the exasperation that caused his hands to tremble suggested that he was speaking impulsively . . . and forthrightly. For the moment at least, he seemed to mean what he said. *You'll get your blessed money back.* He spoke as if he still considered her assets *hers,* instead of *his.* Her heart skipped a beat and then began to thud wildly. Was it possible that he had just wanted a loan in the first place? That he really had intended to ask her for the money, to make her a business proposition?

Just then a familiar figure came racing down the siding toward them. It was Halt, trailed closely by Robbie.

"I was lookin' for ye. Johnson's quit!" Halt panted as he grabbed onto the handrail of the steps.

"Quit?" Bear stepped down with one foot onto the gravel by the tracks. "But he can't just—What the hell happened?"

"Don't know. He left a paper at th' office sayin' he quit—I just found it. Went straight to 'is room at the boardin' house . . . he's cleared out. Paid up his room an' cleared out, survey gear an' all."

"Damnation." Bear pounded the handrail with a fist.

"Who is Johnson?" she asked Halt.

"Our engineer," Bear responded for him. "He surveyed and staked out our first twenty miles, and until yesterday, he headed up the crew preparing the rail bed." He looked at Halt with his chest heaving. "How much did they get done?"

"Don't know, lad," the Irishman said. "Haven't been out there in two or three days." He was already on his way before Bear had a chance to speak. "I'll get th' horses."

When Diamond called after him that she would need one, too, he nodded and waved to acknowledge that he'd heard and would oblige.

"You're not going," Bear declared flatly as he pushed by her up the steps and ducked inside the car. "You're staying right here."

"*No,* I am not." She hurried in after him and dropped her satchel, and folded her arms. "This is what I stayed to see . . . what I suffered ten long days cooped up in a train car to witness. And I'm not going to miss a minute of it."

Bear stopped in the middle of sorting the papers on the desk and looked up. The flame visible in her eyes burned all the way to his soul. She expected him to fail and she wanted to be there to see it. For one fleeting moment, he experienced a deep sinking sensation. Was it already too late? Staring at her, recalling the warmth and tenderness he had once touched inside her, he shook off those despairing thoughts. He was going to build this railroad or die trying.

By the time they set off from Great Falls, heading south and east, their party included Bear, Halt, Diamond, and Nigel Ellsworth, their newly appointed engineer. Following the prepared track bed, they reached the construction camp by mid-afternoon. There were tools scattered hither and yon, an abandoned, half-cleared work site nearby, and not a man to be seen.

Bear called out as he dismounted, but got no response. He and Halt stalked through the camp, ducking into the four tents and locating two warm bodies. When the men were dragged out into the warmth of the afternoon sun and lay sprawled on the ground, it was immediately apparent that they were in no condition to work. The smell of stale whiskey reached Diamond, yards away.

"Falling-down drunk!" Bear grabbed one by the collar and pulled him up onto his knees. "What the hell happened here? Where's Johnson?"

"He run off," the miscreant declared. "Th' rest hightailed it back t' town."

"Where did he go?" Halt demanded.

The fellow shrugged, swayed, and squinted against the sun. "Some fellers rode in t' camp an' talked to 'im. Next thing we knowed, he was packin' it in."

"What fellers?" Halt demanded. "Think, man! Was one of them tall an' lean—dressed fancy an' smokin' a cheroot?" Bear didn't have to see the wretch's nod to know the answer.

"*Beecher.*" Bear stalked toward the edge of the small camp with his hands on his hips, and stood staring at the wind-ruffled prairie grass. "He got to Johnson—bought him off or ran him off, or both. No wonder he was so damned smug this morning. Without an engineer, he figured we would be—" Feeling Diamond's gaze on him, he squared his shoulders and strode back to his new engineer and ordered him down from his horse.

"This is where you start to work, my friend." Bear indicated the roadbed they had just ridden along on their way from town. "What do you think? Can we start building on it tomorrow?"

"I—I—don't see why not." Ellsworth adjusted his spectacles and collected himself. His knees wobbled slightly as he made for the track bed, walked up and down it, and toed out a few clumps of dirt and rock. "The foundation seems solid enough. I suppose we should . . . check the base and see what we're on. I'll need some surveying equipment."

"Get started," Bear ordered. "We'll see you get what you need." He glanced up at Diamond, his mood grim, then turned to Halt. "We'll have to get the men together and send a crew out here. We have to get the cars switched and recoupled tonight. I want to be ready to start laying track at first light."

LONG AFTER DARK, that night, two hulking figures slipped down the dark alley between the land office and the Sweetwater Saloon. They were admitted to the back door of the saloon, where they stood by the door, letting their eyes adjust to the light of the storeroom. Sitting in the midst of those barrels, kegs, and crates of bottles, was a makeshift planking desk spread with a map of the surrounding territory. And poring over that map was Lionel Beecher.

He looked up and pinned them to the spot with a murderous glare. "Sikes and Carrick. What the hell have you two been doing?"

"We had to help switch cars an'—"

"Not that, you numskull—what have you been doing to sabotage McQuaid's railroad? Or did you forget what I'm paying you to do?"

The two glanced at each other and jammed their hands into their trouser pockets. "Wull . . . we jus' got here," the one called Sikes offered.

"Cretins. I'm surrounded by cretins." Beecher wheeled on one of his stone-faced gunmen. "You see what I have to put up with?" Then he turned back, gliding around the desk toward his beefy henchmen like a diamondback ready to strike.

"There were a thousand things you could have done to prevent his damned crane and rails from even reaching here. Uncouple a car or two—cut a brake line—set something on fire—do I have to think of *everything*?"

"Wull—we dumped one o' them carloads o' steel," Carrick offered.

"Not successfully, I take it," Beecher sneered.

"McQuaid—he made us stay up half the night haulin' it back up on th' car," Sikes declared with injury, as if still smarting from the imposed indignity of manual labor.

Beecher stared at the pair. "I see. So you decided not to make any more work for yourselves." He brought a fist crashing down on the desk and they flinched. "Well, the free ride's over for you idiots. I want to see some disrup-

tion, some trouble, some *chaos,* and I want to see it now—
tonight!"

Sikes and Carrick looked at each other, then back at
him.

"Tonight?" Sikes asked.

"It's kinda late . . ." Carrick said.

"Of course it's late . . . and dark . . . and quiet,"
Beecher said with ominous control. "That's when sabotage
gets done—when it's late and dark and quiet and nobody
can see what you're doing!"

"Whadda we do?" Carrick asked, scratching his head,
thinking.

Beecher nearly strangled on his own tongue. "What will
the bastards be using to work? Whatever the hell it is, *get
rid of it!*"

EIGHTEEN

TWO DAYS LATER, down two miles of new track, Bear jumped down out of the sliding door of the kitchen car and noticed the sound and steam from the crane's engine—which had started up only a short while before—was all but stopped. The crane had been moved in front of the engine and was now the leading car of the train. In its present position, it was being used to lift rails from the closest flatcar, swing them forward, and lower them onto the track bed.

Hurrying to the work site, he found a dozen men standing around and sitting on the stacks of wooden ties dumped beside the track bed. A thin, rhythmic clanging was coming from two men pounding a steel spike into the tie that would hold a rail segment in place . . . while the others in the crew watched.

"What's going on?" he demanded. "We've got work to do."

"Yeah," the foreman of the crew said, coming down off the stack of ties, scowling. "We'd be makin' dimes aplenty on them spikes—except, we ain't got tools to do it with. Our spike mauls are gone. All except them two."

"That can't be, there were plenty of—" Bear looked back at the two men who were working, and at the men who were standing around empty-handed. The tools! He bolted for the equipment car with the foreman close at his heels. Half an hour later, empty barrels, wrecked crates, and strong language were all flying from the open door of the ransacked tool car.

Spike mauls—the sixteen-pound hammers used to set spikes—weren't the only things missing. There were only a handful of picks and no shovels left in their cache of tools. The logging chain, rail tongs, puller bars, and gauge bars were missing, and all but a few of the bolt wrenches, ballast forks, and replacement handles had been taken. Several of the wheeled barrows were missing . . . as were the wheels intended for the half-assembled handcar stored in the second boxcar.

"Who the hell was on watch last night?" Bear demanded of Halt, who scratched his head then remembered.

"That'd be Carrick. He had to take a second night of watch when that fella on th' forward crew mashed 'is foot."

Bear tore through the camp looking for Carrick and found him lounging on a pile of wooden ties on the far side of camp. "Where the hell were you last night?" he roared, seizing Carrick by the shirt front and hauling him upright. "While you were on watch, somebody broke into the tool car and made off with half our equipment!"

Carrick paled slightly under his sunburned skin. "I-I-I—didn't see n-nothin'."

"The hell you didn't!" Bear loomed over him and gave him a shake.

"I'm tellin' ya—I didn't see ner hear nothin'." He swallowed hard. "I *swear.*"

Bear searched the man's sullen face for a long, acrid moment. If the bastard was involved in the theft, would he be stupid enough to still be lounging around camp? Bear sensed that the wretch wasn't as dull-witted as he seemed, but that was no proof that he had stolen the tools . . . or helped Beecher do so. He released Carrick.

"If you didn't hear or see anything, it was only because you were asleep on watch. I won't keep a man on the payroll, that I can't trust. Pack up your gear and clear out."

Carrick jumped to his feet as Bear turned away. "It wasn't my fault I got stuck on watch two nights runnin'. Ever'body nods off now an' agin—it ain't fair, McQuaid!"

Bear paused but refused to turn around. "Collect your pay, Carrick, and clear out!"

DIAMOND HAD JUST visited the kitchen car, poured a cup of coffee, and was carrying it up the track for Bear. It was a desperate measure; much too desperate to suit her. For two days she had hardly seen or spoken to him. He had come back to their car after she had retired for the night and left at daybreak each morning. Since he made it a practice to take meals with the crews, she was left with only rare public glimpses of him as he rode back and forth between the crews preparing the roadbed and the crews laying track.

She knew he was desperate to see progress and their first two days had not been especially encouraging. Two miles in two days . . . at this rate they wouldn't make Billings for six months. And they had less than three months before they would have to deal with the threat of snow. And, if Beecher was to be believed, the government land office might even now be moving to deny the MCM the land it was promised, because the track those land grants had been promised on wasn't finished. Bear had to lay track in record time and begin rail service. His only hope lay in picking up the pace as the men settled into a routine.

She had just surfaced from her preoccupation with calculating just how many miles they would have to lay each day, to look at the pile of empty barrels and crates that lay beside the tracks. She didn't see the wooden crate sailing out of the open boxcar door. It shot across her path, hitting the cup she held and pouring hot coffee down her front.

"Owww!" She lurched back and frantically pulled the hot, wet fabric away from her skin. "Ooooh—hot—owwww!"

Bear appeared in the open door and in an instant was on the ground. "Are you all right?" He hovered awkwardly as she fanned her blouse. When it was clear she wasn't badly injured, he vented his accumulated tension in the worst possible way. "What the hell were you doing out here, anyway? You're not supposed to be—"

"Bringing you a cup of coffee," she said, with more than her scalded skin stinging. "You can be sure I won't make that mistake again." She thrust the empty cup into his hands and started back down the track to their car.

"Diamond, wait! I didn't mean—" He hurried after her and pulled her to a stop just as Halt jumped down from the tool car, along with the crew foreman.

"Not a single maul left!" Halt called irritably. "Whoever took 'em knew right what would shut us down prop—" He caught sight of Diamond's stained blouse and red face and Bear's taut grip on her and stopped.

"Somebody broke into the tool car and stole our hammers, rail tongs, pull bars, and gauge bars," Bear said, his grip softening. "I was angry and I didn't see you out there. I'm"—he took a deep breath—"sorry about your clothes."

She looked from Bear to Halt, nodded, and headed for the car. A short while later, after she'd changed her blouse, she heard Halt and Bear enter and head for the desk at the far end of the car. When she stepped out of the sleeping compartment, finishing her buttons, she stopped dead.

Bear was strapping on his revolver.

"Ye cannot do this, lad." Halt planted himself between Bear and the door with his fists on his hips. "He'd like nothin' better—the lyin' thievin' bastard—than to have ye drop everythin' an' come gunnin' for him."

"I'm not going gunning for him," Bear said with a growl. "I'm going to get those tools back. They had to have left tracks."

"You're no Indian or army scout," Halt said, gesturing to the rocky prairie. "Ye could waste weeks out there searchin', and still find nothin'. Except trouble."

That reasoning seemed to take hold as Bear struggled for control. "Fine. Then I'll go into town and see if I can find some more tools." Halt blocked his way yet again.

"Ye don't need barkin' steel to find hammers."

"This is just in case." Bear's gaze hardened as he rested a hand on the walnut handle of his revolver.

"In case what?" Diamond asked, though she already knew the answer. "In case you run into Beecher and his hired guns?"

"A man has to protect himself and what is his," Bear said, eyes narrowing.

"Well, I may be just a silly, sentimental female . . . but in my opinion, a few hammers—an entire *trainload* of hammers—wouldn't be worth dying for."

"She's talkin' sense, lad." Halt felt Bear ease and released his grip on Bear's arms. "I'll go to town instead . . . talk to the stationman at the Chicago Milwaukee and St. Paul, see if they can spare a few mauls an' gauge bars. You got a bigger job right here . . . findin' a way to make sure Beecher don't sneak up on us agin."

"I'll come with you," Diamond said to Halt. When Bear

looked at her with a scowl, she folded her arms and would not be denied. "I have a blouse to take to the laundry."

"HE'S THE MOST arrogant, stubborn, insensitive man alive." She continued her enumeration of Bear's shortcomings to Halt as they bounced and rattled along beside the tracks in a wooden freight wagon that had definitely seen better days. Halt glanced at her from the corner of his eye.

"And inconsistent," she added, gripping the wooden seat to steady herself. "One minute he's reasonable and logical and the next he's a raging wild man—a barbarian—ready to battle the whole world, hand to hand."

"Now, there I have t' disagree," Halt said. "Stubborn, yes. Arrogant . . . maybe. Insensitive . . . well, ye'd be a better judge of that, I suppose, bein' a wife an' all. But inconsistent? He's as reliable as sunrise, Bear McQuaid is. If he gives 'is word, the job is as good as done. And he's fair-minded to a fault. Treats all men—great an' small—like he'd want to be treated."

"Ahhh," she said with an arch look. "Then there's the problem. He treats *women* a good bit different . . . as if we can't be trusted to use the right end of a spoon."

Halt chuckled and shook his head. "He does seem a bit pigheaded, where females are concerned. But that's jus' him, ye see. Independent as a hog on ice. Determined to do things fer himself. The Central and Mountain is 'is life's dream. He saved ever' penny for years . . . ate corn bread an' beans three times a day . . . slept out under th' stars . . . worked till he dropped an' then worked some more. It means more to 'im than anythin' in the world."

Quiet descended as each of them looked out over that rolling sea of prairie grass and conjured images of Bear's determination . . . one from memory, one from imagination. She sensed there would never be a better time or a better person to ask the questions that had been weighing on her for two weeks now.

"The MCM appears to have potential . . . to be a sound investment. Why was everyone so reluctant to lend you and him money?"

Halt sighed. "Bankers. They want control. Bear wouldn't give it up."

"Not even to get the money he needed?"

He chuckled. "Not even then. He's . . . *peculiar* . . . that way."

"Peculiar." She clamped a hand on her hat to keep the wind from taking it and said a mental "Amen." "Halt, how long have you known him?"

Halt thought for a moment. "Seven, eight years. Long enough. I'm not sure I should tell ye this . . . but . . . he's not been much of a ladies' man."

She huffed disbelief. "I saw him and that Silky woman together."

"She's a friend, pure an' simple."

"As I've said before, nothing involving Bear McQuaid is pure or simple."

"Except you," Halt said, glancing at her from the corner of his eye.

"Me?" She looked away, but her ears were burning for more.

"With you, it's about as simple as it gets b'tween a man and a woman." He leveled a look of amusement on her. "He wants ye."

She reddened and stiffened, hoping he couldn't tell that her heart was thumping. "Well, of course. By marrying me, he acquired a huge fortune."

"I'm not talkin' about yer money, lass. He told Vassar straight up, th' first time Vassar suggested ye as an investor, that 'e wouldna romance a woman for money. And he's a man o' his word. More'n once he went to make ye a business offer . . . took ye our maps and plans. Somehow, he never got around to it." He shook his head. "I think 'e just didn't want to ask ye. It scalded 'is pride to have to ask ye for somethin'. Th' man does have pride."

"In abundance."

Two words were all she could manage. What Halt was saying about him seemed to mesh with her own observations. Proud. Independent to a fault. And he had indeed brought her their maps and plans . . . the very ones she had seen that last night . . . With the slightest nudge, she could believe that he might have intended to ask her for a loan but got tangled up in his own stubborn pride and independence instead. *He wanted her.* She stared at the wooden buildings appearing over the next rise, desperate to trust what Halt was telling her and terrified that if she did, she would just be asking for more heartache.

WHEN THEY REACHED Great Falls, they went straight to the train station and located the stationmaster. He was a wiry, nervous sort of fellow who kept his hand pressed to his stomach as if he were always on the verge of dyspepsia.

"Sorry, can't sell any tools . . . against regulations." He slowly backed away. "Have a devil of a time keeping our own crews supplied."

"That's horse—" Halt said, stalking after him. "You got tools, man. I seen 'em in the roundhouse." He glanced at Diamond. "We'll pay top dollar."

"They're not for sale a-at a-any price." The stationman finally smacked into the wall at his back and apparently decided to make a stand. "Regulations is regulations. Great Falls may be just a speck on the Chicago Milwaukee and St. Paul map, but we run tight an' proper. We go strictly by th' regulations."

Halt was suddenly nose to nose with the stationmaster.

"You know we have permission to tie into CM and SP track," he declared. "Ol' Jim Hill himself okayed it."

"Well, he ain't okayed me selling ye any of our tools!" The little man finally found his sticking point and brought his chin up.

Diamond dragged Halt back by the sleeve and insisted they leave before something unpleasant occurred. Reluctantly, he complied. They tried the livery stable, the implement dealer, and—on the off chance—even the general store. No one carried hammers of the weight or configuration they needed.

"We ain't got time for this," Halt said, taking off his hat and banging it against his thigh, releasing a small cloud of dust. "We got to make track. If we don't get the rail laid b'fore snowfall, we'll lose our land grants for sure."

Diamond saw the worry in Halt's face and realized it lay always just beneath that genial layer of Irish glibness and glad-handing. If only there was something she could do to—

"Wait—Hill gave you permission to connect onto his track, right?"

"For a price," Halt said. "He knows the MCM spurrin' off his line will be good for 'is business, too. That's why he allowed it in the first pl—"

"So, if he approved the track, why wouldn't he approve the sale of a bit of equipment? Or the use of it until we could get some from St. Paul or Milwaukee? The stationmaster would have to follow his orders, right?"

"Yeah . . . the little weasel."

A huge smile bloomed. "Where's your telegraph office?"

Soon she was standing in front of the telegraph operator's window finishing the wording of a two-part telegram intended for James J. Hill in St. Paul. Finally satisfied with the wording, she handed it over to the operator.

"How long before we could expect a reply?" she asked.

When told it might be several hours to an entire day, she turned to Halt and smiled ruefully. "While we wait, I need to find a laundry and something to eat."

The Lonesome Dove was one of those mergers of canvas and wood construction that served as buffer between the respectability of the permanent town and the fly-by-night elements in the tents. Halt assured her that despite its location, it served the best food in town, and he proved to be a good judge.

As they finished their ham steaks, mashed potatoes, and scalloped corn, Silky Sutherland entered, wearing a sunflower-yellow dress and hat large enough to save three people from sunstroke. She went from table to table, greeting every diner, working her way across the tent toward Halt and Diamond.

"Well, well . . . if it isn't my favorite Irishman and the Diamond Lady. I hope Lou's feedin' you right." She turned toward the back where a fellow with a towel for an apron was trundling dishes of steaming food out from the kitchens. "Hey, Lou—bring me and my friends here some coffee and cobbler." Then she pulled up a chair and sat herself down with them.

"Don't mind me sayin' so, Finnegan, but you don't look so good." She grinned and gave his hand, on the tabletop, a suggestive stroke. "You ought to come sleep a few nights in a proper bed."

He chuckled. "Whoever said yer beds were proper? A few nights in one o' them and I'd be six feet under. What I need is sleep."

Diamond was jolted to realize that he did look worn. Dark circles were growing under his eyes and the lines in his face seemed to have been etched significantly deeper in the last three days.

Silky looked a bit disappointed and resettled herself on the chair, fluffing some of her yellow ruffles. "Well, I suppose I could provide that, too . . . over at my boardin' house." Then she turned to Diamond. "You, on the other hand, Diamond Lady, look fresh as a daisy. McQuaid must be doing right by you."

"Actually, he's"—she caught sight of Halt's frown and softened her answer—"not sleeping very well, either."

"He always did sleep with one eye open . . . or so I'm told." Silky looked her square in the eye. "Never had the privilege of seein' it firsthand."

Diamond's face flushed with heat. She was both appalled and disarmed by Silky's tacit declaration that she hadn't slept with Bear. Never in her life had she met anyone as brassy, bold, and outrageously plainspoken as Silky Sutherland. In Baltimore she would never have met such a woman, much less shared a table with her. But here, in the untamed, unpredictable West . . .

"Ye wouldn't 'appen to know where we could pick up some spike mauls and gauge bars?" Halt was asking when she came out of her shock. He explained to Diamond: "Silky's something of a businesswoman. Got 'er fingers in nearly ever' pie in Great Falls."

"Eateries." Silky rolled her gaze to indicate the tent around them, then began to enumerate her other enterprises. "A boardin' house, th' dry-goods store, the barbershop, Mrs. Goodbody's baths, most o' the livery stable, part o' the bank, the only hotel in town, and half o' the Sweetwater." Taking Diamond's astonishment for confusion, she explained: "That's th' Sweetwater Saloon. Got a six-foot mirror . . . brought all the way from Chicago. I can provide you a lot o' things, Finnegan"—Silky waggled her artificially darkened eyebrows—"but hammers ain't one of 'em."

"Hammers?" came a male voice from several feet away. They all looked up and there stood Lionel Beecher wearing a freshly pressed suit and a smirk. "Did I hear someone say they needed *hammers*?"

Silky clamped her hand on Halt's wrist, keeping it on the table. "You did. Wouldn't happen to know anybody who's got a few extra to sell?"

"That depends. Who's buying?" The light in Beecher's eyes said that he already knew the answer.

"I am," Diamond declared, stepping in to defuse the rising tension.

"Well, well, Mrs. McQuaid, you do surprise me. I would think a lady of your quality and refinement wouldn't concern herself with such things."

"Mrs. McQuaid is no less th' lady for also bein' somethin' of a businesswoman," Halt said in warning tones. "She 'as a reputation for makin' sound investments."

"Hearing that, I'm doubly surprised to find her interested in the Montana Central and Mountain," Beecher said smoothly, settling his gaze on Diamond while keeping Halt in his peripheral view. "Such a risky venture—out there on the high plains, unprotected from the elements, subject to all sorts of *misadventure*."

"I don't believe you answered Miss Sutherland," Diamond said with ladylike imperative. "Do you have hammers and railroad tools for sale?"

"I might be able to find some, given time and the proper . . . *motivation*."

The way his gaze slid over Diamond made it clear to her that he might prove amenable to a more personal appeal from her. She understood that look, that veiled insinuation; she had seen it a thousand times from men who wanted something from her. Her reaction split instantly into two parts. Externally, she raised her head and rose coolly from her chair, drawing Halt and Silky up with her. Internally, she was wrapping her fingers around the neck of an effigy of him and squeezing for all she was worth.

"The possibility of reasonable profit is all the motivation a true gentleman requires in business," she declared in imperial Wingate tones. "I shall save you whatever effort you might have expended in searching, Mr. Beecher." Her words and icy smile were the social equivalent of frostbite. "I doubt any tool you could come up with would meet my needs."

Beecher went rigid.

"Oh, Lionel, don't take it so hard," Silky said, bursting into a wicked laugh. "Someday you'll find a woman who appreciates your . . . *tool*!" Her raucous reaction caused everyone in the restaurant to turn and stare at Beecher's frozen face.

Beecher turned on his heel and stalked out, but not before shooting a malicious look at Halt and Diamond. It was a moment before Diamond sorted through the exchange and realized what Silky had made of what she had said. The sense of it penetrated Halt's indignation and he hooted a laugh. Diamond bit her lip, her eyes widening at the snickers and guffaws around them. An expanding bubble of tension rose up through her chest and exploded. Her anxiety poured out in clear, purging laughter.

"You're a wicked woman, you are," Silky Sutherland said, taking her by the hands. "I knew I was gonna like you the minute I laid eyes on ye!" As they resumed their seats and were served coffee and cobbler, she continued to chuckle. "That's the best laugh I had in three days. Eat up. It's on me!"

LATE THAT NIGHT, the wagon rumbled back along those twin ribbons of steel that now glinted like silver in the moonlight. Halt drove while Diamond watched for signs of trouble; a loaded rifle lay ready on the seat between them. But the endless dark canopy overhead and the sea of prairie around them were all they saw, and the rustle of windblown grass, the cry of nighthawks overhead, and the occasional howl of a coyote in the distance were all they heard. Slowly, carefully, they inched toward the MCM's camp, and as fatigue threatened to overcome them, they spotted the dark outline of the train and the dim yellow glow of lanterns just over the next rise.

The smoke from dying campfires rose and thinned into the distance. The men sat around them in the early evening, smoking and whittling and listening to one of the men play a mouth harp. As they headed into the dormitory cars and their bunks, they usually left one or two men to watch the fires as they burned down. That evening, with the theft of their tools fresh on everyone's mind, Bear had charged the fire tenders with an official sentry duty and arranged a rotation of shifts.

At the sound of their approach, the sentries sounded an alarm. Men poured out of the dormitories and moments later the wagon was swarmed by sleepy but grinning faces. "Wait'll you see!" Halt called, heading the wagon straight for the heart of camp.

When they rumbled to a stop, Halt climbed back over the seat, seized one of their lanterns, and threw back a canvas tarp to reveal several wooden boxes filled with hammers, tongs, gauge bars and sundry other tools. A cheer went up that brought Bear running with his gun in his hand.

At the sight of them, he jammed the gun down in the waist of his trousers and climbed up on the wagon wheel to look at what they'd brought.

"Hang me, Finnegan—if you aren't the best! I knew you'd find some somewhere!" he called, climbing aboard the wagon to inspect at closer range. His eyes glowed in the lantern light as he made a mental tally. "Where did you get them?"

"The CM and SP," Halt said, beaming. "The stationman wouldn't sell nothin' to me, so yer wife . . . she telegraphed ol' Jim Hill himself, in St. Paul. Told him who she was and what she needed, told him old John Garrett of the B and O was a dear friend . . . an' asked him to author-ize the stationman to sell us tools from 'is roundhouse. By cracky, if he didn' up an' do it!"

Another cheer went up from the men and Bear turned slowly to Diamond, who was still standing on the front of the wagon, holding on to the back of the seat. In the moment he stared at her, the pleasure faded from his countenance, his jaw set, and his shoulders squared, betokening control being exerted inside him. Things got unnaturally quiet as the work crews watched him face his pretty wife and then watched him turn back to the tools with only a nod of acknowledgment.

Diamond watched through a haze of fatigued disbelief as Bear turned away. And she wasn't the only one.

"Go on, lad," Halt said, scowling. "Give 'er a proper bit o' thanks. She earned it this day."

Bear turned on Halt momentarily, warning him off with a glare, but then glanced at the men collected around the wagon, muttering, and apparently reconsidered. He turned slowly to her and seemed to grapple for words.

"I am even more in your debt than ever, Mrs. McQuaid," he said thickly. "I promise, the Montana Central and Mountain will repay you . . . every penny."

To the men watching it seemed an odd way for a man to thank his wife. But to Diamond, who knew from experience and from Halt's words that Bear hated nothing more than to be in another's debt, that statement was like a knife in the heart. She lifted her skirts and stepped over the side of the wagon, searching blindly for a foothold on the wheel. The men nearby rushed to help her down and she kept her head lowered as she thanked them and headed for the car. By the time she reached the steps her tears were rolling freely.

"If ye aren't the stupidest, pigheadedest man I ever saw!" Halt roared, a quarter of an hour later, as they stood in the moonlight some distance from the train. Halt had dragged him out there after the tools were unloaded and the men had drifted back to their bunks, hoping that no one else would hear what he had to say to his partner. "Why didn' ye just go on an' give 'er a belt in th' mouth while ye were at it?"

"This is none of your business, Finnegan," Bear said from between gritted teeth. "And if that's all you dragged me out here for, I'm headin' back."

Halt grabbed him by the arm and found himself restraining both Bear and his own sudden urge to mayhem.

"Yer actin' like a horse's arse, Bear McQuaid. The woman rescues our work schedule an' maybe our whole damn' railroad . . . and all ye can say is ye'll pay 'er back?" Halt brandished a fist. "If ye weren't half a foot taller an' fifteen years younger, I'd thrash you from here to Billings an' back!"

With an oath of disgust, Halt released him and stalked off toward camp.

Standing there in the moonlight, with everything night-washed to shades of black and white, Bear saw his actions in stark relief and his face caught fire.

He had acted like an idiot. At the time, all he'd thought about was the humiliation of having his rich, heiress wife bail out his railroad in front of his entire crew. But the minute the words were out of his mouth he knew they were a mistake. Too cold. Too caustic. Too damned un-grateful.

She was trying to help, he knew . . . the same way she helped missionaries and inventors and fire victims. It was her nature. It was her chosen lot in life. And it was also the surest way for her to dismiss him from her life. If she made him into just another of her charity cases, another investment in "progress," he would lose her altogether. He had to build this railroad by himself and prove to her that he was different from Kenwood and Webster and Pierpont . . . that he wasn't just a contribution or an investment or another need-driven hanger-on. He had to prove to her that he had some worth, some value of his own . . .

SHE WAS JUST trying to help, Diamond thought miserably. The same way she helped missionaries and businessmen and inventors and the poor people who lined up outside her gates. It was just a part of her nature. It was her mission in life. Why didn't he understand that? He was willing enough to take her money and take her passion and take her dreams. Why was he so determined to keep her from being any part of his dream, of the central goal and desire of his life?

She pulled up her skirt and dried her face on her petticoat. She looked around the opulent parlor of the private car and wondered for the ten-thousandth time what her life would have been like if she had been born without money, without the burden of expectation, without the responsibility of constant giving.

Perhaps the fault lay within her. Would Bear have loved her if she had had nothing? Would she have had anything worthwhile to offer him? Her breath caught. Did she have anything now?

The door opened and she looked up from the settee and from the depths of despair to find Bear staring down at her with a turbulent look. In the dim light of the kerosene lamp his eyes shone darkly, his features were taut, his shoulders had lost their squared edge. He looked heart-breakingly human.

She could scarcely get her breath as he edged forward, focused on her, clearly wrestling with something inside him.

"I need to apologize." His voice was low and laden with suppressed emotion. "I was a jackass—a pure jackass—to you earlier. I appreciate what you did. Getting the tools. It's just that . . . well . . . I'm not used to letting other people do things for me. I don't like feeling beholden to anybody. And I already owe you too damned much."

NINETEEN

THAT WAS IT? Explained his way, his harsh behavior sounded somehow excusable, almost virtuous. Diamond searched his countenance and posture, and sensed there was more than that to his rejection of her a while ago. It struck her that even in apologizing, he refused to acknowledge either his true motives or the depth of the pain they had caused. And he obviously expected her to be pacified by that shallow apology . . . made in private, without the audience they had had when he spurned her efforts on his behalf.

Pain-roused defiance raced up her spine, straightening it.

"That's hogwash, Bear McQuaid, and you know it." She was surprised by the vehemence of the words coming from her mouth, but she instantly owned the sentiment. "People do things for you all the time." She rose and faced him with a new sense of strength and clarity. "They wash your shirts and cook your meals . . . they're even building your blessed railroad for you. You don't have problems with people doing things for you at all—not when you're in control of them. But let somebody do something for you that you aren't paying for, that you haven't given orders for, that you can't control . . . and you can't bear it. You don't like feeling beholden? Well, at least that part is true . . . nobody likes feeling indebted.

"But do you honestly think you can go through life paying your own way?" She stalked closer. "Nobody, no matter how rich or how powerful, pays his own entire freight. Everyone has to depend on someone else, sometime."

He stared at her, completely taken aback by her reaction.

"Everyone?" he countered. "Even *you*?"

She drew her chin back, searching herself, testing her assertion against her own experience, her own heart. And she found it appallingly true.

"Even me," she said, her voice softening in spite of her. Then some perversely needy part of her added in a choked whisper: "Especially me."

He came even more alert, examining that half-strangled admission of need. She groaned inwardly. What on earth had she said that for? Her heart began to pound as she noticed him moving closer.

"What could you possibly need, Diamond McQuaid?" he said, every muscle taut and poised . . . for what she could scarcely bear to think.

"Whatever money *can't* buy." She backed up a step then forced herself to stand fast. "Things like friendship and loyalty and caring and joy and love." She lifted her head, struggling to get her thoughts back on track. "No one can have those things by himself. A person needs others to help him claim and experience them."

"And who helps *you* claim them?" He moved still closer.

"This isn't about me," she declared.

"Oh?"

"It's all about your damnable independence." She

jabbed a finger at him. "Your stubbornness . . . your ingratitude . . . your—"

"Stupidity?" he supplied.

"Your stupidity."

"My pride?"

"Your blasted male pride!"

With the naming of each fault he had stepped closer and was suddenly towering over her, radiating heat and tension, demanding her attention and filling her every sense.

"And what about *your* pride?" he demanded.

That brought her up short. "My pride?"

"You can't bear to think I only wanted you for your money. That's what all that fuss was about back in Baltimore."

"That's not true." Her face began to flame.

"The hell it's not. Otherwise, you'd have come out and listened to me like a reasonable person instead of hiding in the privy and crying your eyes out."

She gasped, staring at him in disbelief. "That is the cruelest thing I've ever heard anyone—" She started past him for the sleeping compartment.

"Oh, no." He grabbed her arm and held her. "You're not leaving here until we reach some understanding."

"I believe I've had all the 'understanding' I can stomach for one night," she said, fighting back tears, refusing to break down in front of him.

He saw her struggling with her emotions and realized that the shell she had drawn around her since their wedding night was thinner than he expected.

"No, Diamond, you don't understand at all," he said, his voice and grip both desperate. "I knew that if I asked you about the loan before we were married, you'd end up thinking . . . just what you ended up thinking." He could see that his words made little impact and realized he was doing it again, refusing to confess the truth, failing to say what he really felt. If he had been honest with her before, he wouldn't be on the verge of losing her now. *Tell her*.

"I . . . I wanted *you*. Not your money or your companies. Not your name or position. I didn't want to marry some rich heiress . . . or the progressive owner of the Wingate Companies . . . or Baltimore's famous soft touch. I wanted *you*."

"Then you really don't understand. Because I *am* a rich heiress . . . and a progress-minded business owner . . . and Baltimore's soft touch. That's who I am. If you didn't marry any of them, who did you marry?"

She held her breath. It was the question that had haunted her for years. Her secret despair. Her constant battle. What could he—could anyone—see in her that wasn't some manifestation of her massive fortune?

She really didn't know, he thought, seeing the anxiety in her face. She honestly didn't know what anyone would see in her besides dollar signs. In that moment, he glimpsed the magnitude of the pain and loneliness she had lived with as a child and the depths of the defenses guarding her heart. He began to grope for words and memories to explain, to build a bridge across that sizable gulf.

"I married that little girl who stored her dreams in a toy train car," he said, praying that would make some kind of sense to her. "And who grew up to love railroads. I married the little girl who tried to give away a fortune and grew up to change a whole city for the better with her generosity. I married a smart, stubborn, independent woman who refused to cave in under a mountain of riches and an even bigger mountain of pressures."

She raised her chin to meet his gaze and in it he glimpsed the first flickers of hope. It was painful to witness, but it was the first hopeful sign he'd had from her in days, weeks. And as that small flame struggled and threatened to disappear, he understood that his explanation wasn't quite enough.

"Hell, Diamond, can't you see? This isn't about pride or stubbornness or money or who's going to be in control. It's about this need for you that uncoils out of my gut every time I see you, every time I hear your voice, every time I think about the way you looked that day at Gracemont . . . out by the orchards . . . the day after we were married. It's about the way my blood boils whenever I see you smile. It's about the way I can't wait to see you each morning and talk to you each night. It's about this constant urge I have to touch your skin."

He brought his hand up to trace the curve of her cheek.

She found herself being engulfed in his special kind of sensory heat. Her throat constricted. Her mouth dried. Her insides began sliding toward her knees.

"This . . . this is why I married you . . . why I brought you out here," he murmured, lowering his mouth toward hers. "I'm crazy about you, Diamond Wingate McQuaid. When I said 'I do,' I meant I *do*."

Her resistance was melting. Her much-denied hunger for him and for the closeness they once had shared was rising to the surface to meet his confessed desire for her. Then he pulled her into his arms and kissed her with all the need he'd suppressed and redirected for two long weeks.

This—she thought dizzily as drafts of pleasure tore her senses from their surroundings—this was real. Bear wanted her. Halt was right. He wanted her—*he really wanted her!*

Joy erupted in her and she slid her arms around him, covering, caressing, claiming every inch of him she could reach. His back, his shoulders, his waist, his neck. He was hers; every muscle and sinew, every strained and aching nerve, every proud and stubborn impulse. Just as she was his.

She drew back, her lips throbbing and her eyes dark and glistening. She was his. The fear that had shrouded that fact in her mind and heart was fading. It was an admission, a surrender that both of them were making, and the fact that they were in this growing spiral of desire and acceptance together made all the difference in the world. Surrender, she realized with a soaring sense of freedom, could be a release, an unburdening. And it could be oh, so sweet.

He had braced and lifted her against him, lowering hot, ravenous kisses down the side of her neck and nuzzling open the first button of her blouse. She bent her head back, offering him more, abandoning herself to the pleasure surging hot and viscous through her veins.

She felt herself moving and realized he was half walking her, half carrying her back to the desk at the far end of the car. Then she felt the edge of the desk against her bottom and he settled her on a pile of papers to free his hands. She was trembling as she tried to unfasten buttons, first hers, then his, then hers again. His hands were trembling, too, and he was panting, groaning softly with frustration as he struggled to open her blouse, then loosen her skirt, and then find the ties of her corset.

She laughed softly and licked and nipped at his taut nipple, pushing his shirt back, teasing him with the fact that the task of getting through his clothes had been much easier than his in getting through hers. With a sharp, indrawn breath he renewed his attack on her knotted corset strings and she felt his victory before he knew it had occurred. The garment's grip loosened, releasing her like a reluctant lover, and she sighed as she pulled the boned satin away.

A moment later his kisses and hungry nibbles were setting the tips of her breasts on fire. The erotic well deep inside her tightened, growing hot and moist and ready. She wriggled against the papers beneath her, her body seeking and hungry for sensations only he could provide. Then he thrust a hand beneath her bottom, pulling her up and against him, and she writhed luxuriantly against his palm and questing fingers.

"Well, Jesus H.—"

That appallingly familiar voice and even more recognizable profanity caused them both to freeze. Her heart was pounding, her loins and her lips and breasts were throbbing. She could hear Bear's heart pounding, too, beneath the heavy rasp of his breathing. His whole body had tensed defensively. Shielded by his big frame, she managed to swallow her horror enough to peer around him.

"Oh, Lord," she uttered on a moan.

There stood Robbie in his nightshirt, his eyes as big as saucers.

"Robbie," she said in a hoarse whisper, gripping Bear's arms to keep him from turning. They had forgotten all about Robbie. Clearing the passion from her throat, she managed to sound marginally parental.

"What are you doing out of bed? Get back in bed this instant!"

His lascivious grin faded as he was shoved back into the morass of boyhood.

"Well, I jus' wanted a drink. An' I heard voices and groanin'—"

"Robbie!" Bear thundered, without turning.

"All right, all right—I'm goin'." He turned away with a scowl, muttering: "It ain't like I never seen it done before."

The sound of the door to the sleeping compartment slamming seemed to send a wave of chilled night air over them. They looked at each other, both somewhat embarrassed by the reckless urgency of their desire. But as they gazed into each other's faces, neither showed the slightest regret that their long-banked passions had finally exploded into flame. She straightened and slid her hands down his shoulders. He drew back reluctantly, sliding his hands from her bottom and waist.

"I think this is where it has to end," she said quietly, giving his chest a final caressing stroke.

He nodded, cradling then releasing her chin. "For now."

She collected her garments together and slid from the desk. He watched her sway toward the sleeping compartment and pause at the door to shoot him one last sultry look. When the door latch clicked behind her, his legs felt as if they had turned to rubber.

He reached for the decanter on the shelf and poured himself a large brandy.

"Damned kid."

But by the time he finished the brandy, stretched out on one of the banquettes, and closed his eyes, he was smiling.

THE NEXT TWO days gave Diamond no time to explore or test the understanding begun in the heat of renewed passion between her and Bear. He spent every spare moment leading work crews and solving problems that kept cropping up . . . from a strange spoilage of flour in the kitchen to frequent brawls among the men. By the afternoon of the second day, a general tension gripped the camp and tempers flared like the gusty winds that came barreling out of the west, blowing storms across the plains.

Diamond stood on the platform of their private car, watching a line of forbidding clouds approaching and marveling that there could be enough of them to fill up that enormous expanse of sky. In the distance jagged, luminous flashes of white warned of lightning fast approaching. She went looking for Robbie, whom Bear had put to work carrying water and messages and fetching tools. She found him with a crew of men being spelled by a sister crew. Just as she approached, a scuffle broke out between two men over a missing twist of "chew."

"I saw you with it, Sikes—ye thievin' bastard!" A smaller man was using a finger to drill that challenge into the chest of a larger, beefier fellow.

"Yeah? Prove it weren't mine," Sikes said with a sneer. Then he returned that finger jab to the chest . . . only with considerably more force.

Fists began to flail. Tools hit the ground as both crews flew to separate the two. There was snarling and shoving, and insults were flung from both sides. Bear appeared out of nowhere and lunged into the fray to do some shoving and shouting of his own. Confronted by his formidable frame and fists, the men halted, then slowly backed down. When things were sufficiently calm, Bear drew a deep breath, looked up at the sky, and growled orders to pack it in and stow the tools until after the storm passed. As the men complied, relieved to have an unexpected break, he turned toward the rear of the train and spotted her there, watching.

"It's always something with that lot—they can't go a day without coming to blows over some damned thing or other."

"Maybe it's in the air . . . the storm coming," she said, glancing back over her shoulder, into the wind.

"Maybe," Bear said grimly. Then he struck off down the track to make sure everything was secured before the storm hit. She stared after his snugly molded trousers with rueful longing. At this rate, she would probably see Billings before she saw him alone again.

The storm struck hard and fast, with winds that rocked the substantial Pullman car and made it feel as though the wooden body might be torn from its carriage. Claps of thunder rattled the walls, windows, and floor violently, sending Robbie diving for Diamond's arms. Then the rain came . . . in fierce, driving sheets that lashed the train and camp and soaked the ground at an astonishing speed. A small river formed along the track and flowed swiftly along the barrier of the raised track bed. Then, almost as quickly as it had come, the worst was past. The soft, lingering patter of raindrops against the window and on the metal-covered roof washed away the strain and tension the storm's approach had produced. Suddenly the air was cooler and sweeter.

Diamond opened the door just as one of the men came lurching up the steps. He was wet to the skin and dripping water.

"The boss—" he panted out, wiping his face. "Where's Mr. McQuaid?"

"He went forward to secure the crane . . . must have gotten caught there when the storm broke. What's wrong?"

"Cook!" the fellow called over his shoulder, already headed for the front of the train. "He's hurt!"

Ordering Robbie to stay put, she grabbed the tablecloth she used as a shawl and dashed out into the gentle rain, headed for the kitchen car. A knot of men was gathered on the ground below the open kitchen storage door. Pushing her way through the men, she found their German cook lying on the ground. One of his legs was bent at an odd angle and he was gritting his teeth in pain.

"Schultz!" She spread her makeshift shawl over him, to keep the rain off, and ordered two of the men to hold it while she knelt beside him. "What happened?"

"Danged if I know, mizzus." He sucked air and groaned when she gently probed his injury. "I hear somezing bang an' bang in de storeroom. I tho't das door hass blown open in de vind. I go to shut . . . an' somezing vall and knock me out. Den a barrel come crashin'—*aghhh*!"

"We've got to get him inside." She rose and looked up and down the cars trying to decide where would be the best place for him. "Bring him into our car." She looked around. "And somebody go to town for a doctor."

Bear arrived just as the men were fashioning a make-shift litter to carry Schultz to their private car. Everything stopped dead as the men told him what had happened and what Diamond had told them to do. They watched uneasily between their boss and his wife. Diamond also watched, remembering the last time she had taken it upon herself to make decisions and take action.

After a long, prickly moment, he turned to the men carrying the litter.

"What are you waiting for? Get him inside." He glanced at the rest of those wet, slightly sullen faces. "Who's going for the sawbones?"

Poor Schultz did have a broken leg. And the poor men had a miserable cold supper. Canned beef was cut and served between slabs of day-old bread and stale biscuits left from the morning's baking. The coffee was abysmal, but everyone drank it anyway . . . especially when word got out that Diamond had pitched in and made it herself. Only Robbie was crass enough to complain aloud.

"This grub stinks."

Diamond looked over at Bear and winced. "He's right. It's awful."

Later, after they had cleared the trays and cups and set the kitchen into some semblance of order, Diamond went to look for Bear. He was in the equipment car, preparing the handcar for assembly and trying to locate some spare wheels that might fit it.

"I've been thinking," she told him, knowing she was treading on unsettled ground but heartened by his restrained response to her earlier action. "You have to do something about food. The men won't stay if they don't get better meals than they had this evening." She caught his gaze with hers and held it. "I want to go into Great Falls tomorrow and find another cook."

It was his territory, his railroad, his decision to make. But if he didn't allow her to do this, there was probably little hope that he would ever allow her to be a part of his railroad. And if she couldn't be a part of his railroad, what chance did she have of becoming a part of his life? When he spoke, after a small eternity, it sounded like every word was being strained through a sieve.

"I suppose . . . we have to have a cook."

She released the breath she had been holding. "Then it's settled. I'll go into town at first light." He glowered and inflated his chest as if preparing to object. She folded her arms with determined force. "Or I can be a good little wife and twiddle my thumbs, and let you and your men choke down jerky and dry biscuits for the next two months." She raised her chin. "What's it to be?"

Bear found once more that he couldn't say no.

THAT SAME EVENING just at dusk, Halt came riding hell-for-leather into camp. He had been spending his time in the forward camp, helping Nigel Ellsworth with the roadbed construction. Both he and his horse were spattered and caked with mud and he collected a following of men as he pounced to the ground and roared through the camp looking for Bear.

Bear heard raised voices and hurried out onto the platform of the car.

"There's a flood," Halt panted out, steadying himself on the railing. "Th' roadbed—all flooded! Ye got to come, lad!"

In a heartbeat, Bear was grabbing his hat off the rack by

the door and bounding down the steps. He saddled a horse from the picket line at the edge of the camp, then he and Halt mounted and rode off down the middle of the road-bed. Over two gradual rises and around a set of buttes that formed the edge of a ridge of hills, they glimpsed a river in the distance . . . one that hadn't been there that morning.

Halt led him up onto an outcropping of rock. The scene below caused Bear to shut his eyes and draw a sharp breath. It was nothing short of a calamity. A muddy stream of water gushed along a broad depression that had been barely perceptible before the afternoon's storm. There was water everywhere . . . including inside a tent that had been left behind when Halt, Ellsworth, and the workers scrambled for higher ground.

Bear stared at the swirling brown water, trying to make sense of what he was seeing. "Dammit, rivers don't just happen. Where did all this water come from?"

"Everywhere," Halt said, watching the water rolling over two days' worth of track bed work. "After the storm, we saw a trickle gather an' turn into a small, fast-movin' stream. Then th' stream widened an' before we knew it . . . it was rushin' down the roadbed, tearin' up jack."

There was a good bit more than just two days of bed work at stake here. From this vantage point, it was plain that the surveyed roadbed in the area followed the flow of the water with uncanny accuracy . . . almost as if it had been . . . planned. Bear felt his whole body go weak for a moment. How could Johnson have been so—

A wave of insight broke over him. This was no accident. And it was probably no accident that Johnson, their surveyor and engineer, had run off just as they reached construction of this section of the roadbed. The conclusion was inescapable. Johnson *knew*.

"We grabbed th' tools, wagons, mules, an' horses, struck

what tents we could, an' headed for high ground." Halt pointed to the bedraggled men and jumble of equipment sprawled over a rocky hillside, across the way. "Had to be sure th' men an' tools were accounted for before I could come for ye."

Bear nodded and, with a grim set to his jaw, turned his horse and headed down the rocky slope to ford the river. Nigel Ellsworth met them waving a half-rolled map as they made their way up the other rise.

"There's no mention of it here at all!" he declared furiously, pointing at the lines representing the survey of the surrounding land. "Not a word—not a hint. It's worse than poor judgment—it's outright fraudulence!"

"All right." Bear swung down and reached for the map, bracing himself for bad news. "How bad is it?"

"It's a dry riverbed—the signs were all there, but I—" Ellsworth looked down and reddened with chagrin. "I'm not used to— I mean, usually the survey has already been done—and back East we'd never run into anything quite so—I just accepted the survey and assumed everything was as represented in the charts. He couldn't have missed this." Ellsworth blushed. "I can't believe I did."

"Damnation." Bear exhaled a chest full of frustration as he looked out over the rushing water. "So what do we do about it?"

Ellsworth came to stand beside him, grimacing at the way the water was pouring by. "Actually, the water is down a bit . . . better than it was an hour ago. I think it will drain off quick enough. But it's washed out a fair amount of our roadbed." He looked miserable to have to report: "And it will happen again, every time it storms like this."

The truth was so weighty that for a minute it prevented coherent thought. Bear scrambled for solutions. "What about a bridge?"

Ellsworth glanced from Bear to Halt and back again.

"It's usually dry, but it's still a riverbed. Loose base. Sand and particulates. Not stable without pilings . . . and still likely to be weakened by flooding. The only real solution is to move the track."

Bear rubbed his hands down his face, dreading the answer to his next question. "To where?"

Ellsworth looked around, consulted the map, and scrambled up the slope to fetch his transit and telescope. After a few minutes of sightings and some scribbled calculations, he pointed to a ridge of rock across the way that formed a plateau leading south and east, to the foothills of the Highwood Mountains.

"Given the track we've already laid and our general direction, I'd say that was our best route."

Bear looked to Halt, who nodded, then gave Ellsworth a nod of approval. "As soon as it dries up enough to move the wagons and equipment, we'll take stock of the damage and get started. Dammit—this is going to put us even further behind."

While Bear and Halt rallied the men to begin packing up and made an inventory of what had been damaged or lost, Ellsworth found a flat rock and spread out his maps. He pored over the various maps rendering the local terrain . . . until he came to one that caused his eyes to widen in horror. Checking his transit and position against the darkening evening sky, he confirmed the worst . . . and then took it to Bear and Halt.

"What do you mean, we don't own it? We bought plenty of right-of-way."

"Not over there, you didn't." Ellsworth pointed to the distant outcroppings, then produced the plat map of the area to prove his point.

"Heaven help us," Halt said, staggering back and plopping down hard on a rock. "All that money . . . all that time . . ." He buried his head in his hands.

"The owner—who was it that sold us this parcel?" Bear asked.

"That'd be a fellow named A. J. Hickman," Ellsworth said, reading from the tiny print along the side.

"We have to have a talk with Mr. Hickman. But for now, we need to find out who owns that ridge and the land beyond," Bear declared, pointing to the engineer's make-shift desk. "Check your maps . . . see if it's listed."

BEAR HADN'T RETURNED from the forward camp yet and wasn't there to object the next morning when Diamond ordered Robbie into the wagon and set off for Great Falls with the reins in her own hands. It was early and as the sky brightened and streaked with color, she laid out for Robbie her plans for the morning. They would visit several eateries, sample the fare and find a sound cook—then take the fellow aside and make him an offer of employment.

But her plan ran aground time after time. She was or-dered out of kitchens, or withdrew with her hand over her nose and the specter of spoiled food clinging to her senses. Of the dozen smaller eateries in town, she found none that held the promise of a decent cook. By noon, she headed once more for the Lonesome Dove Restaurant. There, at least, they could find some decent food to purge away the vile impressions they had collected all morning.

As it happened, they found a great deal more.

Owner Silky Sutherland was exiting just as they en-tered. She brightened and greeted them loudly, then ushered them inside. When they were seated and had or-dered, Diamond decided to be straightforward about her problem . . . businesswoman to businesswoman.

"Perhaps you could help us, Miss Sutherland." At the older woman's warning frown, she amended: "Silky. Our cook was injured—has a broken leg—and we're desperate.

I've got to find another cook or the men will start to leave."
She lowered her voice. "Bear needs every man he's got if
he's going to make Billings by snowfall. You wouldn't happen to know where I might find a cook used to doing stew
by the barrel and potatoes by the hundredweight?"

Silky thought for a minute and grew serious as she reflected on Diamond's question. "They're in trouble—Finnegan an' McQuaid—ain't they?" she said.

"They're under the gun," Diamond admitted. "If they
don't get the track laid, they don't get their land grants. I
don't know all the ins and outs, but that Lionel Beecher
has filed a protest with the land office in Washington." She
frowned. "Actually, I know a few people in Washington
. . . I've been thinking that I should telegraph some of
them to check into the situation."

"There won't be no livin' with Bear McQuaid if you do,"
Silky said with a husky laugh. "That is the cussedest, most
independent man I ever known. He once spent an entire
winter outdoors in a tent—because he didn't have money
for both a room and a string of horses he intended to buy
and trade—an' he wouldn't take charity from nobody." She
shook her head. "Not even me."

The food arrived, and as they ate, she turned Silky's
words over. Clearly, this independent streak wasn't a recent thing with him. It went way back. Just how far back?
she wondered. And what could have made him—

"Tell you what, Diamond Lady . . . I think I've got a
cook for ye."

"You do?" Diamond sat up, feeling instantly lighter.
"Where is he?"

"First off, it ain't a *he*," Silky said with a mischievous
twinkle in her eye. "And *she's* sittin' right here." When
Diamond looked dismayed, she chuckled. "I ain't always
been an elegant lady o' luxury." She fluffed her bright purple organdy dress and red and white feather boa. "My ma

was a helluva boardin'-house cook . . . I learned from the best there was. I cooked my way west, until I landed here"—she grinned—"and found me a few profitable side-lines."

Diamond had a hard time hiding her skepticism, but Silky didn't seem to take it personally.

"It's been a while since I rattled a few pots . . . but I'm game." Her kohl-rimmed eyes narrowed cannily. "Halt Finnegan'll be around some, won't he?"

SILKY SAW HALT Finnegan a bit sooner than she expected.

As Diamond, Robbie, and Silky were heading for the dry-goods store to place an order for the things Silky would need, they met Halt and Bear hurrying into the land office. The pair looked as though they'd been dragged across half of Montana and collected a good bit of the territory's topsoil along the way.

"What are you doing here?" she said, looking Bear over with dismay. "I thought you rode out to check on some water at the forward camp."

"It was more than just some water," Bear said grimly. "That sidewinder Johnson routed us through a dry riverbed. The damn thing's flooded out. We have to move the track. And to do that, we have to buy another piece of land." He jerked his head toward the land-office door.

Lionel Beecher stood at the window of the Sweetwater Saloon, next door to the land office, smoking a cheroot and watching Bear McQuaid, his snooty wife, and the others enter the land office. The sight of McQuaid's mud-spattered clothes and boots, coming on the heels of a powerful storm, led him to conclude that McQuaid had just discovered the creative change of routing he had arranged for the Montana Central and Mountain. Engineer Johnson had been prone both to drink and to gamble and was not especially gifted with foresight or intestinal fortitude. It wasn't difficult, really. A bit of liquor, a few losses in a poker game—and a convenient way to cancel the debt . . .

"You're good, Beecher," he said smugly, watching for Bear to emerge and ride south . . . straight into a stone wall. "Too damned good to be stuck out here in the middle of nowhere. Gould owes you plenty for this one."

TWENTY

DANVERS, JIM DANVERS was the name that kept drumming in Bear's head as he and Halt rode south and east, headed for the farmstead of the man who owned the strip of rocky buttes that would provide solid footing for the Montana Central and Mountain. Diamond had wanted to come with him, but he declared that getting the kitchen working again was just as important as buying a bit of right-of-way, and she had reluctantly agreed.

No one had been more surprised at the identity of their new cook than Bear was. But Silky never did the expected . . . always had a few aces up her sleeve. He was a bit unsettled, however, by the thought of her and Diamond getting chummy. He had enough trouble dealing with Diamond now; he sure as hell didn't need Silky giving her pointers!

The Danvers farmstead was typical of those constructed by settlers in this part of the high plains. Most of the buildings were wooden, none of them painted, and some of the earlier outbuildings still rested on foundations of cut sod. The house, at the center of the farmstead, had a front porch and not far from the house was a fenced vegetable garden filled with surprisingly lush rows of green. Danvers obviously had a wife. As they approached, children ran out to greet them—four of them—all of whom looked to be twelve years of age or younger. Then a man stepped out onto the porch with a shotgun cradled in his arm and called the children back, ordering them to get into the house.

"Danvers?" Bear said, reining up some distance away. "I'm Barton McQuaid and this is my partner Halt Finnegan. We're with the Montana Central and Mountain railroad, and we've come to—"

"Don't care why yer here," Danvers broke in. "Jus' turn them horses around and head back where ye come from."

"We've come to speak with you about buying some land . . . the buttes over on your southwest range."

"Ain't for sale." He put his hand on the trigger of the shotgun and swung it around so they could see both barrels. "Now git."

"I don't think you understand . . . we *need* that piece of land. It's mostly rock, no good for wheat or running cattle on. We'd be willing to make you a good price. Cash money."

"Jim . . . please . . ." came a woman's voice from inside the open door.

"Stay inside, Luanna," Danvers snapped, then he brandished the weapon and stalked to the edge of the porch, where he made a stand. "I told ye . . . my land ain't for sale—at no price. Now get outta here, an' leave me an' mine out of it."

Bear dismounted but froze with one foot still in the stirrup at the sound of hammers clicking back behind two steel barrels. He looked at Danvers, really looked. The man was by all appearances a hardworking wheat farmer. Weathered and worn, probably aged beyond his years, with a wife and a passel of kids to raise. There wasn't a farmer alive who couldn't use a bit of cash money. Most went delirious at the thought of selling off a bit of untillable land to a railroad. Something wasn't right here.

"Get back on that horse real slow, mister. And get off'n my land."

As he and Halt rode back toward their railroad camp, Bear kept remembering the look in the man's eyes . . . unnaturally bright . . . tense . . . fearful. Halt must have been thinking the same thing.

"Wonder what's got him so spooked?"

Once the question was asked, answers weren't hard to imagine.

"Beecher visited the other landowners—maybe he offered Danvers more money."

"He didn't even listen to our price." Halt frowned and stared off into the distance. "Whatever it is, it ain't got to do wi' money. I can tell ye that much."

When they returned to camp, Bear headed for their train car to check on Schultz and tell Diamond that he intended to ride back out with Halt to search for alternative routes. He found her and Robbie rearranging furniture and making up the two spare Pullman beds on the office end of the car. His desk and files and bookcase had been pushed to the corner niche behind the necessary, and Schultz was ensconced on the banquette under the windows in the parlor portion.

"What's going on?" he demanded.

"I'm making room for Miss Sutherland." She continued tucking sheets as she'd seen the porters do. "She'll be staying with us while she cooks."

"Staying with *us?* You mean in here?"

"Would you rather I put her in the dormitories with the men?" She raised one eyebrow. "Or perhaps one of the wet canvas tents? How about a boxcar?" He looked as if he would have lain down naked on an anthill rather than say no. Smiling, she nodded to Halt as he entered. "Did you get the land?"

"Danvers wouldn't even listen to our offer," Bear said grimly. "Just gave us a damned good view of his shotgun barrels and ordered us to leave. We're heading out to do a bit of scouting. We have to find another route. There has to be a way through our right-of-way land that isn't a dry riverbed."

Silky arrived later with two kitchen helpers and immediately took up her post in the kitchen car. Diamond found herself assigned tasks, too: setting up the serving tables and locating things in the storeroom. It was there that she spotted the huge, muddy boot tracks. Schultz kept the storeroom pristine and jealously guarded access to it. She stared at those tracks and at the sliding door that Schultz had fallen from. Something whispered that Schultz's accident might not have been so "accidental."

Supper that night was simple but surprisingly tasty. Beef stew with a side of corn bread and apple cobbler. This time, with Silky's guidance, Diamond's coffee was right on target. Better food, the spectacle of Silky's flamboyant style and colorful clothing—which she refused to abandon even in the heat and hazard of the kitchen—and the presence of her two female assistants seemed to improve the men's attitude. The harmonica came out again around the campfire that evening and the men told stories that kept Robbie enthralled until Diamond hauled him off to bed. He fell asleep without even changing clothes.

Morning came deuced early and as Diamond stretched and yawned and poured a basin of water to wash her face, she spotted Bear's berth, undisturbed, and realized he must have stayed at the forward camp for the night. But with breakfast and dinner to prepare and serve, she had no time to think about his absence until late afternoon.

She and Silky carried cups of coffee out to the shaded side of the train and perched on the platform steps of the Pullman car.

"Disaster just seems to prowl the Montana Central and Mountain," she said, mostly to herself. "It seems like Bear and Halt have had just one stroke of bad luck after another."

Silky smiled, watching the horizon. "Don't believe in luck. Never have. 'Luck' is just what folks call it when they don't know what really happened."

Diamond thought on that for a minute, then tallied their troubles on her fingers. "Engineer Johnson ran off . . . the tools got stolen . . . Schultz broke his leg . . . the route was mapped wrong . . . they have to buy more land, but the owner won't sell . . ."

"That's not bad luck, Diamond Lady, that's *mischief.* Pure an' simple."

"But mischief has to be done by somebody," Diamond said.

"So it does."

She sat straighter. "Beecher?"

"That'd be my guess," Silky said, watching the horizon and sipping her coffee. "But McQuaid already knows Beecher's workin' against him . . . doin' everythin' he can to stop this track from goin' through." That conclusion sent a trill of anxiety through Diamond that Silky's next comment did nothing to alleviate. "But they're big boys. They can take care of themselves."

"They're big boys with *guns,*" she muttered. "They can get themselves killed."

Silky smiled. "McQuaid's not about to get himself killed. He's got a wife to be r'sponsible for. An' if there's one thing Bear McQuaid does, it's be r'sponsible. Why, when he was a young fella working cattle—set to roundin' up strays—he stayed out three days in a blizzard to bring 'em all in."

"I'm certain that would be a great comfort . . . if I were a cow or caught in a blizzard," she said tartly. "But since I'm just a woman and a wife, it indicates to me that he doesn't have sense enough to come in out of the cold."

"You'd understand better if you were a rancher," Silky said with a knowledgeable glint in her eye, "who depended on every blessed calf to make yer note at the bank." She shrugged. "It's just McQuaid's way of bein' a man."

Diamond frowned and buried her nose in her cup, thinking on that.

"It's manly to be stubborn and independent?" she said. "To risk your fool neck to bring in a few calves that will fetch no more than ten dollars a head."

"Yep."

"That's crazy."

Silky chuckled. "I never said it wasn't. It's just men. They gotta do what men do. Wreck things. Build things. Protect things. Make things work. Then make things work *better* . . ."

That was what Bear was doing, she thought. Building a railroad. Making things work better. Making Progress. She glanced back down the track his crews had laid. Suddenly, along those tracks she could see future farmsteads and towns and mines and industries. She could see people coming to new lives and fresh starts . . . bringing their ideas, hopes, and dreams with them. And it was Bear's cursed stubbornness and tenacity that would someday make it all possible. The vision, determination, and promise she had seen in him that day in the library had been real.

The last of her doubts about him—his truthfulness and his motives toward her—dissolved. Halt said he had brought maps and papers to speak to her about their rail-

road . . . she had seen them with her own two eyes. He
had wanted to ask her. He had tried to approach her, but
his pride and independence had kept him from mention-
ing it. Now it was that same pride and independence that
threatened to keep them apart.

FOR TWO DAYS he'd been chasing his tail, Bear realized
as he rode back to the main construction camp. He'd been
missing things . . . felt as if he'd been looking through a
dirt-brown haze. A night out under the stars had helped
settle the dust clogging his faculties.

They had looked for an alternative route for the track
and found that their closest suitable land would take them
well out of the way and would involve a bridge they
weren't equipped to construct . . . not in such a short
time. Now, after an entire day in the saddle and a long
night of sleeping on rocky ground, they were back to Jim
Danvers.

"What would make a man pull out his old shotgun and
threaten total strangers?" he asked Halt as they rode along.
"We weren't threatening him."

"Then somebody else must 'ave," Halt responded with a
troubled look.

"Beecher." Bear's features hardened to ruddy granite.
"Damn his hide. He got to Johnson . . . got to our tools
. . . now he's made sure we can't buy land to reroute our
track." He rubbed his hand up and down his thigh and slid
it onto his gun holster. "I've had about all of him I intend
to take."

That evening Bear watched Diamond helping to clear
away the serving tables and put away the kitchen equipment. Her hair was pinned up in a simple but fetching
swirl, her face was moist from the heat, and her eyes were

bright with purpose. She looked like the prettiest, sweetest girl he'd ever seen.

He had been a little taken aback at first by the sight of her with an apron on, hauling trays of biscuits and dishing out plates of stew. He knew how she had been raised; she'd never set a table or carried a dish in her life. But then, she'd always been one to give and to help, and he supposed—testily—that she probably saw this as another form of charity work.

Then, as he watched her carrying around heavy pots of coffee to refill the men's cups, he saw the way the men responded: their smiles, shy nods, and respectful comments. They seemed to stand or sit straighter when she approached. They could tell she was a lady and responded accordingly.

Suddenly he thought of Danvers and Danvers's overburdened wife. He was learning just how much influence a woman could have on a man. When Diamond came toward him with her big enameled-tin coffeepot, he held out his cup with a smile.

"Tomorrow morning," he said, "put on your riding boots and your best bonnet."

"Whatever for?" she asked, leaving aside for the moment the fact that she didn't own a bonnet and wouldn't have worn one even if she did.

He smiled. "We're going visiting."

THE SUN AND Diamond's spirits were both rising when she, Bear, and Halt set off the next morning on horseback, headed for the Danvers farmstead. Despite her tension, she was optimistic that they could change the farmer's mind and felt that a new level of trust had finally been reached between her and Bear . . . for him to be including her in such a vital business transaction.

The prairie was painted with pastel morning colors and the breeze was pleasant. As they came over the last rise, they spotted the farmstead laid out in the hollow below . . . small wooden house, modest barn, three shedlike outbuildings for animals, two corrals, and several grain fields in varying stages of maturity.

Mrs. Danvers, a small, wiry woman with a sun-weathered face, was out in her kitchen garden with her elder children, hoeing. As she spotted them, she straightened and held her hand up to augment the shade of her sunbonnet. After a moment, she gave one of the children a shove in the direction of the barn. Just as Diamond, Bear, and Halt rode into the yard, Danvers himself emerged from the barn . . . without his trusty shotgun.

Bear called a greeting, dismounted, and quickly helped Diamond down from her horse. At the sight of her with the two men, Danvers and his wife exchanged nervous looks and came forward to meet them.

"Barton McQuaid." Bear tipped his hat. "My wife, Diamond McQuaid. My partner, Halt Finnegan. Of the Montana Central and Mountain Railroad." He held out his hand to Jim Danvers. The farmer looked most uncomfortable as he stuffed his hands into his pockets instead of meeting Bear's handshake.

"If you come about th' land, th' answer's th' same. It ain't for sale."

Danvers's wife reddened and spoke up with what Diamond suspected was a rare bit of nerve. "Jim, ye can't be rude t' these folk. They come all the way out here. We kin at least be hospitable." She looked at Diamond and self-consciously wiped her hands down her apron. "I can offer ye some coffee, Miz McQuaid. Would ye come inside an' sit a spell?"

"I'd like that, Mrs.—"

"Don't mean to be rude, missus," Danvers said grimly,

stepping over to take hold of his wife's arm. "But ye can't stay, neither."

Bear stalked forward to Diamond's side. "Look, whatever Beecher offered to pay you not to sell . . . we'll double it."

"We'll triple it," she said on impulse. "We have significant cash reser—"

"Diamond—" Bear seized her arm and when she looked up his eyes were bright with anger. "Why don't you see if Mrs. Danvers will show you her garden . . . or maybe get you that cup of coffee." Combined with his hand tight on her arm, it wasn't a suggestion, it was a command. And a dismissal.

She felt as if she'd been slapped.

"My land ain't fer sale," Danvers said, clearly nervous. "Not even at triple th' price."

"Jim," Mrs. Danvers said anxiously. "We could use th'—"

"Dammit, Luanna, git in the house!" Danvers barked out in exasperation. "An' take the kids. This ain't none o' yor bizness."

Diamond watched Luanna Danvers wilting as she shooed her children into the house and felt an awful kinship with the woman. Bear had just done the same thing to her—put her in her place, albeit more subtly.

"How much did Beecher offer you?" Bear said, searching the man's haunted gaze, stepping in front of Diamond, effectively blocking her from both sight and participation. Through the turmoil inside her, Diamond scarcely heard Danvers's anguished reply.

"He offered to let my fam'ly live t'see another season." Danvers's voice thickened. "And I ain't gonna pass up that offer."

"Look, you need this railroad . . . it will make your land and your wheat and oats that much more valuable.

You can't allow him to threaten and bully you," Bear declared. "Once he starts, there's no telling where he'll stop."

"He won't do us no harm . . . long as I don't sell to you," Danvers said.

Bear tried again. "We can give you protection . . . see to it you have help."

"Fer how long, railroad man? A week, a month, all the way t'harvest? An' what about next plantin' season?" He glowered and said through his teeth: "I said I ain't sellin' to you. Now git off 'n my land an' leave us be."

There was a crackling moment of silence, then Bear turned and seized Diamond by the arm and ushered her forcefully back to her horse.

Through a red haze of anger she managed to find the stirrup and to climb into the saddle, jerking away from his hands the instant she was on board. By the time they rode over the first rise, she had cooled enough to see his action in its dismal context. He hadn't brought her along as a partner, he'd brought her along as a prop . . . something to help him convince Danvers that he was a family man himself and worthy of trust . . . or perhaps something to pacify Danvers's poor, lonely wife. She was supposed to smile prettily and keep her mouth shut . . .

They rode a while in silence and when they came to the trail leading toward Great Falls, Bear looked at Halt.

"Take Diamond back to camp. I'm going into town."

"Don't bother, Halt," she said icily. "I'm not a child. I am perfectly capable of finding my way back to camp from here *by myself*." She kicked her mount into a gallop and raced off without even a look at Bear.

She rode hard and fast for a time, bending to her mount's exertion. She wanted to taste the wind, feel her mount working beneath her, and hear the fierce pounding of hooves . . . hoping the speed and power of riding would purge the hurt from her. But in the end, all it did was postpone the ache in her heart and aggravate the fire in her lungs. She finally had to slow and realized that her urge to action was not yet over.

She had to do something that would force Bear to deal with her . . . something that would make him respect her presence in his life . . . something that would make him admit her to partnership in his precious railroad. Whether she liked it or not, the Montana Central and Mountain was the very core of his life. Until he could grant her a vital and permanent place in it, until he could share it willingly with her, she would always be on the fringe of his life and kept in a small locked chamber of his heart.

She reined up with her chest heaving and her blood pounding in her head. There was one thing the Montana Central and Mountain needed right now more than anything else. Right-of-way. Danvers land. If she could arrange some sort of deal with the Danverses, he would have to see that she intended to help, and that she could be of some value besides money. She had arranged tougher deals than this. A smile and a calm, caring demeanor often made headway where shaking fists and making threats— and riding in with a gun on your hip—had failed.

Filled with fresh resolve and determined to fight for Bear in the only way she knew, she turned her horse and started back up the trail to the Danvers farm.

GREAT FALLS WAS quiet that hot summer afternoon as Bear and Halt rode in. They left their horses in front of the dry-goods store and made their way down the dusty main street toward the Sweetwater Saloon.

"Are ye sure ye want to do this?" Halt said, scanning the street.

"Somebody has to face him down," Bear answered. "Might as well be me. May as well be now."

"Mebee if we talked to th' sheriff—"

"He's probably still sleepin' it off."

The unpainted swinging doors of the Sweetwater Saloon creaked as they entered, but there were only a few patrons at the dozen or so tables and none bothered to look up from contemplating their bottles or their cards. The air reeked of the sawdust used to sweep up spills from the floor, and flies buzzed lazily around the soured remains of beer that had soaked into the unvarnished wooden tables. Bear's boot heels smacked the bare wooden floors and the sound echoed eerily through the mostly empty saloon. He and Halt strode over to the long oak bar and leaned against it. The fleshy, hard-eyed bartender behind the counter mopped his way down the water-ringed surface to where they stood.

"What'll it be, gents?"

"Beecher," Bear said. "Where is he?"

The bartender looked Bear over as if sizing up what sort of threat he might pose. "Don't know where he is. Or when he'll be back."

Bear met the man's sullen glare. "We'll wait."

Every time footsteps were heard on the wooden walk outside or the swinging doors creaked open, Bear felt his gut tighten. But time and time again it proved to be a townsperson walking by or a farmer in town for supplies coming into the Sweetwater for something to quench his thirst.

One hour, then another went by. Near the end of the second hour, a fellow wearing a pair of ivory-handled revolvers entered and headed for the bar. He looked to be straight off the range—his shirt was stuck to his back with sweat and from the brim of his hat to the toes of his boots he was covered with dust. Bear nudged Halt; both of them recognized him from the train station. They tensed and watched the front of the saloon. Soon Beecher appeared in the window, walking toward the doors, his ever-present cheroot glowing a dull red.

Bear scooted his chair back from the table so that he faced the door and then flicked the leather loop off the hammer of his revolver. His every sense came alert; he was suddenly aware of the ticking of the clock on the far wall, of the dusty shine of the huge mirror over the bar, and of the scrape of chairs as two men that had been passing time with cards, near the window, decided to call it quits. He sat rod-straight, his gaze trained on the door.

Beecher entered with three more of his men, all of whom were wearing guns and layers of dust. The three fanned out and dropped down into chairs, calling out to the bartender for a bottle of whiskey. Beecher strolled to the bar, removed his hat, and began to dust his long black coat. As the bartender returned from serving the others to pour Beecher his usual drink, he engaged Beecher's gaze and flicked a meaningful glance in Bear's direction. Beecher turned and stiffened at the sight of Bear rising from a table against the rear wall.

"What?" Beecher said, recovering. "Has hell frozen over already? I must have missed it."

"I'm sure they're keepin' it warm enough for you, Beecher," Bear said quietly, strolling forward. From the corner of his eye, he could see Beecher's men coming to attention, and he heard behind him the unmistakable sound of Halt's revolver sliding from its leather holster. "I didn't come to discuss your plans for eternity."

"I doubt you came to enjoy my hospitality, either."

Bear's smile had nothing to do with humor. "I came to talk to you about my former engineer, Johnson . . . a dry riverbed . . . and an offer you made to Jim Danvers."

"Danvers? Don't recall the fellow," Beecher said with

nasty pleasure. "But then, I've made a good many offers in my day."

"One too many." Bear flexed his shoulders, loosening, preparing. "I've come to see you `.ke back the one you made to Danvers."

"Refresh my memory, McQuaid." The glint in Beecher's eye made Bear's hands clench at his sides. "Just what did I promise him?"

"That his family wouldn't live to see harvest if he sold us his land adjoining our right-of-way."

"It's coming back to me." Beecher reached for his glass and downed the contents. "Not one of my more inspired threats, I'm afraid. He had such a brood of brats, losing only one or two of them wouldn't much matter. And that woman of his is such a pious little drudge, she wouldn't provide much sport. But losing the lot of them . . . even a stoic little worm like him would have to feel a certain amount of discomfort at that prospect."

"You're going to take it back. And you're going to leave town . . . carrying this message to Jay Gould: we're pushing this track through to Billings before snowfall. And there's nothing you or he or anybody else can do about it."

"Brave words . . . for a man outnumbered two to one."

Bear watched the trio of gunmen at the tables sitting straighter, sizing him up, and the ivory handles at the bar squaring off on him, behind Beecher.

"Only two to one?" Bear smiled coldly. "You're not participatin'? For once, Beecher, be a man. My quarrel isn't with them. It's not them I'm callin' a liar and a bully and a damned coward. It's you." He shifted, ever so slightly, so that his right shoulder, right arm, and right hip were slightly forward. His gun felt heavy and familiar on his hip. In his mind, his hand was already snapping up, seizing his gun, and pulling back the hammer as he drew it from its

holster. His shoulders were twisting, his left shoulder jerking back to present a smaller target, even as the powder in
the chamber exploded and the gun recoiled in his grip.

"You in the blue shirt," Bear said, without taking his
eyes from Beecher. "Give him your gun."

There was a long, volatile silence as the gunman looked
between Bear and his employer. Beecher sealed his fate
when he gave a snort of contempt.

"He's not your trained monkey, McQuaid. He's mine."

The flint-faced gunman tossed a speaking glance to his
companions and apparently found them of like mind. He
eased back in his chair and flipped open the buckle of his
gun belt. Keeping his gun hand well away from the revolver, he drew the belt from around him and laid it on the
table. Beecher's face flamed as his hired gunman gave the
weapon a shove toward him.

Beecher looked from one gunman to another, demanding they intervene. Their sullen stares declared that they
saw this as a matter of guts, a test of honor, in which none
of them intended to interfere. Even "trained monkeys,"
their pointed refusal said, had their limits.

"This is absurd," Beecher declared, tensing. "I'm not a
gunfighter."

"That makes two of us," Bear declared with deadly
calm. "Strap it on."

Bear could almost taste Beecher's anxiety, could almost
feel the way his heart was beginning to pound, could certainly see the trouble he was having swallowing. By the
time Beecher moved toward the table, Bear would have
put the odds at fifty-fifty that he would accept or refuse
the challenge.

As Beecher picked up the gun and unbuttoned his coat,
he tossed a speaking look at the bartender, who reached
under the counter and pulled out a shotgun. One fleshy
thumb pulled back the hammers on both barrels at once.

The gun came down to rest on the bar, and the bartender swiveled it so that it was aimed straight at Halt. Bear stepped to the side in order to keep the bartender and Beecher both in his sights.

"Insurance," Beecher said with an ugly smirk. "To keep things fair."

Like hell. If Bear were the one left standing, the bartender would likely cut him down on the spot . . . or so Beecher wanted him to believe. It was pressure that Bear didn't need and helped to even the odds.

With slow, deliberate movements, Beecher buckled on the gun belt and tied it down on his thigh. Then they faced each other squarely, and Bear took a deep—

"Stop!" A blur of green and white, wearing a black hat with a white feather, burst through the swinging doors. Both Bear and Beecher whirled, but only Bear's gun cleared the holster before the face and figure of the speaker registered.

Diamond froze, staring down the barrel of Bear's gun and into his fiercely narrowed eyes. For a moment she couldn't breathe, couldn't speak. Those memorable copper eyes eased, then widened in horrified recognition.

"Bear, you can't do this," she said hoarsely, glancing down at the chilling circle of steel pointing her way.

"Get out of here," Bear snarled, lowering the gun only slightly.

She swallowed the fear collecting in her throat and made her feet move . . . forward. "Please—you have to listen to me—"

"Diamond—dammit!" he roared. "Get out of here!"

"No." She swallowed hard again. "Put away that gun and listen."

"If you don't leave now—go back to camp!"

"No. Not unless you come with me," she said, planting herself directly between him and Beecher. She could see a vein throbbing in his temple and knew she was trampling his manly pride and independence. Better that, she told herself, than trampling across his grave.

"I've solved our land problem." She pulled a folded paper from her skirt pocket and opened it, holding it up . . . partly for him to see it and partly to block his view of Beecher. Exploding forward, he smashed the paper down and grabbed it from her in the same movement.

"Are you crazy? Do you want to get killed?"

"No, I'm not crazy. I'm determined." She pulled on the paper and his hand came up with it. "I was able to arrange a special lease. We won't have to purchase anything. The use of the land is ours for one hundred twelve years . . . until 1999."

He glanced furiously at the paper in his hand, then held it out to Halt, who had risen. The Irishman took it from him and looked it over.

"It's a land lease, all right," he confirmed, his eyes widening. "Like she said. One hundred twelve years. No purchase involved."

Bear looked down at her, then at Beecher, whose face looked like blood on granite.

"Danvers's land, I take it," Beecher said, lowering his gaze to her and his voice to a menacing murmur. "A lease. No *purchase* involved. What a clever little wife you have, McQuaid."

"Go back to camp, Diamond," Bear said fiercely.

"No." She faced him, praying he would read the softer, more frantic plea in her eyes. "I won't go . . . unless you come with me."

"Do go, my boy," Beecher said with a notable relaxation of manner. "There will be plenty of time for murdering me later. Count on it."

As Bear wavered, Beecher ripped open the holster ties, raised both hands into view, and then lowered one to undo the gun belt buckle. The thud and then metallic clank of the gun hitting the floor somehow snapped the last of Bear's restraint.

He jammed his gun into his holster, ducked, and rammed his shoulder into her stomach—hoisting her up onto his shoulder. She began to flail frantically as they reached the door and didn't stop until they reached their mounts and he dropped her into the dirt beside her horse.

"Mount up!" he ordered.

TWENTY-ONE

BEAR WAS FURIOUS enough to throttle her. He ran the devil out of his horse instead, leaving her to trail behind with Halt until they reached camp. He pounced to the ground, paced furiously . . . then charged down the track to the first man he saw with a hammer, wrenched it from him, and proceeded to bash several spikes into unrecognizable lumps.

By suppertime, he had stalked and snarled enough to put the entire camp on its ear. Halt tried to drag him aside and talk some sense into him, but he warned his partner off and continued to work like the proverbial Irish banshee.

He told himself that he'd give both himself and her time to cool off. He didn't need to compound the trouble between them by erupting with all the anger and accusations he felt toward her. She was probably just trying to help, in her own misguided way. He needed to stay calm and collected. He needed to plan out what he was going to say. Their future together depended on him laying down the law and forbidding her from interfering with his railroad and inserting herself into matters as dangerous as those this afternoon.

Then she came around with her big enameled coffeepot and he saw the men turning—none too subtly—to collect his reaction. How the hell had his relationship with her become the business of every man on the crew?

That annoyance was minor compared to what he felt when she swayed over to him with her back straight and her chin raised, looking as if she were doing him a huge favor to be seen in the same territory with him. He glanced up, caught her gaze unexpectedly in his, and felt as if he'd been struck by the blue lightning in her eyes. She was furious with him.

She was furious with *him*!

Broadsided by that bolt of feminine anger, he jumped to his feet, ripped the pot from her hands, and for the second time that day hoisted her onto his shoulder, and carried her off, kicking and squealing in outrage. He stalked through the camp, through the picket lines, through the piles of brush cleared from the track bed . . . out into the twilight.

By the time he set her on her feet, she was well winded and thoroughly rattled . . . unable to do anything but listen to what he had to say.

"What the hell did you think you were doing this afternoon?" he roared.

He had underestimated her ability to talk as long as she drew breath.

"Saving your damnable railroad," she panted out, holding her aching ribs. "Not to mention your stubborn, prideful neck!"

"I didn't *need* saving."

"Oh, yes, you did . . . from yourself, if not from Beecher." She stomped closer. "You were going to shoot it out with him like some hired gun out of a dime novel. Of all the absurd . . . arrogant . . . ridiculous—"

Her tirade poured over him like molten lead. Every nerve in his body was jangling, demanding not just rebuttal but revenge for every insulting word. He grabbed her by the upper arms.

"You don't know what you're talking about," he declared. "Beecher is a mean, dangerous son of a bitch. He'd as soon kill me or you or the Danverses as look at us. It's not the first time he's used threats and violence to try to stop the Montana Central and Mountain and—thanks to you—it won't be the last."

"So you decided to take a gun to him."

"I decided to call him out. It would have been a fair fight."

"If you had killed him, it would have been murder." Her volume was rising steadily. "This is your idea of progress? Making yourself judge and jury and executioner? No wonder your blasted railroad is falling apart."

"It's *not* falling apart!"

"You haven't got a decent right-of-way, you're hardly making two miles a day, and all you can think about is running around waving a gun and playing cowboy," she charged. "And when I try to do something to help—"

"Help?" he roared back. "Is that what you call running smack into the middle of a face-off between two men? This is not 'playing cowboy.' This is not just some damned social disagreement. Out here people live and *die* by their words. You had no right to come barging into something you don't know anything about and clearly don't understand."

"I don't understand?" She wrenched free and stepped back. "I understand that you were about to lay your life on the line because you couldn't bear the notion that you might have to accept help from a mere woman. I understand that you're so blasted determined to keep your precious Montana Central and Mountain all to yourself that you won't let me do anything to help you. That's not only selfish and prideful and hurtful, Bear McQuaid—it's just plain stupid!"

Every shocking word sliced straight to the core of him. *Selfish.* No one in his entire life had ever accused him of that. He'd never had anything to be selfish with, never had anything to withhold from somebody. He'd always been the outcast, the spoiler, the underdog. His entire being recoiled, then reacted.

"Now I'm selfish as well as prideful and stubborn and stupid?" He towered above her, grinding out every unfortunate word. "Well, at least I'm not barging in where I'm not needed."

She stared up at him, feeling those words sinking into the depths of her heart. Not needed. In one horrifying sentence he had summed up their past, their present, and—she now could see—their future. He might want her as a bankroll and a pleasurable bedmate . . . but not as an equal, a partner, a loving and vital part of his life. His railroad was *his* and he didn't need her to share it. In fact, he'd rather see it go under than allow her any part in it.

As they stood there, face to face, chests heaving, confronting the deepest division between them, the sound of hoofbeats came out of the distance, growing steadily. It was a long moment before Bear could pull himself from Diamond's stare to register a light . . . moving along the horizon . . . yellow and eerie gray . . . sparks and smoke. The hurt and anger roiling inside him prevented him from making sense of it at first. It was only his struggle to contain the volatile words in his head that permitted him enough control to finally recognize the shape of a rider on horseback dragging something. Something burning.

She wanted to shake him, to make him turn back to

her, to make him answer all the whys in her reeling mind and heart. But she realized he wasn't just looking away, he was looking *at* something. The brightness beginning to light the horizon seemed oddly gray, though it was nowhere near the recently set sun. He was watching what seemed to be a distant horse and rider. She followed his gaze as he whipped it around to scan the southern horizon, and there was another dark form on horseback . . . with a similar plume of gray rising in his wake.

"Dammit!" Bear pivoted and charged back toward the train, bellowing from the bottom of his lungs "Fire—range fire!"

She stood for a moment, watching those horses and riders on distant rises, realizing numbly that they were dragging something behind them that was setting the prairie grass ablaze. She quickly looked from north to south . . . then to the west, where the dim glow of the sky silhouetted a third rider. Fire. On all sides.

Seizing her skirts, she began to run toward the train. Fire would soon be racing through the dry grasses toward them, closing in from all directions. By the time she reached their train car, she could hear Bear in the middle of camp, roaring orders, and could hear the shouts and scurrying of the men trying to rescue supplies and equipment. She raced toward him as he ordered men into the cab of the engine, and he turned just in time to catch her.

"Get in the car!" he ordered above the chaos. "Seal up the windows!"

"But Robbie—"

"I'll find him!" He gave her a shove in that direction. "Go!"

She barely had time to reach the steps before she heard the sound of coal hitting the metal of the firebox. They were going to try to move the train before the fire closed in. She looked up from the platform and saw the night sky filling with feathers of gray smoke around them. In the last few days they had made so little progress on the track, they had let the engine cool considerably. There was no guarantee they could get it hot enough to generate power in time.

Bear was apparently coming to that same conclusion. He began ordering the men to grab shovels and head toward the fire. Diamond watched them hesitate and look at each other, then at the train that was preparing to move and leave them behind.

"Come on—we've got to build a firebreak—clear the brush out of the way!" Reading their hesitation, Bear stalked back and picked up a shovel himself and started off toward the rising smoke. A handful of men followed; the others hung back, muttering among themselves, uncertain whether Bear's orders would lead them toward safety or toward greater calamity.

Diamond watched with her heart in her throat as they judged Bear's leadership and found it wanting. He hadn't exactly endeared himself to them with his constant pushing and his volatile behavior. And now when the chips were down . . .

Just then Robbie came running up the track and Diamond grabbed him by the arm and turned him back around. "Go find Silky and stay with her!" She gave him a maternal shove toward the kitchen car, then jumped off the platform and headed for the center of camp.

She wasn't entirely sure what she was going to do until she reached the middle of camp and scorched the lot of them with her most compelling glare.

"Well, what are you waiting for?" She reached for the nearest shovel, pulling it from the startled man's grasp. "Let's go."

It took only a split second for them to realize that she was going with her man to fight this fire. If *she* had that much faith in his judgment, then . . . They headed after her, dipping their kerchiefs in a bucket as they went. They spread out into a line, each man keeping within sight of the others. Somewhere along the way, someone handed her a wetted kerchief and she looked over to watch him tying his own over his nose and mouth. She followed suit and soon realized why. The smoke that had seemed so clear and defined was suddenly all around them, threatening to engulf them and take away all sense of direction.

"Clear the brush!" The order came down the line, passed from man to man. "Back ten feet. "Turn dirt only when you have to!"

They fell to work with a fury, pulling clumps of grass, hacking at roots, jabbing spades of dirt from the earth . . . ripping back the dry vegetation with hands and shovels and ballast forks. The smoke thickened around them, threatening to isolate them from each other, and they called to each other to work faster and pull back.

The sharp-edged grasses and tough stalks of scrub sage bit into Diamond's hands and her foot slipped again and again from the shovel, causing her to scar her boots and grit her teeth. Before long her back ached and her shoulders were screaming and her hands and lungs both felt raw. But the earth barrier was widening and when they reached the ten-foot margin she was able to straighten, rest her shovel on her shoulder, and arch her aching back. She didn't have long to rest.

"Good enough here—let's move!" came a familiar roar that seemed smoke-strained and hoarse. She turned to find Bear charging down the line, waving the workers on to a new section. He saw her, standing there with her face half-covered with a kerchief, her eyes red from smoke, and her skirts raised and tucked out of the way, and stopped dead. She was too tired and air-starved to try to evade him. Above the kerchief he wore across his lower face, she glimpsed both fury and pain in his eyes. But a moment later, he waved her and the others on. As she lifted her shovel and hurried past him, he wrapped an arm around her waist and propelled her along with him.

She had no time to think, beyond the fact that he had grudgingly accepted her presence among them. When they reached an area where the fire was some distance away, she took a place in line and began once again to grub out vegetation to extend that fire break.

The digging and pulling and spading and cutting seemed to go on and on. They worked around in a circle until they reached the tracks then hurried across them. Spotting the plumes of smoke on the other side, they staked out a line and began all over again. Just as they were beginning to flag, Halt arrived with a score of men from the forward camp and bolstered their sagging effort.

Nearly two frantic hours after they had begun, the fire reached the first firebreak, stopped, and began to burn itself out. Their only assurance of that was a lessening of smoke in the area they had first cleared. Then the breeze shifted slightly, the smoke began to lift, and they were able to send a detail with shovels right up to the fire itself. The crews beat and shoveled dirt on the smoldering grasses until the greatest threat was past.

Posting linesmen to walk the fire line, checking for re-starts, Bear pulled the kerchief down from his face and waded into the middle of the men sprawled on a gentle slope overlooking what had been their base camp. The tents were sagging and forlorn, there were heaps of crates and boxes here and there, and piles of wood being dressed for ties. He leaned on his shovel, staring out over the smoky, blackened earth that ran like a jagged scar across the rolling countryside. Through the center of that black-ened ring, like an arrow caught in flight, ran a pair of empty steel rails. The engineer had managed to get the engine running and backed the train down the track, leaving nothing visible except the rails they had labored so hard to lay. A track that went nowhere. For a railroad that didn't exist.

He had worked so hard, struggled for so long . . . for what? For a pair of steel rails that ran across a wasteland into nothingness? Unable to bear the sight and the emptiness it opened inside him, he turned away, and spotted Diamond sitting on a rock outcropping on the top of the nearby ridge. She was hanging on to a shovel and had propped her head against the handle. Her forehead and hair were sooty from the smoke and her once-pristine clothes were as grimy as any of the men's.

Never in his wildest dreams could he have imagined her like this. Dirty, exhausted, hands probably full of blisters—for the first time. She hadn't tucked herself safely away, hadn't hidden from the terror around her. She had picked up a shovel and charged into the smoke and flames ahead of many of his men.

Why would she do such a thing? Why the devil would she risk her health and safety to help him save his railroad when—like a giant horse's arse!—he'd just told her that he didn't *need* her?

"You're so determined to keep the Montana Central and Mountain all to yourself . . ." Her face appeared in his memory. ". . . selfish and prideful and hurtful . . ." He *had* hurt her. He had tried to put her in her place, to demand that she sit still and behave like a good little wife while he strutted and roared . . . and floundered . . . trying to prove that there was something of value inside him.

And still she rushed out to help him.

She was who she was, her actions said. He couldn't change that. Nor, he realized with humbling insight, would he want to. Then what was he trying to do? He loved her just as she was . . . the helpful, ingenious, interfering, loyal-to-a-fault, forgiving woman that she was. Loving woman that she was.

He *loved* her.

He suddenly felt as if blinders had fallen from his eyes. A wave of weakness hit his knees. He was stubborn and prideful and ridiculous and selfish and arrogant. And she still came out to help him. He had tried to keep her at arm's length while still trying to hold her. And still she came out to help him . . .

"Bear!" Halt came trudging up the slope, using his shovel as a support.

Bear tore his gaze from Diamond. "Damned good thing you got here when you did."

"We'd 'ave been here sooner, but we run into a bit of trouble. Come wi' me, lad." He struck off for the remnants of camp, pulling Bear along with him. A number of Halt's men had gotten their second wind and shoved to their feet to head back to camp with Bear and Halt.

When they reached the middle of the camp, Bear found two men lying on the ground, trussed hand and foot. Halt rolled one over with his foot.

"Caught them two and one of Beecher's hired guns pourin' pitch over brush . . . preparin' to set it afire and drag it. Beecher's man got away, but we got these two."

Bear stalked closer, scowling at the battered face and recognizing the man. He quickly jerked the other one over and the fellow coughed and spat dust.

"Carrick and Sikes." He wasn't too surprised. "Dammit—I should have known. You two have been nothing but trouble since the day I took you on." Rage filled him. He grabbed Carrick by the collar and hoisted him up, shaking him like a dog does a bone. "You lyin', sneakin', low-down—you tried to burn us out!"

Halt stepped in to keep Bear from venting his full fury

on the pair. When Bear dropped Carrick back on the ground, the thug managed a chilling laugh.

"Yeah, we done it. Set this here fire. Beecher told us to."

"And the tools"—Bear insisted—"you took them, too!"

Sikes snorted, his eyes filled with sullen defiance. "Ain't all we took."

There was a taunt in his tone that made everyone in earshot brace.

"Yeah?" Bear set a boot down on the wretch's throat. "What else?"

There was a long, suspenseful moment while Sikes realized that both the fury in Bear's eye and the pressure from his boot would only worsen. The answer, whispered hoarsely, had the effect of a thunderclap.

"Dynamite."

Bear looked up at Halt, who wheeled and headed for the sagging supply tent. Moments later he was back with a grim confirmation. A good portion of their dynamite was missing. Bear's blood suddenly ran cold in his veins.

"Talk!" He jammed his boot against the thug's neck again. "What's he going to do with it?"

"Too late, boss man." Sikes gave him a malicious smirk that showed the blood on his yellowed teeth. "It's a'ready done."

Bear wheeled, his mind racing, and ordered the camp torn upside down. They were sitting on a powder keg. But as Halt and the men raced to uncover the dynamite, Carrick gave a nasty laugh.

"Ye'll never find it."

Bear looked suddenly at the track—the train! They had planted it aboard the train! As he grabbed a crew of men and sent them rushing to saddle horses, he spotted Diamond and a number of the others returning to camp. He groaned and headed for her—thinking that he had to get her away from the camp.

Then it happened.

The ground rumbled. They felt deep, powerful vibrations that trembled them all the way to their fingertips. The sound seemed to go on forever, quaking them, unnerving them. But then it stopped and all was deadly quiet.

It was a minute before the full impact struck Bear. There had been a blast, but where? His first thought was the train, but there was no light or smoke coming from the horizon north and west, along the track leading to their engine and cars. He scanned the rest of the horizon until he came to an eerie light blooming along the northeastern ridge.

"That's not our track or the forward camp. What could Beecher possibly—" He looked at Halt, then at Diamond, frowning.

"The closest thing in that direction," Diamond said, scarcely realizing what she said, "is the Danvers place."

A few shocked heartbeats passed.

"Oh, God . . ." Bear closed his eyes, but quickly reopened them. "The Danverses. The bastard's dynamited their farm."

For the second time, Bear ordered his men to grab shovels and blankets. This time they mounted horses and piled into the two supply wagons, setting off at a breakneck pace over the rolling plain toward the Danvers farmstead.

Diamond had struggled to saddle a horse, and Bear— thinking of the fire, devastation, and perhaps even death that might lie ahead at the Danvers place—had almost ordered her to remain behind. Then he thought of Luanna Danvers and of Diamond's determined and much-needed help earlier. He shouldered her aside and lifted the saddle into place and tightened the cinch for her. When he helped her up into the saddle and glanced up at her, her eyes were glistening strangely.

By the time they reached the last rise overlooking the Danvers farm, they already knew there was fire, and plenty of it. Columns of smoke illuminated by flames below had been visible for some time, and the smell of burning wood—so different from the smoke of the brush fire—reached them well before they arrived. Still, none of them was prepared for the sight of wooden buildings lying in a thousand pieces all over the yard. Timbers and boards, twisted bits of metal, and charred grain had been blown in all directions. The surrounding slopes were littered with debris and the remnants of the house and main barn were both still burning.

Bear hit the ground running, shouting orders to find both the family and the well. The men found the wooden structure above the well damaged by the blasts, and worked frantically to clear it and rig a bucket line. Meanwhile, all they had were the shovels they brought with them and a few hammers left on the floor of the wagon. They could hear frantic animals trapped somewhere inside the smoke, and in desperation took those huge spike mauls to the still-standing walls of the barn. Wherever they broke through, heat and smoke from the smoldering hay and bedding came boiling out, and they were forced to retreat.

In the heat and confusion, Bear and Halt searched for Danvers and his family. On the porch of the burning shell of the house, they found the farmer pinned under a smoldering beam. He wasn't conscious, but that was just as well; his leg looked badly damaged. They found boards, pried him out of the wreckage, and carried him off to a safe distance. Then, desperate to find Luanna Danvers and her children and fearing the worst, Bear covered his face with his kerchief and went charging into the burning shell of the house.

Heat seared his lungs and drove him back outside, but not before he managed to collect the impression that there weren't any bodies inside. Starved for air and racked with coughing, Bear staggered out to collapse on the ground near Danvers.

Diamond sat by the senseless form of Jim Danvers, wiping his face with a piece of cloth ripped from her petticoat, watching the chaos, feeling helpless in a way she had never experienced before. The Danverses' home had been utterly destroyed. Blown to bits. The unthinkable violence of it shook her to the very core. For the second time that day, she was feeling the wrath of evil unleashed and scrambling to make sense of it.

How could anyone do this to a young family whose only offense was struggling to make a living? No, they had committed one more crime: they had listened to and believed her when she said that leasing the land to Bear wouldn't be "selling it" and wouldn't get them in trouble. How could she have known the finer points of her clever solution would be lost on a man like Beecher?

Then she looked up and saw Bear charging into the burning house and her heart stopped. He was risking life and limb to rescue these people, to make right *her* mistake. Terror gripped her and she abandoned her post by Danvers to pace desperately around the burning house.

There had to be *something* she could do—there had to be!

Frantically she looked around and spotted the men bringing up their first bucket of water. Buckets—blankets—anything they could wet and use for cover. She ran this way and that, spotting a soddy shed and realizing that behind it—protected from the blast—hung Luanna Danvers's wash line. The farm wife had obviously just done her wash—sundry clothes, sheets, and blankets were still pinned to the rope that had collapsed partway into the dirt.

Racing for them, she ripped the linens from the line and headed for the well. The men took them gratefully, ripped several of them in half, and wetted them down. She saved one of the cotton quilts, wetted it as best she could, then headed for the house . . . and Bear.

He was stumbling out of the house as she arrived. When he fell onto the ground near Danvers, she rushed to him and fell to her knees, wiping his reddened face with the wet blanket. He looked up and her heart turned over. If she had lost him to this senseless fire . . . Swallowing down that thought, she looked over at the unconscious Danvers. He had a family, too . . . a wife and children . . . who now were missing.

"I'll be back," she said, scrambling to her feet.

Bear had seen the tumult in her face and felt the anxiety in her touch. She wiped his face with the cool corner of a wet blanket, gave him a look that spoke what would take volumes to explain, then glanced at Danvers and bounded up.

"Diamond!" He tried to call to her, but the smoke had robbed him of all but a rasping whisper of a voice. He watched in horror as she wrapped herself in that wet quilt and ran for the rear of the house. "Damn-fool woman." He gritted his teeth as he struggled up. "Just gotta *help.*"

He staggered over to Halt and grabbed his arm. "Find Diamond . . ."

Together they lumbered around the house, searching through the flickering light and smoke for some sign of her. They finally heard her calling for Luanna Danvers and followed her voice. She materialized out of the choking gray haze and he grabbed her by the shoulders.

"Wait!" she said, fighting his hold on her. "I heard something!"

They went still and an agonizing moment later heard what might have been voices . . . muffled and indistinct. Batting smoke from their faces and trying to breathe only through the wet quilt, they huddled close and listened intently. The sound came again. Even through the roar and crackle of flame and the shouts of the men, they managed to hear it.

"Help! Help us!"

High-pitched voices. Children. They looked at one another, then when Diamond pointed, indicating a direction, they nodded and followed.

As they exited the swirling haze, still half-blinded by the smoke, they could see nothing promising. It wasn't until Halt stumbled and went down on one knee that they realized that they were practically standing on the wooden door of a root cellar. Beams from the exploded barn roof had landed across one end of the doors, sealing the entrance. But when Diamond called out, she was answered by a chorus of voices.

Bear and Halt fell on those beams and debris, scrambling and straining to shove them off the doors. Minutes later, they were pulling Luanna Danvers and three of her children from the root cellar.

"Jim—where's Jim?" she asked frantically as they hurried her around the devastation of her home. When she spotted him lying on the ground in the front yard, she let out a cry and raced to his side. Danvers roused as she cradled him and called his name. When he had roused fully, she fell across his chest, sobbing, and her husband weakly patted her head. Moments later she sat up and looked around. "We saw 'em comin'," she told Bear and Diamond. "Jim told me an' the kids t' head fer th' root cellar. Him an' Daniel—where's Daniel?" She looked first to her husband. "He was with you."

Danvers coughed. "Sent 'im to open th' barn door an' let the horses out."

Luanna Danvers turned in horror to the flaming remains of their barn. "My God. Daniel!"

Barely a second passed before Bear was in motion and calling to ask the men beating at the flames and throwing dirt on smoldering embers if they'd seen a little boy. None had. He ran around the barn and corral, and stopped dead when he spotted the closed barn door. The boy hadn't made it to let the horses out. He must have been caught in the blast.

Daniel Danvers was nowhere to be found. Bear, Halt, and Diamond searched while the men battled the flames. As the fires came under control, some of the men turned to rounding up the animals that had survived the blast. A cow, a few pigs, several chickens that smelled of burned feathers appeared. Then Bear spotted a fellow leading in a plow horse.

"Where did you find him?" Bear asked the fellow.

"Over that rise . . . just wandering." The man pointed.

Daniel must have let the horses out then reclosed the door! They redoubled their efforts. After a time Diamond went back to the distraught Luanna Danvers and her heart ached for the woman. What if it were Robbie who was missing? Thoughts of Robbie and his bag of tricks caused her to straighten and focus on a whole new range of possibilities.

"Does Daniel have special places to hide?" she asked Luanna, grabbing the woman's hands. "Like when it's time for the chores he doesn't like to do?"

Luanna, still somewhat dazed, recalled: "I caught 'im a few times . . . lollygaggin' in one of th' sheds . . . over near the barn."

Diamond ran to Bear and together they headed for what was left of the sheds and searched them, finding nothing until they reached the one closest to the barn. The wood had collapsed over the sod foundation. They had to pull boards away to get to what once had been pegs and shelves filled with half-tanned skins, chains for pulling stumps, carpentry tools, and spare wood. They called the boy's name and after a while Diamond caught sight of a child's worn shoe. Digging frantically through the debris, they located and pulled him out. He was dazed but otherwise unharmed.

Luanna Danvers threw her arms around the boy and sobbed with gratitude, thanking Bear, Halt, and Diamond for all they had done to save her family.

The fires were gradually extinguished, and the breeze cleared enough of the smoke for them to assess the damage. It was nothing short of devastation. Bear's countenance darkened and his shoulders sagged as he surveyed the wreckage. Gravely, he turned to Luanna Danvers.

"I'm sorry for all of this. I promise you, Mrs. Danvers . . . I'll personally see that your farm is rebuilt . . . better than ever."

"It don't matter," she told him with tears streaming down her face. She gathered the rest of her children into her arms and lap and gave them a collective hug. "These here are the most important things we got. An' they're all safe."

"All the same," Diamond put in, despite the lump in her throat, "we'll see you're repaid and that your home is rebuilt. We'll find someone to bring in your crops, if your husband isn't able. You don't need to worry about a thing."

Three of the men were assigned to place Danvers in one of the wagons and drive him and his family into town. Jim Danvers needed a doctor for his leg and the family needed a place to stay for a while. One of Silky's boarding houses would have room for them. With profuse thanks, Luanna climbed up into the bed of the wagon beside her husband and called to her children. They scrambled in, and the family was carried off into the night and into the promise of a future that would be rebuilt.

TWENTY-TWO

DIAMOND AND BEAR were among the last to leave the farmstead. It was so far into the night that it would be dawn before long. Diamond had long since exhausted her second wind and now barely had the strength to climb into the saddle. Still, she reined up on the ridge overlooking the charred and smoking skeleton of the farmstead and surveyed the destruction.

The smell of the burning wood and the roar of the flames would be with her as long as she lived . . . as would the guilt she felt for having talked the Danverses into leasing Bear the land. She heard Bear mutter, "Come on. We've done all we can for now," and she turned her horse to follow his.

They rode in silence for a while, each fatigued beyond reason and operating outside their usual defenses. She was hardly aware of the fact that Bear was leading her down into a shallow ravine lined with scrubby growth that nestled around a handful of real trees. When he stopped at the edge of those trees and dismounted, she watched numbly as he tied his horse and came back to hold his arms up to help her down.

She looked down into his sooty face and his night-luminous eyes . . . eyes she loved . . . eyes she hadn't understood until now . . . eyes she never wanted to lose. The emotion dammed inside her broke free.

"Oh, Bear . . ." Tears poured down her face as he pulled her from her horse and into a fierce embrace. He held her tightly as she released the pain she'd held inside. "It was all my fault, all of it. If I hadn't gone to them . . . persuaded them to sign the lease . . . if I hadn't come into town for you and told Beecher—"

"It wasn't you, Diamond," he murmured, stroking her hair.

"But it was." She clung to him, burying her face in his smoky shirt as she continued to cry. "If only I hadn't been so sure I was right. I should have listened to you . . ." Tears filled her throat, choking off the rest.

When her sobs subsided, he pushed her back and smiled down at her with his eyes glistening strangely in the moonlight.

"It wasn't your fault, Diamond." He stroked the side of her face. "Don't you see? It was Beecher. He's mean and cowardly and unpredictable. The damage had already been done. He had no cause to do this to the Danverses. His quarrel was with me. But he decided that by blowing and burning them out he'd—"

"Strike at you," she said, sniffing and wiping at her wet cheeks. She looked up at him and saw the pain in his face. "If only I had listened to you. All I could see was your pride and how you wouldn't let me be a part of your life. I thought if I helped . . . you'd see that I—"

"That you what? Make a pretty damned good railroader yourself?" He shook his head ruefully and stroked her cheek. "If I'd told you without shouting and storming around like an idiot, you might have listened to me," he said, wincing visibly. "Maybe if I hadn't made it so personal with Beecher. Maybe if I hadn't called him out and shown him up in front of his hired guns. Maybe if *I* had listened to *you* . . ."

He released her and turned aside. His shoulders rounded and his big frame seemed heavy and weary as he headed down the slope to the trickle of water running through the rocky bottom of the ravine.

She followed, feeling the defeat evident in his every move. He was taking it just as personally as she was, holding himself responsible for what had happened to the Danverses. He knelt beside the stream and began to move rocks to dam up the flow into a small natural basin. She could see that he was preparing them a place to wash. It seemed like such an ordinary thing to do, under such extraordinary circumstances. On a deeper level, it struck her that even in pain and defeat, he was doing what he did best . . . taking things in hand, making things happen, making things better.

That was exactly what he had tried to do all along. Make a railroad. Make progress. Make a life for himself and others in a hostile and difficult land.

"Bear?" She made her way through the grasses to the stream bank and knelt beside him on the rocks. He stiffened at her touch and turned his face away. She might have taken that as a further rejection and pulled back herself, if it hadn't been so very clear that he was hurting. She could somehow see through that toughness, that manly decisiveness that he wore like a shield.

"Bear," she said, taking his arm and refusing to release it, "it's not your fault, either. You've done your best. You've started a railroad and worked hard—against all odds—to make it a reality."

"Yeah, I've worked. And I've failed," he said hoarsely, his

entire body tensing against the pain caused by that admission.

"That's not true."

"The hell it's not." He turned to her with his eyes blazing and tracks of liquid glistening on his soot-covered cheeks. "I've stomped and roared and bellowed like a tyrant—I'd have laid that track with my own two hands, if I could! I refused to let anyone help—even Halt, and he's been my partner for three years. If I had listened to him, we would have had any one of a number of loans and the track would have been finished and operation would have started last summer. Every decision was mine. I had to personally supervise every damned signature line, bolt, and I rail." When the insight struck, he could no more keep it inside than he could fly. "I haven't been building a railroad, sweetheart, I've been building a monument to my own damned pride!"

Unwilling to suffer the disgust he knew would be in her expression, he shoved to his feet and stalked back toward the horses. She scrambled up and went after him, dragging him to a halt and planting herself in front of him.

"You're right—you were proud and independent and damned bullheaded. So what? That's not exactly news to anybody, Bear McQuaid, least of all to me. And, yes, a whale of a lot has gone wrong on the Montana Central and Mountain. But none of it was your doing—least of all what happened to the Danverses.

"You just told me that it was Beecher, and you were right. He wanted to stop you, to keep you from building your dream. You had every right to fight for that dream, in any and every way you chose. I was wrong, Bear. There are times when you have to defend yourself and what you're trying to create. Even with force. Even against interfering females who love you with all their hearts but blunder in where they're not needed!"

She realized she was yelling at him and shaking his arms . . . that she'd just roared her love at him. Closing her eyes, she released him.

It took a moment for what she'd said to penetrate his anger and humiliation. How could she stand there with her heart in her eyes, trying to shake some sense into him, fighting her way through both his pride and his despair to declare that she loved him?

How could she love him? He'd deceived, distrusted, and disappointed her. His railroad was a shambles and his life with her even more so. But she was standing there . . . with her heart in her eyes . . .

"Who said you weren't needed?" he said, his hands clenching at his sides.

"You did." She looked up.

"And you listened to me?" His voice softened to a tortured rasp.

"I'm a soft touch, remember?"

The sight of her face glowing through soot and the smudges and streaks of tears caused that ache in the middle of him to spread. She loved him. And it didn't depend on him finishing a damned railroad or proving that there was something worthwhile inside him. She loved him just as he was. Proud, stubborn, arrogant, selfish, overbearing . . .

"And I'm an idiot. You should have better sense than to listen to me."

"You shout. It's impossible not to listen." Through her tension bloomed a pained and tentative little smile. "Just like it's impossible not to love you. Believe me, I tried."

He felt an unexpected and wholly undeserved spot of warmth developing inside that cavernous hollow inside him. Hope. *Please don't let it be too late!*

"Let me into your dream, Bear," she said, so quietly he wasn't sure he hadn't imagined it. "Let us all in. A dream only big enough to hold one person will never amount to much. A dream worth having has room for lots of other people in it . . . especially people who love you."

She stood there in the moonlight, her eyes shining, risking everything to offer him her hope, her faith, her heart. She had loved him enough to adopt his dream as hers, to give herself to it despite his selfishness. She had claimed a stake in his dream, took pride in it, and worked hard to realize it. Just like Halt. And the men in his crews. And the Danverses. They were all a part of what he'd started. And until he realized it and made room for that reality—welcomed it—his precious dream would never come true.

"Will you let me in, Bear?" she asked softly, searching his face.

"You've always been in my heart, Diamond. You're the very core of me. I want you—need you in my dreams and the rest of my life, as well."

He flung his arms around her and held her tightly, pouring his joy out in kisses all over her lips, her face, her hair. She threw her arms around him, holding him tightly, surrendering even her breath to the pleasure of his touch and exuberance of his kisses. Again and again he kissed her; some kisses were deep and soft, some short and playful. He kissed her nose, her eyelids, her smoky hair, her earlobes, and every square inch of her cheeks.

When he finally settled once again on her lips, she kissed him back with all the passion his long-awaited invitation to share his life produced in her. She ran her hands feverishly over his back and shoulders, curled her fingers in his hair, and cradled his bristled face between her hands . . . claiming every part of him she could reach.

When they ended that kiss, they were breathless, weak with desire and fatigue, giddy from lack of sleep, and glowing from an abundance of pleasure.

"Come on!" he said, grinning. "Let's get rid of this soot and salt."

She laughed as he pulled her across the rocks to the small pool he'd constructed. "A pity . . . I was just beginning to like it."

"I think there'll be plenty left after we've washed . . ."

Taking turns, they shed their clothes and stepped into the small bathing pool, letting the cool water and warm hands flow unchecked over them. They dried on what was left of her petticoat and the night air sent them shivering into each other's arms.

Bear made a bed of grass, laid his saddle blanket over it, and pulled her down into a cocoon of smoky clothes and warming kisses. Before long, their bodies were warmed and glowing, drawing on reserves of energy and desire neither knew they possessed.

Their bodies molded gently together, moving, lapping, caressing, merging. It was as if they were making love for the first time. Every sensation was deepened, every response heightened by the strain and terror of the night that even now was passing into the cool promise of another day. As they joined hands and moved together, the first rays of dawn appeared and bathed them first in gray, then in blue, rose, and pink. As the sun climbed above the horizon, they each found pleasure in the other's lavish giving. And by the time the first rays of the sun dipped into the ravine to dust them with morning gold, they were both sound asleep.

FOUR MEN ON horseback moved stealthily across the morning horizon, not far from where Bear and Diamond slept. Behind them on a long lead rope labored a pack-horse burdened with two wooden crates. And on the sides of those crates, stenciled in bold black letters, was the word "dynamite."

As they neared Great Falls, they spotted another party of men waiting on a bluff overlooking the town. Steering around the inhabited area, they headed for that group . . . one of whom had dismounted and now stood with his fists on his hips, like a gaunt, menacing colossus, waiting to hear their report.

"Well?" Lionel Beecher demanded, glaring at the packhorse, then at the lead rider.

"It's all set," he was told. "Jus' like you said. Nobody was there . . . they wus all gone off to fight th' fires."

"And the sod buster? Danvers?"

The leader leaned on his saddle horn and gave a yellowed grin. "They'll be pickin' up pieces o' him down in Wyomin'. McQuaid's crew run over there, all right. Wasn't nothin' they could do. It wus all over but the buryin'."

Beecher smiled and strolled over to a horse that had a blanket-draped human form tied across it. He took one last draw from his cheroot and stubbed it out on one of the small, scuffed riding boots sticking out from under the blanket. The action caused a groan and rustle of protest from the figure, and Beecher smirked and walked around the horse to pull back the blanket. Beneath it was a shock of unruly red-blond hair, very much like Diamond McQuaid's.

"Uncomfortable, my boy?" he asked, fishing through that mop of hair for a face and chin, lifting it up. "We'll try to do a bit better once we get you to the—*e-e-owww*!" He lurched back, shaking his hand, then grabbing it tightly while he bent over and hopped around, gasping out: "He bit me—dammit!—the little bastard *bit* me!" A moment later he grabbed Robbie Wingate by the hair and jerked his head up. "You stinking little turd—you think you can get away with—"

He saw his men staring at him, halted, and dropped the boy's head as if it besmirched his fingers.

"Let's ride," he snapped. "I want to be ready when the fun starts."

IT WAS EARLY afternoon before the whistle of the returning train awakened Bear and Diamond. It was mid-afternoon before they arrived back at the base camp, walking hand in hand, leading their horses, and looking as if they had just set the entire world to rights.

They were greeted nervously by the men in the dinner line, holding empty plates. "After last night th' men weren't in no shape to start work straight off," one of the crew foremen told him, watching anxiously for his reaction.

Were they so used to his temper that they believed he would begrudge them dinner?

"Of course," Bear said, giving the men in the food line a nod and a taut smile. "After dinner. A man's got to have a little something linin' his belly." He felt their questioning looks and paused, taking a deep breath. "You men did a great job last night, fighting those fires. I want you to know . . . the Danvers family is grateful. And so am I."

Diamond, watching from the platform of their car, felt a surge of warmth in her core as the men responded warily to Bear's improved demeanor. Feeling as if a load had been lifted from her shoulders, she headed inside to wash her hair and change her clothes. Thus, she wasn't there moments later when Halt and Bear brought the prisoners Carrick and Sikes from the boxcar where they were imprisoned.

"Lucky for you, your little 'surprise' was a failure," Bear said, standing over them as they were being loaded onto a wagon. "None of the Danvers family was killed. That may be the only thing that stands between you and the gallows."

Carrick looked up with a murderous glare in his blackened eye. "Yeah? Well, it ain't over yet. Beecher's got an ace up 'is sleeve."

Bear cast a look at Halt. Was this a legitimate threat or just hot air?

"Save it for the sheriff, Carrick," Halt ordered, shoving their feet back onto the bed of the wagon and raising the rear board, latching it in place.

"We ain't going to jail," Sikes said defiantly. "You take us in, an' you'll never see that snot-nosed kid o' yours agin."

Bear froze. "What do you mean?"

"That kid. Th' one tha' belongs to your woman." Carrick's grizzled face creased with a smirk. "Beecher's got 'im."

"The hell 'e has," Halt snarled, ripping down the rear gate of the wagon to get at the pair. But Bear wrestled him away from the wagon and dragged him off to the private car in search of Robbie.

Diamond appeared out of the sleeping compartment, freshly washed and in clean clothes, insisting that Robbie was with Silky. But when they checked the kitchen car, Silky hadn't seen Robbie since the previous afternoon, and when they searched the camp and talked to the men, none of them had seen him since the start of the prairie fire.

"Talk, damn you!" Halt roared, charging back to the wagon and shaking Sikes until he was almost too dizzy to speak. "What's Beecher got planned?"

The pair refused to talk. Bear suggested Halt climb into the wagon with him and together they drove with the prisoners off across the prairie.

After a quarter of an hour, they stopped near a rock outcropping and Bear climbed down and walked around, searching for something. When he returned, he said sim-

ply, "This ought to do." He and Halt dragged the pair out
of the wagon and rolled them across the brush and grass to
the base of the rocks.

Between choking on dust and cursing and pleading,
Carrick and Sikes demanded to know what Bear and Halt
were going to do with them.

"You don't want to go to prison," Bear said. "So I've
decided to accommodate you. See those ants?" He scuffed
the dirt with his boot toe and the pair could see red ants
scurrying in all directions . . . including toward them.
"They don't often get a year's supply of fresh meat, all in
one big lump." He smiled fiercely and looked at Halt.

"A pity Robbie isn't here. He'd *love* this."

By the time they returned to camp, they knew that
Beecher had won a small ranch, just north of Great Falls,
in a poker game, and that he had likely taken the boy
there. Word had spread fast through the camp that Robbie
was missing and that someone had taken him. Bear didn't
have to ask men to accompany him; they volunteered . . .
the entire crew . . . to a man.

" 'E's a game little squirt," one of the foremen declared
solemnly, speaking for the men.

Diamond heard that and her throat constricted so that
she couldn't speak. Her Robbie. Her mischievous, infuriat-
ing, sneaky, sticky-fingered disgrace. He had a way of endearing himself to even the toughest of hearts.

Bear was choosing a number of men to accompany him
and Halt and issuing rifles to them when the second part
of Beecher's plan rumbled through the camp. The train
cars swayed on their carriages, windows rattled so hard
they cracked, dishes crashed and pots overturned in the
kitchen car, and tent poles came crashing down. They
staggered and teetered, trying to keep their feet.

When everything quieted, Bear rushed to see if Diamond was all right. Together they turned to Halt, and the

three of them—along with everyone else in camp—looked to the south and east. A huge cloud of dust was rising into the air.

"The forward camp," Bear said. "The bastard blew up the forward camp!"

"Th' camp, hell," Halt said grimly, "he blew up half th' territory!"

Diamond watched Bear staring toward the camp, then looking toward Great Falls and Robbie. Beecher planned well. Everything seemed to be crashing in at once. She saw the pain caused by the decision Bear had to make, and saw him turn from the sabotaged roadbed and set his face toward her young cousin. Her eyes filled with tears.

Bear shouted orders for the men to round up every horse and every rifle in the camp. If they left now, they could reach Beecher's ranch by dusk. Diamond listened to what he said, then headed for their car.

Bear found her there collecting her hat and putting on her leather vest, clearly preparing to ride. He braced.

"What do you think you're doing?"

"Going with you," she declared, her eyes once again that lightning-blue. "He's my cousin . . . my family . . . my charge. And I'm going to help you get him back from Beecher or die trying."

"Now, Diamond . . ."

"Now, Bear," she responded, turning that lightning-blue gaze on him.

Bear expelled a tall breath. "Okay." Before he could add conditions or caveats, she was out the door and down the steps, headed for the center of camp. When he caught up, she was already mounted with the men and waiting.

She focused the attention of thirty determined faces with her question.

"What's our plan?"

• • •

"MISERABLE LITTLE COCKROACH," Beecher spat, pressing a pristine handkerchief to the outer corner of his eye and inspecting the crimson stain it collected. "I ought to start killing him right now. Something very slow and deliciously painful." He slammed the bedroom door and thrust the oil lamp he held into the hands of the man closest to him. "Watch him," he ordered. "If he so much as twitches, cut something off. A finger. An ear. *A leg.*"

When he reached the front room of the ranch house, the main door opened and a grizzled gunman stuck his head inside. "Rider comin'," he announced. "A woman."

Beecher consulted the tarnished mirror hanging over the washstand in the corner, while he mentally went over the list of possible callers. He was totally unprepared for the sight of Diamond Wingate sitting atop a bay gelding, her hair loose about her shoulders and glinting golden in the torchlight.

"Well, well," he said, strolling out onto the aged wooden porch with his hands in his vest pockets. "If it isn't Mrs. McQuaid. To what do I owe the honor of this visit?"

"To sanity and reason, sir," she said calmly, surveying the low wooden buildings that formed the bulk of the ranch structures. "I believe there has been enough violence and bloodshed. I have come to negotiate a truce."

"Things have indeed come to a pass," Beecher said, scanning the road behind her and the horizon, "for the illustrious Bear McQuaid to send his wife to do his dealing for him."

"My husband doesn't know I've come, sir." She lifted her chin. "I daresay if he knew I were here he would soon be gunning for both of us."

"Then he is even more stupid than I suspected . . . to place his hatred of me above his regard for you." He stepped off the porch, eyeing her. "How is it that you can negotiate for him?"

"I didn't say I intend to negotiate for *him*. I negotiate for myself, Mr. Beecher. I am a woman of considerable means. I want my young cousin back. And I can make it very worth your while to deliver him to me safe and sound." She looked around the weathered buildings. "Where is he?"

"Safe," Beecher said with a malicious smile. "I might ask you the same question. Where is McQuaid?"

Diamond hesitated, bristling visibly. "Following his own best interests, as usual. With Robbie missing, he rode out to determine the damage caused by a mysterious blast at his forward construction camp. I was left to take the matter of my missing cousin into my own hands."

Beecher smiled. "Not especially chivalrous of him."

"I confess, he has proved something of a disappointment to me in that regard," she responded with compressed anger in every word.

"And in other regards as well, I take it." Beecher's smile grew. "Won't you come inside and let me show you some true Western hospitality?"

As Diamond held Beecher's attention at the front of the house, dark figures slithered from shadow to shadow across the moonlit yard at the rear of the house. It had taken some time for Bear and Halt to flank the house and barn and bunkhouse and make their way on foot across the open range behind the ranch structures. Clearly, Beecher expected them; he had posted men on the roofs of every building.

Since they knew nothing of the layout of the ranch or of the number of men Beecher had employed, their only course was to move as quietly as possible. But in choosing stealth, they sacrificed speed. Bear had faith in Diamond's ability to hold a man's attention, but would Beecher be-

lieve her story about Bear choosing to deal with the sabo-
taged forward camp over helping her retrieve her cousin?
Would it be enough to distract him into not detecting
Bear's presence?

From corral fence to shed to barn, the men slipped
steadily forward, encouraged by the uninterrupted peace
of the yard. With hand signals, he sent two of the men
who accompanied them to check the barn and two to
check the sheds, while he and Halt headed for the rear of
the house. There they encountered their first guard, leaning in a chair against the rear wall, his hat pulled low over
his face and his rifle lying across his knees. Quickly a
second man appeared, up on the roof, walking back and
forth . . . both awake and alert, scanning the moonlit
landscape. The only reason they hadn't been detected was
the sentry's interest in what was happening between Diamond and Beecher.

" 'At a girl. Keep him talking," Bear muttered as he saw
the lookout give the rear yard a perfunctory visual sweep
and then head back to the saga unfolding on the front
side.

They waited for a signal from the men checking the
barn and sheds. All clear, came the signal. No Robbie.
Beecher was probably keeping him in the house. Bear and
Halt darted across the moonlit yard and crept to the corners of the house. There was no way to entirely surprise
the rear guard. However they approached, he would have
time to make noise or sound an alarm. They would have to
strike fast, get inside, and count on the confusion created
by the men stationed on horses outside the ranch buildings to provide them cover for a getaway.

Taking a deep breath and praying Diamond didn't take
it into her head to try something stupid, he peered around
the corner, gave Halt the nod, and the plan was in motion.

They rushed the guard from both sides, the sound of

their footsteps alerting him at the last minute. He staggered up . . . only to be sent back to finish his nap by the butt of Halt's gun connecting with the back of his head. They caught him and set him back on his chair, propping his hat over his eyes and his gun across his knees.

When the sentry came to investigate the slight noise, all looked just as it had, so the sentry called out to see if all was well. Not wanting to alert Beecher that his hired guns were sleeping on duty, the sentry called down quietly: "Lefty—wake up! Everything all right?"

By the time the sentry realized something was amiss, Bear and Halt were well inside and tiptoeing down the darkened hall, checking doors.

They found Robbie tied to an old iron bed in a dark, musty little room. Bear pressed his finger to his lips, then cut the rags and ropes binding Robbie's hands and feet. It looked as if they might be in for a stroke of luck . . . when Halt impulsively removed the gag from Robbie's mouth.

"I knew you'd come!" the boy croaked out.

A second later, two of Beecher's men were barging into the room, drawing their guns. Bear hardly had time to jerk Robbie off the bed and behind him before his revolver cleared its holster and the crack of gunfire split the stillness.

From that moment, everything happened in curiously distorted time.

Beecher spat out an oath, retreated into the house, and began shouting for his men. Half a dozen men came pouring out of the bunkhouse, brandishing guns and trying to figure out what was happening. The men from Bear and Halt's crew, who were stationed just over the first rise, headed in, firing at the men stationed on the roofs.

At the first shot, Beecher sprang at Diamond—"Treacherous little bitch!"—and managed to prevent her from reining off. After a brief struggle, he pulled her off her horse, clamped his arm around her neck and dragged her into the house. There they stopped dead, confronted by Bear and Halt and Robbie. Beecher tightened his grip on Diamond and shifted slightly so that she shielded him from their line of fire. Then he ripped his revolver from its holster and jammed it into her ribs.

"Well, well, McQuaid." Beecher smiled humorlessly. "Rather clever, all in all. Your wife's plan, no doubt."

"I believe . . . it was a joint plan," Bear said, shoving Robbie behind him and cocking his gun.

"Oh, that is a disappointment." He gave Diamond a punishing jerk, but produced no groan or whimper. "She showed such promise. Now her only possible use is absorbing lead." He backed toward the window, dragging Diamond with him, and looked out. Occasional cracks of gunfire and the sound of horses and men shouting told him that Bear and Halt hadn't come alone.

"Yeah. I brought a few friends," Bear said, moving forward, his eyes riveted on Beecher's face.

"You're just full of surprises, McQuaid. I wasn't aware you *had* any friends." Beecher's features hardened as he glanced at the door. "Come any closer and I'll reduce your friends and family by one."

"Let her go, Beecher." Bear continued to inch forward.

"I'm not feeling particularly suicidal," Beecher said, moving toward the open door, mentally measuring the distance to Diamond's horse, still standing outside. "Besides . . . I rather like the feel of her. One can always tell quality."

"Just as one can always tell coward—" she gritted out before he choked her tighter and cut her off.

Halt, gun drawn, began moving up on Beecher's right

and Robbie, eager for a clearer view, crept out from behind Bear and scrambled toward his left.

"Bite him, Diamond," Robbie blurted out. "He hates that."

"Bloodthirsty little savage you're raising there," Beecher muttered through clenched teeth as he reached the door and glanced over his shoulder. Robbie growled and lunged straight for Diamond, startling them all and loosening Beecher's grip on her.

She dove toward Robbie and they hit the floor together—just as Beecher's gun went off.

Bear had no time to think, only to fire. Once, twice, three times. Twice Beecher jerked with the impact of bullet tearing flesh.

Beecher's gun dropped from his hand and he stumbled backward through the door. He made it to the edge of the porch before he collapsed. There was a moment of utter silence. Nothing moved. Not a breath was taken or expelled. The acrid scent of spent gunpowder filled the dingy room.

Bear rushed to Diamond and pulled her into his arms. "Are you all right?"

"I'm okay, I think." She stood up shakily and her knees weakened with the realization that she had escaped . . . narrowly. Frantically, she ran her hands over Bear and then Robbie. "Are you hit? Did he hit you?"

"We're fine," Bear said, pulling her tight against him, even as she engulfed Robbie. He held them both in a fiercely protective embrace until her tears came and her trembling began to subside. Then he loosened his grip and turned to Halt, who was standing there with a trickle of blood running down his sleeve and a broad smile on his face.

• • • •

IT WAS THEIR number that had won the day for them. The MCM's men had ridden in *en masse*, outnumbering and outgunning Beecher's men by three to one. Halt's injury was a neat flesh wound that he joked would garner him plenty of sympathy from Silky and her girls. Two more of Bear's men had been wounded, neither seriously. By the time Beecher went down, some of his gunmen had already headed for the corral and a quick escape. It wasn't hard to round up the others; several were wounded slightly and the others had no stake in keeping up Beecher's fight. They were just in it for the cash.

Bear's men loaded Beecher and the other wounded into a wagon and headed for Great Falls. Diamond, Bear, Halt, and Robbie followed, arriving in time to pull the sheriff from his nightly rounds of the local saloons. After some prodding, he placed Beecher's men under arrest and posted a deputy at the doctor's office to guard Beecher.

The doctor examined Beecher and announced that the poor wretch would most likely live—and regret doing so. Then he and his wife patched up Halt and the rest of Bear's wounded.

Dawn was well on the way by the time they returned to their main camp, but nobody was ready for sleep. The men were busy celebrating Robbie's return, tousling his hair and hoisting him onto their shoulders, and recounting stories of their great rescue raid to those who had stayed behind. Silky came rushing out in her nightclothes to learn what had happened. At the sight of Halt's bandaged arm, she shamelessly threw her arms around him and declared that if he didn't stop being reckless with his neck she was going to have to wring it herself. Above their embrace Halt gave Diamond and Bear a wicked wink.

Silky insisted on starting breakfast and soon had coffee brewing and biscuits baking. The mood was almost festive as everyone pitched in to help with the tables and serving. All present vowed that they'd never tasted better fare.

It was only as the men were finishing their food that fatigue settled over them. Bear decreed that they would start work again tomorrow morning, saying that the work wasn't going anywhere. His words stuck in Diamond's mind as she watched him moving among his men and then checking the camp to make certain all was secure. The work wasn't going anywhere.

"I'm sorry, Bear," she said, joining him at the edge of the picket line and slipping her arm through his as he looked off toward the forward camp. "I know how much it means to you. We'll get it done."

"We'll have to make seven to ten miles a day to reach Billings by snowfall." He smiled ruefully. "Now that Beecher's going to jail, maybe we can persuade the land office to give us additional time."

"Or maybe we'll get late snows this year," she said.

"Or . . . maybe that dry riverbed will change course," he said, waggling his brows. "Or maybe the track will just start laying itself . . ."

"See there," she said with insufferable optimism. "There are all sorts of possibilities." She pulled him down and planted a kiss on his cheek. "We can do anything together, Bear McQuaid. We make a darn good team." He turned and put both arms around her, gazing raptly into her eyes. She felt the strength and warmth of his chest beneath her hands and her heart skipped a beat. "I know something else we're good at."

"Oh?"

"Come back to the car with me and I'll show you," she said, wriggling out of his embrace and snagging his hand to pull him along.

"Something we can do in front of Schultz and Silky and

Robbie?" he said, holding his ground and giving her a chiding look.

"Oh." She stopped pulling.

"That's what you get for inviting half of Montana into our private car."

"Oh." Into that one syllable was compressed a world of longing. "It will be two or three more weeks before Schultz is ready to move. And Silky is here for the duration . . ." She ran her hand down his chest and sank her fingertips just inside his belt buckle, wiggling them. "Got any ideas?"

An hour later, Diamond stood in the doorway of a boxcar staring at Bear's solution. He'd had the full-sized brass bed in the sleeping compartment dismantled and reassembled in the middle of an empty boxcar.

"Welcome to your home away from home," Bear said, pulling her inside and closing the sliding door behind her. It was almost pitch-black.

"I can't see a thing," she said, feeling ahead of her in the darkness and running into Bear's chest. He chuckled and pulled her into his arms.

"You don't have to."

EPILOGUE

IT WAS WELL past supper that evening when Halt came banging on the door of Bear and Diamond's makeshift honeymoon bower. Diamond lay curled in the sheets, glowing with satisfaction, reluctant to move, while Bear slipped on his trousers and headed for the door. Bear was back in a moment, giving her a brisk kiss on the lips and suggesting that she rise and dress . . . something about Nigel Ellsworth.

"Oh, my heaven—I forgot all about him," she said, hurrying to don her stockings, petticoat, and skirt. "The blast—is he all right?"

"I think so. Halt says he's got news and wants to see us." Bear jerked on his second boot and jammed his arms into a shirt on his way to the door. He paused near the slice of light coming through the narrow opening of the boxcar door. She could see he was bracing for yet another calamity. "Hurry, sweetheart," he said. "I'll wait for you."

Hand in hand, they hurried along the tracks and headed for the center of camp. It was already dusk; the sky was a paint box of extravagant colors and the evening fires were already burning. The men were gathered around the central campfire, where Nigel Ellsworth and his recently appointed assistant sat on a wooden bench, holding them spellbound with unusually animated talk.

They looked as though they'd been dragged through every gulch and gully in Montana: their trousers and coats were dusty and torn, Ellsworth's bowler hat was squashed into an odd mushroom shape, and the pair both had scrapes on their faces and hands. Diamond squeezed Bear's hand and they traded looks of dismay.

"Ellsworth!" Bear extended a hand to the inventor-cum-engineer. "Are you all right?"

"I—I believe so," Nigel said, looking down at his lanky frame with an air of befuddlement. "There was an explosion . . . a *big* explosion . . ."

"We heard," Bear said, a bit dryly. "The camp . . . how bad is it?"

"I'm afraid it's pretty much demolished." Ellsworth winced. "We'd have been demolished with it if we hadn't been off on the far range finishing some survey work."

Bear took a deep breath, bracing, trying not to overreact, when Ellsworth astonished him by breaking into a quizzical smile.

"It's the damnedest thing I ever saw," the engineer declared. "Beggin' your pardon, Miz McQuaid." He doffed the felt mushroom on his head. "The blast took down half of the buttes on the north range of the right-of-way . . . carved chunks out of those buttes like a knife going through butter. It seems there was a soft layer of rock running through the entire set of cliffs, and everything blew out down to that soft layer and then just stopped. It's flat as a fritter. Looks like a damned macadam road. Must be twenty feet across in most places. Won't even have to do any grading . . . just lay down the track!"

"Wait—" Bear grabbed him by the sleeves to hold him

still. "You're saying Beecher blew down half of the buttes . . . and the blast left a ledge of some kind?"

"Slick as brilliantine," Nigel said, scratching his head in wonder. "Never seen anything like it. As soon as we bend the roadbed to avoid that dry river, we'll be building track through what used to be a bad section of solid rock. You gotta come and see!"

All around them the men clapped each other on the backs and talked excitedly about seeing this bizarre twist of fortune for themselves. Bear turned to Diamond in shock that transformed to disbelief, then to a booming laugh.

"Bless Lionel Beecher's crusty black heart!" he roared, picking her up and swinging her around. When he put her down she was laughing, too. "When he finds out what he's done, he'll be furious! He's the only man I know who has worse luck than me!"

As things calmed, Nigel Ellsworth bit the corner of his lip, then called for their attention again. "Ummm . . . there was one more thing . . ."

The look on his face caused Bear to freeze, waiting for the other shoe to drop . . . the one with the disaster in it.

"Yes?" Bear looked at Diamond, then at Halt, bracing.

"As I was climbing around over the blast site, I noticed some rather odd debris." He pulled two sizable rocks out of his pockets and his assistant did the same, holding them out for Bear's inspection. "Now . . . I'm no mining engineer, but . . . don't these look a lot like . . ."

Diamond's heart stopped as she watched Bear's face drain of color.

"My God," Bear said, reaching for one of the rocks. It was meant as a prayer. Halt pushed through to take one of the rocks with the odd blue streak in it from Ellsworth's assistant.

"Sweet heaven above," the Irishman said, giving a whistle.

"What is it?" Diamond demanded, trying desperately not to jump to any conclusions.

Ellsworth looked at her with a faintly befuddled look. "I think it's *silver*. And there's a whole streak of it running through the cliffs the blast exposed."

"Silver? Could it possibly be?" Bear said. "Beecher not only blasted us a roadbed—he blasted us a damned silver mine?"

She took one of the rocks from Ellsworth and rubbed the blue streak with her fingers, feeling its sleek texture. And somehow she knew.

"It's silver, all right," she said. She looked up at Bear and began to laugh. "You're going to be a very wealthy man, Bear McQuaid." Then she looked at the workers around them, beaming at the expectation and hope in their eyes. "In fact, you're all going to be quite well off."

"How do you know?" Bear said, seizing her shoulders and pouring all of his passion for her into that one look of hope, longing, and love.

"Because . . . I'm a soft touch with a 'Midas touch,' remember? I'm the girl who can't even *give* her money away. I've invested heavily in the Montana Central and Mountain. And I always make a huge return on my investments."

"So you do." Bear laughed and took the rock from her and handed it back to Ellsworth. "But, you know . . . you've invested a lot more than just money, this time. You've invested your heart and soul and dreams. And I think it's high time you started collecting dividends."

And he kissed her.

ABOUT THE AUTHOR

BETINA KRAHN lives in Minnesota with her two sons and a feisty salt-and-pepper schnauzer. With a degree in biology and a graduate degree in counseling, she has worked in teaching, personnel management, and mental health. She had a mercifully brief stint as a boys' soccer coach, makes terrific lasagna, routinely kills houseplants, and is incurably optimistic about the human race. She believes the world needs a bit more truth, a lot more justice, and a whole lot more love and laughter. And she attributes her outlook to having married an unflinching optimist and to two great-grandmothers actually named Pollyanna.

And look for Betina Krahn's
next delightful historical romance

THE SWEET TALKER

IN SUMMER 2000